I0779243

ROSEMARY B. ALTHOFF

A Soul's Warfare:
Book 3: The Horned Edge
by Rosemary B. Althoff

ISBN: 978-1-962168-27-4

CHAPTER 1:

BACK ON EARTH …

Thirteen-year-old Patrick Brahmindura huffed as he jogged around the perimeter of his big backyard. *I've got to lose weight. I must have gained ten pounds in the last two months!* Thirteen times around the yard made a mile. He'd laid it out with a ruler.

Frigid fall air seared his throat and steamed out of his mouth, and his right ankle howled because of the old injury when he was kidnapped more than two years ago. *Thanks—but no thanks—to that hot marble I found! I wish I'd never found it!*

To protect his mind from the awful memory, Patrick forced himself to visualize the beautiful things of the world across the universe called Lanthra where he'd had his adventures. Despite everything, he still loved Lanthra. Sparkling waterfalls, delicate ferns, choirs of old-growth trees where the mountains marched rank after rank … Lanthra was the world with eye-popping sunsets and thousand-year-old castles and—*dragons!* Real dragons! He had heard the dragons singing!

Compared to Huntsville, Alabama where Patrick lived, Lanthra was spectacular—and he'd thought Huntsville was pretty. The best part about "The Rocket City" where Dad owned a shoe store was the Sky Bridge not too far from his house. It was an elevated greenway where he could hike or bike around the perimeter of the city. He'd enjoy another excursion to Sky Bridge.

But as Patrick's feet pounded the lawn, the ugly thoughts jabbed into him. That bully in school wouldn't leave him alone.

Patrick stopped abruptly. He leaned against a tree, panting, holding his stomach. The big boy with the blond thatch of hair and the acne called him the "N-word" and threatened to beat him up.

Comfort vanished. Patrick spurted off again, faster and faster until he ran in a full sprint. his lungs burned from the cold, and his chest heaved. Every step hurt, his ankle was on fire.

God, I'm a piece of dark s—! he thought, cursing. But then he cringed. God wouldn't like that. Patrick had said, "I believe in God …," like a lot of people said in church. He shouldn't curse. Nope, he wasn't a good Christian. But God had helped him anyway. He'd rescued all of them when they were in deep trouble on Lanthra and brought them safely home to Earth: Lewis, Gracie, and him.

Thank you, God.

A measure of peace returned. Patrick slowed down to a slow jog. A strong nudge cried, *Stop!* His ankle screaming, he gave up and lurched up the back steps into the kitchen.

*   *   *

Patrick balanced on his good foot and helped himself to orange juice from the fridge and found a leftover biscuit in the breadbox. Then Dad and Lewis plodded into the kitchen from work at Dad's shoe store.

Dad's shoulders slumped. "I'm tired! What a day! I couldn't believe he customers could be so demanding and irritable."

Patrick watched him fill a glass from the dispenser at the refrigerator and heard the clink of ice cubes. "I'm going to watch the news for a while. Before Mom comes home from work, I'll make dinner." Sipping from the glass, Dad trudged into the living room, and soon Patrick heard newscasters chattering.

Lewis stayed in the kitchen. "Where's Gracie?"

"She's at a friend's house, but she'll be home soon." Patrick eyed the big biscuit—but he also noticed gray shadows on Lewis's face. *He's gotten so skinny!*

Lewis leaned on the kitchen counter. "How're you doing, kid," he said and mussed Patrick's thick, dark wavy hair.

"Stop it, bro'!" Patrick swatted Lewis's hand away and packed the whole biscuit in his mouth so that he could hardly chew.

"How's it going?" Lewis repeated. "How was school?"

"Mmmm, same-old, same-old," Patrick mumbled past the

biscuit. He was *not* going to talk about the bully. As usual, he compared himself to his brother. They looked a lot alike: dark-haired, permanently tanned like Dad. But Lewis was tall, while he, Patrick, was short and *plump*. Nobody had ever picked on Lewis, he was sure.

"Tell me more." Lewis's voice sounded quiet but firm, drawing Patrick's attention. Patrick looked up. His older brother held Patrick's gaze to command a real answer. He wouldn't have done that before Lanthra, but now he did; Lewis actually listened to him.

Patrick swallowed and sighed. The bully's words still rang in his head: "You fat n—!" But Lewis didn't need to worry about him. So, he picked something milder to share. "The other kids in geometry class make fun of me when I ask questions. They call me 'teacher's pet.' They say I'm stupid." *And my brother is a math genius. I'll never be as good as he is!*

Lewis countered, "We are *both* talented in math; don't underestimate yourself. Remember this: Because of the space/time difference between Earth and Lanthra, you're physically and mentally more than a year behind the other kids in your class. Don't *ever* call yourself stupid!"

Considering that answer, Patrick downed his orange juice and put the glass in the sink. To get the spotlight off himself, he said, "Okay, your turn. How'd it go at work today?"

Lewis shrugged. "Oh, it was just an ordinary day."

"Hey," Patrick pressed, "you made me tell about school; now you've gotta tell me about work!"

"Okay, okay. Dad was right; customers were odd today. There must have been a full moon."

Patrick chuckled. "That'll do it!"

"Here's one story: I helped a lady try on a pair of spiffy gold-sequined boots, and she really liked them. She smiled like pure sunshine when she came up to the service counter. But just as her card got approved, … she emitted a loud, squishy fart."

Patrick chortled and made a rude imitation of the fart.

Lewis continued, "Her face got bright red and she ran out of the store! Her card was still stuck in the reader, and her shoes lay on the counter."

"Did she ever come back for them?"

"Yes. About ten minutes later, she came back. I gave back her credit card, then she walked away. I called out, 'Wait! Don't forget your shoes!'"

"Did she get 'em?"

"Yep. She came back, grabbed the box, and said, 'Excuse me! I forgot my fart!'"

Patrick cracked up. He held his stomach, laughing until he could talk again. "What a great story! Did it really happen?"

Lewis kept a straight face. "Well, it might have. Oh, the tales those tongues could tell!" His hand patted Patrick's shoulder as he left the kitchen to watch the news with Dad, and Patrick felt warm inside. But then the warmth seeped away and worry came back. Besides worrying about himself, he worried about Lewis a lot but didn't know how to say anything. Because Lewis got so sick after … *Lanthra,* he couldn't work at his big-bucks energy research job anymore. Now he worked with Dad at the shoe store, and Patrick knew he hated it. Plus, late at night just three days ago, Patrick had heard muffled noises coming from his brother's bedroom. *Wow. Lewis is crying!*

And it was all your fault, fatso! the nasty inner critic shot at him. The biscuit Patrick had devoured lay like a doughball in his stomach.

Taking a deep breath, Patrick lumbered into the den to practice the piano. As he drew out his sheet music and adjusted his posture on the piano bench, he imagined Lewis's brilliant brain sparkling with happy thoughts again someday. Patrick had watched videos of real-time MRIs that showed various parts of a brain lighting up as a patient responded to visual, auditory, olfactory, and other sensory stimulation. *How did I know that word, "olfactory?" I must have picked it up somewhere. I love learning about the brain! I want to be a healer!*

Patrick practiced his favorite new piece, Beethoven's "Moonlight Sonata." *This music is so calm and beautiful. It creates the perfect mood to help sad, hurting people feel better!*

* * *

That night after supper while Dad and Mom watched television, Patrick and Lewis and Gracie got together upstairs in Lewis's bedroom. Since his piano time, Patrick's mood had improved. *My life is okay now,* he reflected. *We have a happy family.*

Patrick ticked off the reasons: Gracie at ten years old didn't bother him anymore with teasing, arguing and name-calling like she had when she was eight … *before Lanthra.* No, she and he supported each other—*most of the time.* And Lewis at twenty-four was not too busy to pay attention to Gracie and him.

Smiling, he sipped the cold caffeine-free cola Lewis had served. His bro' acted like a gracious host entertaining visitors. Unlike Patrick's, Lewis's bedroom was tidy. The furniture was just a bed and a chair, desk, and bookcase, but somehow he'd made it look like a Persian palace. Patrick leaned back on plump gold pillows on the soft oriental carpet that his grandfather Gabriel Brahmindura had sent from Varanasi in India. A gold arching floor lamp created a happy circle of light around them as they sat in a circle to talk, and Lewis's little fridge hummed in the background.

"What do you want to be when you grow up?" Gracie asked everybody.

Patrick snorted. *Trust Gracie to dig into people's deep psyches.*

His little sister continued to probe. "Lewis, you start first. You're the oldest. Tell us what you dream about."

Lewis's brown eyes shone as he thought. "Hmmm. All right … I do have a big dream. It's like I've got a "heart-dragon" curled up inside that wants to get out and make me do something great."

"Huh?" Gracie exclaimed. "A heart-dragon? What's that?"

Lewis smiled shyly. "I see the dragon as my ego."

Gracie's hazel eyes widened. "Wow. What's an ego? And how can you have a dragon in your heart?"

Lewis said, "A dragon can be a symbol for a person's self, the 'ego.' Dragons can be good or evil in stories, and people's egos can be good or evil in real life." Lewis imitated a fire-breathing mythical creature. "An evil dragon is an ego that wants to be super-important, even take over the world and seize all its treasures for itself. But a good dragon wants to be the best creature it's capable of being and do great and powerful things to help the world. And because people are complicated—" Lewis pointed to himself, "the same ego can fight with itself to be either good or evil."

Gracie looked clueless, but Patrick understood. "*Ego* is a psychological term," he told her. "I knew that!"

"That's right," Lewis said. "*Ego* means 'I' in Latin."

Gracie twirled her auburn hair, interested. "What does your heart-dragon ego want to do?"

Lewis's face glowed and those dark shadows disappeared. "I want to discover time travel." Patrick guessed that his brother had been thinking about that goal for a long, long time. "I want people to be able to watch the good things in history, not just get bad news on TV. And … I want to influence key events for a happier future." He grinned. "For instance, maybe I could convince Thomas Edison who invented the light bulb to be nicer to Nikola Tesla in the War of the Currents."

"Huh? Who's Tesla? What war?" Gracie's fingers pulled harder on her curly locks.

"Well, it's complicated. Two brilliant guys who had two different ideas about electricity. Just imagine if Edison had supported Tesla's ideas and the two had worked together—"

Lewis stopped mid-sentence. Gracie looked blank, and Patrick felt lost, too. "Okay, I can tell that I'm losing my audience." He pointed to Gracie. "Your turn. What do *you* want to be when you grow up?"

Gracie answered right away. "I wanna be a writer! I wanna make exciting stories and help people …" She paused to think. "Uh, when I was little and read that book, *The Little Engine That Could,* I knew that I wanted to make up stories that tell people …" Her voice trailed off as she thought some more. "Um, I wanna tell people that they can *do* things—great things!"

Lewis smiled. "Gracie, that's a really fine goal."

She blushed, her fair face reddening so that Patrick could count the freckles. "Thank you!"

Lewis turned to Patrick. "Your turn!"

Patrick didn't know exactly how to describe what he wanted to become. He *knew* that there were words for his dreams, but he couldn't get to them. "Bro', I want to … I want to …"

Just then Lewis's phone on the desk warbled a Vivaldi stanza. He held up a finger to tell Patrick to wait. "I've been sending out resumes, applying for a research job," he whispered. "Don't tell Dad—let me do that." He got up and answered the call.

"Hello, Mr. Connors."

Patrick heard *wonk-wonky-wonk,* from the phone, but couldn't make out the words. He saw Lewis's face cloud, then darken some more. "I … I'm going to have to turn down that interview," he told the potential employer. "I agree the position is a good fit in many ways, but your company is tied to the Horned Edge organization."

Patrick sat up straight. Lewis went on, "Mr. Connors, I had a difficult relationship with that, er, movement before, and I can't in good conscience work with them again." Lewis tapped his fingers on the tabletop, shaking his head. "I'm sorry, but my decision is firm." Patrick heard indistinct growling noises from the phone. Suddenly, Lewis exclaimed, "I won't put up with implied threats!" He cut off the call.

Patrick tensed all over. "Bro', you got a job offer from the *Horned Edge?*"

Lewis was breathing hard and sweating. "Not directly. But, yes." He paced two steps. Then he stopped. His eyes glazed; he swayed.

Patrick's stomach lurched. "Uh, Lewis—"

Lewis shrieked.

The ear-splitting sound rang against the walls. Patrick recoiled so hard that he knocked the lamp over. "What's the matter?" he yelled.

But then he saw Lewis's eyes roll back. He toppled backward and his body began to twitch. His arms and legs beat on the floor and his head knocked against the leg of the bed. The metal leg cut his forehead, and a stream of blood trickled down his face and onto the rug.

With a bolt of fear, Patrick leaped up. Gracie screamed and backed away. Lewis jerked like a body in an electric chair. Patrick bellowed, "Dad! Mom! *Help!*"

CHAPTER 2:
MURDER ON LANTHRA

In Bardia on the world named "Horizon"—*Lanthra,* a princess named Miriam—Mim to all who knew her—knew that she had to write a letter to the High Magus Daniel about a desperate matter. This was because she was certain that her father, King Norhe Reynolds, had been *murdered.* And possibly her brother Chris had been, too. *Possibly.*

Mim sat in the royalty's lead carriage with her widowed mother, Queen Katharine. Today's funeral procession was led by, not one, but two white hearses pulled by white horses with white plumes. The lead hearse contained a coffin with the king's body. The other hearse contained a coffin that was empty.

A pale white mist obscured the Winerush River, and its dull clear dew dripped from the rows of blooming dogwoods. *From now on,* Mim thought, *I will hate white. It stands for death; dried, old bones.* After her carriage rolled the carriages of the various Bardian royalty, then nobles rode on horses. Crowded at the tail trod ordinary mourners. The long line crossed the causeway to the cemetery on Gull Island, while memories beat against Mim's psyche.

For, not only had father died a week ago, but only three days ago there came news that her brother Prince Christopher Nathan Reynolds had apparently drowned—*emphasis on the word apparently,* Mim thought, grinding her teeth. And so, since the prince was "certainly" dead, the authorities quickly decided to have a proxy burial of the son along with his father. The thought made Mim's stomach hurt.

The Bardian nobles "knew" that Chris had died because his

bruised, hideously sunburned, and half-dead companion with a terrible story had been found washed up on the seacoast east of the capitol, Kingsport. The young man spent several days in the hospital, but after he could talk, the local authorities rushed him to the palace, with all the nobles and herself gathering.

Her stomach twisted again as Mim recalled Chris's best friend's speech. Hope Lu was her friend, too, the son of a famous sea captain, and she'd hung around with him and Chris often. Even though she was only fifteen, Hope treated her like she was as old as him, that is, eighteen.

Although she was dimly aware that her carriage vibrated and swayed and clacked over the causeway, she saw Hope Lu's raw sunburned face in her mind. Mim replayed his words in her unfortunate clear memory:

"Just one day out from Kingsport," he'd said, "three ships full of pirates attacked our yacht. The *te-sebizor* clubbed most of our mates to death." Hope's face contorted with the emotional pain. "Then they bound about a dozen of us—the so-called 'important' ones—including the prince. I hoped they only intended to sell us at auction in Eleaemana. But one by one we were dumped overboard! Oh, I cannot forget how those evil ones laughed! They shouted, "You're free—now walk home! I was one of the first to hit the water. And I watched my friends drown." Tears rolled down his cheeks. "I do not know how I survived— Radyah must yet have a purpose for my life in this world."

* * *

Now Mim said not a word, and her eyes were dry. She held her mother's hand while the queen wept. But Mim did not cry. She was the strong one; fifteen-year-old Mim was always the strong one.

The procession stopped at the great royal cemetery. Tall hemlock branches dripped down necks or on the tops of umbrellas as the crowd gathered around the white pavilion that held the royal mausoleum. Mim and the queen and her first cousin Norhatha stood inside the pavilion with the pastor.

The pastor gave a sermon. During the long ceremony, the voices of many, many people sobbed in the background. King Norhe and Prince Christopher had been dearly loved by their people and even by people in neighboring countries, so almost everyone cried. But Mim stood stony-faced.

To her ears, the pastor intoned the usual words. In standard church-speak, he talked about Radyah, the singing Lord. He said something about "faith." *Yeah, I know all that,* she mentally growled. *So what? It won't bring Father back. Or my brother Chris, either.* The sermon drifted right through her head like the fog.

*   *   *

Hours and hours after the long, sad, and frustrating funeral, Mim lay on her bed, stiff and unable to sleep. Too clearly, she reviewed all the awful events …

On the Glad-Day, she woke up early to meet her father for breakfast. The king could be gruff and stubborn, but she loved his soft heart. He always listened to her, which was a precious gift for any teenager.

Mim bounced with delight through the French doors toward his suites. Dad typically awoke and was active by dawn. By now he would be in his study, dressed, getting ready for the long day by reading the *LuFared,* the Good Book from Earth while bright morning sunlight streamed through the opened window.

As she walked through the castle, Miriam remembered how healthy he had always been. Most people said that King Norhe Reynolds looked stern, but whenever he saw her, he smiled, radiant to enjoy her company and to tease her about her rich, auburn hair. Father's hair was iron gray, mother's hair fell dark and long as a waterfall. But Mim, their youngest child and only daughter had, to everybody's surprise, turned out to be a redhead. With a loving smile, Dad often told her, "You're a beauty with hair like a quiet sunset."

Struck by an impulse, Mim decided to detour through the courtyard garden. The spring weather was on the brisk side of mild, a little misty as usual in Kingsport by the river, but the clear blue sky vaulted overhead. *It won't take me long; Dad will be finished reading about the time I knock on his door.* Just yesterday, she'd seen big patches of pink, white, and yellow crocuses budding beside the paving stones, and she wanted to see how their blossoms were coming along.

As soon as she stepped outside, Mim leaped back and nearly fell. The flowers were crushed! Ravaged! And on them lay… lay her father's body!

Mim screamed until the windows shuddered. She folded herself into a standing fetal position and wailed. Dad's eyes were open; his awful purple face was contorted. "Help! Help!" she yelled. However, silence pressed around her, as in a death-filled cave.

Maybe he's alive! Mim thought. She cautiously advanced, touched his skin. He was still warm. Hoping, hoping, she sprinted back into the palace to find someone, anyone, who might help her father.

As soon as she sped into the hallway that led to the nobles' quarters, she collided with Lord Broton Sipes, her father's chief adviser. Mim's feet slid on the tiled floor. She landed on her butt; her skirt pulled up around her waist.

Lord Sipes staggered but kept his balance. "Whoa, young lady," the tall, rangy man said in his patronizing voice. "Why were you screaming? Did you see a big bug in the garden?" To Mim's disgust, he stared at her exposed undergarment and smiled. It was not a nice smile. Lord Sipes's eyes gleamed. He wet his lips with his long pink tongue, touched them with his middle finger, and blew her a kiss.

*   *   *

Mim could no longer pretend to sleep. Her heart burned with anger. So, she got up and exited her suite's glass door that led to the castle's waterfront garden. Fog lay thick and cold on the landscaping as she meandered along the long river walk—not the courtyard garden where she'd found Dad; Mim didn't think she would ever go there again. Apparently, her feet knew where she ought to go. The sliding-glass door to Mom's suites opened on the river side, too. To Mim's surprise, candlelight shone through the great window. *Mom can't sleep, either!*

Mim knocked softly on Mom's patio door. The queen's velvet voice called, "I see you, darling. Come in!"

Mim slid the door aside to enter mom's sitting room. Mom's body had gotten thin, yellow, almost emaciated. Her thick dark hair had thinned and roughened, and her patrician high cheekbones bulged through tight skin. No one knew what was making her so ill although the doctors had examined her multiple times. She often felt nauseated, and her stomach hurt all the time.

Mim could not bring herself to think the awful "C-word."

Katharine slumped in a big, well-padded chair. Her maid had made tea, which sat on the side-table untouched.

"Good evening," Mim said as she hugged her mother. "How are you doing today …er, tonight?"

Mom's eyes looked reddened, and Mim did not know if she'd been crying or if it was an effect of her disease. "I'm doing." Her voice sounded weak. "We need to talk."

Mim held her mother's hand, full of questions.

Queen Katharine liked to get right to the point. "Now that your father has died, and I don't know how long I can hang on, I want to appoint someone to care for you. Lord Sipes has been a faithful supporter of our family. I have appointed him to be regent after I'm gone, and he will be your guardian until you come of age. The papers have already been drawn up."

A steel arrow of fury pierced Mim's defenses, and her slim hand squeezed her mother's so tightly that the Katharine cried out, "Mim, what is the matter with you?"

"I'm sorry, Mother! I'm so sorry to hurt you!" Mim massaged Mom's hand. And she was sorry—but she wished she could hurt Lord Sipes.

"We all have had a such a shock, my love," Katharine brushed her daughter's cheek. "I understand how you must feel." Then tears welled out and streamed down her cheeks. She leaned on Mim's shoulder, sobs heaving her body.

But even as Mim held Mom and soothed away the tears with a lace handkerchief, she saw a dark, frightening web pattern in her thoughts. Whispers, innuendos, absences, and presences shouted that the hasty coroner's report lied. *Murder!* An even worse idea came to mind: *Broton Sipes, that nasty B. S. killed the king! And maybe he arranged a deal with the pirates who killed—no, captured Chris, the heir to the Bardian throne, just so that he could get himself appointed regent.*

Her stomach sank as she thought, *Lord B. S. wants to seize the kingdom!*

Mim knew the English insult that came with those letters. She relished it now.

Mim also knew her history. She connected the dots. In her high-level classes at the University from Daniel the High Magus himself Mim learned that cruel, demon-worshipping Horned Edge magi in Tor used the advanced—but illegal—ancient technology to connect with Earth last year. They allied with similar fanatics from Earth to conquer both planets by exchanging advanced weapons and invading strategic countries.

Mim learned the mechanics of the Horned Edge plan for Lanthra. First, they'd seized the College of the Magi up in northwest Bardia near Tor and held Daniel hostage. Then they convened a "kangaroo court" assembly of the magi in Tor with him as their captive key leader. The Horned Edge almost became the ruling sect on Lanthra! But their plot failed. Mim remembered with a tickle of pride that a woman—the High Magus Daniel's daughter, Deirdre, had foiled the Horned Edge's plans by persuading Mim's stubbornly neutral father to send the Bardian army to Tor to rescue Daniel.

Since the Horned Edge's attempt to control all the Lanthran magi—and therefore Lanthra—had failed, they … they were planning to control Bardia, the seat of the Magi!

Mim's moment of wholesome pride fled. She shuddered as the pattern she induced from the king's murder expanded its scope. *Saoma-worship and the Horned Edge movement is resurging in the southern nations; it has even risen up in southern Bardia. And B. S. admires the Horned Edge. I even heard him say once, "They certainly know how to control their countries!" Does that mean that Broton is a covert Saoma worshipper? And—is he part of a second plot even bigger than I can imagine?*

The queen was quiet now, and her head drooped. Her breathing slowed; she warmed and slept. Leaning back, still holding her mother's hand, Mim considered. *What are my options? I can't solve Dad's murder by myself. I can't stop a Horned Edge plot to take over the throne—or worse!*

As she sat next to Mom and stroked her hair, Mim's eyes narrowed. She calculated. *Who can help me?* Her first cousin Prince Norhatha came to mind. But Norhatha, only three years older than Chris, had left Bardia to work a farm in the country of Polunking. She thought, *Maybe Norhatha's passion would bring him back. I know he loves us. But … no. My cousin is so busy and distracted, newly married with another child on the way … I'm sure that he cannot help.*

The faces of her more distant cousins and uncles, even those of the servants, soldiers, friends, and anybody, anybody who might help ran through her mind at top speed. Mim discounted each one. They were distant, incompetent, deeply grieving, clueless, or allied with Lord B. S. No one, not even the queen—especially sick Katharine—stood out as a helper.

What shall I do? What shall I do?

While she stewed and moved chess pieces around in her mind, Mim began to smell a sweet aroma. *Huh?* She inhaled. It was not her mother's perfume, and certainly not her own. The odor was flowery and minty, familiar. It reminded her of mom's mother, Grandmother Anne.

Breathing deeply, Mim wondered if the smell was real. *Whether it is or not* ... she felt her mind calming down. She felt her heartbeat slow. The prickles of fear eased.

A lattice of relationships formed in Mim's thoughts. Her grandmother Anne was a Forschwynn, the sister of Edwin, who was best friends with a certain important, very important power in Bardia, even in the whole world ...

Mim reviewed his strengths. First, he had an awesome reputation. A skilled court diplomat as well as a wise scientist, he held the whole world together with persuasion, not coercion. Mim knew him personally from taking his classes in political management and Earth Studies at the university in Kingsport.

Just as Mom raised her head and reached for her cold tea, Mim pictured the one person that she absolutely knew she could trust: Daniel, the High Magus of all Lanthra! Mim decided, *Daniel. I will send for you. Please, please come!*

CHAPTER 3:
STRUGGLING WITH MENTAL BACH

Patrick yelled for help while Lewis continued to convulse. Footsteps pounded on the stairs. "What's the matter?" Dad shouted as he ran into the room. Patrick tried to grab Lewis's arm to help him, but got knocked on the nose and backed away.

Dad stepped in. Patrick heard Dad mutter, as he turned Lewis on his side, "I thought he was over this!"

"Dad, what's wrong?" Gracie sobbed, tears streaming down her cheeks.

"He's having a seizure. Let me handle this," Dad ordered. "He's had them before, and I know what to do. We can't stop what's happening. But we can help Lewis from getting hurt." He stuffed a pillow between Lewis's jerking head and the bed frame. Lewis continued to convulse. A big blot of blood seeped into the pillow.

Dad and Mom surrounded Lewis with pillows as he flailed. Gracie huddled into herself, arms across her chest. Patrick tried to help with the pillows. Once again, he got hit on the chin.

Suddenly, Lewis's body quit shaking. He lay limp, gagging, snorting with deep breaths. Patrick saw his lips smacking, frothy saliva escaping his mouth.

"Dad!" Gracie howled. "Lewis is *dying!*"

Dad felt Lewis's pulse. "No. He's not okay, but he's not dying."

Mom stated, "I'm going to call 911—right now!" She sprinted downstairs. In half a minute, she shouted, "They're on their way!"

*   *   *

A crappy week after Lewis's seizure, after playing video games in his bedroom, Patrick drifted downstairs to the living room to practice the piano. It was a Steinway baby grand, and he loved it. On most days, when his fingers pressed, punched, and tickled the keys, the piano made beautiful sounds. He practiced, practiced, practiced for sheer joy. But not today.

Today, sitting at the baby grand piano, Patrick fumbled the chords and scales. He closed his eyes. His hands quit playing, and he rested his forehead on the keyboard. Tonight was the fall recital. *Argh ...*

*   *   *

It was time to go to the recital. Dad drove all the Brahminduras to Patrick's piano teacher's mansion. Patrick's stomach roiled through the ride. He muffled a burp. *I shouldn't have eaten that third dinner roll.*

"You're going to do great, bro'!" Lewis told him as the family got out of the car. He looked all right now, but Patrick knew he was on a lot of meds and couldn't drive anymore.

When Mrs. Arson opened the front door, Patrick saw that she wore a pale lavender long dress with sparkling amethyst jewelry and a silk bow in her tall beehive dyed red hair. She reminded him of a certain unpleasant amethyst cave chamber ... "Come in, come in!" she ordered, smiling. Patrick's family filed down the hallway to a large formal parlor stuffed with people.

Conversations buzzed; adults sipped from wine glasses and kids chugged down some kind of nasty sour ginger ale. Mrs. Arson's dark pink lipstick coated her front teeth as she smiled and greeted the guests.

Eventually, the crowd seated themselves around the upright piano. Mrs. Arson gave a short speech. "Welcome, everyone, welcome. Tonight, we have some special guests! Children, I expect you to do your best!" She introduced several important people from the crowd, and when Patrick heard their names, he closed his eyes. *Oh great. The governor, a senator. No pressure.*

At her prompting, child after child went up in turn, played a short, memorized piece, then bowed and sat down. As the star pupil, Patrick was to go last. Mrs. Arson beckoned. Patrick rose from his folding chair. He stumbled once, but made it to the piano and took his seat. *I can't mess up. I've gotta do this right.* Taking a deep breath, without sheet music, he zoomed through the *presto* tempo.

He was doing great! He was more than halfway through the sonata! But then … Patrick's mind went blank—empty as the void of space! He stopped, lifted his hands, tried to remember what to do … and failed. So he swept a great, loud *glissando* and jumped up from the piano. He started to rush back to his seat, but Mrs. Arson glared at him. He stopped and bowed. People clapped. While Patrick slunk back to his seat, he thought, *I'm a toad. A great, fat toad.*

Once they got home afterward, Mom hugged him. Dad and Lewis patted his shoulder. Gracie exclaimed, "You were doing great! But why did you stop?"

Patrick snapped, "I just did, that's all. Leave me alone, *Greasy.*"

After he said that, he felt like a … *toad as in u-r one.* He snarfed down some chocolate cake that Mom had made for this special evening. It sat like lead in his stomach as he went upstairs to bed.

*   *   *

Piano lesson day rolled up again. Mrs. Arson had selected a new piece for him, and Patrick had practiced it, but …. *I've just got to make up for messing up Mrs. Arson's recital.*

"Now, Patrick, get out your new music," Mrs. Arson said.

In his most polite voice, Patrick said, "Before I play that, I want to play the 'Moonlight Sonata.' I ordered the Beethoven book myself and paid for it with my allowance. And I've practiced and practiced."

The aristocratic lady with her beehive hairdo frowned and snapped, "You should have been practicing your piece for the recital! I had the mayor of Huntsville *and* the governor of Alabama, *and* even our senator! He especially wanted to hear my star pupil play."

Patrick retorted. "But I did practice! I just blanked out!"

Mrs. Arson's lip-sticked mouth hardened. Patrick noticed that she didn't always color inside the lines. She hissed, "Go ahead. Play your new piece."

Patrick took a deep breath and began. He thought the music was flowing nicely when, in the middle of the sweet melody, Ms.

Arson's long scarlet fingernails stilled his hands. Her voice cut like a razor. "Patrick, you will never be a concert pianist. You are just not good enough."

* * *

Patrick came home from the lesson and ate a pudding cup plus he chugged some sweet tea. His feet took him around to the piano. "Patrick, please play me that new Beethoven song," Gracie asked from the sofa. "I liked that one."

"I don't wanna'."

"Please!" she begged.

Pushing back too fast from the piano, Patrick knocked over the bench.

"What's wrong?" Gracie complained. "Why are you so crabby?"

But Patrick didn't answer. He left the bench where it was and stomped upstairs to his bedroom. Slamming the door, he flung himself onto the bed. *I'm never going to be good at the piano. I should quit taking lessons! Or maybe I should give up playing the piano forever!*

* * *

It was Friday afternoon after a long day in the nineth grade—and more insults from the bully. Patrick threw his bookbag down on the chair in the hall and limped into the kitchen. He saw Gracie, who had just come home from sixth grade. "Hi," she said, pouring herself a glass of milk. "How's it going?"

Patrick thought, *Horrible,* but he didn't say it. He couldn't meet his sister's eyes as he grabbed four cookies.

Gracie noticed. "Honestly, Pat, what's going on? You look like you stepped in doggy doo!"

"Don't call me Pat! My name is Patrick!" he snapped. Turning away, he started to storm up to his room. But then he heard a hurt little squeak from his sister, and he stopped. *Don't take your problems out on Gracie.*

He sighed and turned back to her. "It's me and the piano. I'm no good at music. I think I'm going to quit."

Gracie stamped her foot. "You *love* music! You're amazing!"

"No, I suck!"

Gracie started to blurt out something, but then she stopped

and cocked her head. "Okay … what happened?"

The closet of shame began to open in Patrick's mind. "My piano teacher told me that I was no good. She wouldn't even let me play the rest of my lesson."

"That's so stupid!" Gracie exploded. "Are you just gonna' quit piano? You *love* that! Honestly, bro', you need to dump that teacher!"

"But suppose she's right?" Patrick threw back at her. "I should quit and save Mom and Dad their money!"

Turning away, he trudged upstairs to his room and flopped onto his bed. It was hard to think, hard to understand what he felt. His stomach hurt, so he curled up into a ball.

Patrick's tears began to flow. He stuck his head into his pillow to try to quit crying, or at least keep everybody from hearing him. "I'm no good!"

A calm voice talked in his thoughts: *You are not* great *at playing the piano—yet—but you want to do it. That makes it okay.*

"Huh?"

Sometimes what you really want to do is what you should do.

He sniffed and wiped his nose on his sleeve.

So what do you want to do? the voice continued.

"All right, I really wanna play piano for people. I do want to play concerts. But what does that amount to? Who cares?"

You do, and Gracie and Lewis and Mom and Dad, too.

Taking a deep breath, Patrick sat up. A quote rose in his jangled thoughts, something he'd heard Mom say. *"Music soothes the savage beast."*

When did she say that? Some time back, Mom and he had visited Grandma at the nursing home. Grandma didn't have dementia, but her roommate did, and it was bad. The old woman got agitated, even yelled at him and swore when he tried to talk to her. That rattled Patrick, but he also wished he could help her. When Mom and he left, Patrick asked, "What can anyone do to quiet down that old lady?"

Mom answered, "The nursing home plays music for her. It always quiets the lady when she gets so anxious. They have a great music therapy program there, and that's why I chose it for my mom."

"What's music therapy?" he asked.

"They've learned that music helps ease the pain of people with Alzheimer's and even post-traumatic stress disorder," she said. "Some colleges offer a degree in music therapy."

Now as he sat on his bed, an idea sparked in Patrick's heart. *Music therapists could help people like Lewis, my brother who makes himself act happy around us but has seizures and even cries at night.* Patrick's thoughts hardened into a resolve: *Maybe I could heal people's minds with music, even if I can't play like Mrs. Arson said. Forget what she said! I'd like to become a music therapist.*

A kind voice inside, soft and sweet like Gracie's added, *And ... maybe you can be a concert pianist, too!*

*   *   *

Patrick's stomach tickled with nerves as he opened the heavy door of piano practice room number eight at Oakwood University. The university's music department had a whole building, and on one wing were eight of these practice rooms, each containing a shining black Yamaha upright piano, well-tuned, ready to play. Patrick's new music instructor, Jordan Washington, was already waiting for him.

Jordan Washington looked older than Lewis, maybe in his mid-thirties. He had rich brown skin and a thick crown of braided black hair. Right away, Patrick noticed the music teacher's long-fingered, chiseled hands, and compared, *My hands look like fat paws compared to Mr. Washington's.*

"Thank you, Mr. Washington, for letting me have lessons with you," Patrick said. "Here's a first payment." His Apple Pay app sent the fee to the tall, lanky African-American graduate student.

"You're kindly welcome for the lessons. Please call me Jordan." The piano teacher smiled, and his face, brown like Patrick's, glowed with accepting warmth. Gesturing toward the padded piano bench, Jordan indicated that Patrick should play, while he took a gray folding chair close by.

"I'll call you *Mr.* Jordan." Patrick's heart fluttered as he sat down on the bench. He thought, *I'm going to mess up. I'm only thirteen. I'm not that good. I'll never make a concert player. He's going to tell me to go back home and wait until I grow up.*

Mr. Jordan said, "Here's how I want us to start with this lesson. I see that you've brought a sample piece that you've played before. Good! I want you to play it for me. I'll listen to get an impression of your style and skill, and we'll go from there."

"Okay, Mr. Jordan." Patrick reached down into his backpack. He drew out a big binder and took out an intermediate level gospel arrangement of "Abide with Me." *I really need to calm down right now.* His hands trembled. *I'm going to butcher this music.*

But the teacher sat with an open posture and his eyes were kind. "Relax, Patrick. You've got this."

Taking a deep breath, Patrick settled on the bench, opened the sheet music, and placed his fingers over the keys. He played the hymn arrangement. Once he got into it, his mind began to relax. Patrick survived the entire piece without faltering. At the end, he let the last chord hold its sweet fermata. When he looked at Mr. Jordan, the man had his eyes closed and a smile on his face.

"Patrick, you've got it down. Now let me tell you what I've observed about your style."

Oh boy. Patrick tensed and prepared for the worst.

Mr. Jordan spread his arms. "You like to play 'wide.' Your arms, your legs, your posture are wide. That means that you are a confident player and like to show strength."

"Really? Wow. You mean it?" Patrick began to glow inside.

"Yes!" Mr. Jordan emphasized. "Your skill level is intermediate at this time, and you chose a great piece to match your ability. I'll teach you how to sharpen your skills. Soon, I believe, you can move on to an advanced level."

Patrick leaned back, his thoughts far away. *I could play for church. I could play for sick people, too, and help heal them. I could play for Lewis.*

"Now," Mr. Jordan said, reaching into a briefcase, "I want you to play this new piece for me." He handed Patrick a book: *Two-Part Inventions* by J. S. Bach. "Let's hear the first one."

Patrick started playing. At first the music had appeared simple, but after a few measures, he began to struggle. The fingering was hard. He was used to pressing the damper pedal down, but it made a mess of the frequent changes of key. He stopped, turned around toward Mr. Jordan, and sighed. "This is *hard!*"

"Yes, it's harder than it looks at first glance. However, mastering Bach's music will teach you accuracy. You already play with great emotion. But I want you to improve your accuracy and crispness in handling the keys as well." Mr. Jordan gestured toward the piano bench. "Let me have your seat. I'll play it, and then I'll turn the piano back to you."

They switched seats. When Mr. Jordan played the first *Invention,* Patrick heard sharp staccatos and a clock-like steady rhythm. It wasn't all the same volume; there were loud phrases, and very soft phrases. The music flowed like a stream from the instructor's hands. "Wow," Patrick said. "You're great! I could never play like that!"

"I believe that you can, and sooner than you think." Mr. Jordan got up from the piano, closed the music book, and handed it to Patrick. "The book is mine, but you may keep it until I can order one for you. The cost will be added to your lesson fee next month."

Patrick accepted the loaned book. He was excited, but he was scared, too, while he put the book into his backpack. *How can I ever learn to play like Mr. Jordan? The music is only two parts, but it's* hard*! I'm just not that good.*

Apparently, Mr. Jordan read his thoughts, because he said—and his voice was sharp, "Besides mastering notes, you have to master what goes on in your head. You have to change every negative thought to a positive one, saying that you're good at music, that you've got this. Practice the thinking even more than playing the piano!"

Patrick moaned, "I don't think I can."

Mr. Jordan folded his arms, so Patrick took a deep breath, and said, "Okay, okay. I'm a good player. I'm going to be advanced, and I'm going to play concerts."

As they left the practice room, Mr. Jordan shook Patrick's hand. "You're a good musician, maybe even a great one. Just believe in yourself. You'll do fine. Now remember, play Bach's *Inventions* staccato, with an even rhythm, no pedal. Don't worry about being fast yet. Observe the dynamics carefully. And ... about that 'Abide with Me' arrangement that you've already mastered ... right away, schedule yourself for a performance.

CHAPTER 4:
THE CURL OF DATA

A loud *buzz!* from the home phone distracted Lewis while he listened to his brother practice the piano. He'd resonated with happiness and excitement because the Baroque rhythm of Bach's inventions matched his thought pattern … and distracted him from certain dark memories. *Argh! I'm not going to answer it,* he decided. *The computer home manager can take that call.*

But the phone kept ringing. *If that's the Horned Edge-affiliated company that called before … before my seizure … And if they knew I had this, they'd come after me even harder!*

Lewis's heart beat faster. His right hand patted his back pants pocket. There was a little flimsy piece of plastic in there, a souvenir from his previous stay in Lanthra. Its atomic structure held the complete design for the Lanthran technology that enabled instant space travel. If only he could …

"Somebody, answer that phone!" Patrick yelled.

The blasted phone went on making a racket, and now it was impossible for anyone to concentrate. Lewis rose from the sofa and made his way to the kitchen to answer the call.

"Hello?" he growled.

A man's voice answered, "Hi, I'm Eric Mansfield, the music team leader at Christ Methodist Church." Eric sounded mature, but probably younger than his forties. Lewis pictured him as a white, medium height, generic person.

But, inside Lewis cringed at the term "Christ Methodist Church." He'd been an atheist 'before Lanthra,' and during the greatest suffering he'd ever endured, had begun to believe that Christianity might be true. But "church people" made him uncomfortable. *Church people can be so dogmatic. What does this guy want?*

Eric asked, "May I speak to your brother Patrick?"

Dumbfounded, Lewis could not answer at first. *Eric is calling* Patrick? Then excitement filled his heart. *He's recruiting my musical genius brother!* "Just a moment. I'll get him for you."

"Patrick!" he called, "It's Eric the music leader from Christ Methodist Church. This call's for you!"

Grinning, glad for Patrick's opportunity, Lewis brought the phone into the living room. Patrick took it and put the phone on speaker.

Eric's mellow voice said, "I have an idea, and I'd like your answer. You are the right age to fit into our youth band, and I want to develop you as our assistant keyboardist. Would you be willing to play preludes and offertories for our worship services? Not every service yet, but at selected worship events."

"Um …" Patrick gulped. "Uh, I would try."

"You'll be fine. No criticism, no sarcasm, just a performance. Would you select a piece related to the Advent season before Christmas? I'll schedule you for the second Sunday this month, just before the sermon."

"Really?" Patrick squeaked. He lowered his voice and tried again, "Do you really think I could do it?"

Eric said, "Sure!" I was at your recital, remember?"

Lewis saw his brother cringe. "Oh. I didn't see you that night. And I, er, goofed up."

"It's normal and common to draw a blank under recital pressure," Eric emphasized. "It takes time and repetition to develop your performance mentality. I thought you were awesome!"

Patrick took a deep breath.

Lewis pictured Eric's calm face, his positive encouragement that had impressed him the few times they'd met. "Do it, Patrick, do it!" he whispered.

Patrick swiped one hand through his thick, dark brown hair. Trying to sound assertive, he answered, "Wow. Okay, I will. Let me start, and if that goes well, then maybe I could play more often."

Eric said, and Lewis's heart echoed in agreement, "You'll do fine, Patrick! Thank you for agreeing to help us with the music at worship. I'll send you a quick text with the schedule, theme, and so on."

"Wow," Patrick repeated. "Thank you, Eric!"

"Thank you, Patrick! And Jesus bless you. You are loved." Eric ended the call.

Lewis high-fived his brother. "Way to go, my modern piano virtuoso!" Patrick smiled and jumped up and down like a happy puppy, wincing as he came down on that injured ankle.

*   *   *

On Sunday Lewis sat with his family in comfortable theater-type seats at their huge Methodist church. Soft recorded opening music soothed the atmosphere while people chatted. Ahead, high over the altar, a big screen showed serene pastoral landscapes. At his right side, Gracie sat rapt in the moment; Lewis knew that she loved the latest Christian praise and worship songs. On Lewis's other side, Mom and Dad smiled. With a little tug of joy, Lewis watched their hands touch. It always pleased him when they showed their love for each other. It made him want to touch Deirdre.

Deirdre! Will I ever see you again? I miss you so much! He remembered her long honey-colored hair, her steady green-gray eyes, her sumptuous curves. She was his first and only true love. Miracle of miracles, she loved him, too! But—and Lewis's heart sank—*Deirdre is on Lanthra and I am on Earth, the planet of the Curse.* His hand crept toward that back pocket. *But, if I could develop this, if I could make a partial connection, then Deirdre could have a Zoom-type meeting. I couldn't touch her, but I could talk with her!*

Twang! Squall! Massive sound waves blasted from the big speakers when the worship band began. Lewis's hands clenched, sweat broke out, and he took deep breaths to calm down. The band played very well, but the volume was much, much too loud. The cacophony drove Lewis toward a panic attack. He gritted his teeth and hugged his knees, trying to control himself.

His phone buzzed in his pocket. The caller ID showed a number from Space X. Lewis knew the call was from their hiring manager regarding his application for a physics research position. *I've got to get out of here and answer this one.* The phone kept buzzing, and he slid out of the pew and stepped fast to the back of the church.

"Hello, this is Lewis Brahmindura." His chest revved with excitement. *I may finally get back into my field!*

The hiring manager said, "Your credentials from Dr. Zhartha are awesome! You're quite a talent."

Lewis stood up very straight, smiling, expecting to schedule an interview. *And get out of the shoe store!*

The manager continued, "I'm sorry, but we have decided to turn down your application. You've been politically compromised and are no longer a good fit for our company."

A few words later, the phone call ended. His throat tight, Lewis debated sneaking out of the church to the car and waiting until the service was over. But, after a deep, deep breath, he made his way back to the pew. The music team had started up another enthusiastic and loud song, but Lewis chose to endure.

Eventually, to his huge relief, the praise and worship torture ceased. The band withdrew. There was a welcome silence, then it was time for an offering. Lewis pulled a twenty-dollar bill out of his pocket. When he looked up again, he startled because his brother Patrick walked onto the stage, limping a little.

His brother sat at the grand piano. Lewis smiled, job-rejection shock soothed. *Way to go, bro'! This is going to be good.* Then Patrick put his hands to the keyboard and played the song he'd been practicing at home so often: "Abide with Me." The tune sounded simple, but the arrangement ran and chased the melody with what sounded to Lewis like mixed classical and rock styles. "Patrick's song reminds me of a Christian 'Classical Gas,'" he whispered to Gracie.

"What's that?" she whispered back.

"Never mind." Lewis leaned back, closed his eyes, and absorbed Patrick's music. *My brother, my thirteen-year-old brother already has such talent!*

While Patrick played, Lewis's memory took him to one of the happiest moments of his life: Lewis held his love, Deirdre. She had chosen *him.* Deirdre had chosen *him*—the geek with the pocket pencils and the coffee stains on his white shirt. And she was a Lanthran noble, daughter of the High Magus Daniel. His beloved was trained in Earth lore and Earth languages, a skilled swordsman, and soft as a velvet pillow. They held hands while the

Bard of Bardia, young Sir Thomas Forschwynn, played his lute for the crowd so that Deirdre's and Lewis's hearts beat together. *If only I could savor one of her spicy kisses again!*

The last note of Patrick's music hovered pianissimo over the audience, and Lewis slowly, slowly exhaled. Now that he was back on Earth, he had a mission, a mission from the God he'd didn't understand but had barely begun to trust.

While the worship service continued, Lewis's hand slipped into his pocket and fingered the curl of silicon. It felt like a mere plastic candy wrapper, but its atomic and even subatomic structure was a schematic for all the technology that he needed to connect to Deirdre. *If only I could develop the data ... If only I had a job where I had the right equipment ...*

At that moment, the great dragon of his heart's desire stirred in his soul and told him, *Your dreams can come true with that curl of data. I have a purpose for you. Not only can you create instant space travel, but you can enable time travel.*

Lewis touched the curl of data in his pocket again. *May it be!*

*   *   *

Monday's weather was cold, clear, and intensely bright. On the way to the store—Dad driving—Lewis saw a weird pattern in the glare. *Not another seizure!* he prayed. But it was another seizure. His brain exploded; he blacked out.

When consciousness returned, Lewis found himself lying down on the back seat of Dad's car. He felt like he'd been tasered. The car door on his side was open and Dad bent over him, his brown face tense, even horrified.

"Did it again," Lewis mumbled. His forehead hurt. When he touched it, he felt a large lump. "Ouch!"

"You really had a good one," Dad quipped, trying to lighten the moment. "It's good that you had your seat belt on, or you'd have blown out the windshield."

Lewis took a deep breath to steady himself. "I feel better," he lied.

"I'm going to call the emergency services."

"No. I'm okay now."

Dad hesitated.

Lewis insisted, "I'm okay! I don't need to go to the hospital;

I need to work!"

But Dad took him home to rest, and Lewis was secretly glad.

* * *

More seizure meds, Lewis meditated the next day as he brought out boxes of women's new stylish boots. *They must be working because I feel groggy.*

He set down the boxes and began to stack them. Then it occurred to him that he might have lost his curl of Lanthran data during yesterday's seizure! Lewis's hand dived into his pocket. *Still there.* He sighed with relief.

Suddenly he sensed a presence and turned. *Wow!* A beautiful woman stood in front of him. *Wow again.* She was tall and slender, with thick, long, wavy honey-blond hair. Her subtle makeup and gold dress totally complimented her perfect face and figure. "H… hello," Lewis stuttered. "How may I help you?"

"Do you remember me?" the young woman asked. "I'm Peggy Gnudst, the pharmacy representative who visited you in the hospital." Peggy's smile radiated like warm sunshine. "I know that was two years ago, but I really enjoyed meeting you."

Lewis remembered the hospital, but not her visit. The whole hospital experience was foggy because two years ago when he'd returned from Lanthra to Earth, he was so sick with pneumonia that he thought he would die, and so did everybody else.

"Lewis?" Peggy's voice interrupted.

His thoughts jerked back to the woman waiting for him to speak. "Um … hi. How are you, Peggy?"

Peggy smiled. Her eyes shone. "I'm fine, thank you. I was in town visiting my uncle, and heard you were here."

Lewis drew a blank. "How—

She explained, "My uncle's wife once worked for Dr. Zhartha on the energy project, and she told me about you. Plus, I never forgot our visit, even though it was two years ago. I really wanted to see you again."

"Er, …" Lewis began, but Peggy continued, blue eyes twinkling, "Besides meeting you in the hospital, I saw you in the news. You're the brilliant physicist who disappeared for two years! The news said you and your siblings had been kidnapped by terrorists who made you work for them. That must have been an awful experience!"

Lewis nodded. There was a silence.

Then Peggy handed him her business card. Besides her photo and name, "Peggy Gnudst," he read, "pharmaceutical representative." Lewis's eyebrows rose when he saw the logo for Gnudst and Cranz Pharmaceuticals.

She touched his arm in a friendly way. "Are you free for lunch today?"

Lewis considered. *Dad and Mom keep telling me that I should get out more, make some friends. It's nice that we both have a tie back to Dr. Zhartha and my old job.* "I am free, if you can wait about a half-hour until I finish stocking these shelves."

"Great!" Peggy touched his arm again with her delicate long-fingered hand. Lewis noticed a pale place on her ring finger and guessed that she had either broken an engagement or had divorced. His heart quickened, both with empathy—and with excitement. "When you're ready, I'll drive us to the City Cafe Diner."

Dad's whole store brightened, and Lewis began to look forward to being with her. Plus, the City Cafe Diner had great reviews and he loved Greek food. His mouth began to water. "Thank you, Peggy," he said.

*   *   *

After Peggy left the shoe store, she found the corner coffee shop. There she ordered a skinny latte, sat in a dark corner, and pulled out her phone. "I've met with him," she whispered while she sipped her latte. "He's agreed to go out with me for lunch today."

"Good," she heard. *"Call again and report after you've had a chance to talk with him. And make sure you arrange a next-time meeting with Mr. Brahmindura. We want him.*

"Oh, I will, I will. By the way, he's really cute."

The person on the other end of the call hung up.

*   *   *

At the diner, Lewis ordered a gyro and cheesecake, and Peggy ordered a Greek salad. They chatted about small things.

As he bit into his gyro, Lewis couldn't help but notice that her dress style had a nice "V" neckline, and his eyes couldn't help but follow the line downward. Her gold dress perfectly enhanced her skin and hair, and the subtle brown eye shadow made her large

29

eyes even more luminous. Lewis closed his eyes. *Deirdre, I love you. I don't want anyone but you.*

Peggy asked, "What happened to Dr. Zhartha's big energy project? I haven't heard about that lately."

A muscle twitched in Lewis's jaw. "It was discontinued. Apparently, people were afraid that the huge power that we could access from the Earth's gravity would destroy the planet."

Out of habit when thinking about gravity, his hand crept toward his pocket to feel the curl of data that he always, always carried with him. Peggy's eyes followed his movement, but she didn't remark on it.

Peggy supported her head on her hand so that her beautiful hair hung over her shoulder on that side. "Tell me about your family. Do you have a partner?"

"Yes," Lewis answered, but he chose not to elaborate. A lump blocked his throat, and he had trouble swallowing the bite of his gyro. Wiping a bit of tzatziki sauce from his chin, he gulped and finally got the bite down. He hoped Peggy didn't notice.

But she did and she smiled. He told her a little about his parents and Patrick and Gracie. Then he reciprocated, "Tell me about yourself."

Peggy began, after a small bite of her salad, "I live in Newark, New Jersey. My dad is the CEO of the pharmaceutical company that I represent."

Lewis nodded. "I saw that on your card. I'm impressed!"

"Don't be. I'm just a pharmacy rep—but," her eyes flickered, "I'm very good at my job." Her expression darkened. "My parents are divorced, and my father has a new 'trophy wife.' She is actually only one year older than I am. And she wears loads of jewelry and smells like a tank of cologne." Peggy wrinkled her nose. "Angie doesn't like me, and I don't like her." Her eyes narrowed, and for a millisecond Lewis was reminded of an angry cobra.

Dismissing the alarming image, he commented, "That's too bad." It didn't seem fair that his family would be intact and happy but hers was broken and bitter.

"Never mind. I like my job, introducing drugs to doctors' offices, hospitals, and clinics, meeting all kinds of people. I'm an extrovert. I like people and I like to party." Peggy smiled.

"Speaking of parties—will you come to come to my uncle's party this weekend? My guest?" Her hand briefly touched his knee.

Lewis nearly jumped. He immediately thought of Deirdre, his Lanthran love, and felt guilty. *I miss you so much!* However, a rational-sounding voice in his head urged, *Come on, Lewis. Get a life! You aren't abandoning Deirdre! You should go to the party.* He answered, "Sure, I'll go. Thank you for asking."

CHAPTER 5:
JOB OFFER

Peggy's sleek red Porsche pulled up at her uncle's house. Nestled at the base of a big, forested hill, the three-story house looked decidedly genteel when Lewis compared it to his family's modest suburban home. Passing rows of parked high-end Mercedes, Teslas, and two Lamborghinis, Peggy settled into a parking spot under the porte cochère. "We are here. This is my uncle Maynard's house. His partner is Adrian—but call *her* 'Trudie.'"

Lewis nodded. *Why are you so nervous?* he asked himself. *You've travelled; you've met people of every kind.*

A soft inner voice brushed his soul. *A lot has happened to you, a lot of bad, bad stuff. You're not recovered yet, Lewis. And you're afraid of being judgmental.*

He followed Peggy up the steps to the private entrance. Its door was painted dark green with a large stained-glass window. In the center panel hung a door knocker—a brass handle shaped like a tongue protruding from a gargoyle. Lewis stared, gulping. The snarling demon face leered at Lewis as Peggy grabbed its "tongue" and rapped on the door. He knew it was probably just a humorous detail based on the legends that gargoyles protect a property against evil spirits, but the nasty thing still gave him the creeps. *Okay, you're not in a dungeon. Today's a nice, sunny day, you're with a beautiful young woman, and you get make new friends.*

Maynard Gnudst himself answered the door. "Come on in, *darling,*" he cried. As Peggy stepped forward, he hugged his niece and pecked her on the cheek. Then he turned to Lewis. "Who have we here?"

"This is Lewis Brahmindura," Peggy answered.

"Glad to meet you," said Lewis. Thank you for having me here."

Maynard winked at him.

They passed through the kitchen, which was crammed with jovial people. "Come join the party!" Maynard boomed. He led them into the living room. Chatter filled the huge space. Blackout curtains on every tall window choked off most of natural light, but plenty of candles dotted glass tabletops. He and Peggy jostled among people drinking coffee, martinis, colas, wine, and mixed drinks of every kind. Peggy pressed a glass of wine at him and he took it. Lewis knew that he shouldn't drink because of his meds, but he was reluctant to tell about that. "Serve yourselves," They loaded porcelain plates from a long smorgasbord table.

"Here's Trudie now." Maynard called his partner over to meet Lewis. "This nice young man came with my niece Peggy." He hugged Trudie, kissed *her* on the cheek, patted the other man's butt.

What in the world have you gotten into? Lewis wondered as he shook Trudie's hand, rattled with sudden homophobia. Since returning to Earth, he had been reading a modern-translation Bible. In the letter to the Romans by Paul, he had encountered a discussion of homosexuality. If the Bible was true, what should he feel about Maynard and Trudie? Judgment? One concept from Romans had stuck in his mind: "Nobody is righteous." *In other words,* he thought, *don't single out one doctrine's people-problem to judge someone. All people are problematic.* The higher thought, the better thought, he knew, is *Love one another*. Trudie smiled, and his soft dark brown eyes were warm. His handshake was firm, cool, and dry.

Lewis's emotional lurch relaxed.

Peggy saw someone she wanted to talk to and excused herself. "Lewis, enjoy yourself. I'll be back with you in a jiffy." She squeezed through the throng.

"Tell me your name again," Trudie asked. His tenor voice sounded smooth, cultured, and he had a faint Central European accent.

"Lewis. Uh, Lewis Brahmindura."

Trudie's eyes widened and his mouth dropped open. "Lewis

Brahmindura?"

To Lewis's surprise, Trudie pronounced his last name correctly. "You are the famous physicist who worked on the Dr. Zhartha's energy project two years ago—you were going to make a singularity to power the whole world!"

"Well …," Lewis began.

Trudie invited, "Sit with me and tell me about yourself. Here, this place will be relatively quiet, and we can talk."

Balancing a soft drink plus a plate of fancy crackers, caviar, a wedge of cheeseball, and several stuffed mushrooms, Lewis joined Trudie in a corner that contained two chairs and a cushioned settee. The area reminded him of a coffeehouse. It made him feel more at ease.

His eyes sparkling, Trudie sipped peach brandy from a big snifter and began the conversation. "I read in *Wired* magazine about you. The article said that you were the genius behind the idea of using the Earth's center of gravity to create endless energy. You're so young … maybe twenty-four?"

Lewis nodded.

"Let's see if I can remember properly … you went to Stanford to study physics in the Honors program. You graduated summa cum laude in two accelerated years, at the top of your class, and you were only twenty years old! Then you were immediately hired for the experimental energy production project."

"Yes." Lewis sipped his caffeine-free cola and ate a mushroom.

Trudie went on, "I'm a physicist, too. My work involves, well, global observation and navigational systems." He lowered his tone, "A lot of what I do is classified. Your work was, too, I imagine."

"Yes," Lewis commented. He felt flattered and wary at the same time. "What company do you work for?" Mentally, he warned himself, *If he works for the Shields weapons manufacturers, I'm out of here! They threatened my family if I didn't work for them! That company even allied with the Horned Edge to take over the world!*

Trudie said, "I work for MayFari Schematics Company. Not the home furnishings one, but a space contractor."

Lewis took a deep breath and felt his chest relax.

"We specialize in the electronic components of satellites." His tanned face blushed a little. "Defense satellites."

Lewis had never heard of the company. But it sounded interesting.

"But I don't want to get into details of *my* work," Trudie said. "You are much more interesting. What have you been doing lately?"

Lewis noticed with relief that Trudie avoided talking about his infamous disappearance which the news had reported as "Energy Research Physicist Kidnapped by Terrorists." *Good! I don't want to go there.*

Staying general, Lewis talked about his family: his parents, Patrick, and Gracie. That, he knew, was a safe topic, and one he could get enthusiastic about. Then Trudie asked him, "Where are you working now?"

Lewis composed his thoughts and, after a brief struggle with embarrassment, disclosed, "I help my dad with his shoe store. I'm clerking, selling, stocking, helping with paperwork. It's low-key employment … just right for me these days."

But he knew deep in his heart that the shoe store was *not* "just right" for him. The dragon of desire that pushed him every single day to yearn for his goal would not let him rest. *Time travel. I want to enable time travel. I don't know why yet, but I think the desire is a God-thing.*

Suddenly, as if his psyche had been kicked, Lewis blurted, "I'd like to get back into the physics field. Actually, I've been sending out resumes."

Trudie's eyes gleamed. "If you are thinking of physics work, have you considered biophysics? Peggy's father is hiring biophysicists right now in a study on a new treatment for genetic muscle degeneration diseases. I know you've been a theoretical and particle physicist, but …" he smiled, "helping people with Alzheimer's would be a worthy task."

Curiosity stirred, and Lewis shifted, almost dropping his plate. "I suppose the human side of physics needs to be explored, too. I confess I've concentrated on the mechanical system."

Trudie sipped his brandy, then raised his head. "Perhaps it is time to move from the shoe business to really working in your field. And," he laughed, "you know the old adage: 'It's easier to get a job when you already have a job.'"

The sudden opportunity hit Lewis in the gut. *Maybe I can work my way into time travel through biophysics. Yes, it's a sidetrack, but ... Maybe I can get there this other way.* Something in him checked "negative," but he could not pass up the chance to get out of the shoe store.

Trudie pressed for a decision. "I'm sure that I could put in a good word for you with Roger Gnudst—he handles the techie side and Ted Cranz handles the marketing. Your excellent reputation speaks for itself. Might you be interested?"

Lewis's dragon stirred. And it was not happy. Lewis felt it like a ripple in his mind, saying, *Do you really want to detour from your real goal?*

He argued. *I'll get back on course. It's just a few twists and turns away from time travel physics!* A pressure inside contradicted that statement, but he pushed it back.

Head whirling, Lewis made a sudden decision. "Would you be a reference for me?"

"I can do better than that. I will talk to Roger *right now!*" Immediately, while Lewis watched, Trudie made the call.

Chapter 6:
GRACIE'S GRIEF

Gracie stretched and practiced yoga on a mat in her bedroom as usual before breakfast. Movement felt good. Her supple limbs moved like poetry. She started to ramp up her exercise, trying more difficult poses and holding them longer, but then she heard Mom call, "Breakfast is ready!"

Smiling, Gracie thought, *We have a happy family. I love 'em so much!* She snickered and added, "Even Patrick!"

In the kitchen, the Brahminduras munched cereal with milk and bananas before heading out to school and work. It was not a fancy meal, but they were *together*. No one said much for a while in the silence of happy eating. However, soon Patrick poked Gracie's side. "How can you stand to eat that granola? It's just a teeny amount in your bowl. You're going to starve before lunch at school!"

"It's filling, and it has protein and fiber. You can't say the same with your sugary, vitamin-added mush!"

"But look here." Patrick grinned as he got up and grabbed a large, stale leftover pastry from Sunday breakfast. He took a huge bite, chomped, and swallowed. "I've got reserves, *Greasy!*"

"And I've got health, *Patty!*"

Dad interrupted. "Enough!"

Gracie gave her brother a dirty stare, but she quit fighting. So did Patrick.

As they packed lunches and got ready to go, Mom told them, "I have an appointment this afternoon, so I won't be here when you get home."

Mom worked several evenings during the week as a

librarian, so Gracie did not think this was unusual. On those evenings Dad stayed home and made supper. As she slid a trapper into her bookbag, Gracie mumbled, "What kind of appointment?"

"I have a medical appointment," Mom replied.

Gracie froze. She asked, "Are … are you okay?"

Mom shrugged. "It's just a mammogram."

Lewis, wrapping his sandwich, spoke up. "What's going on?"

"Oh, I found a lump, and I want to check it out."

Gracie dropped her bookbag. Her stomach dropped, too. She gulped, her throat getting tight. She saw Patrick run a hand through his dark wavy hair, as he did when he was unsettled, and Lewis did the same. Dad frowned.

Mom gave them a half-smile and picked up the keys to her car. "I'm fine. Just being careful. Now, let's go."

But Gracie remembered that Mom's mom, Grandma Anwen, had died of … *It's gotta be just a lump,* she thought. *It can't be*—she couldn't even think the awful "C" word.

*   *   *

That evening before bedtime, Gracie sat before her little desk in front of her computer. She wrote a few words of her newest story: an adventure about a girl who fought an evil dragon—a Cancer Dragon. But after listing the beast's dark gray scales, long coils, bony wings, clawed feet, sharp fangs, long forked red tongue, and scorching breath … and, and …, her mind shut down. She let her hands drop away from the keyboard. Nothing, not one word about the brave girl would come.

Mom might have cancer, she groaned. *Mom might have cancer. She might get really, really sick and even … even*— Gracie couldn't bring herself to finish the thought. Mom had told them that she'd had a biopsy. She'd know the results tomorrow. Gracie's dinner curdled at her thoughts. She remembered Mom's pale, haggard face, her limp hug before withdrawing from them all and going early to bed.

Scowling, Gracie saved the few words of her dragon story and started a new blank document file. The white page glared at her, empty, like her head.

Hmmm. Her schoolteacher had suggested that she write about herself. So, Gracie began to type: *In the spring I'll be eleven, and after school's out for the summer I'll start sports. I can play in the softball league. I can run track, too!*

Encouraged, Gracie sat back and thought about what it felt like to run on her long legs. She was tireless. She felt great!

But her good thoughts lasted about two seconds. Bezuby—her word for "awful"—thoughts began. Gracie knew, she *knew* that Mom had cancer.

Gracie sighed. Her effort at writing got stuck in muck. While she twirled her hair, she heard Patrick playing the piano downstairs. *Okay, I'll go in the living room and read a book while I'm listening to him,* she decided.

She went to the living room, sat on the sofa, and opened *The Hobbit* by J. R. R. Tolkien. The ticking of Bach's music began to irritate her reading rhythm, and she complained, "Can you play something else?"

Gracie saw her brother frown, anticipated a smart remark. "Okay," he answered.

Surprised, Gracie pleaded. "Just—please play something calm and smooth." She returned to reading as Patrick shuffled through a couple of music books. Then a song came pouring out from the piano. It was a new one, a flowing contemporary version of "I Will Lift Up My Eyes."

As she listened, Gracie delved into her book. The sofa felt nice and warm, and she began to enjoy Bilbo and the dwarves. Her mind soothed like putting cream on a burn as Patrick's melody flowed. All at once she sat up. "Hey! I've got an idea for a story!"

"That's good," Patrick replied, not paying much attention.

Gracie raced upstairs. She knew exactly what and who she was going to write about: Daniel the High Magus, her Lanthran friend and protector. She'd been his "daughter" when they'd ridden as hostages toward the Moorway swamp with its mosquitoes. And, when they were kept in a castle prison in a tower, Daniel helped her escape from the evil Lord Charon. *Nothing* was going to block her story this time, not Mom's sickness—nothing! *This* story had a happy ending.

CHAPTER 7:
A NAUSEATING WEDDING PLAN

On Lanthra, Princess Miriam read Daniel's return letter. She then lowered her head between her hands, slumping. Her long auburn hair fell forward and served as a curtain while she thought. Outside her suites, rain hurled in sheets upon the sliding glass doors that overlooked the Winerush River.

The letter from the High Magus was short, warm in tone, yet business-like. Anyone reading it would see a simple greeting and notice of a visit from her respected mentor. No, the letter itself wasn't the problem. Mim's heart sank because the seal was upside-down and fell off when she handled the envelope. Daniel's letter had been opened and read by "someone" before it was delivered to her.

What can the High Magus do to help me? Are all the rulers here corrupt? My father the king is dead, and the heir has been murdered or taken prisoner. There is such evil in this place! I can hardly endure it; my heart aches and my stomach burns. The Horned Edge has infiltrated the palace. I can trust no one except Mom, but I can't tell her what I know because "they" would kill her.

Mim had a good idea who "they" were: Lord B. S. and his cronies.

She laid down Daniel's letter and paced. Rain thundered outside, a heavy and steady rain with a howling wind. Condensation obscured the sliding glass doors to the outside. But agitation made her want to bounce off the walls of her suite. *If only I could walk along the river front! Then I could think! If Daniel were here, how could he help? Think, think, Mim. Come up with a plan!*

Her mind roiled. Her gut twisted inside.

"Never mind the rain! I *will* walk outside!"

In the bottom of her oak bureau lay hiking clothes, including sturdy rain gear. As she opened the drawer, she muttered, "The storm isn't dangerous; it's just unpleasant. And I feel unpleasant. So, I'll prepare and go walking now. Right *now!*"

Mim put on her old clothes, her boots, a blue scarf, and pulled up the hood of her rain gear. Pulling open the sliding glass door to her patio, she leaned out and looked both ways.

Rain, rain, rain. Mim stepped outside, closing the door. Rain pounded and wind beat against her. Mim exulted in it; the weather matched her mood. Paralleling the Winerush River, she walked fast, keeping her back to the wind. It was raining so hard that she could hardly see the river. Even through the oilskin suit Mim was getting soaked. She didn't care; she just walked faster toward the gazebo and the garden. In the summer, she loved to visit there; a food cart sold snacks, cold drinks, and ice cream, and interesting people gathered to talk. But, not right now! *Thank goodness, I'm alone! I need to think!*

It was spring in Bardia. Azaleas bloomed profusely, pink, coral, red, white, even orange. The crocuses were well up, and daffodils smiled along the walkway. Her plans figured no clearer than ever, but the beauty of nature encouraged her. Mim's hurried steps slowed for a moment. *Daniel said he would come soon. I can hang on until then.*

*   *   *

The rain drove down harder than ever; so, returning to the palace, Mim decided to slip in through the kitchen area. The cooks and staff should be on break at this mid-afternoon hour. Water puddled onto the tiled floor as she took off her oilskin cloak. *Somebody might slip.* Taking a mop from a cupboard by the stove, Mim began to clean up the puddles.

The sound of heavy steps and a drawling male voice drifted through the hallway: "How long before *Hegofean* Dancing Dan arrives?"

"Only two days, my lord," said another voice.

Egad! Mim exclaimed to herself. *It's Sipes and his toady Emmet! Lanky, lewd Broton Sipes! Nasty pasty doughball Emmet!*

Her chest burned at the insult B. S. had used on the High Magus. But she held back. They sounded as if they were coming into the kitchen!

She crouched near the huge stove but continued to mop. The scarf concealed her auburn hair. The old clothes were unremarkable. Sipes would think she was just a servant girl cleaning the kitchen before the dinner shift began.

"Hmmm," Sipes murmured. "I will make the announcement tonight. We've got to act *now,* before the nosy *zitta* tongue gets here. He's the only one who could stop us now."

"Does anyone know yet what you plan to do?" Emmet asked.

"Oh, the rumor has been started. Even the queen has heard it."

Well, I haven't heard the rumor! Mim thought. *What is this slimy snake about to do? Another murder?*

Lord Sipe's voice continued. "The menu is planned, the announcement is writ, the clergy are ready." He sounded very pleased with himself. "Did you prepare the gift for the bride?"

"Not yet," Emmet mumbled.

"Hurry on it! We've got to be ready this very night, and the ceremony will be held tomorrow afternoon!" Now Sipes sounded snippy.

Mim's heart raced. *Sipes is getting married? To whom?*

Footsteps retreated. The two men were exiting the kitchen, and Sipes was drawling again, but this time there was a sting in his voice. "Put a guard on the princess. We don't want her to get away until the wedding is complete."

Mim froze. *Who is going to be the bride?*

"You've had this planned for a long time," she heard Emmet say.

"Oh yes. That little red-headed beauty will be delicious to bed."

Mim's heart pounded so hard that she was sure Sipes and Emmet could hear it. She cowered, nauseated, nearly throwing up. Swallowing hard the nasty bile, she waited until there was no more noise in the hallway. Then she put away the mop and fled out into the storm.

*   *   *

Thunder rolled. And rolled again. Rain pounded anew, A sharp *Crack!* made Mim jump as she slid open the door to her palace suites. Shivering, not even bothering to shed the wet rain gear, she dripped her way into her bathroom.

I cannot trust my lady-in-waiting, Mim knew. *Emma may not be part of the plot, but she's loyal to Sipes and his followers. She and so many people seem convinced that B. S. is the next Beautiful Savior instead of the next—* she thought a dirty curse. *Nothing I can say will change their minds.* Her stomach heaved. She leaned over the toilet to release the bile in her stomach.

I've got to leave; I've got to leave right now!

The hood fell over her eyes when she was throwing up. Her long red hair had even strayed into her dirty mouth. Mim yanked off the oilskin coat and flung it onto the tiled floor. But an idea came to her. Grabbing scissors, she hacked at her hair until only an inch or so was left on her head. Shining auburn locks curled on the floor; untidy shorn hair haloed her face in the mirror. "I don't want *anyone* to know what I'm planning, including Mom," she murmured, and gathered the mess of hair into a small sack to throw away into the river. "It will only be putting them in danger."

Mim grabbed some personal items and shoved them into her pockets. "Darwin's dad's ship is in port. We've never met, but Darwin is a strong connection! I'll sail away with *Westwind.*" Stepping back into the storm, she ran to the east toward the docks, away from the gazebo, away from the garden, away from home.

CHAPTER 8:
RINGS

Patrick stewed during every mile of the fourteen-hour car trip to Newark, New Jersey. *Lewis accepted that crazy new job. That's wrong, wrong, wrong!*

The boring highway corridor in November offered a view of bare trees. And more trees. Hills, yes, but all gray. Not only that, but it rained. His family headed for a big Thanksgiving holiday new-job reception for Lewis—*except for Mom.* That was another "stew" ingredient, and Patrick blamed Lewis and Dad. *She's got breast cancer, bro'! She'll have surgery as soon as we get back, and chemotherapy after that! Mrs. Clark is with her, but we're going to be gone for four days!* Images of Mom's pale face haunted his thoughts. Even competent, caring Mrs. Clark staying with her wasn't the same as having the family close by.

As the green Tesla hummed and bounced up US-81, Patrick's heart ached. Plus, he had terminal TB … Tired Butt. But he clamped his lips shut. Now was not the time to say anything, even though the anger built up every mile.

His ankle smarted like fire when his family walked into the Hilton Newark Airport Hotel. But Patrick didn't even care when now, sitting on one of the queen-sized beds in his and Lewis's room, he pounded a pillow and exploded, "You're gonna to switch to a job in a drug company? Lewis, your train is off the track! What about that heart dragon that you told Gracie and me about, your dream of time travel? And … you're leaving us when Mom needs *all* of us!"

Patrick rubbed tears away. When he looked up again, he saw that Lewis had quit scrolling through his email. His brother lowered his head, eyes half-closed. "I need a job," he stated. "And here's one just waiting for me. It's connected with physics. It'll give me opportunity, income, and connections. I can get back on track later." He turned toward Patrick. "I'll be available for the fam'. I'll call often. And I'll fly home if—"

"That job's a dead end!"

"No, just a short bend in the road," Lewis argued.

"Have you told Peggy about your real dream? She's, like, your girlfriend now, you know."

"We're friends, just friends," Lewis insisted.

But Patrick saw his eyes shift. He couldn't hold back. "Peggy! She hangs all over you! What happened to Deirdre?"

Lewis flashed, "It's been two Earth years since I last saw Deirdre! She hasn't contacted me; *no one* from Lanthra has contacted me. And Deirdre has probably met someone else by now. Besides, you remember that Earth is the planet of the Curse—"

"Yes, I remember! 'Earth is the planet of the Curse; don't go there.' But High Magus Daniel said we might see the Lanthrans again. And bro', you've been literally sitting on that plastic curl containing Lanthran instant space travel technology for two years and haven't even approached anyone to make it happen!"

Lewis's face reddened, his jaw tightened, and he started to snap back with a reply. Patrick steeled himself for a rare but scalpel-sharp rebuke.

But Lewis held back. He took a deep breath, relaxed his jaw, and then he said, "You must really care a lot about me to give me such an honest raking over the coals!"

"I do care! You're my brother!"

"Hey Patrick," Lewis's voice softened, "you've been playing the piano like a master, pursuing your dream. But I've been sick at home having seizures or plugging away in Dad's boring shoe store. Oh, I can't tell you how many times I've wanted to take that Lanthran locating system to some authority, but …" He shook his head.

Lewis continued, "Can you imagine me, an unemployed physicist, going to somebody in the U.S. government and saying, 'Would you help me develop the technology for instant space travel between any two locations mapped in the known universe?

And, by the way, it's from an alien planet.' They'd think I was a nut! It's not realistic to think I could get the support and the several billion dollars I'd need for the project."

"If you don't do anything," Patrick warned, "somebody might steal it!"

"Don't think that I haven't thought of that!" Patrick noticed Lewis's hand creeping toward his back pocket.

"And that Peggy—"

"As far as my relationship with Peggy goes, I've been lonely. I don't want to two-time Deirdre, but Peggy's a good friend—"

"Have you kissed her?" Patrick shot.

A knock on the door startled them. Dad stuck his head inside their room and said, "Time to go to the reception downstairs. Are you ready?"

"Okay. I'll put on my tie," Lewis answered.

"I'm not ready," Patrick complained. "And do I really have to wear that suit?"

Dad gave him the *look*. "This is a formal reception. We have no time for thirteen-year-old whining."

*　*　*

Soon the four Brahminduras entered the hotel's reception hall for the new-job party. Patrick and Gracie followed their father into the big, lavishly decorated room. A buffet table was set up along one wall with an enormous bouquet of white roses. Arrangements of chairs and sofas grouped within range of the food. Guests stood in large groups with wine or martinis or china plates of tempting appetizers.

Patrick eyed the goodies, and Lewis went to find Peggy. When Patrick scanned the crowd, he groaned. "Gracie, we're the only two people in the room who have to stay away from the champagne."

"Hmmm."

Patrick considered his little sister. Gracie had been awfully quiet on this trip. He figured that, like him, she was upset about Mom's nasty cancer and about Lewis's stupid new job. Gracie could be a real pain. But he approved her new beige dress that complimented her auburn hair. Gold and glimmering opals adorned her earrings and necklace; she could have modeled for a catalog.

Patrick's mind drifted into comparisons. Even at age ten, Gracie was taller than he by several inches, plus she looked fit and trim. Patrick touched his pudgy stomach.

Fighting the unpleasant prick of low self-esteem, Patrick stood near the punch table to people-watch. Everyone had dressed to the teeth, one level below "formal wedding." *Wow. They've gone all out to welcome Lewis. What do they expect? An engagement announcement? Argh. I hope Lewis and Peggy never come to that!*

He pulled at his choking tie, trying to relieve the pressure. Standing around made him feel like a wallflower, and … pain shot up his leg as if a sword had slit up his ankle. "Ouch!" he blurted. "Gracie, I've gotta find a place to sit down."

She turned toward him, her hazel eyes darkened with concern. "Okay, Patrick. Let's go sit down."

Patrick limped to the chairs, following Gracie. The stabbing ankle pain subsided after a while. Gracie got pop and hors d'oeuvres.

Patrick nibbled on a petit-four. Gracie sipped a cola and ate some baby carrots.

He had just tried a bite of caviar on a cracker when he froze, nearly choking on a salty swallow of fish eggs. *Rings!* "Gracie!" he whispered, trying to hide his pointing finger, "Look at those!" Patrick gulped,

At least a dozen people wore gold bands on their right hands. All the rings were set with a black diamond. At first, Patrick had written that detail off as "wealthy people in a club." But he'd seen those rings before in a very dark place at a very dark time, and he shivered. "Look at all those rings! These people are Horned Edge!"

"You're kidding!" Coming of her blahs, Gracie turned fully toward him.

"No! Talk about the Deep State, the Illuminati …"

"Huh? What's that?"

"I think the Horned Edge is *It!* They're like termites! The internet says they've infiltrated the government, the schools, the businesses—all over the place!"

"Why are you so upset about *It?*"

"Remember how on Lanthra we found out that the Earth is the planet of the Treasure? Of all the places in the universe, it's strategic for control."

Gracie's eyes widened. "Oh, I remember!" She shivered. "That's scary."

Patrick nodded.

"What can *we* do?" she whispered.

"We've gotta get Lewis to see what's around him. He's so infatuated with that new job and that Peggy lady that he's oblivious to everything else."

"But when how—?"

"Right now! Let's go!" Wincing when he stood up, Patrick made his way through the well-dressed, smiling, and loudly chatting crowd toward his brother. Gracie followed.

Lewis stood in a small cluster of people, including Peggy's father, Roger Gnudst, who had his arm around the petite twenty-something wife with the platinum hair. Patrick's eyes narrowed when he saw Peggy take Lewis's arm. He surged forward, but Gracie held him back.

"Wait. We need to get Lewis *alone* to warn him."

For too long, Patrick jittered at the edge of the grown-ups' circle, wanting to be noticed. But Lewis glowed as if he were enchanted. Patrick saw his brother put his arm around Peggy's shoulders, his face a little flushed and a lot animated. Patrick groaned, *Oh no, they've let him drink alcohol. I sure hope it doesn't act up with his meds!*

Just then Dad stepped forward. He interrupted the circle of conversation, holding a gift-wrapped box toward Peggy. "My wife Cora bought this for you."

Peggy smiled as she accepted the gift. But when she began to put it on a side table, Dad stopped her. "Please," he urged, "Please open it now."

Peggy beamed, and even Patrick had to admit that she was a beautiful woman. Long, honey-colored hair rippled down her back, and her short peach-sequined dress barely covered her long, shapely legs. Peggy's blue eyes sparkled as she deftly pulled away the ribbon and loosened the paper wrapping. The box itself was white wood, with ornate flower scrollwork etched into its surface.

A woven cloth bookmark in gold and white thread lay on top. Peggy cried, "A lovely gift—the box is a gift all in itself!"

Then she opened the lid and lifted out a white-covered book embossed with gold lettering. Patrick recognized it: A *Bible.*

Peggy's jaw dropped. Handling the Bible with the enthusiasm of smelling a dead fish, she dropped it back into the box.

Dad didn't notice. He smiled, focussed on the Bible. Lewis radiated, too. But Patrick noticed Roger Gnudst frown. The platinum blond wife giggled, rolling her eyes.

Clueless, Dad beamed. "Cora had your name engraved on it."

In a flash, Peggy smiled and held the Bible to her chest. Then she wrapped Patrick's father in a huge hug. "Thank you, thank you, Mr. Brahmindura! What a wonderful gift—and so personal!"

"Call me Frank." They let go of each other. Peggy began clinging to Lewis, a winsome, loving look on her face.

Patrick added another item to his warning-list for Lewis. *Watch out for Peggy. That lady is not what she seems!*

CHAPTER 9:
CAPTURED

Eventually, the new-job party began to break up. Patrick saw Peggy tap Lewis gently on the elbow and point at the clock, and his brother nodded and loosened his tie. Roger Gnudst began shaking hands; people started leaving; finally, the room was almost clear.

"Hey, let's have some family time now," Lewis suggested. "After all, tomorrow I move into my new apartment."

Dad shook his head. "You kids get together. I need a nap before we go out to dinner."

Patrick thought, *Finally! I can warn you, Lewis. It may not be too late for you to back out of this trap!* "Sounds great! Lewis and Gracie and I can hang—"

Peggy interrupted. "Gracie's coming to my girls' party. That's the plan."

Gracie gave Patrick a resigned frown and shrugged. But Patrick grinned when Lewis said, "Well, it's just you and me, bro'."

*   *   *

Outside the Brahmindura's hotel room, it was wintry dark already and sleeting. Patrick sat on the queen bed in his and Lewis's room, his back propped up with pillows and his bare feet elevated. The ankle's throbbing eased.

Lewis leaned back in the office chair, his lean legs crossed. "What's up with your ankle, Patrick? You limped like an old hobbit without a cane all the way down the corridor."

"You know my ankle's been 'shouting,' as Grandma Lewis used to say." Patrick quickly changed the subject. "Funny …" he added, "I never noticed it before. You are named after Mom's family!"

"Yes," Lewis nodded. His brown eyes twinkled. "And I've been reading C. S. Lewis since we returned from … well, *that* world."

"Oh—*The Chronicles of Narnia,*" Patrick remembered. "Yeah, I like those."

"Actually, I'm into *The Screwtape Letters,*" Lewis said. Patrick saw his brother shiver. "The letters from a senior devil to a junior tempter makes bezubs—the demons of Earth—real to me. C. S. Lewis uses a lot of sideways humor to lighten up the conversation, but the bezubs are still unpleasant."

The mention of "bezubs" opened up a terrible memory. Patrick ventured, "Remember that night? You know, up on the mountain when they were going to kill us."

Lewis nodded, and Patrick went on, "I still have nightmares about it. The bad guys had us tied up and they were going to make a sacrifice to their god *Saoma*. But you saved my life!"

"That wasn't really by *my* power." Lewis held Patrick with his eyes. "Even though I didn't believe that God exists, I prayed that night. Then God let me speak and whatever it was I said somehow made Barth reconsider what he was going to do."

Patrick got quiet. He couldn't find words. Somehow his idea of God had gotten tangled up with the frightening part of the adventure. He wanted to ask Lewis more about God and Jesus and all that Christian stuff. Lewis, after all, was one of the most brilliant people he'd ever known, and if he believed that God stuff, that would mean a lot. But—

This is the time to tell him about those Horned Edge rings, came the thought. Patrick began, his voice dropping to a near whisper, "By the way, bro', did you notice people's hands at your new-job party?"

"No," Lewis answered, eyebrows raised. "What are you talking about?"

"Lots of 'em were wearing—"

"Patrick!" Lewis interrupted. He pointed.

A movement in the corner seized Patrick's attention. It was like a hologram, but the image got clearer, and he gasped. A large oval glowed. "Speaking of bezubs …" he shrank away from the sight.

A hostile presence flowed from the oval. It felt spooky, malicious, hateful, and much too familiar. *It feels like the Thing that threatened Gracie and me when we found the hot marble!* Sliding off the bed, Patrick edged toward the door as if backing away from a coiled, hooded cobra.

"I see it, too," Lewis whispered. He, too, edged away from the oval.

Patrick's skin crawled. Terror squeezed his heart; he began to tremble as two huge blue man-like forms appeared in the oval. "Blue People from Lanthra!" The blue males radiated power and a purpose-filled malice. One of them stepped forward; Patrick saw its horny toenails sticking out of the portal.

Lewis yanked open the hotel room door. "Patrick," he yelled, grabbing his arm, "run!"

They made it out of the room just a few inches ahead of the brutish *homo azure*. Patrick's sneakers and Lewis's well-polished shoes pounded through the corridor.

"To the stairs!" Lewis held the heavy exit door so that Patrick could rush through, then covered the rear.

The stairway smelled stale, like the air seldom circulated around the cement, and a hint of verboten cigarette smoke lingered in the turns. They had nine floors to descend to the ground level.

Patrick raced down the stairs, taking two at a time. *Surely the clerk in the lobby will call the police!*

In the stairway a few floors behind, he could hear the pursuers' heavy tread. Lewis and he slammed through the exit at the lobby level.

For this once, there was no one at all in the lobby, not a hotel customer, not a clerk. The whole area was empty. "Help!" Patrick shouted. But there was no help. The hairy Blue males burst into the lobby.

Lewis and he pelted out the automatic sliding glass doors to the front parking area. Freezing air pierced Patrick's clothes and lungs; an inch of slushy snow soaked his bare feet. Lewis and he sped toward the road, hoping for a restaurant or a gas station— anywhere that they could find somebody who might help them.

The pale city-lit cloud cover plus the haloed streetlights gave him plenty of light to see and be seen, but he saw no people, no one at all! There was just Lewis and himself and the two huge Blues in a deadly serious chase. Patrick's nose and throat burned. Gasping, he groaned because that ankle started to scream. *How long can I go on? Is there any place to hide? No.* Landscaping included only a row of winter-bare small trees plus a few droopy azaleas.

"Head for the highway! Hopefully someone will stop!" Lewis called from just behind him.

Right at the ramp leading up to the highway, Patrick's ankle gave way. His leg crumpled under him, and he fell on his side onto the icy berm. With a screech of tires, a car swerved to avoid crushing his head. The driver leaned on the horn, the honk's Doppler effect distorting the sound as the car weaved away. Patrick forced his body up again. As he limped along the roadside, he screamed, "Help! Help!" Lewis, beside him, waved his arms to flag down a car.

The Blues caught up with them. Patrick felt a massive burning hand grab his arm—but then it let go.

Lewis faced both attackers. For a moment, the Blue males hung back, intimidated. Patrick hoped they'd back down, even slink away. But then, red eyes gleaming, they drove forward, long arms reaching for them.

Lewis sparred with them; his cold expression threatened no mercy. One of the Blues whimpered in dismay and drew back when Lewis took a swing at its hideously contorted face. But the other massive thug caught Lewis's arm, kicking Lewis's foot, and threw him over his shoulder like a martial arts expert. Lewis flipped down onto his back in the slush. Then the Blue kneeled on him and began to tie his hands with a scarlet cord.

Recovering, big as a muscular blue locomotive, the other male grabbed at Patrick. Patrick slipped away. When the Blue came at him again, he fought kicking and hitting like a cornered cat. No good; the Blue knocked Patrick's head onto the road and put its knee on his neck.

Meanwhile, cars swerved, changed lanes, honked, crashed into each other. A huge truck eased past the mess to within ten feet of Patrick and the Blue brute who held him down. But instead of helping, the truck's driver gawked, rolled down the window, and drew out his smart phone.

Patrick hollered, "For God's sake, help!"

But although onlookers watched, amazed, not one came to help. Patrick, suffocating in a knee press, face down in the snow, felt a huge jerk, as if his whole body were a tooth being yanked out of an anesthetized jaw. He saw the snow and slush go gloomy, and then he felt himself slide out of the world.

CHAPTER 10:
WESTWIND

The clouds were still pouring rain when Princess Miriam of Bardia reached the Kingsport docks. Even though it was late afternoon, the sky loomed dark as twilight. She tightened her raincoat and edged along the riverwalk examining the ships. *Where is* Westwind? *Will Darwin's dad lit me aboard?* She scanned the walk before and behind her. There was no pursuit.

Near the end of the riverwalk, she read *"Westwind"* in big gold letters on a clipper.

The Winerush River lapped against the ship and the thick dock pilings. On a sunny day, it would look majestic with all its rigging against the sky; today it was a complicated dark mass.

"Hurry, hurry," Mim murmured as she looked both ways. "I must get away from that awful B.S." *Westwind* rested, sails furled, secured to great bullocks—and the two obligatory watchmen apparently had taken refuge inside, because there was no one in sight. Lord Broton Sipes had not found her … yet. But he would have noticed her absence by now. Her lady-in-waiting would have come to her suites to dress her for dinner. The silly woman would be surprised at Mim's absence and tattle immediately to Sipes.

Silent as a moth, Mim flitted across the gangplank to the ship's deck. *I must get below deck; I must hide until the ship sails.*

The cargo hatch was closed but not locked. Scanning the deck, Mim still didn't see the watchmen, so she lowered herself into the darkness of the hold. The inside smelled like fragrant soap. Captain Lu was trading the soap that the Blue People made from the oils of *rethe* plants in Moorway's swamps up north in Tor. It was the best in the world. Mim knew it would fetch a fine price wherever *Westwind* traded. And … *if* … she could hide undiscovered until *Westwind* was too far away to turn back, she'd be helping to unload heavy boxes of it as a deck hand.

Mim evaluated her ability to pass off as a boy. Her hair was shorn. She was petite, which meant that her breasts were hidden by her baggy shirt. And her slim body was strong. She could pass as a teenage boy.

Feeling her way around the crates, she found a place to nest in a corner. The rain gear would have to do as a blanket and pillow—once it dried out. She had no food, no water, but that was somewhat reassuring. There wouldn't be much pee or poop to excrete. Mim determined to "hold out and hold on" as long as possible. Even with her adrenaline still pumping, her body shaking, she told a lame joke to herself. "Hold out and hold on in the hold." Then she drew a sharp breath. *Stupid joke.*

A distant voice in her soul reprimanded her. It sounded like her father. *Never call my daughter 'stupid!'* But he was dead, and a would-be tyrant controlled his palace … and aiming to control the kingdom. Mim began to cry.

*   *   *

Tide going out. The muffled sounds of shouting sailors stowing the gangplank and raising the anchor came through the thick hull to the hold. Finally, a loud, sharp *thud* of battening down the hatch resonated into Mim's hiding place. She was locked into the hold.

Soon, *Westwind* caught the current in the Winerush River and headed toward *tessappa,* the ocean. Mim had sailed before, but not in such a close, stuffy place. She felt nauseated, and the sickness in her belly wouldn't go away. By the late afternoon, while the ship reached the river's mouth and passed into the ocean, Mim couldn't control the seasickness anymore. She managed to leave her nest, but what happened after that, and after that, was nasty. The hold began to stink.

Once her empty stomach finally quieted, Mim returned to her nest and lay down. But as soon as she tried to rest, little clawed feet scurried not far away. *Rats!* She tensed all over and hoped they were more afraid of her than she was of them. If any rodent approached, she'd smash it with her bare hands!

The next day. Mim awoke with more nausea. The ship

surged, heaved, swayed, pitched, rolled, and yawed. *Westwind* must have ventured far out into the open ocean—and into rough water. Her stomach was empty, but she retched up the "nothing" anyway in her stinking place. And thirst tormented her throat. She felt her tongue swelling and her lips cracking. *I have to make it through another day,* she told herself. *It's just what I expected.* But her soul and body were weakening.

Day three. Mim was sure she would die here in the dark. Thirst, stink, nausea, terror. She knew—she *knew!*—that if she got any weaker, she would die, sealed into this soap-smelling tomb. When *Westwind* reached port, the dockworkers unloading the crates would find her bloated body, half-eaten by the ship's nasty rats.

Struggling, she inched her way up the hold's ladder to the hatch. Mim pounded on the metal and croaked, "Help, help! Let me out!" Nothing happened. She beat on the hatch, screaming.

The hatch opened so fast that she nearly tumbled back into the darkness. Strong hands heaved her out of the hold.

CHAPTER 11:
THE GIRLS' PARTY

The drink of choice at Peggy's afternoon party was slo gin. Gracie didn't know what that was, but she was too shy to ask. It was probably some kind of fruit juice. With the black-out curtains drawn and stubby candles lit, Peggy's apartment felt spooky, as if they were going to pretend it was Halloween instead of nearly Thanksgiving. Gracie wondered what was going on. A little fear scrunched in her tummy, until …

… Until Peggy's friend Monica put a hand on her shoulder and insisted that she join them in a game. Monica directed Gracie and all the other girls to sit in a circle on the thick carpet. "Here are the rules," Monica told them. "Each of you has a little glass filled with sloe gin."

"What's that?" Gracie asked Monica.

"It's called a shot glass."

"But," Gracie persisted in a soft voice, trying not to be young and stupid, "What's slow gin?"

In the gloom, she couldn't see Monica's face, but her voice was smiling and light. "It's a sweet drink, very sweet. You'll like it. Okay here's the game: We'll play Trivial Pursuit. If you get the answer, we just ask a new question to the next person. However, if you *don't* get the answer, you drink up your glass."

The game started. Gracie got her answer twice. But she missed her answer the third time around.

"Okay, Gracie, take a drink," Monica ordered.

Gracie obediently downed the liquid. It was thick, rich, sweet, a little tangy, and tasted way better than pomegranate juice. "Hey," she exclaimed. "That's delicious!"

Another trivia question came. *Wrong again.* She had another drink. *This stuff tastes sooo good!*

And so the game went, round and round, until everyone got loud, talking and laughing at the guesses. Gracie wasn't sure what was going on with her head, but it felt good. The fears about Mom's illness faded into the way-back of her soul, and she decided to enjoy the moment. Instead of swimming in misery and scared like she had been since … *well, since the awful "C,"* Gracie felt happy—*happy!*

Way too soon, the game was interrupted when Peggy tapped Gracie's shoulder. "Time to go! We only have about twenty minutes before dinner. The rest of you are welcome to stay here at my apartment and party. Just lock up when you go. See you all later, ladies."

Gracie got up and waved at the circle of her new friends to say goodbye. In the candlelight their eyes glittered like critters in the woods. "I've gotta go."

They waved back, giggling. "Thank you for bringing me to the party," Gracie told Peggy as they left. "I had a great time!" Her brain was spinning, but she felt very merry. She held tightly onto the rail as she followed Peggy down the stairs and out to Peggy's car.

*   *   *

"Did you like the party?" Peggy asked in the ladies' bathroom at the hotel, adding the finishing touches to her makeup. She wore a sparkling short black dress. Her blond hair waved down her back. Gracie thought she could model for a catalog. *Wow. She's beautiful. Patrick's down on her, but I think she's cool.*

"Yes! The party was loads of fun!" Gracie exclaimed. "I've never done anything like that game before, and I've never had … uh, what was that drink?"

"Just a sweet cordial that women love."

Gracie didn't understand "cordial," but she licked her lips at the remembered taste. Her head still felt a little—well, a lot—woozy. That was good. It made her forget … *Mom's cancer.*

"Time for you to get little primped up for the dinner," said Peggy, turning and scrutinizing Gracie. "Can I give you a touch of makeup? You—let's see, you're ten years old? Not quite ready for a coming-out party, but certainly attracting the boys."

Gracie blushed. "Okay."

Peggy got out a new gold-bronze lipstick. "Here, try this."

Gracie let her apply it to her lips, then stood patiently while a soft brush highlighted her cheeks, and a tiny brush added some dark brown mascara to her eyelashes. Just then a jazzy ring tone interrupted them.Peggy smiled. "Just in time. We're all finished here."

She took her phone out of a black purse while Gracie smiled at her own reflection in the mirror. *Hey, I look like a model, too! I like Peggy and her friends so much! Patrick's just being paranoid.* But then something in the stillness and rigidity in Peggy's stance caught her attention.

Peggy cried out, "Oh no. Oh no!" Her face had gone white. She listened a minute longer and then said, "Yes. We'll meet you in the hotel lobby."

Gracie raced after Peggy to the lobby—and stopped abruptly when she saw Dad there, clothes a little rumpled, hair messy. His wide brown eyes stared at the large television screen.

The news showed the outside of the hotel, with a gaping crowd gawking from the circle drive at vehicles with flashing lights. Police had blocked off the hotel entrance. There was little to see beyond the confused people besides snow and slush and typical highway scenery.

"What's going on?" Gracie asked Dad. But he ran his hand through his hair again and didn't answer. On the television, a news person commented in a solemn but urgent voice, "It is unknown what the fight was about, but the two who disappeared were Lewis Brahmindura and his brother Patrick. A phone camera caught the scene."

To her horror—the hair on her head actually stood up—Gracie watched her brothers running up the side of the road, pursued by two huge … "Blue people!" she cried. On the highway ramp, her brothers fought and lost. She watched Lewis being bound, Patrick seized. Suddenly, her brothers and their Blue captors disappeared. They were gone, just plain gone. The news feed kept showing the clip over and over, while the journalist speculated on what might have happened.

He went on, "Lewis Brahmindura is the physicist who

disappeared five years ago, along with his brother, his sister, and a friend who was Lewis's co-worker. The Brahminduras returned after two years with a story about being captured by terrorists, possibly due to Lewis's research work, and the friend has never returned. Now it appears the strange and weird has happened again to this family."

Gracie felt a huge rebellion in her stomach. Leaving the breaking news report to Dad and Peggy, she ran into the bathroom and was sick.

CHAPTER 12:
THE HOT MARBLE AGAIN

Light exploded when Lewis passed between worlds. A heavy velvet "something" brushed against his skin. Reality appeared. He lay face down on a hard stone floor. A burning, dead weight like a hot sack of sand pressed him down. With a ton of man—no, a Blue person!—on top of him, his chest couldn't fill enough to get a good breath.

Numb shock faded into analysis. *We're in Lanthra again.* This was not comforting.

In a few minutes, the weight lifted. Lewis took a breath. By now he could operate in cool mechanical operation, although his heart pounded in his chest, demanding more air than he could obtain. Lewis's hands were under his chest, still bound tightly together by the scarlet cord. He worked the cord, hoping his captor wouldn't notice. Turning his head slowly, he saw Patrick.

The boy stood nearby. A hairy Blue person was fitting metal cuffs onto his wrists. Patrick appeared dazed and unsteady, his rounded, pleasant face tense.

I've got to help my brother! Lewis mentally shouted. But he had to wait for an opportunity.

Lewis's Blue brute raised him up to a stand, and he sucked in several deep breaths, alternately choking and swallowing, steadying himself outside as well as in. When he felt able, he examined his surroundings.

He and Patrick were inside a spacious, rococo styled room. He stood on an intricate mosaic in jeweled colors. Tall pillars held up a vaulted ceiling. But the walls—the walls had been painted with frescoes of demons like Mayan gods eating terrified people.

Lewis trembled and thought, *I'm in hell!*

No, he countered, *I'm in a place like hell*, and forced himself to return to calm. *Where is the technology that brought us to this world that names itself Lanthra? There, on the left.*

Lewis noted a black stone hulk—a control panel. *That's like the one I used back in Lord Charon's cave chamber.* Inlaid on the mosaic floor circled ornate silvery rings. Maybe three meters from the control panel stood an upright obsidian slab. *Okay. I know what to do.*

A deep underground well tapped into the continuous instances of singularities at the planet's center of gravity. The power from that core's horizon, no larger than a speck, could resonate the connection between points in space—allowing instance travel.

Lewis examined the control panel, planning his move. *What's different about that control panel?* It was awkwardly low, as made for a midget. He'd have to bend down to reach it, but Lewis intended to reach it, and the sooner the better.

By the control system, a small man held up an amber object like an ordinary marble. Lewis nearly salivated. *The hot marble! I need that to get Patrick and me back to Earth.*

The Lanthran magus bowed like a magician after an impressive trick. Lewis noted his orange robe with a scarlet lining to the sleeves. *He's from the southern continent—Swetha. But who's that other guy?*

Near the magus stood a huge *homo sapiens,* more than seven feet tall. White linen robes wrapped tightly around his barrel chest. A gold crown and loads of jewelry showed that the guy was a ruler, maybe even a king! He held a wicked iron scepter. But the man smelled sour, like old armpit and crotch sweat. Long, greasy black hair curled around his shoulders, and his oily beard covered his chest. A large gold ring pierced his nose. There was a bugger on it.

The king seemed familiar, but Lewis couldn't quite place him. He strove hard not to be terrified when the man pointed his scepter at him. *Stay calm.*

The king stared at Lewis with narrowed black beady eyes. He said in broken English, "Do ya not remember me? I am Baron Nargoleh Layhew. And now I be *Tot-Baon,* High King of the Isle of Mercy, a master of *Saoma*'s Horned Edge."

Lewis remembered Nark Layhew. He swayed, mind darkening, but the thug squeezed his neck, forcing him to be still.

"*Eaye* murdered my brother, Barth. And I will have my revenge."

Horrible scenes from the last time he was on Lanthra, a prisoner, scalded Lewis's mind. Nark's brother had kidnapped him and Patrick. Barth had mocked him, tortured him, threatened his family.

Lewis tightened his self-control and asserted, "Nark, I didn't kill your brother."

King Nark glowered, emanating waves of hate. "*Ditfama!* Whether t'was your hand or not, it doesn't matter. He died, and— *Lew-iss*," Nark hissed, "ye were there. Ye destroyed me, forced me out of my home. Howe'er," the awful man pointed toward the locating console and its obsidian monitor, "I'm more powerful now than ever. Let me show you. Then I will hurt you."

Lewis cringed as Nark growled to the magus, "*Lua ye, Fean Holdi. Til, forde fortilla.*" Nark's dialect sounded a little garbled compared to what Lewis had learned during his days as a magus on Lanthra, but he understood.

Tempted to explode into panic, Lewis grappled the fear that shook his body. He closed his eyes and prayed with all his soul as he, once the proud, self-reliant atheist, could never have done before, *Dear God, help us now. Especially keep Patrick safe, even if I have to die.*

His emotions stilled. Lewis relaxed even though he was bound, even though the Blue person next to him squeezed its hot hand around his neck. Rational again, he sent a desperate question to the God he'd barely begun to know. *Why? Why are we here again?*

A gentle voice inside stated, *Of all the billions of people on Earth that this locating system could have transported to this place, you and Patrick were chosen. What appears to be an unpleasant coincidence has "powers and principalities" behind the scene. But I am* the *Power, and I am with you.*

But God—

There was no answer, only more calmness. Lewis told God, trying not to quiver, *Okay, God, you had better be stronger than*

Saoma and King Nark!

At that moment, the little magus put Earth's marble back in a case on the wall. Nark called out, brandishing his scepter, "Show what I can do. Show them Wega, *Fean* Holdi!"

Lewis gritted his teeth. *I need that marble to escape!*

"*Alor! Wega!*" Lifting a second marble out of the case, Magus Holdi got ready to connect again. He inserted the marble into the control console. Lewis remembered that Wega was the copper-colored moon, one of Lanthra's six moons. It had been explored and mined as a productive source of copper, gold, platinum, rare earths, and many types of jewels.

The ancient technology is back in Lanthran Horned Edge hands. Their plot to conquer Lanthra carries on, Lewis groaned inside. *And if Lanthra falls, Earth will go soon.*

The obsidian monitor glowed. There appeared a beautiful orange-gold moon in a black sky dotted with myriads of bright stars. The stars looked like plain round dots … and somehow this was important! Lewis had admired this view of Wega himself, back when he was a magus working in Charon's amethyst cave chamber. But there was something wrong now about connecting to moon Wega. It had to do with those hard, brilliant stars. Lewis fought his fear to work out what, while Magus Holdi adjusted the controls on the console.

On the huge obsidian monitor, the moon's image grew close. It shone like a new penny. Rich ores wove through the mantle onto Wega's surface. The copper had never turned green or dull because there was no oxygen, no air—"*No air!*" Lewis shouted. "*Don't connect!*"

But Magus Holdi had already enabled the full connection. A mighty wind swooshed his robe; he tottered as the vacuum of space began to pull him in. Nark grabbed a pillar. The Blue persons rushed to protect their king. Patrick fell, and Lewis felt himself being dragged toward Wega's shining image. Magus Holdi said something like "*Oops!*" but then was sucked into the deadly void.

Lewis struggled to free his hands. He couldn't. Yet *someone* had to save Patrick, and he was the only one who could do it. But it meant getting to the low console despite the wind whirling into the vacuum of space—It would be like ballet in a hurricane.

Hitting the right control with tied hands would be tricky; he had to touch the *exact* spot to close the connection. Plus, he needed to anchor himself while he managed the disconnection or be sucked into the vicious vacuum like Holdi.

In a flash of thought, Lewis knew that running forward would cause him to be yanked into space. But—*Baseball! Slide to home base for the winning score!* The low control center would stay him for a moment—just long enough, he hoped.

Lewis dived toward the console. Shards of loose matter flew past him into space, to eventually fall into Wega's gravitational field. Through the open portal, he saw the body of the magus floating away, quickly dead, he hoped, because death in a vacuum would be excruciating.

As Lewis slid across the slick mosaic tile, he focussed on the small circle on the control panel that would shut off the connection. If he missed it, if his tied hands hindered his desperate effort, they'd all be sucked into space, their blood boiling in their living bodies until … until they died.

The wind got more violent; he could hardly see as his hair whipped over his eyes. *Ready, aim, fire* … Lewis stuck out his bound hands and let his right index finger slam against the small spot that would close the nexus.

Immediately the air stilled. *Thank you! Thank you! Thank you, God!*

What a mess. Debris littered the great locating chamber. *Patrick is alive! I'm alive!* But … so was Nark and the two Blue thugs. Disgusted, hot with anger, Lewis saw that the Blues had abandoned the manacled boy to steady their ugly master. *My brother could have been killed!* But … that gave him an idea.

Lewis hauled himself to his feet. He hardened his face and projected all the authority of a high magus. Everyone froze, even Nark, waiting for orders. As clearly as possible, Lewis spoke in classic Lanthran, *"Alor, siapplaya oma."* To Patrick, he ordered, "Come."

Patrick's shocked expression relaxed just a little, and he nodded.

While his brother stepped forward, Lewis turned to the cabinet on the wall that held the *noretha*—the marbles. The cabinet was new, as if made just a few days ago, and the marbles inside lay like smooth jewels, each in its own case. *Rats!* They weren't labelled. His heart sank. If he'd been managing this system, the Lanthran script would read, *Pigolanor* for the special marble: "Earth: Don't go there!" But there were no labels, none at all. *Stupid amateurs,* he yelled inside, *I don't want to connect to another atmosphereless moon or some poisonous gas planet!*

Acting majestic, Lewis extended a confident hand into the cabinet for *Pigolanor,* hoping for some clue, and he got it. One amber marble was still very warm to the touch. *The hot marble!* He palmed that one. "Let us go home, dear brother," he said to Patrick in lordly English and stuck the hot marble in the slot at the control console. Lewis's skilled fingers brushed the controls, and the monitor's obsidian surface began to glow.

Still projecting the authority of a high magus, of a person with absolute power, he stroked his fingers across the console as if expertly playing a harp. The obsidian monitor showed a beautiful blue Earth against the background of space. Lewis sighed with relief. With a deft movement, he focussed until he saw the Newark highway ramp where he and Patrick had been captured. The ramp's slushy snow now churned with people and car tracks. "Come," Lewis ordered, grasping Patrick's cuffed hands, and he drew his younger brother toward the nexus.

"Thanks, Lew—" Patrick started to say, but never finished. A Blue male jumped forward and seized the boy with its great azure hair-covered arms.

"No!" Lewis yelled. But he had already begun to pass into the nexus. He could still see Patrick; he reached to grasp his brother.

Smirking, the Blue person holding Patrick raked its fingers at random across the control panel. The nexus closed. Light exploded, heavy velvet stroked his skin, and Lewis found himself back on Earth.

*   *   *

Earth's winter air was frigid. Lewis shivered with cold and shock as he lay in the slush. *I'm right back where I started, but it's been hours since I left, Earth time.* Cars and trucks and even semis parked along the berm end-to-end, maybe twenty of them, some of them smashed. The guy with his recording smart phone was still there. When he saw Lewis reappear, the man gaped and kept making his video.

Rows of police cars, lights flashing, filled the ramp and blocked access to the highway. Lewis saw Dad talking to six policemen. Dad wore his dinner clothes, but his tie was loose and crooked. His dark face had set in grim lines, but Dad's eyes glistened with tears.

Lewis saw Gracie, too. Tears flowed down her cheeks as her auburn hair whipped in the bitter breeze.

Lewis pulled himself to a crouch onto the wet road, hands still bound in front of him with that stupid red cord. The cool, quick, analytical brain function that had saved him shattered. Emotion erupted from wherever he had stuffed it, boiling through his mind and into his heart, and he staggered forward, crying, "Dad, Gracie, I'm here!" He had arrived safely through the marble's nexus, but Patrick remained on the wrong side.

Chapter 13:
TRAFFICKING PATRICK

Patrick's head whirled and his heart sank, heavy as a boulder, to see his brother disappear without him. He was stuck on Lanthra—by himself! And he was the prisoner of the meanest, ugliest brute on the planet!

King Nark demanded in a scraping metal voice, *"Dedileh bibat!"* In a tight grip, a Blue thug dragged Patrick forward by the manacled hands. Patrick's feet scuffed through debris until he stood in front of Nark, and then the Blue person pressed its burning hand on Patrick's head so hard that he knelt.

Nark loomed over him, stinking like a smoking tire, and his black hair hung in a thick tangle. He roared and gripped Patrick's chin hard, forcing him to look up, "I am the *Tot Ba-on!* The High King! Even the *bizeor* serve me in my domain!"

Those beady eyes grew cunning. "So, the *sebizor* who killed my brother has a little brother, too." His great gnarly hand traced Patrick's cheek with one dirty fingernail. Patrick jerked back, and Nark laughed. "And how shall I get revenge? He killed my brother; shall I kill his?"

Patrick's mind took in the words, but it was as if his brain had become a chaotic mess. He heard a stabbing voice inside accusing, *You should be brave like your brother Lewis and find a way to escape.* But his knees shook.

"Nay." Nark chuckled, a throat-clicking sound that was worse to Patrick than the grating laugh. The king addressed the Blues, "Mark him as mine. He shall serve me on The Isle of Mercy. And … after many years, I will show that Lewis what his brother has become." He laughed, swept his arm in a dismissive gesture. Patrick's captor pulled him up by his thick hair and dragged him out of the locating chamber.

* * *

Too many things happened next. They exited the horrible chamber into a large courtyard. Sunlight blasted Patrick's eyes. An intensely blue sky domed overhead; palm trees hung limp without any breeze; tropical humidity made him break into a sweat.

In a high wall studded with shards of glass stood a wrought-iron gate. Patrick winced at the cruel spikes on top and the leering demon face around its lock. *What waits for you inside?* the demon voice sneered in his mind. He imagined torments, humiliations …

Patrick balked. A Blue brute pulled him forward. "No!" Patrick kicked and flailed, but the blue males seized him and pushed him through the gates which locked behind them. From the courtyard they entered a dark, shabby green room where the stucco-covered walls peeled away with smelly tropical rot. Patrick saw several benches inside, and tables with tools like dental equipment. *They are going to torture you now. You will sob and cry and plead for mercy, you fat little wuss!*

A scrawny human with a scowling face and big biceps motioned toward a bench. Then Patrick saw the bottles of ink, needles, a lit candle, and a razor on the torture table. *They're giving me a tattoo!* That was worse than torture; that was permanent. Patrick fought as they stripped off his shirt. No good.

They strapped him down, his face smashed into a little oval pillow. One Blue gripped his head, and Patrick began to feel the razor shaving the back of his neck. *A tattoo. Oh, God, no.* He recalled a seminar he'd attended at church about human trafficking. The stories had horrified him then, moved him to deep empathy for the women and girls—and boy—tied up and tattooed with the mark of the "owner" on their necks. And now it was happening to him! He smelled rubbing alcohol as a cold liquid scrubbed the back of his neck. Then a pen nib began tracing an outline. Patrick tried to struggle away, but the thug pressed so hard on his head that he could suffocate unless he gave up.

Next, stabs like fire ant bites punched his skin. The scrawny man was doing this by hand, like the tattoos were done before electronic tools had been developed on Earth. Patrick's tears welled out onto the pillow. He clenched his jaw, but he couldn't stop crying. They were forcing a new identity on him, a slave mark, and he would bear it for the rest of his life.

After endless pricking, the blue male's burning hand let go of Patrick's head and pulled his head up by the hair. The tattoo artist held a hand mirror in front of his eyes to reflect one behind his head. On the nape of his neck, Patrick saw a large black "N" with a snake coiled around it. Patrick inhaled a shuddering breath, disgusted at the mark, angry at himself for being so helpless. *Oh, yes, you are scared, aren't you, little fat boy?* his nasty inner voice mocked.

He was terrified. He was a slave.

Chapter 14:
AN ALLY

Five hundred Lanthran *linath* from terrified Patrick, Mim sat anxiously on a hard chair in front of the ship's captain in his cabin. Her body shook despite the blanket wrapped around her shoulders. She stank; she was so humiliated at her vomit-covered, greasy-haired, raunchy condition that her insides squirmed like worms. Two of the crew stood between her and the door.

From behind a great desk, *Westwind*'s captain held her with steady dark eyes. Although Mim could hardly hold up her head, she felt speared by that gaze; she could not glance away. The captain resembled his son Darwin, with jet black hair, a straight nose, thick eyebrows, and the Asian features of the sea-faring families on the northern coast. Silence and his long, long scrutiny stretched out until Mim could stand the tension no more.

"I'm sorry," she croaked. A crewman had given her water, but thirst still burned in her throat.

Westwind's imposing captain finally spoke. "'Tis too late to turn around to Kingsport, if that's where you are from. We are well on our way to Eleaemana. I must consider what to do with you and how to return you to your family." His chiseled lips twisted, and Mim flinched, fearing some dreadful plan to ship her right into the lascivious, murderous hands of Lord Broton Sipes. "I'm inclined to set you down at the nearest port, which would be Newton, in the Eastmarch Province, and hustle you back home."

Mim's heart pounded. Her breath came fast and shallow, and her face must have turned gray, because she felt a gritty blackness filling her brain.

But the captain noticed, and his face softened ... a little. "I am Captain Lu, master of this ship *Westwind.* We will'na jettison you. 'Tis a fair journey from Newton back to your home, I expect, and you have'na money."

There stretched another drawn-out pause. Miriam recovered a tiny thread of composure and rehearsed her plan to get as far away as possible from Sipe's disgusting marriage plot. She opened her mouth to begin the cajoling argument.

Like a hawk, Captain Lu pounced. "Who are you, *lassie?*"

Deflecting his "lassie" probe, Mim talked fast to spin the fake identity she'd made up when she ran away. "I'm not a girl! I'm Michael Redman. My dad and mom are dead. My uncle is my guardian, but he's a beast when he's drunk and beats me. I can't go back! Make me one of your crew. I have a little experience with sailing, and I know how to climb a rigging and brace a sail. I know all the knots. I'm small, but I can be useful! Yes, I stowed away, and I owe you for passage. I can work for you until my debt is paid off."

Captain Lu's face did not soften. "Tell the truth, *lassie.*"

Fear pierced Mim's heart. Her hands trembled, but she stuck to her story. "Please, please, Captain Lu. Don't send me back. I'm Michael, eighteen years old. I'm just small for my age. And I ran away from home for a good reason."

Captain Lu repeated, drawing out each word, "Who. Are. You. Lassie?"

Mim crumpled and would have burst into hysterical tears if she wasn't so dehydrated. She covered her face with the blanket. Breathing in and letting her breath out slowly, she peeped out and whimpered, "I ... I'll ... tell you, but ... Please! Let me tell you in private!"

Another long silence swelled in the room. Captain Lu jerked his chin to the crewmen. "Verra well. Wei Chou, and Spinner, step outside and close the door until I call you."

They left, shutting the cabin door. Captain Lu ordered, "Begin."

Mim took a deep, deep breath. It was hard to speak because her throat was so tight with a great, big lump of fear, but she confessed, the words spilling out, "I ... I'm Princess Miriam Reynolds. You've never met me, but I know your son, Darwin."

Captain Lu registered surprise.

Mim continued, "Lord Broton Sipes murdered my father the king, and that … that *rat* is well on his way to seizing the throne, if he hasn't already done so. My mother Queen Katharine is sick and weak, and my brother Prince Christopher is reported to be dead—your own son was with him!"

Mim kept talking. She told her belief that Chris was alive; she even forced herself to tell the ugly, repugnant, obscene overheard detail about Sipes intending to wed and bed her. Hiding under the blanket again, she confessed, "That's why I left the palace and hid on your ship."

Silence ruled again until Mim began to squirm inside.

Then Captain Lu said gravely, "I believe you, my lady."

Mim stammered, "Call … call me Mim. I … I'm just Mim now until I can get help. I need big help, *big* help. I need to stop Lord Sipe's plot. But I don't know how. I wrote High Magus Daniel, but I ran away before I heard from him so I don't know—"

"Enough, my lady." Captain Lu raised one hand. "I believe you. And I shall call you 'Mim Redman.' There is no need to tell the crew who you really are. Your name will be entered in the crew list, and a princess you will be no longer—for them—until 'tis time."

Still shaking, Mim wriggled until she sat up straight. This time her words came out clear and strong. "Captain Lu, anything you can do for me will be much appreciated, not just by me, but by Bardia."

The captain said, "Bardia, and much more than Bardia is at stake in your situation."

Tentatively, Mim asked, "Sir, why does the Horned Edge want to ruin my country? I know they support Sipes and want to control Bardia through him."

Captain Lu's chiseled lips quirked. "One, Bardia has a strategic location, a jumping platform for the rest of the world. Two, our country has rich resources. And finally, Bardia is the home of the College of the Magi, the seat of all the Lanthran magi.

"I feel so small! How can people like me hold the Horned Edge back?" Mim cried.

To Mim's vast shock, the captain rose. He walked slowly around the desk. Mim tried not to shrink back.

Then he bowed low before her. "In honor of your parents, and my son's dear friend Prince Christopher, I will help you. I will help my country, my world—and you—with my life!"

Mim, struck dumb, nodded.

Captain Lu continued with an arched eyebrow, "Like you, I do not believe that your brother is dead. He would be a crucial piece in a very large plot, much too valuable to kill. My best guess from my son's report is that the king of the pirates, Nargoleh Layhew, has captured him. Nark's lair is on the Isle of Mercy off the Ploiyon Jetties in Eleaemana. That's where my cargo is going: to Eleaemana! The coincidence—nay, not a coincidence, but Radyah's own arrangement! I'll make inquiries when we reach port. Then … we shall see what we can do."

Mim repressed a sob. Finally tears escaped her eyes and ran down her cheeks, and she wiped them off with the blanket. "Thank you! Thank you!"

Captain Lu called the crewmen back into the room. "Lieutenant Chou, please escort Mim Redman to the passenger cabin that is vacant. That will be her quarters. Bosun Spinner, outfit her with whatever she needs. Make sure she has privacy to bathe and dress." He added, "And when she has readied herself, introduce Mim to Cook Reeve. She'll help him in the kitchen and will serve the crew's meals."

Mim got up, tightening the blanked around her. Her nasty clothes still stank, her body felt miserable—but her soul had lifted, and she could hold her head high. Getting the truth out lightened her heart. And now she and Bardia had an ally.

CHAPTER 15:
INTERROGATION

In the biophysics laboratory at Gnudst and Cranz Pharmaceuticals, Lewis looked away from the brand-new super-resolution fluorescence microscope and rubbed his eyes. It was just 8:30 a.m.; he been at work for a half-hour and already he felt exhausted. He rubbed his cold hands on his white lab coat and looked around the lab. Art-wise, it was dull: no paintings, no Christmas decorations, just work cubicles. Architecture-wise, there were white painted walls, white ceiling tiles, cubicles containing desks with computers and microscopes and other white-coated technicians. From Lewis's desk, he couldn't see the doorway that led to the interesting room with its fancy research equipment, including a Fourier-transform ion cyclotron resonance mass spectrometer. That was too bad, because he wanted to see it. The cyclotron used some of the science Lewis had used in Lanthra for instant space travel. *If only I could use one to develop that data curl I keep in my pocket! I could rescue Patrick!*

Lewis could look out of a window from his swiveling ergonomic office chair. *It's another wintery gray day in New Jersey. Every* day since he'd started work, his heart sank like a soggy log. *I cannot help Patrick. I hate what's happening to Mom with her breast cancer. I feel so cut-off from Dad and Gracie!*

You are at work! his inner parent reminded him. *So ... get to work!*

Lewis put his face back down to the microscope. *How can I work with my brother missing and my mom sick with cancer?* But, in a few minutes a flicker on the slide caught his attention. An inexplicable niggle of curiosity tickled him, and he focused the microscope's view. On the slide lay a brain sample with 3D images of a folded aggregate molecules formed by an amyloid-β peptide filament—a protein found in Alzheimer's disease. An idea grew. Lewis switched the sample from an abnormal structure to a normal structure. And again. And again.

The thought burst into his brain: *Suppose I could use AI to record a 3-D atom-by-atom model of this deformed amyloid protein and another of the normal protein. Then I could do a time-lapse study of the deformation process. The 3-D study may give me a clue to a molecule collection that could neutralize the destruction of healthy proteins ... and lead to a drug that would halt the progression of that terrible disease! Maybe ...*

His phone rang the Vivaldi *Spring*. Lewis startled, his thoughts broken. Muttering an imprecation against himself for leaving the phone unsilenced at work, he answered the call. "Hello? This is, uh, Lewis Brahmindura. Who ... who is calling?" His normally pleasant baritone voice broke, and he chastised himself, *I'm a mess. I want to recover enough to do my job! And develop the Lanthran technology. And find Patrick! But where will I start?*

"Mr. Brahmindura, I'm Special Agent Dante Sheldon, FBI. We need to ask you a few questions at the FBI headquarters in the Claremont Tower." The deep official-sounding male voice on the phone left no room for argument.

Lewis sat up straight. "I will make arrangements to come in tomorrow ..."

"No." The FBI agent brooked no argument. "You need to come in this morning. Now."

Before Lewis could protest, Sheldon stated the clincher, "We have already cleared it with your employer."

Lewis consulted his watch. His brilliant insight about a cure for Alzheimer's had vanished and was replaced by a powerful ache in his chest. *Patrick is missing. I wonder what the FBI has to say. Has someone found his body?* "Very well, I'll see you in a half hour. It's at the same place I went on the day I, uh, disappeared, right?"

"Right."

There was no friendly "'bye," just the emptiness of the cut-off connection.

Lewis powered down his computer. Dread made him as mindless as a mule in blinders, and his actions followed in an automatic order: He hung up his white coat. He swallowed the last of a cup of sweet, creamy, tepid coffee and put the dirty coffee mug in the break room sink. After calling a Lyft, he grabbed his raincoat with the winter liner. His heart sank like a heavy doughball, and he realized he was frightened.

*　　*　　*

Lewis sat on a hard chair facing Special Agent Dante Sheldon's desk. The small gray-and-white room seemed too brightly lit, and there was very little in it except the desk, two chairs … and a blank wall behind him, probably concealing onlookers. Sheldon, a big African American man, frowned. His well-cut expensive brown suit smelled faintly of Axe men's body spray.

"Mr. Brahmindura," Sheldon began, "You just started working for Gnudst and Cranz Pharmaceuticals as a biophysicist."

"Yes. That's right."

"Aren't you researching Alzheimer's proteins? Biophysics is a whole different field than you were in before. You've sidetracked."

Lewis kept it simple. "That's right."

"Before your first disappearance two years ago, you worked on energy research. And this report indicates that, after you were kidnapped, you worked with terrorists on … space travel technology?" The last words dangled, demanding an explanation.

Lewis decided to tell as much of the truth as he could and see where it got him. "Yes, two years ago, I was kidnapped and forced to work for terrorists—and they held my brother and sister hostage to make me comply." At the thought, his stomach hurt. "And, yes, I worked on space travel technology."

"Did you see the same people as before when you disappeared this time?"

"No. This recent time, some guys came out of nowhere, chased my brother and me, caught us, tied me up, and took us with them. I managed to escape. Patrick didn't." Lewis's heart felt like a heavy stone.

"How do you explain disappearing into thin air?" Sheldon countered, leaning forward.

78

This was the tricky part. *Should I tell what I know?* Lewis decided to be blunt. "Both times, our captors used very advanced technology that makes connections that enable instant space travel. We passed instantly from that highway ramp into their, er, place." *I can't tell them about Lanthra,* he thought. *He'll never believe me—and if he does, it'll open a great can of maggots.*

Sheldon snorted, "That's highly improbable."

"That's what happened."

"How do you know?"

Lewis confessed, "I've used that technology. I'm familiar with it."

"How can you say you know technology that lets people teleport from place to place? Sounds like science fiction."

"It's science, not fiction! I did work with instant space travel after I disappeared the first time two years ago." *Keep answers short; you don't need to go into how you'd mastered the advanced technology of the ancient magi on another world!*

"So, this disappearance *is* connected with the last one two years ago," said Sheldon. He leaned back. "I don't believe in coincidences." His dark brown eyes ran up and down Lewis in a critical evaluation. He still frowned.

"Possibly," Lewis agreed. "My, uh, recent captors used the same space travel technology, but this time they were not necessarily the same people." A little voice in his mind said wryly, *But probably the same supernatural agencies are involved, with their ongoing purpose of conquering Earth and Lanthra.* Somehow, he didn't think talking about the paranormal entities he called "bezubs" would fly with Mr. Sheldon.

"Then how do you explain—"

"Frankly," Lewis broke in, "I just want to find a way to rescue my brother. You could only help me find him! If I had access to the technology—"

Sheldon leaned forward. "I believe you know more about what happened than you've been letting on."

Lewis glowered at him. "What do you mean?"

Sheldon leaned back. His right hand, Lewis noticed, had balled into a fist. *He's angry,* Lewis realized with a jolt.

"So, shall we treat the incident as a kidnapping?" Sheldon fixed sharp eyes on Lewis. "Kidnapped *again* by terrorists because of a secret technology that you just happen to be an expert in, even though you're not working in that field at all anymore? How are you involved?"

Lewis returned, "A kidnapping yes. But—this time—not because of my expertise in technology!"

Sheldon dug for more truth. "Mr. Brahmindura, I think you are hiding something. You never divulged any names of these terrorists or what group they might have belonged to. In the previous disappearance, your friend Mr. Jontz never returned, and you stated that you do not know where he is or what he is doing. And, as for this latest disappearance, you and your brother were kidnapped in full view of others, and your brother is still missing. What's your pattern?"

"There is no pattern, no tie between the two events."

"You admit, then, that you had no deliberate part in the plan?"

"Right! It was a *kidnapping!* I didn't *ask* to be chased through the snow, tied up, and hauled away! And I want my brother back!" Lewis sank back in his chair. He wished he could weep.

"The question is …," drawled Sheldon, "how are *you* involved in this? How did you mean to gain anything by having your brother and you kidnapped?"

"*What?*" Lewis shouted, anger rippling through him and clenching his stomach muscles. "Are you insinuating that I might have *planned* it all?"

Sheldon's eyes were half-closed but completely alert. "Since you yourself brought up advanced technology in this discussion and mentioned experimental subjects, I can't help but wonder if you know a lot more than you're letting on, Mr. Brahmindura." He shuffled his chair, which scraped unpleasantly. Standing up, he wrapped up the interview. "I will bring in some experts and continue this discussion later."

"I've told you—"

"We'll see you next Thursday, same place, at 8:00 a.m." Special Agent Sheldon showed his white teeth. "And don't disappear before then."

CHAPTER 16:
"HE'S AWFULLY CUTE!"

After the interview with FBI Special Agent Sheldon, after pacing with his brow knit through the rooms of his apartment, Lewis grabbed his phone. He wanted comfort, someone to help him calm down after the unsettling interview. And Deirdre was far, far away. His first calls were to his family. But he kept getting voice messages; no one was picking up. *Argh.*

Lewis wondered how his mom was doing. Did she have to go to the hospital? Was she having intravenous chemo right now? *Argh!*

Then he called Peggy. "Can you come over tonight?"

"Aren't you coming back to work today?" she asked. "What's going on? Where were you? I missed you in the break room."

"I've told my supervisor that I'll be back early tomorrow. But I'm fine. Just want to talk to somebody."

"I'd be glad to come tonight," her melodic voice assured him. "What time?"

"How about 6:30 p.m.? I'll have supper ready for us."

To get home, Lewis's Lyft had to drive a stop-and-go road. It caught every light red. Plus, three cars had wrecked each other in the middle of an intersection. Lewis's insides felt raw. His chest tingled, a muscle in his face kept twitching, and his stomach burned. He realized that it was lunch time and longed for a cup of hot, sweet tea and the toasted coconut ladoo lunch leftovers. *Hurry up traffic!*

At one particularly long red light, Lewis began to mutter a

pungent curse. But when he noticed activity in front of a large white stone church on the corner, he held back.

A huddle of people worked outside in the cold drizzle, putting up a life-sized Christmas crèche scene. Lewis saw painted figures of Mary, Joseph, and baby Jesus, a group of shepherds and some sheep, and the three magi and their camels. *Magi. Could the magi in the Bible have come from Lanthra?* He watched as they arranged greenery over the stable, attached a star, and stacked several bales of straw. The people joked and smiled despite the weather, smiling, laughing, joking with each other. They would probably go inside afterward and enjoy hot chocolate and a nice lunch.

Lewis wondered whether the church had a nice Christmas Eve service, and then felt an odd longing. *You haven't been to church since ... Maybe you could take in a service this Christmas. It's coming up soon!* At that moment, before he made any decision one way or another, the light changed, and the car accelerated.

*   *   *

"What is that *smell?*" Peggy exclaimed as she entered Lewis's apartment that evening.

"I'm cooking a chicken curry." Lewis stepped out of the one-butt kitchen to greet her. He wore a white chef's apron over his black t-shirt and old jeans, and he held a ladle of the curry, a little of which dripped onto his front. "Would you like to try a bit before we have supper?"

Peggy wrinkled her nose. "Not if it smells like *that.*" She sat at the small table in the kitchen-side corner of the living room and sat down. Her place was already set with tableware, cloth napkins, a Corel-ware plate, and a sweating crystal goblet of ice water. Lewis took pride in his presentation. On the table sat small dishes of various sauces and spices on the table, pita bread, hummus, and a large bowl of basmati rice.

"I'm sorry for my outburst." Peggy's lower lip stuck out just a little. "I've always been a picky eater." She laughed. "You know, chicken nuggets, pizza, hot dogs, and meatballs. I'm not into spicy foods, either."

Lewis swept away the comment with a gesture. Digging inside his refrigerator, he found no hot dogs, no nuggets, but he did have ... "Would you like some scrambled eggs and cheese?"

Peggy brightened. "Oh, don't go to any trouble for me."

"Honestly, it's no trouble," Lewis insisted. "Here, I'll make a three-egg omelet with cheese."

"Make that a two-egg omelet." Peggy smiled. "And I'll try some of that rice. It smells different … sort of *fragrant*."

"It's basmati rice." Lewis wanted to please his girl … his *friend*. He scrambled two eggs and served them on her plate with a modest spoonful of rice. Then he sat across from her and served himself a large helping of rice with the chicken curry. Saliva filled his mouth as he anticipated the rich, heavy, savory flavor.

"Lewis, you need a napkin," Peggy told him after his first bite. "The curry juice is running down your chin."

And it was. The curry adorned his face and on the tablecloth. "Oh, pardon me!" Wiping himself with his napkin, Lewis rose and dabbed at the table's spill.

He began to relax as they ate and chatted about work. Peggy glowed. Lewis appreciated her perfect outfit: A dress in a pale-yellow fabric printed with white roses. She made the dreary weather bearable.

"Your hair is getting long," she noticed.

"Yes," Lewis admitted, pulling it back and fumbling around for an elastic tie. "I haven't found a barber yet."

"Oh, I have a hairdresser that could make you look, well, less nerdy." Peggy texted the contact to his phone. "I want you to keep some length—maybe grow it to shoulder length—but you can keep that natural wave. If you'd take on the Steve Jobs persona, you'll be a stunning East Indian male model."

Lewis didn't know what to say. He appreciated the compliment, but a memory filled his thoughts. He put down his spoon and let its mist envelop him. Lost in the past, he pictured Deirdre's eyes when she and he walked together in the university park before the ice storm—on Lanthra, on their first date. He wore a white dress shirt, a dark gray vest and pants, and knee-high boots. A flowing black cloak covered him against the wintry weather. That evening, for the first time ever, he was deeply aware of his appearance, and in her eyes, he saw a very handsome man. *Then again,* he thought, *Deirdre always saw me as handsome, even when she saw me naked, bone-thin, coughing up blood, nearly dead after being a prisoner in Lord Charon's cave chamber.*

He heard a *click* and came back to the present. Peggy had snapped her fingers. "Where were you?"

Lewis stuttered, "Um … I … I was just back in the past." He hadn't told Peggy about Deirdre. He had told Peggy some very bare details about his kidnapping a year ago and less about his work for "the terrorists." Whenever he talked about himself, she always paid rapt attention, asking penetrating questions. He knew that she knew that he avoided a lot of topics. But the longer he knew Peggy, the more he revealed himself. *Maybe I can tell her about Lanthra tonight,* he thought.

She reached out to him across the table, and he took her soft hand. For a moment, neither spoke, as Lewis caressed her fingers.

After the feast, Peggy dug into her huge handbag and pulled out a bottle of Pinot Noir. "Where are the wine glasses that I gave you at the party?"

He hesitated. *You're taking some strong meds for your seizures, and they won't mix well with alcohol.* Then Lewis decided to please her. "I'll get them."

Peggy pulled out a bottle opener from her bag and expertly opened a bottle of the dark red wine. She poured a glass, filling it, then moved to fill the other wine glass. But Lewis felt a tic of alarm. "I can't drink alcohol. I take meds."

"Surely one glass of wine won't hurt you," Peggy said, looking into his eyes, sending a message of warmth and welcome. "I just want to celebrate this moment."

"Okay," Lewis agreed, "I can handle about two ounces."

She poured the Pinot Noir.

After they clinked glasses in a toast, Lewis downed his two ounces. The wine tasted smooth, like cherries with a subtle forest flavor. Lewis accepted a refill, a larger one. But when Peggy began to pour a third portion, he held his hand over the wine glass. "I must stop now."

"Okay, I understand,"

Peggy said. Her eyes shone and she chattered as Lewis put the dishes in the sink.

"Let's move to the living room," Lewis suggested after he'd cleaned up the table. Peggy and he sat on his dark gray sofa, side-by-side. He asked, "Would you like to watch a movie?"

"No, thank you. Right now, I just want to be with you." Peggy snuggled against his left side and drew an afghan over their laps.

Lewis became acutely aware of her warmth. He liked it. They clasped hands under the afghan, and his hand lay on her knee.

Peggy talked about her family for a little while, which she described as "dysfunctional."

Lewis listened with occasional conversation notations such as "uh-huh," but few interruptions. The wine, the warm food in his stomach, and Peggy's soft body snug against his made him sleepy.

He jerked to awareness when Peggy asked, "Have you found your dream job here? Or …" she paused, handling a delicate subject, "do you wish you had your old job?"

Lewis straightened. He began to move his hand toward his pocket, but then shoved down the urge. *Nope. Can't show anybody that curl of data yet. Too explosive. Too dangerous. The Horned Edge would love to get it.*

Peggy had certainly felt the movement, but she did not comment. She nuzzled Lewis's cheek with her temple, and her rich blond hair smelled like a flowery meadow. Their connection was intimate, warm. He felt a surge of desire—both a compulsion to confide his soul with her and, yes, physical sexual desire.

"I do wish I had my old job," he confessed, shifting on the sofa to control his excitement. "I'm trying to give this one my all, but really I love … my dream is …" He sighed and took the leap. "I was working on instant space travel. I know how to send people and objects through large distances—without a car, without plane, without a rocket. You can simply walk through a connection."

Suddenly realizing the implications of his disclosure, Lewis sat up, fully awake and a little scared. Once again, his hand crept toward his pocket. "Peggy, I've told you classified information! It is very important that you do not spread it; keep it between us. The FBI knows, Homeland Security knows—but I don't want that information to get to the Horned Edge!"

Peggy's eyes widened and shone with affection. "Lewis, I promise that I will keep that between us." Her slender hands enveloped his. "I promise! And I am so proud of you!"

They sat, hands clasped, silent for moment. Lewis wanted to kiss her. He imagined her pink, soft rose-petal lips brushing against his, a surge of … *No!*

Shaking his head to clear it, he took a deep breath. "Peggy, I need to get to work early tomorrow. I have a lead on a new direction for my research on Alzheimer's disease, plus I …"

Peggy was direct. She squeezed his knee under the afghan, then released her hand. "I want you, too. But perhaps best not tonight. We both could use a good night's sleep, and it's getting late already."

Lewis and she rose. They hugged, and Lewis couldn't resist giving her a kiss—a quick taste of her sweet mouth. Peggy gathered her coat and purse and stepped toward the door. Then she held back. "Wait a minute. Where is your restroom?"

"First door in the hall on the left. I'll get my coat, and then I'll see you down to your car."

Lewis went into his bedroom to get his coat. A caution brushed his mind, and he pulled the curl of data out of his pocket. *I need to keep it secret, keep it safe.* As quietly as possible, he opened his bureau drawer, and hid it in a pair of rolled up socks.

*   *   *

In her private meantime, Peggy got out her phone. She texted to her contact, *He's been working on instant space travel. And there's something secret in his right pants pocket. It may be a thumb drive.*

The terse answer came back immediately, *Very good. Proceed to the next step.*

Feeling playful, Peggy replied, *Do I have to? He's awfully cute! I hate to hurt him.*

Her contact hung up.

Rolling her eyes, Peggy sent one more text to a different number.

CHAPTER 17:
THE ISLE OF MERCY

Westwind sailed toward the southern Lanthran continent, and the weather stayed fine. Mim decided to hang out—after she'd worked in the kitchen and served the crew their midday meal—at a nook on the starboard bow, near the figurehead of the *foroyon,* an angel.

On Earth, the *foroyon* might be a cherub (a "love butt," as Mim called those flying naked babies), or perhaps a sweet, winged woman. But on Lanthra, a *foroyon* took on the form of a stern warrior. The figurehead's great wings stretched back and upward as if slicing the wind, and its right hand held a long sword with a real shining steel blade. Mim exulted to think about the protective angels. They would protect her when she searched for her brother. Not only that, but they would protect Chris.

In her shady place at the rail, Mim stood on her toes and strained her eyes at the horizon, anticipating *Westwind*'s destination: the great city of Kyrie in Eleaemana. There, *Westwind* would trade Torish fine soap and Bardian iron tools for tea, coconut fiber, and jewels. Captain Lu had said that they'd arrive today in the afternoon. And Captain Lu also had promised to inquire at the Bardian embassy for news about Chris.

I wonder what Eleaemana looks like? Lush tropical growth? Verdant hills, black volcanic sand beaches, and bright sparkling water? The map of Eleaemana shows the huge Thesare Bay with lots of islands, including the Isle of Mercy. Captain Lu says that island belongs to King Nargoleh Layhew.

She shivered. *Chris told me about King Layhew. He said the king's a monster, a smelly giant with a depraved soul who flays his prisoners. Oh, Chris, if you're there, I hope we find you soon!*

At that instant, a white pelican flapped so close that Mim ducked. It perched on one of the angel's outstretched wings, clamping a wiggling fish in its beak. As she watched, the pelican swallowed the terrified fish, which would pass into its gullet alive and be digested.

Mim gulped, too, identifying with the fish. *Is that an omen? Am I going to get caught like that fish?* She imagined Nark seizing her if she ventured onto his island. Obscene and disgusting possibilities crawled through her mind. People back in Kingsport had whispered so many horrible tales about what Nark did with his female prisoners—

"Land, ho!" The lookout up on the crow's nest shouted. Mim's entire being shuddered, and she ran to the rail.

The first land drew near: Jagged hills of black rock spotted with gray bushes. Mim's spirit sank. "I thought it was going to be beautiful!" she cried to the *foroyon*. This ugly desolate coast glided by on and on. *Westwind*'s progress slowed; Mim heard the captain, the pilot, and First Mate Wei Chou converse in serious, low tones. *Westwind* must have dangerous rocks and reefs to clear—or maybe, she feared, the ship would be seized by the pirate king before it reached the port.

Two hours passed and the afternoon sun beat down. The ship crept along the rugged landscape. Anxious, imagining a pirate attack, Mim scanned the Thesare Bay, running from starboard to port and back again. No marauding pirate ship appeared. Finally, with a gigantic sigh of relief, Mim saw the Ploiyon Jetties, rows of long white cement structures built out into the bay. She counted twenty-eight sailing ships docked there now, sporting their complex rigging. Stevedores like little brown ants carried cargo onto or off some of the ships. *Westwind* drifted toward the last jetty, and Mim's heart beat faster.

A young sailor named Alli, maybe in his early twenties, joined her to watch the docking process. "Where is the Isle of Mercy?" he asked her. The teenager smelled like salt and sweat doused with men's beauty oil, and Mim wrinkled her nose. Alli liked to flirt—not too openly, lest he catch the captain's attention.

"The Isle of Mercy is on the port side," she said. Alli edged closer. Mim dodged into the shade under the *foroyon*'s port-side wing. Alli moved with her, smiling with a wolfish flash of even white teeth. Mim knew that he knew he was handsome. Gritting her teeth, she tried to ignore him.

In the distance to her left, she saw a forested cone rising behind a stony spear of land. For a place with such a horrible reputation, she recognized its beauty. Mim's breath came quicker as *Westwind* closed on the jetty. *Will we find Chris there? How? If that nasty pirate rules the island, how will we even get on it?*

With a slight bump, *Westwind* settled alongside its unloading dock. "All hands on deck!" the first mate ordered. Alli muttered a regretful expletive as he peeled away to obey. Dragging herself away from the view of the Isle of Mercy, Mim followed.

At attention in her place beside the ship's cook (and a good distance from Alli), Mim focussed on Captain Lu's declarations. The captain, taller than most of the crew, projected calm and authority in his dress uniform. He announced, "Ye have four days in this port. The day after the Glad-Day, *Westwind* shall sail with the late morning tide—which will be at the fifth hour. Do not—I repeat—do not leave the city of Kyrie. If you do, 'tis possible that slavers will take you. They will sell you to Swethans, and you may never break free from the hard labor that your masters force on you. Am I understood?"

Mim could swear that Captain Lu looked directly at her. *One way or another,* she thought, *I have to find Chris. But who will help me?*

Captain Lu waited for questions. Several sailors raised their hands. Mim fidgeted, tapping her toe while obvious and mundane discussions of port rules, crew's pay, and honorable behavior in a foreign country followed. Yet Captain Lu did not show impatience; he answered the same repetitive questions over and over.

The briefing took an hour. Mim perspired in the heat; her chemise stuck to her back and her shirt showed sweat rings under her arms. *How will I even begin to find my brother?* Her thoughts chewed her many questions, and her stomach flopped at the idea of going ashore with no plan. When the briefing broke up, she slipped between the sailors toward Captain Lu.

He looked down at her as Mim hurried her many questions, "Captain, where shall I go after the ship is unloaded? Where can I sleep? And who will help me—"

Captain Lu's eyebrows drew together. "Help close up the kitchen first. I want it clean and tidy during our leave. After the unloading is finished, I'll give you instructions. Privately!"

CHAPTER 18:
FORCEFUL RECRUITMENT

Frigid air smacked Lewis's face and neck and seeped through his coat as he and Peggy descended side by side down the steps of his apartment building to the street below. The skimpy overhang allowed drizzle to dampen his hair—but although he noted the discomfort, suddenly he didn't care. Shining in the lamplight, Peggy could have been a film star. He walked the gorgeous young woman to her car and decided to kiss her … cheek.

But she turned her head, and his motion turned into a full kiss. He felt her eager lips, breathed her gardenia scent. Aroused, Lewis leaned forward and embraced her. The kiss tantalized him; he kissed her again, deeply this time. When the black Volvo pulled up next to them, he didn't notice until too late.

Two men grabbed his arms. They pulled them behind his back and clamped handcuffs onto his wrists. His old shoulder injury screamed with pain; Lewis panicked. The fight-or-flight instinct made him struggle while an inner voice mocked, *Just wait until they torture you. You'll tell them anything, give them anything they want.*

As "they" hurled Lewis into the back of the Volvo, Peggy cried, "Don't hurt him!" Lewis became aware through the pain that she was with him in the back seat. But closing his eyes, he writhed from the shoulder agony and a horrible old memory surfaced:

With a stretching noise, the pulleys lifted his arm backward. The pain began.

Images surged of a huge implacable man with overly red lips, of chains in an amethyst cave chamber …

And then Lewis smelled rotting leaves. A rippling red light filled his vision. He gasped … He heard Peggy shout something, and then his universe blanked out.

* * *

Lewis woke with a blazing headache. He heard a sound like a scared puppy's whimper. The whimper was his. Behind him rumbled what was probably a big furnace. He smelled the sterile concrete and dust and guessed that he was in a basement somewhere under an apartment building.

Lewis opened his eyes, and harsh light hit his face. He blinked. The glare came from a clamp lamp angled into his face like an interrogation light. When he could focus, Lewis saw a shadowed concrete wall beyond the light with no markings, nothing to see but some old paint cans in one corner and assorted trash in another.

Next to him, he heard, "Lewis! Lewis! Are you okay?"

Peggy sat on a wooden chair. Her hands were cuffed together, her rich blond hair tousled, and mascara had smeared under her wide blue eyes.

Lewis's hands were cuffed, too. He still wore his coat. A rivulet of sweat crawled down his face, so that he dipped his head against his shoulder to rub it off—and yelled when pain stabbed inside both his brain and his shoulder joint.

"Lewis, are you okay?" Peggy cried out again. Her voice sounded husky, strained. "Lewis!" she exclaimed again, "I was afraid you were dead!"

Lewis took a deep breath before he could answer. "Fine," he lied. "And what about you? I'm so sorry …"

"Oh, I'm hanging in there. I'm so glad you're okay!"

It occurred to Lewis that it was ludicrous to be "fine" and "okay" when you found yourself a prisoner in an unknown basement. He wanted to comfort her, because he was sure she didn't feel like laughing. "Peggy—"

Measured footsteps approached from behind. "He's awake," said a male voice. Lewis detected a soft accent. It sounded familiar, but he couldn't place it. Gaelic, perhaps?

"Yeah, it's about time," commented a deep gravelly voice. "After that seizure in the car, he blacked out and stayed out. We had to carry him into the building."

A tall, slender man flanked by two tall, husky men came around in front of Lewis and Peggy, backdropped by the wall. That infernal glaring clamp lamp put them in shadow. Plus, black hoodies and masks shadowed most of their faces, yet their eyes glittered like monsters in the dark. Lewis could see that the tough guy on the left had a smashed nose. The menacing man on the right had huge biceps.

Lewis asked, oddly calm inside, "What do you want? Why are you doing this?"

"Would you have come willingly?" said the man with the accent, who appeared to be in charge.

Lewis admitted, "No."

"There are many who would seize you because of what you know, Lewis Brahmindura," the Leader Man told him. "And many would do much worse to you—and those you love." His voice softened, almost tender. "We will not hurt you, not now, not ever."

Smashed Nose approached and removed the handcuffs from Lewis's and Peggy's hands. Lewis rubbed his shoulder and wrists, but he listened as Leader Man continued, "We want your cooperation with a big project—the same research that you've wanted to do throughout your whole adult life. If you help us, we will help you."

Lewis looked into Leader Man's dark, fathomless eyes. *Do I know you?* "What project?" he asked with the minimal words of caution.

"The Horned Edge project."

Lewis's insides crawled as he remembered his encounters with the Horned Edge from his past ... misadventures. *Will he threaten my family to force me to work with them?*

Leader Man asserted, "We want to heal the world! This era is the opportune time, even the perfect time. It is time for drastic change."

Against the backdrop of the concrete wall, Leader Man stood like an orchestra conductor, gesturing with graceful long-fingered hands while he painted a symphony of concepts for Lewis to process. "There are so many horrors in the world! Do I need to list them? The powers of this Earth promote terror to keep people afraid and helpless. But our Horned Edge organization will curb violence. We will promote the general prosperity."

Lewis blinked away tears; his eyes watered because his seizures always ended with such bad headaches. He used his freed hands to rub his head and face.

Leader Man went on, "Do you know that many of the world's serious incidents are engineered ... *on purpose to maintain control!* Serious dangers, horrific accidents, and acts of terror—on purpose! They unsettle people, confuse them, until they move in to control them."

Lewis knew many people who held that to be true. Their fingers pointed in all directions. "Is there indeed a hidden central agency involved?"

"Yes! Some call them the Illuminati. Have you heard of them?"

Lewis blinked. "Yes." He knew from raw, painful experience that secret organizations wanted to control the world—make that *worlds,* to include Lanthra. "But the Horned Edge—"

"Yes! Yes, our Horned Edge! Through us the Illuminati can be overcome! The world's problems can be managed! We plan to develop instant space travel—teleportation if you like—specifically for that purpose. Just imagine: We could move law enforcement immediately to take out terrorists—as soon as they are spotted, even teleporting into the area before a single shot is fired! We could instantly move food and shelter to disaster-stricken people! We have funding. We can get the equipment." His voice lowered, intensified, "But we need your expertise."

Despite his horror at being a captive, Lewis thought, *With that funding and equipment and expertise, I could find and rescue Patrick!* For a moment, working with the Horned Edge sounded possible. Maybe he could believe Leader Man?

Peggy interrupted, "What's going on? I don't understand!"

Leader Man ignored her. His voice deepened and softened even more. "You, Lewis, and I are Patriots. We look back to the principles of the American Revolution to reestablish freedom, godliness, and democracy to our country, our United States of America. Just as our founders did in 1776, we want to establish order based on those basic principles. And we have allies in every country. Soon, true democracy can spread throughout the world."

Patriots? Freedom, godliness, and democracy? A big knot of doubt rose in Lewis's aching brain. He asked, "What do you mean by 'godliness'?"

Leader Man stepped forward. The glaring lamp showed that he smiled. "God is the Transcendental Other. He has all power, he is everywhere, he knows everything. We worship the true God, the One who rules the universe. Remember, God is a construct to understand the incomprehensible Other, but that entity is real. We honor him by being free ourselves and helping others. This God does not demand tribute, does not set up cruel laws. Where there is no sin, there is no need for law. God's people are free."

Lewis retorted, "But you put handcuffs on us; you kidnapped us! Did you do that in God's name?"

"Yes," Leader Man admitted.

"You're Horned Edge!"

"Yes. If you value God, you will be, too, Lewis."

Silence filled the clammy basement. Leader Man said, "You are a very talented man, Lewis. It would be a serious mistake to suppress your talent rather than use it to help correct the Earth's wrongs."

Lewis closed his eyes. Despite his crazy situation, he felt the flattery sink in. Leader Man urged, "Lewis, your life is precious. Use it well. Honor God. That is godliness."

Doubt struck Lewis's heart. *I've had trouble with the way Christians tend to coerce people to have faith in Jesus. Perhaps there is more than one path to heaven besides Jesus. Is this guy telling the truth?*

Peggy burst into the conversation. "Don't force Lewis to do anything! Don't hurt him!"

"Would we have really have to threaten him to do what he loves?"

Lewis thought hard about Leader Man's words. *I could rescue Patrick!* Meanwhile, a constant rumble from the massive furnace vibrated in the basement. Suddenly the vibration stopped. Lewis heard a faint ticking as the furnace cooled. Then silence stretched out.

Leader Man spoke to Peggy again, his slight accent more pronounced. "Lewis wants—he *yearns* to bring about instant space travel as he was doing before. His work for your father's company is a sidetrack. It's a worthy endeavor, but it is not Lewis's God-given purpose."

Peggy began to blurt something, but, ignoring her and focusing on Lewis, Leader Man continued, "Don't reject us until you know us."

Lewis considered. *Maybe the Earth's Horned Edge is different than Lanthra's Horned Edge. What if I got everything backwards? Are they able to help me find Patrick?* Underneath, a more self-centered voice added, *And realize my dreams!* "Tell me more."

"Lewis, with the funding we can supply, you can continue the research you had started under your employer Dr. Zhartha two years ago. We can help your mother with her medical bills … her chemo is going to be very expensive, and your father's shoe store alone will not earn your family enough to keep them out of debt. Your brother Patrick is missing? We'll help find him. I know that he and your sister Gracie are bright; they can have the best college education. We'll also have a place for them when they are older. And remember—you will be serving God as well as fulfilling your deepest desires."

Lewis's heart surged with hope and fear. "You'd … you'd help me find Patrick?"

Leader Man nodded. His eyes glistened, and Lewis wondered if he was moved to sympathy.

"Lewis, you and your brother Patrick disappeared, kidnapped by—of all things—*Blue* people. You escaped, but he did not come back with you. Listen! With the funding and help we can give to develop the technology to search and cross space, we promise that you'll be able to find him and get him back home."

Lewis started to speak, but Leader Man made a cutting motion. "We are finished now. Think about our offer, Lewis. You will not regret it."

*　　*　　*

The black Volvo twisted and turned through dark, damp streets. Freezing slush coated the roads. From glimpses of the skyline, Lewis recognized that they were in Manhattan somewhere, heading for the Newark-New Jersey Turnpike. He still had no idea where he'd been. They were taking him back to his apartment, but, in a figurative sense, he wasn't sure where he was going. *Should I join the Horned Edge? Maybe this is God's way of getting me back on my—His—mission!*

He and Peggy sat once again together in the back seat. Peggy snuggled against Lewis and dozed. Lewis relaxed, took deep breaths, and his headache eased. Peggy's warmth comforted him. *She's been a trooper,* he thought. *She stayed with me.*

Through the forty-minute drive, Lewis reviewed the encounter with the Horned Edge trio in the basement of who-knows-where in New York City. They'd kidnapped him, yes. But … what that Horned Edge leader had said made sense. *Down to the depth of my soul, I want to develop that instant space travel technology and find Patrick. Perhaps the Horned Edge truly worship God. Maybe their strategy of keeping peace by preventing abuses is a reasonable way to go. A benevolent control with freedom for all well-intentioned people sounds possible.*

Then Lewis noticed that his arms and legs were shaking. *No! Not another seizure!* But the physical sensations felt different; they came from … a gut response to trauma. *I've been terrified!* Lewis realized. *These people kidnapped us!* His shaking stopped. He felt stronger. *I'm not going to join the Horned Edge. I've got to find another way.*

The Volvo dropped him and Peggy off at the lamplit curb in front of Lewis's apartment. After it drove away, Lewis gently placed his hands on her shoulders and gazed into her wide eyes. Hers were moist; she had been crying. Moved with compassion, he kissed her forehead, and Peggy drew into his embrace.

Suddenly Lewis's phone burst into Vivaldi's *Spring.*

Startled, he stepped back. "Who could be calling me after midnight?"

Apparently, it was a junk call, because when Lewis answered it, the caller immediately disconnected. But he found that his hands were shaking.

Peggy put her arms around him and raised her face for another kiss. "Perhaps we could go up to your apartment?"

"Dear Peggy," Lewis sighed, pulling away, "I'm exhausted. I need sleep!"

A flash in her eyes might have been anger. "I'll see you tomorrow, then."

She leaned into him for a last long kiss. She nuzzled his neck, squeezing Lewis in a big hug. Then, with a big sigh and a glance up toward the bedroom window, Peggy put on her coat. Lewis walked her downstairs and watched as she got into her car and drove off.

Lewis entered his apartment building's voice-controlled front door. He took the elevator up to his third-floor apartment. As soon as he let himself in, he hurried to his bedroom and checked his sock drawer. The curl of data lay tucked inside the pair of blue socks, just as he had left it. Sighing, Lewis stumbled to bathroom to take four Ibuprofen. Then he went to bed, but did not sleep.

CHAPTER 19:
SOOTHING THE SAVAGE BEAST

Summer on the southern continent of Lanthra was awful. Patrick scratched the tattooed "N" on the back of his neck; the slave mark itched like crazy in the tropical heat. Trying not to think but thinking too much, he trotted the prerequisite three steps behind his new master, King Nark, escorted by burly Blue warriors. Compared to the huge Nark, he felt like a captive hobbit with an orc. As they crossed the long, wide causeway that led from Nark's island to a whole new country, Patrick wondered, *Can I run and hide in Eleaemana? Would they help me if I tried to escape?*

For the first time since his captivity in—not on—Nark's Isle of Mercy, Patrick had a broad, unwalled view of the outside world. Still hurrying to keep up, he shot glances at the scenery. On Nark's island rose a mountain forested with palms near the beach and, on the higher slopes, great trees like rosewood and mahogany. Patrick liked big trees. The island was pristine because—as Patrick knew too well—all of its inhabitants lived in the many underground chambers, hollows, and bubbles inside the inactive volcano's granite bedrock.

Around the causeway, the sea water lapped clear blue and green. Patrick saw enormous crabs on the rippled sand, burying themselves into the rippled, white sand bottom that was punctuated by patches of sea grass. A long gar slid past. A school of minnows turned and flashed in the space vacated by the gar. A little thrill moved Patrick at the beauty of nature.

Overhead soared an intense blue sky punctuated by rising white cumulus clouds. Patrick guessed that those were destined to be afternoon pop-up thunderstorms. He liked thunderstorms, too.

Just being active, being outside helped his numbed heart rise. Straight ahead on the Long Beach gathered hundreds of gulls, and a flock of dozen white pelicans glided overhead in a row.

Fear eased in a little corner of Patrick's brain. Creation's beauty always helped him feel … close to God. *Are you there, God? Or are you way out in space somewhere?*

Pain distracted him. His ankle hurt from the long walk on the causeway. He began to limp.

Patrick tried to speed up despite the howling ache, and fear crept back in control because he'd been slapped whenever they thought he was disobedient. This very morning, when he slipped and said the forbidden name "Nark" once in Nargoleh Layhew's presence, one of the specially bred huge Blue servants back-handed him. The broad slap had hurled him to the stone cave floor, and he'd skinned both knees and one elbow.

When the long causeway ended, King Nark, Patrick, and the Blue retinue passed under a guarded but open bronze portcullis. The portcullis led into the great, wealthy Eleaemanan city of Kyrie. Nark did not rule here. Many of the Eleaemanan people still worshipped Radyah, so Patrick knew that Nark would probably not let the Blue guardian hit him here. He hoped.

Where are we going? Patrick wondered. Nark had not told him anything about their errand. *Can I run away and hide?*

A short distance into the city, past rows of neat, attractive Eleaemanan shops, the retinue stopped at … just another shop. Palm trees shaded the entrance. Like the other shops, it was attractive, with white, crushed-shell walls, a blue door, and window boxes with pink and orange succulent flowers. One of the Blue slaves opened the shop's door, and Nark plus Patrick and his enormous Blue guardian minus the retinue stepped inside.

The shop's interior was white, cool, and austere. Patrick smelled a citrusy incense. His bare feet enjoyed the polished hardwood floor. On elegant side tables sat blooming white orchids. Whatever the place sold would be expensive, he figured. *Why in the world did we come here? There's nothing to buy!* Dread crawled in his belly. *What is Nark going to do to me here?*

Then Patrick saw a young woman in a white sari sitting behind a counter. She got up, curtseyed low. "Your Majesty, to what do I owe the honor? May I offer you a refreshing drink?"

Patrick understood everything. He was getting good at Lanthran again.

"Aye."

"Please, wait here for a moment."

The woman disappeared through a bead curtain into a further area of the shop. She returned with a female Blue servant. With a gesture instead of her voice, the woman, who moved with the deep authority of wealth, told the Blue servant to bring chilled coconut-mango water. The Blue servant stuck out her long red tongue and wiggled it in compliance. Patrick's mouth watered. *Will I get some? No.*

Nark lowered his bulk onto a giraffe-skin covered chair. He received the sweating glass, pressed it to his broad forehead, then gulped down the contents.

Patrick stood by the wall next his guardian. He was thirsty. His skinned knees smarted. His bum ankle ached, but the worse sensation was the grip of fear that never left his chest. *Will Blue Boy find a reason to hit me again? And what is Nark up to? Will I get a drink?*

He came to attention when the woman approached with a tray, licking dry lips. But she invited, "Your Majesty, let me show you something."

Nark rose. His dark, deep-set eyes flashed at Patrick. "Come with me." He gestured to the Blue guardian. "Stay."

Patrick followed Nark through the beaded curtain, dread growing like black mold. *What will he get? Instruments of torture? Chains? Or will he force me to get another tattoo?*

Behind an ornate gold screen stood a plain door to the back of the shop. Patrick balked, *No, no, no!* But Nark grabbed his hair and dragged him through the menacing door.

Once inside, Patrick startled. The great back room was full of musical instruments. He saw racks of horns, trumpets, lyres, harps, and wind instruments of every kind. But in the middle of the room Patrick saw … dozens of pianos! He forgot that he was a slave. Impulse drove him to the one piano that called to him so strongly that it shouted in his heart.

He fingered the smooth finish of a full grand piano covered with a white veneer, gleaming and smooth. He knew the veneer wasn't plastic; Lanthrans had no plastic because they had little to no petroleum. Was it ivory? Or—more likely in vegetarian Eleaemana—the gorgeous white veneer was plant-based. He delighted to see that, just like any Earth piano, its keys were in the proper spaces.

Patrick sat down on the piano's plush white leather-padded bench. Automatically, his hands began playing the song he had memorized: Beethoven's "Moonlight Sonata." He closed his eyes to let the music pour out of his soul—or rather *into* it to comfort him.

When he opened his eyes again, Patrick dared to turn toward his master. Would he receive a blow to the side of the head for his impertinence? Or worse?

Nark's fearsome head bowed, greasy hair hanging over his eyes. The king's full lips twisted in a relaxed smile. Nargoleh Layhew, the treacherous, dark, cruel ruler of the Isle of Mercy, was happy.

*　　*　　*

The piano was transported to the large Royal Chamber in the heart of Nark's island. While Nark conducted his business day-after-day, Patrick played music in the background.

Contrasted to the horrible locating chamber, the Royal Chamber was almost lovely. The best smokeless oil burned in gold sconces in the broad, high stone walls. Tapestries hung to soften the underground chill. King Nargoleh Layhew sat high on an ornate, gilded throne. The king addressed dignitaries and a horde of magi in their colorful robes, and Patrick caressed the piano keys to provide the appropriate mood. The piano had come with a pile of Lanthran sheet music based on Earth-type notation. Patrick learned the songs as fast as possible.

And Patrick listened to the chatter and negotiations around Nark while he played no louder than *mezzo forte*. Because he was immersed in Lanthra—*again!*—he could understand much of what was said. Most of the conversation sounded boring: Shipping terms, Lanthran acronyms, grumbles about supplies and trades.

But one afternoon, Patrick's ears pricked with attention when he heard "Bardia" repeated over and over. He didn't dare to quit playing, but he eavesdropped on their speech, which got angry, even violent with Lanthran expletives. The hairs on his neck rose in a prickling chill. Nark and the magi were talking about "invasion" and "conquest."

Patrick's insides burned with the frustrated urge to action. *I've got to warn Bardia! But how can I get away?* Nark kept him nearby day and night. He might as well be chained, because at night he slept with a mean Blue guardian on a mat in an alcove of Nark's bedroom. Plus, Nark had promised with a red gleam in his deep-set beady eyes that if Patrick tried to escape, very, very bad things would happen to his feet—and hands.

CHAPTER 20:
THE INTERVIEW

After the recruitment effort by the Horned Edge, Lewis's work week crawled by. Finally, the dreaded Thursday morning rolled up again, and he was supposed to see FBI Special Agent Sheldon. Thinking about everything too fast, too hard, he dropped his breakfast toast butter-and-jelly side down onto his charcoal gray suit. After he sponged off the mess, Lewis abandoned the toast without tasting it.

The view as he rushed outside to his Lyft was gray, and his soul felt gray, too. All the recent snow had melted except for patches; rain drizzled onto the messy, dirty sidewalk. That decrepit Victorian house for sale across the street exhibited chipped gray paint and a rutty yard. Lewis felt like that view. *I will not, I will* not *tell Mr. Sheldon about getting recruited by people from the Horned Edge.*

*   *   *

To Lewis's surprise, this Thursday morning, same time, same place, Special Agent Sheldon was not present to meet him. When he entered the office, he was confronted by not one, but three inquisitors. "Have a seat," they said, and he sat.

Lewis faced two men and a woman in the room with the viewing wall. *Are they Horned Edge? Will they press me for a decision to join them ... right now?* But they smiled and chatted small talk with him. His jittering left knee relaxed ... a little.

Suits and ties and white shirts and a distinct aura of training shouted, "Federal employees!" regarding the two men. But the petite thin woman was different. She might be about sixty, with an austere face, thick white hair pulled back in a braid, and she

104

wore a smart navy-blue dress suit. Acute intelligence shone in her gray eyes. Lewis thought, *I like her.* The woman examined Lewis and fingered notes into her iPad.

The interview began. Lewis determined to stay polite, even though the thought made his heart pound: *If anyone threatens my family, I'm getting up and walking out!*

"Mr. Brahmindura—may I call you Lewis?" began one of the men, the leaner and lighter of the two.

"Where is Special Agent Sheldon?" Lewis asked abruptly. "And who are you?" *This is so similar to my encounter with the Horned Edge, except for the handcuffs.* Even the office's flat gray color reminded him of that basement.

"Special Agent Sheldon brought us in to talk to you," answered the lean man, without answering Lewis's question. "I'm Bruce Patterson. Call me Bruce. My partner is Dave Cortez and our associate is Dr. Jane Moritzer from Cornell University. She is a consultant for us. First names are fine here. We're from Homeland Security."

Lewis reminded himself again to be cautious. *Just because they say they're from Homeland Security doesn't mean they're friends!*

"Special Agent Sheldon invited us to take on your case because of your previous experience. What happened to you recently is so similar to what happened to you two years ago that we cannot imagine there is no connection. You were apparently kidnapped by terrorists back then, and this time you were kidnapped again in public by *blue* people!"

Lewis's throat thickened, remembering the *latest* incident, one that he was determined not to describe. He nodded.

"Please, tell us your version of your most recent kidnapping."

You mean, my next most recent kidnapping. Lewis decided to tell them as much of the truth as possible. He was tired, yes, *tired* of tippy-toeing around trying to decide who to tell what.

"Mr. Bruce, two blue—yes, *blue*—males appeared out of nowhere in our hotel room. Patrick and I ran, but they chased us. We got as far as the highway when they overpowered us." Lewis paused, shuddering. "Th … then we all disappeared into a who-knows-where locating chamber, er, a sort of control room for instant space travel."

The two federal agents leaned forward. The woman pursed her thin lips. "Yes," Lewis emphasized, furrowing his brow in the intensity of his speech, "in … instant space travel is possible. And aliens from other worlds are real!"

The conversation paused with a virtual thud. Bruce and Dave exchanged a long look. Dr. Jane, unperturbed, wrote more notes.

"Go on with your story," Bruce prompted.

Lewis took a deep breath, then began, "Everything started when an ugly king-person with a grudge against me ordered for Patrick and me to be, er, fetched. That was done; we were captured. Then—at the king's command—a half-witted scientist played around with the technology that connects distant points in space. The mag—the man connected directly to an airless moon. The vacuum sucked him into space. His blood boiled …"

Everyone grimaced, including Lewis. He went on, "Because everyone was so shocked, I engineered an escape, but at the last second one of the Blue goons grabbed Patrick, and the nexus closed on me. I found myself back on the highway—without Patrick. That's the story."

Bruce and Dave raised their eyebrows. Dr. Jane glanced at Lewis with a keen eye and paused in her notetaking. "That is quite a far-fetched tale," Bruce commented.

"That's what I experienced! B … but the big question isn't whether I did anything wrong the last time I was kidnapped or this time. The real question is how to get Patrick back home!"

Bruce and Dave crossed their arms. They sat up in their chairs and frowned. Dr. Jane kept writing notes.

"What can you tell us about the blue creatures?" Dave asked. "We saw the viral video. They were covered with blue hair with white crowns. They wriggled long red tongues and wore no clothes."

Lewis nodded. "Yes, the Blue people … they're from another planet. It's … complicated." Musing on Lanthra and forgetting the present, he slipped his hand into his back pocket. He fingered the small coil of flimsy plastic that recorded everything a scientist needed to duplicate the Lanthran technology that allowed instant space travel. *If only I could develop this, I could rescue Patrick!* His mother knew that he had a piece of plastic "trash" that he carried everywhere. But neither she nor anyone else, he hoped, realized how important it was.

Coming back to the here-and-now, Lewis saw three pairs of eyes scrutinizing him. He bit his lip and tried to think about what he could or could not say. And he knew their eyes had followed his hand.

"What do you have in your pocket?" Bruce asked.

"Um, just some loose change. And a candy wrapper."

Bruce frowned. "We can't do much to get your brother back until we understand what *really* happened to you."

Lewis ran his hand through his hair, wishing he could tear it out. "I've told you everything that happened."

He was leaving out a monster-of-a-tale, the story of his experiences on Lanthra—another planet!—in a cave chamber. And these people's questions made it clear that they knew he held it back. Lewis groaned. *Am I going to have to tell them the entire hot marble story from beginning to end? With Lanthra, magi, dragons, and bezubs? They'll think I'm crazy!*

Dr. Jane had not spoken the entire time. She now affirmed in a cool, precise voice, "Lewis, I *do* believe you. And it's clear that you know far more than you're telling. However, until you come clean with us, we won't be able to help find your brother. You are a brilliant scientist, you have worked with cutting-edge technology, and to have you disappear twice like this is not a coincidence. To develop instant space travel"—she stared pointedly at his pants pocket—"our enemies would indeed kidnap you again, and …" Dr. Jane paused, catching Lewis's eyes as if she could read his soul. "They would threaten your family. If they are keeping your brother prisoner somewhere, they are probably threatening you already. We need to know the whole story."

Lewis couldn't answer. His hands began to shake. He clenched them together, but Dr. Jane noticed. "You are trembling, Mr. Brahmindura. There is something big in there, something that needs to come out."

She glanced at her iPad. "According to our records, you never saw a psychologist after your first ordeal. Yet you came back critically ill, having seizures, and Dr. Zhartha terminated you from the energy project—with good recommendations, I must add."

Lewis said nothing. *What shall I do?*

A quiet answer came: *Work for them.*

But I don't know them! Are they Horned Edge or some insidious competitor? I cannot trust my own country!

Dr. Jane continued, "You exhibit pressured speech, and your doctor suggested that you may have post-traumatic stress disorder in addition to your other ailments." She reached into her black alligator-skin briefcase and came up with a business card. "Here's the name of a psychologist who helps us out from time to time. I strongly recommend that you follow up with an appointment as soon as possible."

Bruce pinned Lewis with a serious stare. "In fact, whether or not you are detained for more questioning depends on you making that appointment. Someone from our office will call you tomorrow to find out when that appointment is scheduled."

Dr. Jane handed Lewis the psychologist's card. His hands still shook, but he managed to tuck the card into his wallet. *Why am I so upset? What's wrong with me? I'm usually so calm when I'm in danger. Or ... am I in danger?*

He asked, "Am I free to go now?"

Bruce looked at Dave and Dr. Jane, and they nodded. "For now," Bruce said. "Expect to be followed. We don't want to lose you again."

*   *   *

On the way to work after the morning interrogation, Lewis's Lyft had to travel the same stop-and-go road. The Buick again caught the stoplight red in front of that big church that he'd noticed before. As Lewis sat in the Lyft's back seat, numb and scared, he saw that the decorators had put up many lights in the trees and wrapped the trunks and branches with close coils. *I'd like to see that at night. The days are so gray and short in this time before Christmas.*

Just before the light turned green, Lewis resolved that he'd find out if the church had a Christmas Eve service. Carefully, he noted the sign on the corner: My Redeemer Church, and he decided to call the church office for information. *You don't want to go,* a nay-saying thought told him. *You'll stick out like the proverbial sore thumb. People will greet you with virtual claws and teeth, drooling, "potential new member to fill the pews and give money."*

Lewis wavered. But he'd felt so awful after the interrogations and seeing the happy people decorating the church grounds had picked his soul up considerably. He decided, *I will go to their Christmas Eve service.*

CHAPTER 21:
LITTLE PRAYER

Gracie had a headache, and she never got headaches. Well, almost never. She'd had them often since she started drinking at Peggy's party. This one just would not quit; it grew in her head like a poisonous toadstool on rotten wood. By lunchtime at school she felt nauseated. The hot lunch menu was deep dish pizza. *It smells like cleaning fluid.* She couldn't eat. Everything looked disgusting. The pain kept getting worse. By the time she got on the bus to go home, she could hardly see to climb up the steps and get a seat.

I want a drink, Gracie wailed inside. She put her hand on the top of her head and that made it feel a little better. However, she couldn't go around with her hand on her head. *I need a drink. But how can I get one?*

A silly idea came to mind. At first, she discounted it. But, as her head pounded, she began to entertain the plan. *Go to somebody's house with loose rules on alcohol. Now!*

Calculating, Gracie considered all the factors. Dad wouldn't be home from work until suppertime. Mom was sleeping—or throwing up from the chemo. No one would care if she didn't show up immediately at the house. Gracie hated the empty-feeling house, anyway. All her favorite things there groaned, *Your Mom is dying.* The bus driver might notice if she got off at a different stop, but she could explain it as visiting a friend. *What friend? Oh, I know. Brad.*

Brad lived two bus-stops away from her. The skinny kid was older than Gracie, about Patrick's age, but she knew him from riding the same bus all the time. Gracie looked for him among the bus seats.

Ah! There he is, two rows back, talking and being loud with his buddies. She didn't care for Brad. He told lewd jokes. He cursed. He smelled funny, like nobody did the laundry at home. Sometimes he got into fights. But he probably had alcohol at his house, and that would do.

The bus stopped at her chosen place. Blinking away the pain, Gracie picked up her book bag. "I'm getting off early to visit my friend," she mumbled to the driver as she stepped to the street. The woman didn't comment.

Brad and two other guys and a girl got out behind Gracie. In this neighborhood, the houses had scraggly bushes and needed paint; at one house, little trees shot up from its foundation.

"Hi, Brad!" Gracie approached the kid, and made her face look extra-friendly.

Brad stared at her bug-eyed. Then he leered, "You coming over for an afternoon romp?"

"Did I hear there was a party at your house?"

"You and me, we can make a party."

"Got anything worth coming over for?" She hoped he would mention *beer* or *wine.*

"Well, of course! Me!"

Gracie walked with Brad, her heart racing. Everything here seemed gray and dingy, and that wasn't just because of the overcast sky. Stepped-on blobs of gum decorated the sidewalk. The few plants or trees were brown and frost-bitten. Cars swished past, so did trucks and vans and another school bus. She kept tight hold of her book bag in case she needed to bean Brad with it.

A little voice inside suggested, *Turn around and go home! Take some aspirin, get a snack, and change into your running clothes. You'll feel better.*

Instead, she and Brad stopped at a two-story building. The first floor was a tavern. And taverns had what Gracie wanted. Brad pointed to the second floor with the shades over the windows. "I live up there. Come on in, my dear." He leered at her.

Gracie swallowed a surge of disgust. She followed him through the door up the grimy steps.

*   *   *

The door on the second-floor landing opened to a living

room. Right away, Gracie wrinkled her nose: The stained and worn shag carpet in mottled orange and brown smelled like rotting leftovers. Plus, the air reeked of cigarette fumes. But, when she noticed the cold, sweaty can of Budweiser in Brad's hand, she forgot the odors.

The kid jittered and grinned as he gave it to her, glad like a child to have company. In his other hand he had another beer.

"Where are your parents?" Gracie hoped to drink a lot of beer; but she also wished there was an adult available to regulate Brad.

Brad shrugged. "Mom's probably at work—or shopping. She likes to shop-til-she-drops or runs out of money. Dad? Who knows. He's been gone for years."

"When do you think she'll get home?" An anxious knot hurt her chest. But Gracie sipped the beer and stood with Brad in the middle of the living room.

"Oh, sometimes she gets home for supper, sometimes not until late at night."

Gracie gulped and nearly spewed. *Oh great, you're completely alone with this kid.*

Ripped cushions, used tissues, old microwave trays, and other rubble covered the sofa and two chairs. She saw no vacant sitting surface. Brad lowered his wiry frame to the carpet. Gracie did, too, after flicking away a dead centipede.

"Well, darling," Brad drawled, puffing out his chest, "Want to see the bedroom?"

"No," Gracie stated. "I don't."

At the moment Brad seemed less randy than talkative. Gracie figured that he had few friends and fewer supportive adults. While they drank three more beers—each, the older boy went on and on about his dog that had died last month and the dead goldfish he'd flushed down the toilet. He offered to show her his ferret, which Gracie was sure contributed to the odor, but that meant going into the bedroom. "No thank you. Not this time."

"You mean that you'll come back?" Brad's deep-set green eyes widened but then narrowed as if he were calculating a strategy.

Gracie drank down the last of her beer. Her head floated; she liked it. "It's time for me to go home."

But Brad put his hand on her knee. Gracie brushed it away. "No need to hurry," Brad told her. "Mom won't be back for hours, and besides, she doesn't care what we do. Just stay a little longer. I'll show you a great time." His eyes narrowed like a predator, and alarm built up so fast that Gracie stiffened in temporary paralysis.

Leaning forward, hand still on her knee, Brad crooned with a blast of sour beer breath, "You're beautiful, you know."

Gracie shivered. This was going too far. Brad moved close that they reclined cheek-to-cheek. Before she could stand up and get away, he nuzzled her ear.

"I've gotta go!" Gracie sprang up, knocking Brad away.

"Aw, just a little nookie, darling? You'll love it."

"Brad, I've gotta go home right now!" But Brad exuded lust; she could see it on his face. Her mind sped to consider her options in case she needed to fight him.

Brad was older than her, but he was only about her height. He was wiry, though. Gracie set her jaw. She'd wallop him if he tried to molest her.

He must have read her determination in her eyes, because he didn't attack.

"Bye, Brad," Gracie said, and sped out the apartment door, taking the stairs two at a time. When she reached the sidewalk, she sprinted down the street. But Brad didn't follow her.

Gracie walked about a mile until she approached her house. She had a half-hour total before Dad came home. Mom might be wondering where she's been—or, maybe Mom was just conked out. *Never mind. If they ask, I'll just say that I was late because I'd been talking with a friend—and it's true. Sort of.*

*   *   *

Soon Gracie stood in the shower, soaping off the stink. Her head felt dizzy and when she toweled herself, she wobbled. But then she felt more than heard the garage door open. *Oh boy, Dad's home.* She'd lie to Dad and try not to talk to Mom at all.

As she pulled on her pajamas and slippers and slipped on a robe, she thought of a cover story. *I've been sick all afternoon.* It might explain why she acted a bit unsteady, too.

With her plan in place, Gracie went downstairs.

"Hey, Gracie," Dad greeted when she came into the kitchen, "are you all right? You're wearing your pajamas already." His brown eyes with their crinkles at the corners shone with concern. And his thin face had gray shadows in the cheekbones from worrying about his family. Gracie hated herself, but she had to lie.

"Hey, Dad," she said, faking squinty eyes and putting her hand to her head. "I didn't feel so good at school today, and when I got home, I went right to bed."

"What's the matter?" Dad asked, anxiety all over his face. He came over and gave Gracie a hug. She held her breath so he couldn't smell the beer.

Stepping back, keeping her head down, Gracie told him, "Nothing much, Dad. I just don't feel good. I wanna go to bed early."

"Shall I bring you up some chicken noodle soup and hot sweet tea?" he pressed. Gracie winced. He sounded like Mom. But Mom was sick and—just as Gracie had calculated—sleeping.

"No, thanks, Dad. If I get hungry, I'll come down and make a sandwich." Slumping, Gracie trudged upstairs.

From her bedroom she heard clinks as Dad opened drawers in the kitchen. She heard the microwave and smelled a chicken breast frozen dinner. Dad would be all right. He would take care of himself—and Mom. She got into bed.

The buzz in her head made life bearable. As Gracie lay down, she thought, *So far, I'm doing okay. I don't drink every day and I haven't tried drugs ... except, well, twice.* One girl she'd visited had shared her mom's Oxycodone.

Gracie wanted to drift off to sleep, but she couldn't. She missed Patrick and Lewis horribly. The house was deadly quiet without them. And with Dad depressed and Mom sick as a dog from chemotherapy, her life compared to eating cardboard while watching a wretched game show. And she couldn't do a thing to feel better—except numb her heart.

But maybe Jesus can help you, said a dim little glimmer of positive thought. *Just ask him.*

"I don't wanna pray." Gracie mumbled. "God, you don't do anything. You're invisible and you're useless!"

Try me, came the reply.

Although she pounded her pillow in frustration, Gracie prayed for the first time in weeks. *Okay, okay! Here goes. Bless Dad—and Mom. Keep Lewis safe. And bring Patrick home.*

It was a pitiful excuse for a prayer, but Gracie couldn't think of anything else to say. Taking a deep breath, she asserted, *See, God? I prayed.* Her body grew warm, her dizzy brain emptied, and a few minutes later, she was asleep.

CHAPTER 22:
LEWIS CELEBRATES CHRISTMAS

"You want to do *what?*" Peggy exclaimed when Lewis told her his plan in the break room at work.

"I want to go to the Christmas Eve service at Redeemer Church downtown. I've already called them; it's at seven o'clock tonight!" Lewis sipped his coffee with one hand—the coffee was rather burned, so he'd put more sugar in it than usual—and wrapped the other around Peggy's shoulders.

"Lewis, we can't go," Peggy told him, leaning into his embrace. "We have an important party tonight, remember? My dad and Mr. Cranz have spent a lot of time and money on putting it together for all the employees."

Lewis had forgotten. An inner voice said, *You're a newbie around here. You would be wise to meet friends at Peggy's Dad's party.* He wavered. He had just decided to bypass his idea and go to the party, but then he felt a different, softer nudging inside. *Try the Christmas Eve service. It's only this time. You won't know if you don't go.*

He came back to his resolve. "We can still go to the party," he said, smiling down into her lovely face. "The party people won't care if we come by after the service."

"I don't want to go," Peggy answered. Doubt darkened her voice, and she crossed her arms. "I can't imagine anything I want to do less than go to some stuffy half-baked Christmas ceremony at a decaying old church."

Images of hokeyness and acute embarrassment inside an unfamiliar moldy building barraged Lewis's mind. He could see her point. However, he could not forget the *good* feeling he'd had whenever he passed that church. He told Peggy, "I think it'll be fun. It's as if that place has been calling me."

She drew back and questioned, "Are you're having a religious experience after ... after we were—"

"No, I'm just—"

"You're just giving me a hard time." Peggy acted as if she were teasing, but he saw she was half serious. "We're busy enough this Christmas. Work is so demanding these days. I've got five clients to push drugs to this afternoon in three different hospitals." Peggy rolled her eyes. "Besides, I can just imagine trying to tell people at the party where we'd been, as if we were ... well, church people."

For some reason, the harder Peggy pressed him, the more convinced Lewis felt that he should go. And this conviction felt ... appropriate. "I've made up my mind," he said, standing straight. Then he smiled. "But I want you to come with me."

Peggy tensed, her hands with those perfect nails clawed, and for a moment Lewis saw her as an angry fox. But, to his great relief, she relaxed, caressed his brown eyes with a soft affectionate gaze, and put her hands on his shoulders. "All right, for you. Just for you."

As she left, Lewis took a deep, deep breath, held it, and let it out, wondering why he felt like he'd been in a battle instead of making a date with a gorgeous, vivacious woman. Since their scary session together with the Horned Edge recruiters, they'd gotten more and more physical. That last kiss had been wonderful! His whole body tingled with the memory of it. And she'd stuck with him, helped him. Was his growing decision to remain aloof from the Horned Edge driving a wedge between their ... friendship?

Your romance, a thought corrected his mind. *Be honest, Lewis. You're falling in love with her.*

*   *   *

That evening at Redeemer Church, Lewis took a program and a candle and led Peggy into the church's sanctuary. He wore his dark slacks and trusty charcoal sweater; she wore fashionable tawny tights over her long, shapely legs, a gold big-shirt, and a glittering red pashmina around her neck. "You look fabulous," he told her as they filed inside. She gave him a quick kiss on his cheek.

It was about ten minutes before the start of the Christmas Eve worship service, and the place was filling up. "I don't want to sit so close to the front!" Peggy whispered when Lewis took her hand and led her up the right aisle.

"There's no room anywhere else," Lewis murmured. "Besides, I can see better up here." He felt excitement picking up in the air, the warmth of a crowd along with the fragrance of candles and festive greenery. People all around chattered in low voices. He saw lots of Christmas ties and Christmas sweaters. One bent old man using a candy-cane striped walker with a horn even wore a Santa hat. Lewis's mood rose. *Christmas! I love this season! I'm so glad to try something different after ... losing Patrick.*

Lewis took the second seat on a pew; Peggy sat next to him by the aisle. "Can you see all right from here?" he asked, sliding his arm around her shoulders. To his surprise, she now felt stiff with tension.

Peggy put a hand up to her head. "I'm getting a headache. It feels like one of my migraines is coming on."

"Do you have any aspirin?" Lewis asked. Her eyes squinched with pain, and he caressed her forehead. Yet, the general uplifted atmosphere in the church infected him. *I wish Peggy could enjoy this.*

"Aspirin!" Peggy shook her head. "That wouldn't even put a dent in the pain I get from my migraines!"

A family of six hovered next to Peggy in the aisle. "Excuse me, but may we squeeze in?" the mother asked with a shy smile. Peggy stood up, Lewis stood up, and they let the cavalcade edge past.

Pleasant introductory music started. An organ high in the back of the church played the "Canon in D" by Pachelbel. After a while, a children's choir joined into the organ music and sang one of the parts, *"Merry Christmas!"* Lewis smiled. Around him, people got quiet, while latecomers squeezed into the available spots.

He let his eyes rove around the altar area. It was a feast of Christmas beauty. Flaming red poinsettias filled the sanctuary, great gold bows hung from the chandeliers. Up by the altar stood a large manger scene. A live Holy Family gathered around the wooden, straw-filled manger, and Lewis noted with delight that they were dressed in contemporary clothes. Joseph, standing, wore jeans and a dark sweatshirt. He held a glowing flashlight and seemed worried. Mary sat by the manger, wrapped in Joseph's coat. She wore a loose blue sweater and a long gray skirt. Her dark hair was long and bedraggled, like she'd come through a real labor and delivery. Mary viewed the manger, rapt with wonder as her hand caressed the tiny fingers of a baby figure. The baby doll Jesus looked like a newborn wrapped in a yellow and blue baby blanket with ducks on it. As Lewis watched, the shepherds with staffs entered, wearing cargo pants and padded jackets like outdoorsmen. The wise men came in from the other side, wearing expensive suits like executives. *How creative!*

Delighted, Lewis started to comment to Peggy, but she frowned and said, "I've got a splitting headache and I feel nauseous. Oh, my! I've got to go—now!" Springing up, she thrust her candle at Lewis and hurried down the aisle toward the back of the church, nearly knocking down a late lady wearing a glittery red Christmas dress.

Lewis, in a quandary, started to stand up. He wanted to stay and enjoy the service, but … *Peggy must feel awful; I'll go to her.* Then he realized that she was most likely in the ladies' bathroom.

Just then the lights dimmed. Lewis sat down. The Christmas Eve service was starting.

Thus began an hour of wonder. Soon his soul became immersed in the experience. Someone had written an original musical score that told the Christmas story. Adults and children sang in parts.

What stood out for Lewis was a recitation. The bulletin had printed the text of a summary of Christian beliefs called the Nicene Creed. The pastor—a vigorous black man in a crisp white chasuble—picked up the baby from the manger and held it while a reader said from the front,

I believe … in one Lord Jesus Christ,
the only begotten Son of God,
begotten of His Father before all worlds,

God of God, Light of Light,
very God of very God,
begotten, not made,
being of one substance with the Father,
by whom all things were made;
who for us men and for our salvation
came down from heaven
and was incarnate by the Holy Spirit of the virgin Mary
...

The Nicene Creed's words mounted like huge pillars carved out of granite. What Lewis had come to believe as a vague, shadowy ghost began to solidify. For once, he understood the basic Christian teachings about Jesus, and they floored him. "Peggy!" he whispered, wanting to share his great emotion with her, but she was not there.

For the final event of the service, the sanctuary lights darkened. While soft music played, ushers came down the aisles and lit the first candle in each row. Lewis was more aware than ever of Peggy's absence as he leaned over to get his candle lit. He turned to his neighbor and passed the little flame; the man turned to an eager child, and so on down the row until all the candles were lit. Like the kids, Lewis turned toward the back to see the host of candle flames. *I wish Peggy were here,* he thought regretfully, but still enjoyed the moment as everybody sang "Silent Night" a capella, led well by the choir.

CHAPTER 23:
A BROKEN ARM

After a benediction, the Christmas Eve service was over. Lewis filed toward the rear of the church, searching for Peggy. In the crush of people, he was afraid he might miss her, but after several minutes he spotted her off to one side on a sofa in the anteroom.

Her eyes were puffy and red.

Lewis hugged her and asked, "Are you all right?"

A glistening tear crept down her cheek. "No. I feel horrible." Then, with a weak smile, Peggy added, "But I still want to go to the party."

Lewis took her arm and led her through the exuberant crowd to the waiting ride.

*   *   *

Lewis tried to enjoy the Gnudst and Cranz Christmas Eve party, but after the worship service his perceptions had changed. The conversation sounded loud and shallow and the whole point of people's behaviors seemed to be the consumption of lots of alcohol. Because of his seizure meds, Lewis knew he should not drink alcohol. After one small glass of Pinot Noir to satisfy Peggy's urging, he stood to one side holding a cranberry juice and watched Peggy socialize. She had recovered from her headache, and she was in her social element.

The party dragged on toward midnight. To Lewis's growing concern, his beautiful companion imbibed freely. She laughed, slapped shoulders, patted a few butts, and chugged back onion-graced martinis.

Lewis thought, feeling anxious for his sake as well as for hers, *Is this the life I've chosen?* The intuition grew that he wanted something different. He'd crossed an abyss to walk with the angels while he was a prisoner on Lanthra two Earth years ago, but more and more he seemed to be wandering into a dead-end canyon.

After two hours, Lewis could stand no more of the banal party. Going over to Peggy, he said softly, "I'm ready to take you home. I've already called our ride."

*　*　*

In the cab, they snuggled. Lewis brushed her neck with kisses. She held him, drew his face toward hers, and kissed him deeply. "Let's stop by my place for a while," Peggy breathed.

Lewis's heart rose as she led him into her apartment. Perhaps they could put on some music, sit on her sofa and talk and kiss and ... his thoughts moved toward her bedroom.

As soon as they entered the kitchen, she poured each of them a glass of dry Riesling. Lewis rationalized that one more drink wouldn't set off a seizure. His mood was fine silver, a full moon glinting on puffy clouds. He kissed her again, and let one hand feel her soft, smooth thigh.

She responded with a sigh of pleasure. "Oh, Lewis, that feels nice. Let's—"

All at once, Peggy stopped. She set down her glass so fast on the kitchen table that the wine sloshed out. "Wait a minute. I have to tell you ... First you dragged me to a lousy hokey church service, where I promptly got sick, and then you moped around at the party. I was just getting into the fun, and you had to leave early. What's going on with you?"

Lewis wanted to share his heart. *You're right; we need to clear the air. And then we can ...* He decided to share a true, deep emotion. "I've been thinking a lot. When Patrick disappeared—"

"Yeah?" she interrupted. "Well, *that* sure was weird."

Confused by her abrupt changes, Lewis began, "Huh? What—"

But Peggy headed for the living room, and he followed her. She talked fast, "I had hundreds of nosy clients saying, 'Oh, dear, are you all right since your friend Lewis disappeared?' You were quite the sensation—on national television, no less! That guy put his phone video on YouTube and got three million hits. Since then, every time I have gone to an office or hospital for my job, I've been embarrassed out of my mind!"

Lewis decided to stay patient. "Peggy, I miss Patrick."

"Okay, so you miss your brother," Peggy agreed, but without a lot of sympathy. She pulled away from him and stood by the sofa, swaying a little.

Lewis had been deeply moved this evening, and he thought that if he explained it would mollify her new mood. "This winter has been depressing. Since Patrick got kidnapped, the FBI and Homeland Security have been questioning me. And then the Horned Edge grabbed us and began to recruit us. I was so confused! So, when I saw that church decorating for the Christmas season, something got stirred up inside me. I wanted—"

"Ow!" she complained, putting her hand up to her head. "My headache has come back. I want to take another Vicodin!"

"*Another* Vicodin?" Lewis exclaimed.

"Keep your voice down!"

"But you had quite a bit to drink on top of that headache medicine you took before the party! Maybe you should—"

"How dare you criticize me!" Peggy flared.

"I'm not—"

"I'm not the one getting hauled in by the police, the one who lost his own brother in the stupidest way imaginable!" Her thick blond hair seemed to bush out around her face and her eyes narrowed. Her pink tongue pointed at him like a cobra about to strike. Lewis suppressed a jump back.

Trying to calm her down, he soothed, "Okay, maybe it's not the best time to talk right now." He longed to go back to the way this evening had started: Happy. Romantic. And, yes, sexy. "Tomorrow is Christmas Day. We have plans to go to brunch with your dad. "That'll be fun. Now, would you like a cup of coffee?"

She leaned up and thrust her face close to his. "You're telling me that I'm drunk? Aren't you?"

"Yes, maybe a little." *Maybe a lot,* an honest voice in his mind said.

Peggy's eyes glittered and she took another step forward, pushing him backward. "You think you're so righteous, don't you?"

Suddenly, her clenched fist smacked him hard on the chin. He stumbled back. She swung again and hit the side of his head. "Ow!" He crouched to avoid another blow. "Peggy, stop it!"

But she grabbed the pole lamp and knocked it across his

shoulders. The lamp broke into sections and the shade spun off across the room, shattering a glass on the table. Lewis was afraid to hurt her, but she was hurting him. Her face crazed, Peggy used the pole like a spear, aiming at his eye. Lewis tried to fend of the pole with a cushion, but she caught the fabric with it and tossed the ripped cushion away. Foam stuffing scattered everywhere.

"Peggy, stop it!" he yelled. When the pole came at him again, Lewis caught it and yanked it out of her hands. He dropped the ruined lamp to one side. "Peggy! Please! Let's just talk it out!"

She screamed and picked up a jagged shard of the broken glass. Lewis had no choice but to back into her bedroom. There was nowhere else to run. As she advanced, Lewis retreated some more, toward her closet, afraid that she would stab him. He felt his emotions freeze on hold, and every second stretched out into infinity. All he could think of was stopping her madness.

Peggy sprang toward him. Lewis pulled open her closet door and leapt inside. But the door wouldn't close. She blocked it with her foot and ripped his sweater with the shard. Then Peggy aimed for his face. Lewis dodged. "Stop it, Peggy!" When he pulled back as far as he could go, his shoulder knocked her clothes rack from its seat, sending Peggy's coat hangers, dresses, pants, skirts, shirts, sweaters, and accessories crashing on the floor.

"Look what you did!" she screeched. She rushed at him again, glass shard aimed at his neck, her mouth twisted and eyes glaring. Lewis swung the clothes rack like a baseball bat to fend off her attack.

The rack struck Peggy's hand and made the glass shard fly across the room. But she clawed her fingers and tried to rake his eyes. Another blow with the rack banged her wrist ... hard. "You broke my arm!" she shouted, "you son of a —!"

"I'm sorry, I'm so sorry," Lewis cried. However, he didn't put down the clothes rack in case she attacked him again.

Holding her wrist, Peggy seemed to shrink back into her usual size. She mumbled, "You scum, I'm calling the police!" Her face crumpled, and tears rolled out of reddened eyes.

Lewis stood in the wrecked closet, gripping the clothes rack, while Peggy fumbled for her phone. First, she snapped a photo of him. Then, she dialed 9-1-1. "My ... my boyfriend beat me up," she sobbed. "He broke my arm!"

CHAPTER 24:
JAIL

Swirling red and blue lights smote Lewis's eyes through the front window outside Peggy's apartment. He lowered himself onto the sofa, head in his hands, while the police came thumping up the stairs. The ugly thought flashed that he lived on Earth, the home of the Curse, the headquarters of the *bizeor* that infest human relationships—including his.

"What's going on here?" a deep male voice growled from the hallway.

Lewis raised his face from his hands and stood up. He saw blood on his hands … his own blood. Peggy gave him a dirty stare and unlocked the door, letting in a tall, broad police officer. Another officer, also tall and substantial, came in and rumbled at them, "What happened here?"

Without immediately answering, Lewis examined Peggy. Her hair wild and her eyes red, the young woman held her arm and whimpered. He wanted to go to her, but the look she threw at him was a stab. "We had an argument," he mumbled. "She and I … it was over nothing. Just a very bad evening after a party."

The police officer who had addressed him bristled with gun, riot stick, and handcuffs. He showed his badge, examined the scene with a sweep of his eyes, then turned to Lewis. "Aren't you that guy that disappeared in November and came back?"

"Yes, I'm the one," Lewis said, resigned to notoriety.

"What happened here?" the other officer asked Peggy. He held a tablet.

Peggy's face twisted with pain. "My boyfriend got mad at me, called me names." As the officer keyed notes, she burst out,

"He came at me, shook me, backed me against the wall, and raised his fist. When I pleaded with him to stop, he tore up my closet, pulled the rack out, and hit me with it."

"What about this damaged lamp and broken glass?"

Lewis started to answer, but Peggy jumped in first. "He went wild! That … that skinny rat started hitting me! And I had to defend myself." She sniffled. A big tear rolled down her cheek. "He's threatened me before, but this time he really lost it."

Stunned, Lewis opened his mouth to protest, but nothing would come out.

"My arm—it hurts so much! I'm sure it's broken." Peggy wailed.

The officers glared at Lewis. When they turned to Peggy, however, their faces softened with sympathy. "And your name?"

"Peggy Gnudst." She spelled it for them, her voice weak and low, while the officer wrote on his tablet.

"And your name?" he growled at Lewis.

"Lewis Brahmindura."

"Spell that."

Lewis spelled out his name. He gave up on explaining his side of the story. *You broke her arm.* He hung his head, noticed again that his hands were bloody. *Caught red-handed,* the ironic accuser continued, but the joke was not funny.

"Ms. Gnudst, you need medical attention. Do you intend to press charges?"

Peggy's icicle gaze speared Lewis. "Yes."

"Very well. Turn around, Mr. Brahmindura."

Lewis slowly stood and turned, and the officer nearest him cuffed his hands behind his back. The shoulder that had been injured under torture in Lanthra years before complained, but Lewis did not say anything. His brain felt immersed in a thick fog. Everything moved in slow motion; voices sounded under water. The officer grasped his elbow and marched him out of Peggy's apartment.

"Do you have anyone who can take you to a doctor?" he heard the other officer ask Peggy.

"I'll call one of my girlfriends. Brittany—I can depend on her to get me to the ER," Peggy answered.

As Lewis passed her at the doorway, he turned. "Peggy, I'm

so sorry."

She grimaced, her pretty mouth curling with derision. "Merry Christmas!"

*   *   *

Lewis sprawled, exhausted, on the cushioned slab that served as a bed in jail. The overhead light was too bright; it hurt his eyes even when he closed them. There was a sink and toilet by the bed—no privacy. Today was Christmas Day. Several drunks were stuffed in the cell with him; one of them smelled terrible, with ripe feces and vomit creating a palpable stench in the room.

When Lewis imagined the questions he was going to get, the judging stares of his coworkers—not to mention his employers, he fought a retch. Just a few weeks ago he had started at Gnudst and Cranz, and they had thrown him a lavish "new job" party. Some associates had commented that he and gorgeous Peggy were the perfect couple. Plus, they—or at least he—had really been falling in love. Now he was cast in the light of "abusive boyfriend." Lewis groaned and faced the wall.

"Mr. Bramin—how do you pronounce your name?" a hard voice came through the bars.

Like an automaton, Lewis answered, "Brah-min-du-ra."

"You can go now."

Lewis blinked. He sat up.

"Ms. Gnudst has dropped all charges."

Keys clanked, the officer ordered everyone to "stand back!" and his cell door opened. The news didn't make Lewis feel any better. In fact, he just felt dead as an old dirty plastic bag squished in mud. But he got to his feet and put on his jacket. Stumbling like an old man, he followed the officer out into the station area.

"May I use the phone?" he asked, his voice rasping.

The officer, the tall, broad one who had cuffed him in Peggy's apartment, scowled. "All right, Mr. Brahmindura. I'll give you back your own phone."

The officer handed Lewis his cell phone and other items from a labelled bag where they had put the contents of his pockets. *Who can I call in Newark?* Lewis wished that his best friend Fred was around, but he had left Fred behind in Lanthra two Earth years ago. Now it seemed that all his friends were Peggy's friends, and he didn't feel enthusiastic about seeing any of them. *Who can I call?* He thought. *Mom and Dad are all the way down in Alabama.* For a while he drew a blank. He couldn't think of a single soul in the Newark area that he was willing to ask to pick him up from jail in the wee hours of Christmas morning. He decided to just call a taxi.

Soon a taxi arrived. Lewis went out to it—the night air was very cold, and damp and the sky was overcast—and told the Sikh driver his apartment's address. The driver nodded and they zoomed off.

CHAPTER 25:
HELL IN MIND

Lewis awoke late on Christmas afternoon. Slashing between the darkening drapes, a sliver of light smote Lewis square in the eyes. His head throbbed with unwelcome consciousness, and with disgust he groaned, "It's Christmas. What an atrocious holiday!"

The radiator cranked; its vibration put him on edge. Trying to tune out the noise, he flopped onto his belly and pulled the covers over his head. When he got hot, he threw the covers back, lay still, and stared at the wallpaper. It had paisley patterns within patterns, and he dimly remembered that another time in a more pleasant mood he could use chaos theory to come up with an equation to explain those infinite patterns—but not now. In fact, the visual "noise" made him afraid that a seizure might strike. Quickly he shut his eyes.

For a while, Lewis managed a twilight sleep. However, the sleep evaporated, replaced by acute, wakeful discomfort. Peggy's attack, her lies to the police, and his gut-wrenching shame over breaking her arm haunted his mind. Plus, the bed sheets were tangled; his skin felt oily, and he had not undressed before going to bed, so his clothes bulked around him.

A glance at his watch showed him that it was going on two o'clock in the afternoon. Groaning, Lewis got up. His wrinkled clothes reeked of his cell mate's body odor.

Then the front doorbell rang. Lewis stumbled out of bed, unlocked and pulled open the door.

A tiny Asian woman with a ponytail and bright eyes greeted him. "Merry Klistmas!" she said. Her name tag read "Binh." She wore a silver cross. Her smile faded when she saw his face. "You okay?"

"Sure, fine," he mumbled. "What do you want?"

"You asked for me to come," Binh said. "To clean after your party."

"Huh?"

But the little woman pulled a large cart of cleaning equipment, and she was determined to do her job in his apartment. Lewis sighed and let her start. Cleaning would only take about a half-hour, and then he could get another round of sleeping misery. As Lewis settled onto his sofa, the cloud in his mind intensified. *I didn't arrange for anyone to come and clean on Christmas day!* But Binh had shown up, and he didn't have the heart to order her out.

Binh dusted all the light fixtures, wiped all desk surfaces including his computer screen, mopped the floor, and at last chirped, "I done now."

Lewis paid her cash. "Jesus bless you, Mr. Jones," she told him as she left.

He started to exclaim, "Who?" but the elevator door closed, and Binh was gone.

In the silence left behind, Lewis hated himself; he wanted to implode like a black hole sucking all light and matter into itself. Short and simple: he wanted to end the pain. *Why did I come to this place?* The honest answer pounded in his brain: *I came because I wanted to follow Peggy to Newark. I also wanted to do something—anything—besides work in Dad's shoe store.*

Suddenly, an urge pushed through all other thoughts. *I want to die.*

Images of ways to do "It" flicked past: *I could buy a gun and some soft-point bullets, put the barrel to my ear, and pull the trigger. I could buy a big container of bug spray and drink the whole thing. Or—*this idea struck him—*I could step in front of a vehicle on the road. And this apartment is near a busy street.*

"Do It," he mumbled.

Do It! The inner urge echoed.

He could jump in front of a big truck out on the road and feel much better. Lewis went to the window. A dark cloud slid over the too-bright sun. All at once heavy rain came down, some sleet mixed with the rain. But there were lots of big trucks on the road, and Lewis could think nothing but death.

Planning his death scratched an intense spiritual itch. Stepping to the apartment exit, Lewis put his hand on the doorknob.

*　　*　　*

He exited to the street. Lots of cars and trucks zoomed past, splattering rain with their tires. Just a few yards more. And … there was a semi …

"Hello, how are you?" a well-dressed couple greeted him as he stepped toward the curb. "Fine," Lewis mumbled. They smiled and kept going. But the pull of suicide had been interrupted. He felt icy sleet hit his neck and slide under his collar, and he ran into the building.

Back in his apartment, Lewis wandered into the living room. Flipping channels with the remote, he searched for something mindless to watch. There was a Christmas Day parade. *Flip.* The cooking channel had a Christmas feast. *Flip.* Lewis turned to a news channel. Fortunately, he did not see himself on the news. A murder took up the publicity—depressing enough, but at least he didn't hear a report about himself disappearing, dying, or being involved in "domestic violence." *I wonder why Peggy dropped the charges?* Briefly he considered calling Peggy. If only they could patch things up, get back to "normal" … That idea snagged in his chest. Before the fight, at the party, something new had started speaking to him, and it was speaking to him now. *You're not going to do It.*

Death had to have the last word, *Not yet, anyway.*

CHAPTER 26:
THE RECOVERY MEETING

Gracie ran straight up to her bedroom after school. As she sat down to her desk and cracked open her laptop, she took a deep breath and let it out slowly. *Where shall I start with my new story?* She thought. At first her shoulders drooped, but then she sat up straight. *I'll just start anywhere.*

She tried a description from her time on the world named Lanthra, a happy, "rainbow" one. *Sadie Gregory hugged me every morning before I went to school. She was—is—beautiful. Her long black Hawaiian hair flows all the way down her back, and she keeps it in a braid. I can imagine a red hibiscus flower in her hair. And her cooking! She's a vegetarian and I'm still a carnivore, but her casseroles, muffins, corn, puddings, fruit, homemade breads: All yummy!*

Something like a fly buzzed in the room. Not only was the noise irritating, but she imagined a big, fat bug that bit and left its dirt everywhere. She was familiar with that sound, and all that she could think of were *bezubs!*

Gracie knew about the demons that controlled Earth. She'd fought a big one on Lanthra and won, so that Lewis and Patrick got rescued when they were prisoners. But she'd never told anyone about that battle, not even her brothers. The memory of the demon's perverted scorn made her skin crawl. The images squatted inside her like muddy concrete blocks covered underneath by earwigs and grubs and swarming ants ... *Never mind, people don't need to know what happened because that story is absolutely awful.*

The fly noise began again in her bedroom. She felt the insect land on her forehead, and it bit her! "Ouch!" When she raised her hand to her face, Gracie saw blood on her fingers. She'd been thinking of demons—and now a real horsefly badgered her. *Those blasted bezubs!* She thought of her mom and dad, and stressed-out Lewis and disappeared Patrick. *They're attacking my whole family!*

After she smeared some Benadryl cream on her fly-bite, Gracie returned to her story. She forced herself to write the first images that came to her head.

Mom has breast cancer. She's taking chemo, but it's bad. The doctor said it got into her liver and her bones. And sometimes she's vomiting and sometimes she sits up in bed and reads, but most of the time she's asleep. She can't eat much because she's got no appetite, and the food runs right through her. Nights are tough. I've heard her in the bathroom ... Gracie paused, not wanting to continue the memory of that noise.

Then she began to write once more. *Once a week she goes and gets a new treatment that lasts for hours. And after that she's sick. And then for a couple of days she's recovering some, then comes another treatment. It's been ages since we had a real talk. Okay, okay, it's my fault. I don't want to be near her. I can't stand how it makes me feel.*

And I miss Patrick. Sometimes my brother gets my goat, and we fight. But I wish he was home. That viral video showed him and Lewis getting captured, disappearing, and then Lewis came back—without him. Who knows what Patrick's going through now? He could be—

She heard light footsteps coming upstairs and stopped writing. It was Mom.

"Gracie, it's about time to go."

"Huh?" Gracie kept her eyes on the computer screen.

"Gracie!"

Gracie slowly turned her head. Mom stood in the doorway. Her pretty oval face was pale, with dark shadows under her eyes. That beautiful red-gold hair had fallen out and she was bald under the hat. Mom's arms and legs were thin as sticks. Gracie's stomach squinched, and she turned back to her writing. *I wish Mom would go away and leave me alone,* she thought, but felt horrible about the idea. A new, sinister thought entered her mind

… Maybe if Mom dies, I'll feel better.

"Dad and you and I are going to the meeting." Mom sounded rather sharp.

"Now! Time to go!"

"I don't wanna go," Gracie mumbled.

"You're going." Mom's words were final.

Gracie sighed, put away her stuff, making unnecessary noise, and followed Mom downstairs.

*   *   *

The evening sky was dark blue with hard-looking stars when Gracie and her parents entered the church social hall. Not her own church—thank goodness!—but some nondenominational church on the edge of town. Although she couldn't quite shake the cloud of resentment in her chest at being dragged to a stupid meeting, Gracie had to admit that the big room was attractive. She saw elegant sofas and chairs arranged in sets with side-tables and colorful Tiffany lamps. The light, fresh cream walls had huge floor-to-ceiling windows, and she saw pots of healthy real tropical plants. The bougainvillea was blooming optic pink. *Like a Lanthran sunrise,* she thought with a little surge of pleasure.

Mom and Dad sat on a love seat; Gracie plopped down on an armchair. Other people filled up the other places to sit. Gracie figured that she was the youngest person there. She noted a couple of teenagers about Patrick's age and two young women who looked like Lewis's age. Everybody else—about twenty people— were adults and old people. Gracie heard a subdued buzz of conversation, but she didn't feel like saying anything. *I'm just a turd.* Remembering the whole drinking spree, all the lying and cheating and stealing, filled her with sick shame.

The meeting's leader chatted with other people. She was either one of the church's pastors or an elder; Gracie didn't know. *I don't much care, either!* But she couldn't help but notice that the woman was attractive. She wore her thick, naturally blond hair up in a chignon and looked stately in a fawn-colored dress suit. Because of her confident stance and her elegant jewelry, Gracie figured she was a high-society lady, rather like Deirdre except taller and at least forty years older. A deep part of Gracie's insides wanted to be that lady, a leader who helped people. *Sorry,* her shame mocked. *Remember—you're a piece of crud.*

At starting time, the leader stood up and began in a carrying voice, "Good evening. I'm an associate pastor here, a licensed counselor, and the host for your Family Recovery meetings. What I'd like us to do is go around in a circle and introduce ourselves. I'll start, and then we'll go around clockwise."

Everybody quieted. The leader began, "My name is Madeline Grayce. Besides having a full-time practice in counseling and pastoring at this church, I'm also divorced with four grown kids—that's a long story. I am an alcoholic, but in recovery for thirteen years."

Gracie gasped. *She's divorced and an alcoholic?*

The circle introductions began. Gracie fidgeted in her armchair, trying to figure out what to say. Her stomach growled with hunger, and the snack she'd had before the meeting was gone, consumed, digested, disappeared. *Am I an alcoholic?* she thought. *Well, I don't want to admit it, ... but ...*

Despite her inner chaos, Gracie paid attention when a teenage boy with dark hair like Patrick began to talk. "I watched my older brother get shot. One minute we were in front of the house playing basketball, but then a car drove by, and I heard a *bang!* My brother was dead."

That sounds like what Patrick went through when he was captured with Lewis, she thought.

One of the older people droned on about her terrible experiences, and the leader kindly interrupted the monologue. "Thank you for sharing. Next, we'll hear ..." Madeline gestured toward the person to the left.

This person was a female about Lewis's age, that is, mid-twenties. She said, "My name is Karla, and I was raped by a neighbor when I was eight. I didn't tell anybody, and the neighbor moved away. But the shame didn't go away. I started using drugs just to feel normal. Then, when I got a boyfriend, I got pregnant. Before I could think about it much, he said that he'd only stay with me if I got an abortion—right away, I did. He left me anyway. Now ..." Karla broke down, sobbing into her cupped hands. Several people in the circle came to her and hugged her and prayed for her.

Gracie's attention focussed on Karla's statement that she had been abused when she was eight. *That's how old I was when*

I fought with that nasty demon! But my story is so unreal. How can I tell it?

Karla quieted, and the sharing began again. Sitting next to her on the right was Dad. What would he have to say? His life, frankly, was kind of boring. Gracie glanced at him sideways. His face was grave. *What must he think of me after ...* Her eyes fixed at a tiny stain on the carpet. As she stared, it seemed to grow and grow, a sinkhole of shame. Her mind felt darker and darker.

Dad's turn came. She expected him to say something simple and throw the turn to her, but he didn't. "I'm Frank Brahmindura. I drank myself silly in college, lived with a girlfriend, smoked, went to classes drunk—when I went at all. I failed all my classes and dropped out of school."

Startled, Gracie shifted in her chair. It squeaked. *Dad was like* that?

Her father went on, "But when I married Cora, I quit drinking. I took a manager's job in sales, and I began to get prosperous. Then, when my oldest kid, Lewis, was tiny and we didn't get enough sleep, I took some sleeping medications. I worked long, long hours starting up my store, and I took more pills for more energy. Cora can remember those times. Lewis might remember. I wasn't a nice person. But one day I said 'yes' when my wife asked me to go with her to church. It was a miracle that I even went! The sermon that day captured my heart. It was about how my Father God is not angry with me; He loves me. After that, I kept going to church. I also joined a 12-Step group. I straightened up. But I am heartily sorry that I didn't continue going to meetings after Patrick and Gracie were born. I didn't start drinking and drugging again, but if I'd kept going, my family might never have ..." His voice broke. Gracie heard a sob.

Peeking at her father through her thick auburn hair, Gracie saw a tear trickle down his cheek. *Dad, an alcoholic and a pill addict?*

Dad squeezed her hand. "Your turn. If you don't want to say anything, say 'Pass.'"

Gracie opened her mouth to say, "Pass." Instead, what came out startled her. "I fought a big demon once. I won. But it was so awful that I've been a ... ashamed ever since. And when Mom got sick, I just couldn't handle it anymore. It was like the demon was back. I started drinking."

She burst into tears. She sobbed until her insides hurt, her nose ran, and her face puffed up. Dad hugged her; Mom hugged her. A number of people in the group came up and joined the hug like they had for Karla.

Somehow Gracie felt cleaner after her crying explosion. Two more people shared—but she was so full of her own emotion that she couldn't pay attention—and then Madeline wrapped up the meeting. "Thank you all for coming tonight. Continue to come to the meetings, because recovery is not an event; it's a process. God bless you. We'll see you next week, same time, same place. And then we'll learn and practice some communication habits, both to other people and inside our own minds. Those skills will strengthen our ability to fight stinking thinking and the addictions that follow it."

Soon after Madeline's closing remarks, the meeting broke up. Gracie pushed open the church glass door, and immediately a waft of deliciously fresh air cooled her face. The sky was so clear that it was nearly black, with the stars intense. She could even see the Milky Way overhead. And in the south shone a big white star. *Probably Venus,* she thought. *Lewis would know.* A rush of sibling-love welled up in her. *I'll call him as soon as I can.*

CHAPTER 27:
A STEP OUT OF HELL

The whole rest of Lewis's Christmas afternoon dragged by. Night darkened his room, but he only managed a twilight sleep. The urging voice came back. Over and over it demanded, *Do It!*

At least twelve times during the day he thought of more ways to do It. There was always the highway again with its lethal cars and trucks. *Let's see ... F=mv², where v² is the speed of a vehicle in meters per second squared and m is its mass. Suppose the vehicle just went the speed limit. The impact would be more than enough force to kill me.*

But Lewis shook himself. *Nope! No!* Some invisible force in him fought with the strong idea of self-murder.

Loud Vivaldi music startled him: His phone! Swinging his legs off the bed, Lewis sat up. His heart beat, regularly and loud, like Edgar Allen Poe's "Telltale Heart."

"Peggy? Could she be calling me?" Lewis's chest tightened and his jaw clenched.

The phone rang and rang. He did not answer. Soon the phone silenced. He thought, *Deirdre. My true love. Why did I abandon her for anyone, anyone at all?*

Lewis knew why, and tears came to his eyes. Racked by deep guilt, he rocked back and forth with his arms squeezing his chest. *I felt lonely and deprived and tried to fill up the void with infatuation, eye candy. My new job took me away from my support system. I followed Peggy, and I chose work, however "noble," that side-tracked my real dreams. Since my former boss, Dr. Zhartha, rejected me after ... after Lanthra, I've been playing the tiny whining violin of self-pity.*

He groaned and cried aloud, "Deirdre! I miss you so much! But I live on the Earth. Every time your beautiful Lanthra connects to this planet, bezubs pass through. I can never see you again! I vowed to be true to you … just in case … in case by a miracle we could be together someday. And I've betrayed you!"

At that second, his phone rang out Vivaldi's *Spring* again. Lewis's whole body jolted. Fumbling, dropping the phone once, Lewis managed to answer the call.

"Hello?"

"Hey, Lewis, this is Gracie." His sister's voice sounded bright, like a happy yellow warbler.

He croaked, "Hi, Gracie."

"How are you?"

"Fine," he lied.

His little sister's voice declared, strong as a grownup's, "I *know* you're not fine. You sound like you've been smoking cigars for forty years. So, tell me what's *really* going on."

Lewis waited a long time before he answered. *What can I tell her? I've never could fool Gracie; she senses what I'm thinking more than I do.* His little sister waited patiently for him to speak. Finally, he gave in. "Peggy and I had a fight. And I broke her arm."

Gracie exclaimed, "Bummer!" Then she prompted, "Tell me about it!"

Lewis told her about the fight, in short words that a ten-year-old girl could understand. After he finished, there was silence on the phone. He wondered if the call had dropped. "Hello? Gracie, are you there?"

Gracie finally talked. "I'm awfully worried about you. Do you want Dad and me to come up there?"

Lewis's heart swelled with pride that little Gracie would care for him so much. But he hated the thought of imposing on his family. "No, I can handle it."

More silence. When Gracie replied she sounded strained. Her young girl's voice stammered. "I … I … I have to tell you what *I* did."

It was Lewis's turn to listen while she told him her holiday "activities." He caught his breath when his little sister confided that she had started drinking and had even taken some drugs. She described the lying, the sneaking.

"Why, Gracie," Lewis retorted. "Why?"

She didn't answer right away.

Lewis wondered if the call had dropped. "Hello? Are you there?"

But then he heard her breathing. "Well," she finally answered, "when Mom got sick, I felt so scared. I got into the whiskey that she keeps for the fruitcake. Then I did it again, later, at … at a party. And then I visited some kids at school who had alcohol. The last time was … with a boy who … made a pass at me."

"What?" Lewis exploded.

But while he sputtered, Gracie kept on talking, "I won't lie anymore. It makes me feel like dirt. And I asked Jesus to help me."

"Oh, Gracie!"

"Mom and Dad took me to a recovery meeting for families. The leader says that drinking and drugging is a family problem, and … anyway, it starts from deep, bad emotions. Lewis, since Patrick got captured and you moved away, our whole family went bonkers …"

"Oh, Gracie," Lewis moaned. "Of all the people in the world, I would *never* have thought that you would do that."

"Yep," she said. Then her voice sounded stronger. "I'm an alcoholic. And I haven't had a drink in a whole two weeks."

*　*　*

After Gracie's call, Lewis took a deep, deep breath. Good memories and thoughts disintegrated the black slime from his emotions. He remembered times with his family, joking and playing games, eating meals together. Those moments were a slice of heaven.

He said out loud as his heart lightened, "I feel alive! And the Christian creed at that Christmas Eve service boomed out to me: Jesus is God of God, Light of Light, Very God of Very God!"

Lewis walked over to his desk. Out of a drawer he withdrew his journal and, opening to the last entry, he exclaimed, "I haven't written anything since October! Well, time to catch up."

He sat and wrote: *I don't understand all that Christian doctrinal stuff, but I believe that it is true. God is the creator of the universe; it didn't all happen by itself. When I was a prisoner on Lanthra two years ago, surviving torture, surviving a desire for suicide, even murder, I knew beyond doubt that the devil is evil and that he is real. But the Christian creed tells me that Jesus is real and much stronger than the devil.*

I still have issues with you, Jesus. I don't understand all the killing in the Old Testament. I really don't understand why you let such evil things happen today. But I have to believe that you are alive and with me. Back in the cave chamber when you took me across the abyss of Hell to the "good side," I dared to tell you that I didn't like you very much. Yet you didn't jump on me with anger or hurl lightning at me.

You've let me get stuck in a corner—again!—and I need to get out. Please help me let go of Peggy and be faithful to Deirdre. I ask that you'll somehow bring Deirdre and me back together again. Please be with Patrick and protect him against evil. And ... thank you so much for rescuing Gracie!

Putting away the journal, Lewis grabbed the Bible his parents had given him from his bookshelf. He got off the chair and sat on the floor, like he used to do to play with toys when he was just a kid. The first verse he saw when he opened the Bible at random was Psalm 14:1, *"The fool has said in his heart, 'There is no God.'"*

Lewis did not like to hear that he had been a fool. He snapped the Bible closed. Opening to another page, he read: *"But we preach Christ crucified, to the Jews a stumbling block and to the Greeks foolishness."* He didn't like that, either. But after he mulled over the concept for a while of "Greeks," the thought occurred: *I have been a "Greek." I thought I was wise, I thought I could understand the universe by being a very smart physicist. But I left out a very important and real thing from my equations and grand theories: God.*

Taking the lotus position, Lewis closed his eyes and talked to God. *Dear God, I want to trust you. I know that I've been a proud fool. I reckon that's what is called "sin." Anyway, I want to believe in you. I've heard the words, "Jesus died on the cross to save me from my sins." Please forgive my sins and take me with you to eternal life.*

He opened his eyes. "Oh boy. I'm a Christian. And I'm supposed to remember that—even around my friends and associates."

Lewis knew he had a lot of deep processing to do. He couldn't possibly write down all that was going on inside; it would take days! And … he was hungry. His stomach whined and pained and nagged.

His bank account had enough balance to cover the rent, but not much more. His credit card wasn't maxxed out, but it already had a plump charge on it from the new AI program. And he might be fired from his job at Gnudst & Cranz any day now. *Maybe I have change enough to get something from the vending machine in the building's foyer.* Thrusting his hands deep into his pants pockets, he felt for change. Lewis also felt a paper card. It was the card that Dr. Jane Moritz had given him, the one that recommended he see a psychologist: Dr. Greer.

"Oh great," he said aloud. "I'm supposed to call that guy. Or *else!*" The Homeland Security people had made it clear that they would pull him back in for some serious detention if he didn't follow up on an appointment.

Stomach growling, Lewis descended into the apartment building's foyer, got a Cola from one vending machine and a package of crackers from another, and retreated back to his apartment. The meal, poor as it was, helped. He sat at his desk and began to speak a voice note into his phone. "Tomorrow, call … let's see … Dr. Greer the psychologist and make an appointment. Call the Homeland Security and FBI people and tell them you've made that appointment."

And after that—"Call Dr. Zhartha and tell him about that coil of data I've been hiding."

There. An action plan. He felt better.

CHAPTER 28:
DR. JANE

The workday after Christmas was cold and overcast, with a forecast of snow mixed with rain. Lewis hadn't been fired—yet—and he went to work. The day dragged with dread. But no one stared at him or commented; Peggy wasn't around; he didn't get called to Mr. Gnudst's office. It was just another day with electron microscopes and computer analysis ... except for one thing.

Lewis retrieved from the company database a chemical analysis of defective brain amyloid proteins associated with Alzheimer's in various stages of development. He added compositions of natural protein molecules and sent everything to his home computer. *If I can use AI to simulate a normal protein atom-by-atom and also AI some other models of the defective ones, I might be able to find out what is deforming the amyloid. There are probably several factors involved, but an AI atom-by-atom simulation could be a step in developing a treatment that could halt or prevent the progression of the disease!* The idea filled him with new excitement. If he had to be side-tracked in his dreams, let it be toward something worthwhile.

After work, the moment he returned to his apartment, he took off his coat and beelined for his laptop to reconstruct the molecules. Just as he sat down, Lewis's phone rang. *Could it be Gracie again? Or Mom and Dad?* Smiling, he dug it out of his pocket.

When he glanced at the ID, Lewis groaned. "Homeland Security wants another interview."

He answered the call. "I've already made an appointment with the psychologist for tomorrow afternoon," he said in a flat tone and thought, *I'd rather not talk with you.* It was true: He'd called the psychologist's office, explained his situation, and they had made a special hurry-up appointment just for him. But the caller, dogmatic Mr. Cortez, had a firm purpose.

"This isn't about the psychologist's appointment," Cortez growled. "We need to meet with you tomorrow. I repeat, that's *tomorrow* at ten o'clock, at the office where you were before."

Lewis had originally planned to take that morning off to work at home on his idea. His plans were going awry—and Mr. Cortez made it clear that showing up was not optional. He sighed. "Okay."

Conversation over. He had another interrogation to look forward to, and after that, a session to analyze his post-traumatic stress-damaged self.

*　　*　　*

The next day before he left for his Homeland Security appointment, Lewis felt thin and stretched inside. He hadn't slept well, dreaming that an angry mutt chased him through some woods. *Coffee! I want coffee!* He made himself a cup of very strong, very sweet coffee with his French Press coffeemaker.

While he sipped, he looked longingly at his computer. *No time for the AI simulation.* Instead, he doodled on some paper, trying to come up with some brilliant insight. *Alzheimer's characteristic deformed amyloid molecule in the brain ... What deforms it? What proteins and processes? How can those be inhibited?*

But he found it hard to concentrate. *How is Peggy?*

So far Peggy had not communicated with him at all, not even once. Nor had he dared to call her.

Lewis sagged. *You broke her arm!* "All right," he told himself. "I will call her ... after my appointments."

He finished his coffee and stood up. There was one item from the past that Lewis had held onto: Bobbie the teddy bear that little Gracie had given him years ago. Bobbie had been exiled to the bottom of his closet in a plastic bag *because he'd been ashamed of him when Peggy was around!* Lewis only had a few minutes before he had to scoot off to the Homeland Security appointment, but he took the time to pull out the bear.

"Bobbie," he said, "I'm sorry. I want to do better from now

on, but I'm in a mess."

Bobby agreed, *You are a mess.*

"I wish I could somehow help Patrick come back."

Bobby contemplated him with his inscrutable brown teddy bear eyes. *What are you doing with that Lanthran technology stored in your sock drawer?*

Lewis asserted, "Bobby, it will take millions, even billions of dollars to recreate that Lanthran locating system, even if I had the resources. And time!"

The bear was unsympathetic. *You're already talking with government people. I'm tired of you sulking and being helpless. Tell them what you want.*

Lewis grinned and put the bear front and center on the kitchen counter.

* * *

Interrogation again. The same people, the same place. Bruce Patterson, Dave Cortez, and Dr. Jane Moritzer listened as Lewis (*again!*) told his story. "I've already told you everything," Lewis began, but they wanted to hear it all from the top. When he repeated, "The scientist connected to space, and the vacuum began to suck the air from the room," they told him to stop.

"Connected? How do you mean, connected?" asked Dr. Jane.

"How much do you want to know?" Lewis came back at her.

"As much as you can tell me," she stated.

Lewis dug into his back pocket. "Look at this."

Cortez sniffed. "Looks like a candy wrapper."

"No," said Dr. Jane. "It's too long and curly."

"It's a template with the design on the atomic level of a system that can connect you instantly to any mapped area in space."

The group looked at him with their mouths open. "Huh?"

Patterson, quiet as usual, shook his head.

"You're crazy," Cortez said.

"He's not crazy." Dr. Jane's eyes widened. "Tell me more!"

Lewis began. He could see that Dr. Jane followed him but the other two did not. Their faces registered patience, however, as he lectured without downsizing the scientific terminology: "When stimulated with ultrasound, the system this flimsy piece of plastic shows the detailed schematics ..."

After ten minutes, the group still listened, and Dr. Jane stayed attentive when Lewis wrapped up: "The system's technology uses power from a singularity at the center of the planet to create gravitational resonance according to the pattern on the map of a crystal neural network. Did you follow that?"

"Yes," Dr. Jane said comfortably. "And what you've said raises lots of new questions."

"Such as what?"

"Is that technology from Earth?"

Lewis nearly choked. He cleared his throat and answered truthfully, "No."

"Then what planet are you talking about?"

"Um . . ."

They all waited.

"Um . . . It's called *Lanthra,* which means Horizon."

Silence draped the room. Dr. Jane stated, "Since I choose to believe what you are saying, I must infer that during your disappearances you travelled through a door in space, from one planet to another, without a spaceship."

More silence.

"That's right," Lewis said. He didn't know what else to say, but then his conversation with his teddy bear came back. *Be assertive. Ask for things.* His heart leaped and he cleared his throat. "I could duplicate that technology on Earth with the right resources."

Dr. Jane smiled. "That's exactly what I was hoping you would say."

CHAPTER 29:
LEWIS SEES A PSYCHOLOGIST

The next day, Lewis took a Lyft to see the psychologist, Dr. Greer. He jittered and frowned and grumbled all the way there. "I don't want to lie on a couch and talk about my mother."

Your mother has aggressive breast cancer, and she's dying. Since when have you called her? The thought glared in his head, and, feeling a pang of guilt, he gritted his teeth. Lewis's ride caught red stoplight after red stoplight. He muttered, "Those lights—It's as if some sadist timed them to all turn red on purpose when I'm coming down this road."

It started to rain, a misty pervasive dampness. The temperature outside was bone chilly at 34° F., and Lewis started to shiver. His bones ached with cold. Even the roaring heat in the car didn't reach through his skin.

The Lyft got him to the correct office complex. Lewis found the right door. A metal plate on the wall by the elevator listed many professionals, including Dr. Greer. Lewis pushed the button for the third floor, and the elevator lifted.

When he reached Dr. Greer's office, Lewis rubbed his arms because of the burst of cool, business-like air that did nothing to warm his bones. The office smelled like polish and leather upholstery. Was that undertone odor a tang of nervous, edgy clients? Hanging his coat on the branched stand, he checked in at a pebbled glass window that barely opened so that he could see the receptionist inside. Automatically, he informed the person, "I'm Lewis Brahmindura, here to see Dr. Greer."

When he finally focussed on the receptionist, Lewis's heart squinched. The young woman who checked him in and handed him his intake papers reminded him so much of Deirdre that at first he thought she must have crossed the void of space to Earth. The young woman was young, pretty, and well-endowed, with long blond hair curling over her shoulders. For a moment he was speechless.

The receptionist didn't notice his stare. "Fill these forms out and return them to my window. Dr. Greer will see you shortly after that."

His heart beating fast, Lewis found a seat on one of the hard chairs, spurning the sofa. He balanced a clipboard on his lap. With the provided pen he began to fill in the intake papers.

The process took him some time, and even though he tried to breath smoothly, his heart pumped hard, his stomach fluttered, and he tried not to think of Deirdre but it was impossible.

Oh, Deirdre, I have been unfaithful. I have been such a fool. Can you ever forgive me?

The form asked him questions about his moods, his medical history, his family's medical history, his medicines—all of them, even over-the-counter—and a twenty-question examination of his thoughts over the last two weeks. When Lewis got to the one that read, "I have had thoughts of killing myself," he hesitated.

Should I lie? Mark "never" instead of "twelve times a day?"

An invisible strong presence joined him in the waiting room. It reminded him of the inner dragon that had overcome him when he was a prisoner in Lord Charon's palace. The dragon had forced him to feel his emotions like barbed wire in his soul.

Lewis struggled. "Go away!" he said aloud. The five other people in the waiting room stared at him curiously. Lewis ducked his head and thought, *Get lost! Leave me alone, dragon!*

However, the presence only grew greater.

Lewis breathed fast, almost panting as his hand holding the pen wrote. He marked the suicide question in bold capital letters and several exclamation points: *EVERY DAY!!!* Finished, he sprang up from his chair and thrust the clipboard and questionnaire into the receptionist's window. The woman who so painfully resembled Deirdre grabbed it before it struck her nose.

"Thank you, Mr. Brahmindura. Dr. Greer will call you when he's ready."

Lewis didn't have to wait long after he returned the form. A side door opened and a medium tall, curly-haired man in a brown suit appeared. He used one finger to push up his eyeglasses and smiled. The gesture immediately reminded Lewis of Patrick. "Hello, Lewis. I'm Dr. Greer. Come on in."

Hurriedly, his long legs tangling, Lewis jostled himself to his feet and stumbled through the doorway after Dr. Greer. Down a corridor and one left turn later, he was in the psychologist's office.

"Have a seat."

There was a sofa in the office, but Lewis chose a chair, a gray leather armchair. As his eyes roved around the room, he noticed a well-stocked bookshelf against blue walls that contained, not only professional books, but also classic sci-fi books by Robert Heinlein, Isaac Asimov, and Ray Bradbury. In spite of his surly mood—or was it fear?—Lewis softened inside. Other office ornaments included two real and healthy ficus trees, several original paintings of Atlantic beaches with pelicans and sea turtles, and a real salt-water aquarium. Dr. Greer himself sat beside a small desk, facing Lewis.

The psychologist said pleasantly, pushing up his glasses, "So tell me what's been happening with you lately."

Lewis groaned.

Dr. Greer waited, so Lewis started, "I had a fight with my fiancée—er, friend—and I lost my brother in another world. Where do you want me to begin?"

"Let's try the fight with the friend since you mentioned that first."

Lewis summarized that too-recent evening when he'd taken Peggy to a Christmas Eve church service. She'd started a migraine and took Vicodin. Right after that, at the office party, she had ingested alcohol on top of the Vicodin. Next, at her apartment, her behavior had changed drastically. She and he argued briefly—and then she attacked him! "I've never seen her like that before! Peggy's eyes … they blazed at me. She came at me with some broken glass. I swung the clothes rod from the closet at her, and it stopped her, but … the rod broke her arm. She called 9-1-1; the police came. I was arrested and went to jail. But Peggy dropped the charges."

Dr. Greer started to comment, but Lewis rushed on, "However, well before that, the police were already involved with me. The FBI and Homeland Security got dragged into my life because of my missing brother *and* my past history of disappearing off the face of the planet *and* because I … I've had a lot of experience with some high-security physics research. One of the people who interrogated …er, interviewed me said that I had pressured speech and that I might be suffering from post-traumatic stress disorder, and they ordered me to call you." Lewis paused.

Dr. Greer remained in listening posture. Lewis blurted, "It seems my whole family is messed up! Mom's got cancer—I haven't called her in way too long—and Dad says that Gracie's not acting like her usual happy self; her grades are going down and she spends all her in her room and won't talk to Mom. Then Patrick has been kidnapped—oh, I hope he's okay!" Lewis suddenly found that he was standing up and breathing hard. He ended his outburst with a short, curt, "And here I am."

"That is quite a story." Dr. Greer's face was open, nonjudgmental. "You do have pressured speech. Your chart says—shouts—that you also have thoughts of suicide. And, those, with other symptoms, are signs of PTSD. The first thing I want you to do is to promise that if you think of suicide and have a *plan* that you will call me. Otherwise, go immediately to the emergency room and check yourself into a hospital."

"You mean the fifth floor?" Lewis asked. He felt his lip curl.

"Whatever floor it takes," Dr. Greer said. "You may also call 9-1-1." Seeing the skepticism on Lewis's face, he emphasized, "It's that serious. Promise to me right now."

Feeling abashed, Lewis made a formal promise to take immediate, concrete action if he had any plans of suicide. When he finished speaking, even making a reminder to that effect in his phone, the psychologist continued the session.

"All right, you've told me about the fight with the woman … Peggy. What experiences did you have when you 'disappeared off the face of the planet,' as you put it?" Dr. Greer pushed up his glasses and waited.

Lewis read his expression as mild, amiable, curious, and serious all at the same time. He decided to give the man the straight story and see if skepticism would take over.

"I literally travelled to another world, Dr. Greer. It is called Lanthra. They were expecting us because they could see us with their technology, and they sent soldiers to pick us up."

"'They?' And 'us?'"

"The Bardians. And maybe the Torish, too. My brother Patrick, my little sister Gracie, and my friend Fred. There was a fight, an ambush at the ford of the Winerush … Er, I'm stumbling all around trying to describe what happened."

"No problem. Just say whatever comes out." Dr. Greer listened while Lewis told the story about how he rode a horse at night over a river on another planet. He described the wild screaming, the arrows flying, people dying. He'd been so worried for his loved ones that he couldn't feel glad when they all survived—except for the lieutenant Rel who'd saved him from capture. Lewis's telling didn't follow a straight line. Dr. Greer asked a few questions, and he backtracked to answer.

Dr. Greer finally stopped him. "Our time is up for today. But you certainly have more story to tell."

Lewis asked, his heart beating fast from the adrenaline rush of remembering past terrors, "Do you believe me?"

"Yes!" Dr. Greer sat up very straight. "I *know* you are telling the truth. I'm amazed, but I believe you. And I'm sure there is much, much more to tell."

"That would take years," Lewis said.

"It would be important work," Dr. Greer emphasized. "Lewis, you have had terrible experiences. You have hardly begun to talk about them. And I have something to say that you need to hear."

Lewis leaned forward. "What?"

"Note this: People who have suffered extreme trauma don't heal instantly. Recovery takes time—sometimes a lot of time. Recovery also takes soul work, feeling those emotions and learning how to respond to them rather than react to them. My diagnosis is that you have post-traumatic stress disorder along with your seizure disorder. However, instead of letting your past bully you, you will learn to manage your past—and yourself."

Lewis struggled to understand. "I knew that people don't get over trauma right away, but Dr. Greer—it's been two years!"

The psychologist nodded. "Yep. And for two years you've been stuffing all those feelings. You—and your family—are only beginning to heal. Well, you can't control your family or Homeland Security or the FBI or Peggy—but you can control yourself. You can recover. And that recovery will have a huge impact on the people around you."

Lewis opened his mouth to argue, but Dr. Greer pushed up his glasses and pointed to his watch. "I have 'homework' for you, and then I want to see you once a week for a while. We can meet virtually if you cannot come in person. Now, for your homework: The next time you have a big emotion— and I believe you're full of big emotions—write whatever comes to mind. Write *anything*: What you remember, how you felt, concrete impressions of sight, sound, smell, taste, and, importantly, anything it reminds you of. Don't worry about complete sentences, spelling, and grammar. Just write. Then bring what you wrote to your next appointment."

He ushered Lewis out of his office and accompanied him to the door. Lewis made a return appointment, a standing weekly time for Tuesdays at 8:00 a.m. He was going to have to get up excruciatingly early, but it was the only slot when he could see the psychologist and still get to work on time. *I'll have to get a flex-time deal at work for those mornings. My boss will probably ask embarrassing questions, too, doggonit. Everybody at work will guess what's going on. And what am I going to do when Peggy comes back to work?* He cringed at the images.

It was raining when Lewis got into his ride. The driver put the car into automatic mode. The Lyft needed minimal driving, using its sensors to keep it moving appropriately along the chosen route in traffic. What used to be merely road reflectors now also served as signals to the car's navigational system. Lewis briefly thought of the hot marble, a navigational tool based on gravitational resonance, and wondered how its technology might work for traffic control. *Could a marble be placed in each vehicle, and monitors like signal readers set up along highways?*

But his mind couldn't concentrate right now. Lewis stared at the passing buildings and trees, replaying his session with Dr. Greer. The psychologist reminded him so much of Patrick that his stomach hurt. He pictured the flimsy plastic-appearing curl of data that he kept in his pocket or his sock drawer. *Will I ever be able to reproduce the Lanthran technology, build the sonic computer plus all the trappings, and find Patrick?* That outcome seemed possible since his interview with Dr. Jane *et al.*, but was Patrick still alive? Could he even find him after the years it would take to build such a system?

As Lewis got to the stop-and-go section of road with all the unkindly timed stop lights, he felt his stomach contract painfully. It growled. *I've had nothing to eat but a cup of coffee since breakfast.* Suddenly he brightened. *I'm hungry! And that's good! Talking to Dr. Greer must be helping me!* He wanted to eat an unlimited pile of pancakes swimming in butter and syrup. *There's a pancake house along this stretch. I'll stop there.*

"Driver," he called, "let me out at the Pancake House."

The car pulled into a restaurant parking lot. Cold, gusty rain came down hard as he ran to the building and hurried inside.

The usual restaurant transactions took place. A mature and friendly hostess seated him at a booth with "We'll be right with you, love." One cheerful server brought him hot coffee; another server took his order. A nice restaurant, not a chain, either. The coffee tasted wonderful. "Aaah," Lewis said to himself, "Hot coffee: A wonderful and pragmatic event that precedes heaven." The bit of whimsy made him pause. *Where have I heard that before?*

Suddenly he knew. His mother liked to say it. A wave of guilt rocked him, coming up from deep within. *Mom! She has cancer, is run-down with chemo, and I haven't called even once!*

Writhing, ashamed, Lewis spilled hot coffee onto his shirt. "Ouch!" The server came and gave him a wad of napkins. As he cleaned himself, a rational thought came to him. *Okay, admit you are guilty, Lewis. But just because you haven't called doesn't mean you can't call. You know that she loves you. Also, she is being treated with the best medical advances, she was healthy before this illness began, and you may keep her into her old age.*

Besides, as a Christian you believe in the resurrection of the body: Hers—and yours!

Comfort and even a tang of delight warmed him. Lewis reflected that, no matter what happened with his mom's living or dying, hot coffee would always be able to recall for him the fragrance of his mother and a sharing in a joy beyond their messed-up physical existence.

Quickly he began to tap notes into his phone. First, Lewis scheduled a call to Mom—for today! Then he wrote a note: *Grief hurts. When Mom got cancer, I assumed I'd lost her forever. Yet, if there is a God, then He has Mom in his keeping. He is strong. Medical science has evolved far in treating cancer, and she has a good chance of recovering. Also ...,* he grimaced but resumed his thought. *Even if she dies, I will see her again.*

Taking a deep breath, Lewis resolved, *When I call her, I'll be able to tell her all about these last few weeks, and maybe she'll give me another of her memorable messages, one of those short pithy statements that puts everything into perspective.*

Service was slower than he'd anticipated. While he waited, Lewis kept writing in his phone journal. *When I told my story to Dr. Greer, I thought that I was just relating the facts. But now I realize how scared I'd been. That means that I have a habit of sucking up my fear in order to function ... and then forgetting or neglecting to feel again after. Somehow my body knows the emotion is there, though. The trauma lurks inside. It affects my sleep, my dreams, and my behavior.*

The server put a steaming pile of pancakes in front of Lewis. *I think Dr. Greer is going to be like my dragon. He's going to make me feel—and I will hurt.*

A calming statement settled into his psyche: *Yes, you will hurt! However, like the experience of drinking this very fine coffee, some of the pain will be mixed with joy.*

Lewis took another sip of the rich, steaming brew. There— let this memory be an anchor to remind himself of something good. Then he poured syrup on his pancakes and began eating.

CHAPTER 30:
DEIRDRE

Once again at work, Lewis stared at brain cells and proteins and ß-amyloid molecules *ad infinitum* through the scanning electron microscope and on the computer analogs until his eyes blurred. He thought, *Everything I'm doing here is based on light. But the Lanthran system is based on sound. What would it take to watch the detailed processes of the brain's proteins at the subatomic level? Even the quark level?* That technology was within his reach … wasn't it?

Lewis tried to hold onto the creative thought, but all thoughts bogged down, filtering through heavy emotional fog. Ashamed and tempted to hate himself, he recognized that he had sat on that curl of data for *two years* and kept telling himself that developing its technology into reality was impossible. He'd been passive. He'd let his true dream slip away.

Pulling away from the screens, he wondered when he could relax. He checked his schedule: Next, a discussion with his research team. After that he had a conference call with some MRI people, and another with a couple of Alzheimer's researchers in California. There was a meeting after that with the researchers about clinical trials on a new medication that might slow down the horrible disease.

Getting up to stretch, Lewis fingered his back pocket. *Amazing*—Dr. Jane and Homeland Security gave him permission to develop his Lanthran technology. They implied that they'd connect him with the resources. But how long would all that take? And would he have to quit his job?

Another thought crept in; it was a real downer. It made his

stomach sink and his skin crawl. *Powers and principalities will most certainly want to control the project once I get going on instant space travel technology. They could move weapons, not to help stop wars, but to reach specific locations to conquer territory. Can I trust my country? Can I trust* anyone? Lewis shivered. *The Horned Edge don't all wear rings. And those who do aren't all in one place—they're in many, many places. Suppose they are associated with Dr. Jane? I like her, but I don't know her.* Lewis did *not* want to work for *any* agency that planned world conquest, but … he might give in if they threatened his family.

Just then, he got a text. When he read it, his stomach flopped.

> *Dr. Zhartha is giving a lecture at Harvard in a few days. We've scheduled you a spot. Air tickets are already reserved. Regards, Dr. Jane.*

"Wow," he muttered. "If Dr. Zhartha gets on the project with me … Wow."

Lewis made a decision. He would work on developing the Lanthran technology—no matter what. But he was too distracted to work anymore today; he'd go home and make some calls. Striding to the administrator's office, Lewis asked that his part in the conference calls and meetings be cancelled for today and rescheduled.

The administrator Georgia raised her sculptured black eyebrows and questioned in her svelte voice that was so effective with the clients and researchers, "What's going on, Lewis?"

Lewis knew it was a bold but caring question. Everybody had already heard on the grapevine about Peggy and him having a fight. Everybody knew he was the strange guy who had publicly disappeared around Thanksgiving and then reappeared without his younger brother. But he couldn't openly tell the truth about what he'd be doing. Even his supervisor could be Horned Edge. "Thanks for asking, Georgia, but I just can't go into it. Tell everybody that I'm not feeling well and that I'm going back home."

Georgia's eyes widened and her jaw dropped. "Alabama home?"

Lewis startled. "No. Just local apartment home. And just for today.”

*　　*　　*

Damp from the drizzle outside, feeling like his soul flew high with expectation, Lewis clumped up his apartment steps to the third floor. He pulled out his keys and turned them in the upper and lower locks of his door, thinking, *It's time to check on that lecture by Dr. Zhartha. And I want to rehearse my request about him helping me develop that curl of data into a whole system for instant space travel.*

The door opened; Lewis stepped inside. He stepped into the small kitchen, set his keys down on the table.

A lilting female voice from behind him said, “Lewis?”

Jumping with a bolt of adrenaline, he spun around. “Peggy!”

But the woman in his apartment was not Peggy.

“Oh my stars, *Deirdre!*” Lewis's eyes took in his beloved. She wore a mid-length blue dress suit—Lanthran style—and a warm gray stylish winter scarf that highlighted her peachy skin and blue-gray eyes. Her golden hair hung in waves to her waist. She not only had all the right curves in the right places, but he delighted in her characteristic straight, assertive stance. “How in the world—” A blazing light exploded in his brain.

*　　*　　*

When Lewis came to, lying on the floor with a powerful, agonizing headache, he saw Deirdre again. “Are you real?” he croaked.

Deirdre knelt near him, dabbing at his face where he had slobbered and frothed. When she saw that he was awake, she very gently touched his hand. “My love, …”

“How in the world did you get here?” But talking hurt. Lewis closed his eyes because of the pain.

Deirdre told him, keeping the story short. “You know there's a working locating system in Nutman; you helped build it! For more than a year I've planned to see you—ever since you left Lanthra, in fact. Our friend Fred helped me look for you, and I judged that it is time to be with you. Fred connected to Earth and let me pass through the nexus to this place. All the arrangements are made—even with my father and sister—and I've been open about what I'm doing. I've left Lanthra behind, Lewis, and for

157

better or for worse, I'm living on Earth."

"But—"

"Yes, I know that I'm on the world of the Curse! But I'm counting on its Treasure to guide us and protect us."

"What about the practical details? You need ID, a place to live, income …"

Deirdre smiled, and her bright grin made her look very young. She had the poise of a mature woman, but Lewis remembered that she was only about twenty-two in Lanthran years. "I came prepared for this adventure," she told him. "I know that I have a Lanthran accent and some gaps in my English … what is the word? … *idioms,* but my ID and living arrangements are all taken care of. Yes, I'm legal. My Lanthran people have worked hard for me to find you, dear Lewis. Plus, although I do not lack for funds, I have a job as a teacher at Essex County College in the University Heights area for a remedial class. I'm teaching English composition."

Lewis imagined Deirdre's fair skin and blond hair contrasted with the predominantly Black and Hispanic students who would fill the remedial college classroom. He thought of her, who had never driven a car or operated electronic machinery in her life, managing Smart Boards and computers and so on for classes. "But … How … When did you start?"

She kissed his forehead. "At the beginning of January. Can you get up?"

Lewis eased himself up, was able to stand, but then he collapsed onto the sofa. "Oh, Deirdre, I'm still in shock!"

She moved toward the kitchen. "I'll make some *tac*—I mean, coffee."

In a few minutes, Deirdre had two mugs of coffee ready, plus some snacks, and brought it all on a tray to Lewis in the living room. Drinking the coffee together and eating a small snack of tangerines and string cheese, they sat together on the sofa and talked as if there had never been years of time and space between them. Lewis was amazed that they felt so close. There was no interpersonal barrier between them, none. They "fit" together so well that relating to her was like cream and sugar in coffee.

"How did you manage to insert yourself so well into an Earth identity?" Lewis asked. He helped put away the snack remains, although a dull ache still spasmed behind his forehead.

Deirdre smiled. "Maybe I can tell you later, but not now. Just know that, on Earth, my name translates into Deirdre Celeste Higgins." Her smile arched further. "And the Lanthran root of Higgins is 'goat herder.'"

Lewis took her hand and brushed it with his lips. "I love your name."

They headed back to the living room and sat once more on the sofa. Lewis breathed in her fragrance; it reminded him of cinnamon with a hint of cardamom. He told Deirdre bluntly, "Because I despaired of ever seeing you again, I began a relationship with another woman. I dated her; I have kissed her, and I would have had sex with her. I thought that I was in love with her! Can you and I go on together after that?"

Deirdre's gray-blue eyes sparkled as they met his. "Earth's bezubs have been chasing you, have they? Welcome to temptation!"

"But—"

"Temptations are going to come at you time and time again. The real question is this: Do you love me enough to fight them and *tell* me about what's going on inside you?"

Lewis could imagine himself giving in to all kinds of bezub-talk, from despair to lust to passivity. He remembered all the times he'd wanted to kill himself. His body felt again the excited stirrings he'd had every time he'd seen and especially touched Peggy, and his imagination knew the memories of what he'd wanted to do with her.

When he came back to the present, he saw that Deirdre was waiting for him to speak. He gulped. *Can she love me the way I have been behaving?* "Deirdre, I'm so ashamed …"

Her reply was fierce, "Shame is *not* in our picture. It is *never* in our picture. That is one of the few absolutes. I love you as you are, without condition except that you promise to tell me what's happening inside you. No, I cannot demand that you must drag out your every single passing thought! However, your deep feelings, especially when something bothers you, must be open with me."

It struck Lewis hard to think of shame as something to be denied, even fought against. He could remember the shame he'd felt in the cave chamber submitting to Lord Tahei Charon's will, enabling the plans to conquer Lanthra and Earth. Resolving to write that memory with its strong emotion down for Dr. Greet, he began to steady himself. "Yes, Deirdre, no more shame. And I have to tell you what I'm thinking and feeling instead of hiding or assuming that you can guess what I'm going through."

She scooted toward him and Lewis did also until they snuggled while they talked. "Eventually we have to decide where our relationship will go," Deirdre began.

Lewis decided to practice the deep sharing she'd asked for. His eagerness made the words come out fast. "I want us to promise ourselves to each other. When we're ready, I want to marry you, and if possible, have children. I want you to do what makes you happy, while I … I give in to my inner dragon."

Deirdre raised her eyebrows. "What do you mean by 'dragon'?"

"My dragon is that part of my soul that wants to be my real self, with all that's possible. It sounds strange, I know, but I think that the dragon is what the Holy Spirit is trying to make me become. Not a demon dragon, but a healthy, er, *ego.*"

In answer, she kissed him. The beautiful young woman next him felt so warm and good! Lewis continued, "You know already that I have a copy of the Lanthran *thoyo-on* and that I've been encouraged by Dr. Jane Moritz to develop it. Doing that would mean quitting my job and stepping far, far out of my comfort zone. Before … before Lanthra, I lead amazing physics research projects under my former boss, Dr. Zhartha, but I'd have to actually step into his shoes and start from the ground up."

"You aren't actually starting from scratch," Deirdre told him. "You will have help from all sides!"

Lewis stroked her soft hair. "Deirdre, I told you what I want about our relationship, and then I side-stepped instead of letting you talk."

He saw that she closed her eyes, committing herself to her next statement. "I want to be your wife, and you to be my husband. I want to have our children."

Lewis pushed a little. "When?"

But Deirdre put a finger on his lips. "We will, we will. But let us make firmer plans the next time we get together. Lewis, I'm not going to live with you in your apartment; I have my own place.

We are both going to be busy, you with your *thoyo-on* project, and me with teaching. And then we can plan a time and a home for us."

A home for us, Lewis echoed in his thoughts, smiling. He rested his chin on the top of her head as she snuggled into his shoulder. Deirdre and he sat that way from a long time. Then she turned her face toward him, and they kissed again. *She has such an exciting tongue!*

CHAPTER 31:
THE OTHER PRISONER ON THE ISLE OF MERCY

Patrick was still stuck on Lanthra, and every day was horrible. In the large chamber under the Isle of Mercy where King Nargoleh held court, Patrick played the piano. Nark preferred relaxing music. Patrick guessed that he needed the soothing strains to calm down. For instance, when his councils were not going well or profits were down, the king's face turned puce and the huge, greasy, frightening man screamed at his advisers.

Today, business came and went, and Nark seemed lethargic, letting people talk and talk without much reply. Patrick had no idea what was going on in the man's warped mind. So he played on and on, as well as he could—he was getting very smooth and skilled from all the practice—until a new group of people came in, all wearing the gold Horned Edge rings with the black stones. Dressed in the cordovan robes with brilliant indigo sleeves of the magi from Swetha.

They consulted today with Nark the plans to conquer their world, Lanthra. The idea included artificial insemination to multiply the Blue People. They'd force Blue People into the armies—and to provide more sacrifices to Saoma. The demon god was entrenched in Swetha, gaining strength in the southern Lanthran countries, and his zealots concentrated hard on Siphe, Raphe, and Poiemana, the peaceful but malleable pastoral lands across the ocean.

To conquer Bardia, however, would take some doing. The Bardian army was strong, though not large. That *nobbo,* High Magus Daniel, that dictator over the scientific world and the chief disparager of their exalted principles, must be killed and his locating technology in the College of the Magi seized. Plus, since Bardia had won the war with the oppressive Torish barons, the *Tiorpatath* citizenry were largely loyal to Bardia and were a force to be reckoned with. Not only that, but the Bardians' beloved bard, young Sir Thomas Forschwynn, was active all over those northern countries, and his songs rallied the *Radyah*-worshipping heretics against *Saoma.* He had to be neutralized. That faithful slave of his, the technology-savvy *subua* Fred Jontz from Earth could possibly be captured and used to manage the technology of the connection to Earth and the exchange of weapons from the Bardian hub.

The Swethan magi talked on and on. Nark perked up. They began to discuss some upcoming sacrifices to persuade Saoma to bless their plans.

Their plotting made Patrick sick to his stomach. He struggled to control himself. Then, while he played, Patrick's nose caught the intense odor of fear through the heavy incense that Nark burned in the chamber to conceal his rank body odor. His Blue guardian was terrified! Blue People were the favorite material for the sacrifices, as the Horned Edge followers did not regard them as fully people.

Patrick felt sympathy for the guardian even though the Blue person had been cruel, and he had been tempted to hate him. He still cringed to remember the very large, muscular Blue person clenching his fists and menacing or even actually hitting him on an ear. When the 'mute' guardian communicated, his long, long red tongue came out and wagged with an amazing range of vocabulary, calling Patrick fat, stupid, slow, disobedient, smelly, and a total loser who would never, ever be anything other than King Nargoleh's captive blob of hairless brown human.

But now, over the weeks since he'd been Nark's prisoner, Patrick had seen his Blue person soften towards him. When Nark raged, they feared together; when they had a moment without the awful pirate king, they had actually begun to converse in Blue people sign language like … like friends.

During the prolonged planning for sacrifices, Nark glanced at the guardian. *Maybe,* Patrick thought, *he smells the fear, too..* The Blue Person shrank back to the chamber wall as if he wanted to become invisible. Patrick knew that the *homo azure* was as much a captive as he was … and, worse, a possible sacrifice to

Saoma.

The Swethan magi's voices rose. When Patrick caught the gist of the vehement discussion, his hair prickled all over his head and down his neck. The Horned Edge allies on Earth used the tactic of "divide and conquer." They encouraged people to hate each other, playing on fears and prejudices and stereotypes until violence broke out and they could blame the 'other side'—usually calling them vicious names. Then they claimed to be the trusty solution. Earth's Horned Edge were the "good guys," serving God and Country, champions of the "Right." When chaos got big enough, the weapons-making Shields who worshipped Saoma would formally organize to declare war on key opponents.

The Horned Edge on Lanthra had failed to divide since the Bardian-Torish war, so they would just conquer. However, … Apparently the ancient locating technology in Swetha did not work. The magi at its site could not repair or operate the Swethan *thoyo-on*. To help them conquer Lanthra they needed King Nark, ruler of the amazing space-connecting technology on his Island of Mercy because right now that was the only quick way to communicate with their distant Horned Edge allies.

Glorying in their attention, Nark sat with an insolent turn to his red lips. Finally, he spoke. "My *thoyo-on* is fine, but I, too, need an expert to operate it. There is one available, on Earth … and I have his brother."

Patrick's blood froze. He stopped playing. *Lewis! He wants to use my brother for their war.* More than ever, his stomach felt nauseous.

Nark signaled displeasure at Patrick, who immediately began his music again. Nark commented, "I do not have the *fean* now. He has moved from his place, and I have not found him."

One of the magi, a dark fellow with a hooked nose, said, "Since your system works, we can bring that Fred here after we invade Bardia. He will work the *thoyo-on*. Just join us when we sail to Kingsport."

Nark's eyes gleamed and he nodded.

"You'll still be in control of your country, still "owner," just lending aid to the Swethan Horned Edge," the Swethan magus assured the pirate king. Patrick thought, *Fat chance! If you listen to them, Nark, you'll lose your kingdom, even find yourself dead.*

The magi began once more to plan to urge Nark's partnership in the invasion of Bardia. They had a fleet and wanted Nark to add his ships to theirs. And they had a puppet to put on the Bardian throne. The heir had apparently drowned after being taken prisoner by pirates.

Nark broke in. "I have the young prince, Christopher."

What? Patrick inwardly gasped.

"Where is the *biaya*?" Hook-Nose asked.

"He is my prisoner. I have a special sea-cave for him." Nark began to boast. "He cannot get out. He is chained. When high tide comes, he must breathe through a tube. If he does not drown, he will be a fine puppet." Behind the dirty beard, Nark's smile showed sharp, big yellow teeth, as if he were delighting in the desperate state of his captive prince.

Patrick was ready to throw up. Swallowing bile, he played a few unrelated chords. The Swethan magi murmured at Nark's disclosure. Then they began to press him on details, aiming for him to give up some measure of control over his very functional locating system.

An idea came to Patrick. It was a way to rebel, to interrupt, and possibly stop Nark from agreeing to let the ruthless Swethan magi control his *thoyo-on,* which would be a crucial deciding factor in the invasion. He'd play a new piece of the sheet music that had come with the grand piano.

Trying not to rustle loudly, trying not to pause too long, Patrick slid the sheet music out of the piano bench. He knew exactly what he wanted to play. It was a fast, loud, crashing Hungarian Dance by Brahms that Nark himself had bought, not knowing a thing about reading sheet music. The lively sounds would reflect the hot surge of rebellion that Patrick felt against Nark, the Horned Edge magi, and their horrible plans. So far, he hadn't practiced the piece, but he felt sure that he could muddle through the score.

He began. Sneakily, he started it *mezzo piano.* As the rousing melody flowed along, he added passion. Soon, Patrick had the volume up to *mezzo forte.* Nobody seemed to notice.

When he heard the magi press for a starting date on their nefarious invasion, he crashed chords triple *fortissimo.* In his mind, the delirious Hungarians danced like dervishes, spinning and leaping and shouting while their audience rattled tambourines and pounded on drums. And while he played, the chamber, a natural bubble cave in the island's living rock, resonated so profoundly that the sound amplified to painful decibels.

Around Nark's throne, the conversation abruptly stopped.

Patrick pounded on through a few more measures, then he felt everyone's eyes on his back, and he paused. He was afraid to look at the magi and the king directly. Holding his breath, he willed himself to turn his head—just in time to see Nark move. The pirate king slowly rose to his gigantic hulking height. His greasy locks flung around as he shook his head. He advanced, breathing hard, his face white with anger—which was even more scary than the irate red face Patrick had seen before. The man's huge hand held ... a large knife.

Nark loomed over Patrick, who cringed, his eyes bulging. There was nowhere he could run, even if he were allowed. His thoughts locked into darkness, his body froze; he prepared for the cut.

The pirate king stared at Patrick's hands with angry laser focus. One of his mighty paws with its long, sharp fingernails gripped Patrick's right arm. The man's strong, sour body odor filled Patrick's nostrils so that he almost gagged.

Feeling that hot vise on his arm, Patrick closed his eyes, trembling. There was nothing he could do to resist; he was about to lose his hand.

CHAPTER 32:
THE LECTURE

"There is no big black hole per se at the center of this Earth to power a new system for tapping energy from the Earth's core," Dr. Abel Zhartha stated at the Harvard lecture at the Black Hole Initiative.

Lewis, who had taken another personal day from work and had flown to Harvard University just to attend this lecture, shifted uncomfortably in his seat. Much of his experience in Lanthran technology for instant space travel supposed that planets greater than a certain mass contained a singularity. He had thought that Lanthra, which was larger than Earth, had a black hole in its core with an event horizon capable of powering the gravitational resonance to open spatial connections. Now Dr. Zhartha was shooting Lewis's foundational theory to pieces. *But the thoyo-on, the 'Toy," works. How, is that possible?*

Then Dr. Zhartha announced, "here is, however, an infinite series of tiny, short-lived singularities at the center of Earth's gravity that connects to the collection of black hole 'pins' that hold the universe together. We've accessed the power of gravitational resonance another way: Using both orbiting and underground foci tuned to distant but massive black holes and joined with the Earth's own center of gravity, we direct the resonance and amplify it, just like substations do the electric power generated by, for instance, a hydroelectric power plant. And there's no carbon footprint. It is ideal power generation."

Lewis's ears picked up. *The power is available for my locating system to become a reality! I've got to talk with Dr. Zhartha at the end of this lecture!* He thrilled with excitement as his former boss set the pointer to the big Smart Board. Space photos appeared with a chart connecting dots.

Dr. Zhartha's wrinkled old face smiled, and he chanted, pointing to each relay:

"Earth's center of gravity resonates with the
Sun's center of gravity that resonates with a
Series of singularities spread about the
Sagittarius A* black hole in the center of the
Milky Way"

"The universe isn't random," Dr. Zhartha explained. "It's like a fish net with the ropes tied at nodes. At the nodes are the black holes. So, although there's not a single big black hole at the center of the Earth, there is a system of black holes that we are able to use for power."

A thin middle-aged woman asked, "But why is the universe expanding so fast? Isn't it flying apart?"

Dr. Zhartha said, "I believe that it is stretching at its nodes, like a net full of fish, not flying off in all directions."

"That's scary," a male scientist with heavy dark eyebrows commented. "Suppose the connections were to snap? Break a hole in the net? Would the universe collapse or perhaps snap together like an elastic band and destroy itself?"

Dr. Zhartha shrugged, and he still looked happy. "That's beyond my ability to predict." He smiled. "The universe is designed to hold together."

Someone in the back of the room called out, "Are you promoting Intelligent Design?"

With no evidence of shyness, Dr. Zhartha nodded. "That is my conclusion." Lifting his chin at the whole crowd, he added, "But whether you believe in God or not, the technology works." He advanced the board to another image.

Lewis found himself squeezing his hands together and leaning forward at his seat. His soul took in the lecture with a great *Amen!* And his hand crept to the curl of plastic in his back pocket. He made his hand return to the table. *Uh, no,* he warned himself.

Leave your pocket alone. You know there's a couple of Horned Edge people, even in this crowd. You find them everywhere these days.

But his heart raced, his hands clasped tightly, and his right toe tapped fast. Yes, he had thought that there was a black hole at the center of the Earth. He had figured that to access it and power his space travel system would take decades of building taps into the Earth's core. But the project could take place much, much sooner with a relay system guided by the James D. Webb telescope. According to what Lewis had read before coming to Harvard, Dr. Zhartha already had a new facility in Texas and was ready to go forward with his research. Lewis could dovetail onto his old mentor's research—and actualize all the data in that curl. He had much, much to add to the space travel initiative.

Lewis soaked up all he could from the lecture and waited patiently during the many questions. He waited some more as the various scientists and students and techies swarmed around Dr. Zhartha after the lecture was done. The tall, talkative guy with the eyebrows had practically cornered the scientist. The man went on and on.

Lewis decided to interrupt. He hurried to within two feet of Dr. Zhartha, inserted his body into the other man's space, raised an arm to cut off the talker's invisible interpersonal connection. Then he looked Dr. Zhartha in the eye and asked, "Is there any way we could work together on your project?"

To his delight, the grand old man smiled at him and stuck out his hand. "Dr. Moritz has already contacted me about that. You're in."

Lewis smiled back. And when he withdrew his hand from Dr. Zhartha's, the curl of data was no longer in his palm.

CHAPTER 33:
THE RULER

Leaving the hall, Lewis strode across campus, his heart singing. He had plenty of time to make his flight back to Newark. He felt great! After weeks of freezing drizzle, the sun shone, and the branches of the wintry trees traced intricate patterns on the sidewalk. Lewis inhaled fresh air; he reveled in nature as he walked.

He was back on track with his life! He had already made an appointment with Dr. Zhartha in Texas at the new, restored Super Collider for next Tuesday, and his old boss would show him the progress they'd made at duplicating the technology Lewis had carried from Lanthra. As for reaching his dream of enabling *time travel* … instant space travel was the first step forward.

Yes, he thought, *I've been playing at biophysics, and Alzheimer's research is certainly needed. But it's not in line with the dream that God has given me, the one that just won't go away …*

There was just one big catch. *I've got to give my notice at work.* His high thoughts fell away. Before he reached the intersection where he planned to meet his Lyft, Lewis stopped abruptly. *Oh! I've got to talk with Peggy's dad! As soon as I get back to Newark, I've got to give him my notice. And I've got to share my ideas for furthering Alzheimer's research.*

He wavered. *After my fight with Peggy, Roger might not want to talk with me.*

But a small voice inside prompted, *Try, anyway.*

His mind raced. *Mr. Gnudst needs to hear what I have to say. With time travel controls and atomic resonance measurements, we could watch back into the process that forms the Alzheimer's producing beta-amyloid proteins, and we should see exactly what's screwing up the normal proteins. There must be more than one factor, but those should be predictable. Pharmaceuticals may be developed to halt the progression of that disease or even prevent it from starting in risk-prone individuals! I've got to tell ...*

Lewis swept his phone out of his pocket to call Mr. Gnudst. He reached a recorded greeting. Hanging up with a brief message, Lewis then called Mr. Gnudst's secretary. "Hi," he began, "I'd like to make an appointment with Roger Gnudst."

Just as the secretary finalized the appointment and said the "goodbye," a heavy hand gripped Lewis's left shoulder. He spun around, but a quick grab snatched his phone away. "Mr. Brahmindura, come with us."

There were two of them, two large men in bulky dark coats. And one of them pointed a gun with a silencer at his heart.

Lewis tensed. *Can I run?*

But the other man who was now putting Lewis's phone into his own pocket stated, "You're too valuable to kill, but you could certainly endure a bullet in your knee."

They seized his arms, and a black Lincoln swept up to the curb. One of his kidnappers opened the car door while the other pushed his head down and shoved him hard into the back seat. The gun man sat in back with Lewis while the other hopped into the front passenger seat. Everything happened so fast that Lewis could not cry out or struggle.

The car drove off.

*   *   *

The kidnappers made no effort to blindfold him or gag him or restrain him other than buckling his seatbelt and securing the car's child lock as they rode down the Cambridge streets. Instead they talked as if negotiating a business deal ... at gunpoint.

The man with Lewis in the back seat had a thick-lipped mouth under a thin-trimmed black moustache, some pock marks on his cheeks, and close-cropped black hair. His suit smelled faintly of garlic. Lewis categorized his appearance as *mafioso*. When the Lincoln turned a corner, not too fast, not too slow, the sun reflected off the man's ring. A ray like a laser smote Lewis's eyes.

"We hear you are going to work with Dr. Zhartha," Mafioso said pleasantly. The right hand holding the gun was steady.

To control the alarms banging in his chest, Lewis took a deep breath and went into "cool" mode. "Why do you say that?" he asked. He saw signs for BOS airport, and it was getting harder to control the flutters in his stomach. "And where are you taking me and why?" He already had a basic economy flight back from Boston to Newark that day, but he was sure that the kidnappers did not plan to kindly give him a ride to it.

Mr. Mafioso smiled with his full lips. "It is necessary for you to work for us. We have a goal with a due date. And—since you worked for Lord Charon and our organization before—we know that you are very experienced in the mechanisms of instant space travel."

The man's words stabbed into Lewis so that he could not speak. His jaw literally dropped. When he recovered, he stammered and lied, "Who is L … Lord Charon?"

The kidnapper in the front passenger seat turned his broad clean-shaven Slavic face to stare at Lewis, "Don't play games, *Fean* Lewis!"

Lewis made sure his voice was flat when he answered, "I will not work for the Horned Edge."

Slavic Face snorted and rolled his eyes. The gun that Mafioso pointed at him never wavered. "Yes, you will. That eager handshake you had with Dr. Zhartha told us that you are dying to get back to work in space travel physics. You can work for Dr. Zhartha. And everything you do will be supervised by us. And the outcome will belong to us."

Silence reigned in the car. It was a short trip. Lewis's stomach flip-flopped when he saw that it was turning, not to the main terminal, but to Harborside Drive. Even there, the car did not park, but Slavic Face and Mafioso ushered Lewis out quickly at the curb and the driver took off.

They walked him to a Beechjet parked near a hangar. Its clean, white interior exuded a "new plane" odor. Somebody had spent a lot of money on him. Lewis felt like his head was floating and reminded himself to breathe. *Deirdre,* he thought, *I hope they don't know about Deirdre.* But he guessed that he'd been under surveillance for a long, long time by the FBI, by Homeland Security, by the Horned Edge, and even by the media. They certainly did know about Deirdre.

Mafioso directed Lewis to a seat in the back of the jet, in a spot where he couldn't see out of a window. He sank into plush, cool white leather. Slavic face sat beside him. "Fasten your seat belt now," Mafioso ordered. Lewis complied.

To his surprise, a tall, leggy young beauty in a tight black dress approached down the six rows of seats and leaned toward him. "Would you like a drink? Wine, beer, or a mixed drink?"

Too astounded to speak, Lewis shook his head. Mafioso and Slavic face ordered liquor, and she returned to the front of the plane.

For a couple of hours, the plane hummed through the sky. Lewis's captors sipped their drinks and chatted in what Lewis guessed was Russian. No one cuffed him or tried to control him. Except for the ever-present gun—whatever type it was, it was large, dark, and deadly—they acted like they were just on an elite business trip.

This type of jet has about three flying hours of range, Lewis figured, as the jet engines began to whine. *We're probably staying in the United States.* It was a small comfort. They took off with a low-pitched roar.

*   *   *

One hour later, Lewis felt the plane descend. "Prepare for landing," the announcement came, and he buckled his seatbelt.

The jet hit the tarmac with a gentle bump and rolled to a stop away from an isolated hangar surrounded by forest. As they disembarked from the Beechjet, Lewis breathed clear air. He noticed that bright sun was lowering to the horizon. Weather-wise, it was a pretty day. Kidnap-wise, nothing had changed. Another car, another road trip, another hour.

The sun set as they pulled under the porte cochère of an enormous stone chateau. Lewis counted eighteen windows on the soaring front before Mafioso grabbed his arm and pulled him out of the Mercedes. The chateau's front door opened as Lewis and the kidnappers drew near, and there stood … Lord Tahei Charon.

Lewis stopped, speechless, as if bolted to the ground. The Lanthran ruler's chiseled face, his long silky hair, the tall elegance were the same. So was the affectionate regard in the man's brilliant, dark eyes. Different only was his attire: Instead of a Lanthran Horned Edge magi's robe, he wore black jeans and a long-sleeved white brushed cotton shirt, slim fit with an Italian line. Lord Charon's fine-fingered hand with its large ring touched Lewis's shoulder and he said, in a faintly Gaelic-like accent, "Come in, *Fean* Lewis."

*   *   *

Everything came together in Lewis mind as Lord Charon led him into the house's impressive foyer. The Horned Edge of Earth, the Horned Edge of Lanthra: It was a huge twisted, pervasive organization dedicated to conquer the two worlds and restore its brand of 'peace.' And its head was Lord Charon, its unifying principle: total control, and its guiding spirit: *not* the one Lewis trusted.

They all passed under a crystal chandelier and into a spacious, contemporary living room. Everything smelled fresh, as if cleaned professionally and often. Thick gray velvet curtains draped the floor-to-ceiling windows and softened the dark gray walls. The air smelled fresh with a faint scent of myrrh. Gold and silver Tiffany lamps made the ambience warm.

Lord Charon directed Lewis to a white circle sofa and sat close beside him. His liquid eyes sparkled. "Good to have you working for us again," he said in beautiful English, with a faint Lanthran accent that sounded rather Scottish.

Lewis forced himself to inhale, then replied, trying to sound firm, "I cannot work for you, my lord. That time is over." But when he heard himself addressing Charon by his Lanthran title, "my lord," he inwardly groaned. *How easy it would be to fall back into the spell of this Machiavellian ruler. I should eat and drink nothing while I'm here—as long as Charon keeps me prisoner. Last time, he drugged me, and I was completely compliant.* The prospect of being drugged alarmed him to a near panic.

Charon played hardball, threw a hundred mph pitch. His voice very gentle, he held up a photograph and said, "Yes, you are working for us now."

Lewis glanced at it and froze. The photo showed ... *Patrick!*

His younger brother's face contorted with pain and fear

174

while … *Oh my God!* His neck was being tattooed with Nark's serpentine "N." Lewis's vision broke into a mosaic pattern. He was terrified that he might have a seizure. *No, no, no! Oh, help!* he mentally cried.

Charon put away the photo. "*Fean* Lewis, not only shall you have your heart's fill of physics research, but you will also help establish world peace. Earth's United Nations does not accomplish that. Only our world-wide government does. We have advanced into every area of the Earth's powers. Our reach includes politics, courts, schools, churches, and much more. We control many countries already, and soon we will control this one. *Fean* Lewis, you can have a large part in creating world peace."

Lewis breathed again to calm his racing heart. "Lord Charon, you ruled your Lanthran country through absolutism and coercion. Your laboratory featured chains, yes, *chains* to bind the sacrifices of Blue People you offered to your god Saoma!"

To his surprise, Lord Charon chuckled. "Yes, Saoma was pleased." His face radiated a type of joy—or maybe it was fanatic fervor.

Lewis forced himself not to show fear. "You do not need coercion to accomplish your rule. It's counterproductive; it only produces terror. In contrast, the Council of the Magi on Lanthra operates through persuasion, as does the government of any democratic country on Earth—"

"Persuasion, Lewis?" Lord Charon raised a fine eyebrow. "Think again! The Council of the Magi—Daniel's magi—used fearful force and put to death some poor souls on Lanthra who transgressed the ban on electronics! And also …" Charon showed his white, even teeth " … their war hurled out one certain scientist who defied the defunct, passé One Law" and connected to your Earth."

Lewis countered, "Those 'poor souls' used the ancient technology to torture the Blue People! And weren't *you* that defiant scientist?" Anger rose up in his gut. It burned into his arms, his hands, which clenched into fists. "You didn't mention that your persistent dishonoring of the One Law paved the way for invasion by demons from Earth. Or that you disobeyed the law against electronics because you wanted weapons for world domination. Remember the chains in your cave chamber? For human sacrifice? Many Blue People died there. You fastened those chains around *me!* If that isn't coercion, I don't know what is!"

Charon scoffed, "The Blue People are sub-humans! They are barely sentient."

"Your sacrifices were made to a demon you call *Saoma!* He—it—is nothing but a cruel devil! The Horned Edge worships Satan!"

"No. You completely misunderstand. *We* worship the true God. Not three gods, but one Unity, a Transcendental Other. The Christians are the ones who demonize whatever they don't agree with. They persecute and torture the people who have different beliefs."

Lewis opened his mouth to counter Charon's logic, but shut it when Lord Charon shifted toward Lewis so close that Lewis felt the ruler's warmth. "Time out, dear *Fean* Lewis. Let me offer you some ice water. Talking religion and politics is thirsty work."

From a large crystal-and-silver pitcher, Charon poured two glasses of ice water. He raised his glass, drank deeply, and then offered a glass to Lewis. His fathomless eyes crinkled in a grin. "It is not drugged."

Lewis's throat ached with dehydration, but he was afraid to drink. Staring at the refreshing-looking ice water, he kept his hands at his side.

Lord Charon went on, "Christian history is full of brutality. Remember the Spanish Inquisition? The burning at the stake of John Hus and William Tyndale, among too many others? The Salem witch trials that pressed women to death so that greedy men could seize their property? The Trail of Tears where soldiers brained babies to keep the mothers moving in the sad procession? Saoma is not *that* God! Nor is he the red-horned demon that you imagine. That corpse named *Jesus*—and any fanatic that follows him—is the demon!"

Lewis could not answer.

"Join me, Lewis," Charon pleaded. "You know that we together can heal the world."

Lewis wavered; words stifled in his throat. *Argument with a madman at gunpoint is no argument; it is foolishness.* Charon's

Lanthran associate, Nark, had Patrick in his power; he could kill the boy—or worse. Plus, the Horned Edge could reach his family in Alabama. *Oh, what if they threaten them! What if they take Deirdre!* His heart thudded. *Should I pretend to join them to save my loved ones?*

Lewis felt as if he had slammed into a stone wall. *I've given in to coercion time after time to save my family, and I've cooperated with the devil with the idea that I could undo the bondage later. So, ... do I want to do that again? 'Protect' everybody, including myself?*

It's time to let Me protect you all. Lewis felt the voice more than heard it deep in his heart.

But if I do not cooperate with The Horned Edge ...

The answer came: *You have been controlled by fear long enough. Do not live in fear.*

Relaxing his fists finger by finger, Lewis closed his eyes. *How can I trust You, God? I know that evil happens too often; I realize that you aren't a protection vending machine. Suppose these people carry out the threats they make against me?*

There was no reply except a deep, deep silence in his soul.

Lewis rehearsed the grand words that had so impressed him at Christmas: *You are 'God of God, light of light, very God of very God!' If you cannot help me and the people I love, no one can!*

Taking time to answer, Lewis breathed slowly. Lord Charon had folded his hands and waited. Again, the thoughts challenged Lewis's resistance. *If I bow to him as master again, will I do the great things I dream about? Will my efforts help this sick Earth experience a long peace?*

Lewis finally asserted, "I know those horrible historical events of persecutions are true. And once upon a time I agreed with you about Christians being demonizers. But what you are saying about Saoma is not true. Jesus is the Lord of the universe. He's alive! He's God—he made the whole universe, and if there are multiple universes, he is God of all of them! And he is *love*!"

Lewis focussed on Charon's brilliant, fathomless eyes, forming an intense link with the man. "The people who support the Horned Edge are prideful people who are certain that they are *right*. They are people who hate anyone who threatens their control and their extremist principles. They say they believe in

God, but they are really like the old scribes and Pharisees, willing to contort the truth. Those people substitute their own made-up laws for good laws. They use coercion to keep in power, willing to manipulate or even kill innocent people."

Lewis's voice rose with passion. "I used to be like you. I used to want to *be* you. The brilliant scientist, dedicated to saving the worlds through my own ideas of what is right and wrong. But today my heart is aching with pity and compassion, because your soul is in danger, Tahei Charon. I want you to be safe. I want you to trust that Jesus exists, and that he is good. But as for your command that I must work for you: I cannot belong to Jesus and work for the Horned Edge, no matter how you may threaten me and those I love!"

Charon blinked. Those dark eyes moistened. Lewis wondered if the ruler had genuinely heard him, had softened.

Then Charon turned away, breaking the bond. He said, pointing to Mafioso who stood nearby with the gun, "Take him away."

Mafioso stepped forward and put the gun to Lewis's temple. "Kole," he growled to Slavic Face, "let's walk Mr. Brahmindura outside where the blood won't get on the sofa."

Kole came to Lewis, grabbed his collar, and jerked him to his feet. Charon, too, slowly stood. He walked out of the living room, and Lewis was flabbergasted to see that the ruler was crying, big tears rolling down his cheeks.

Lewis walked with them stiffly, his head high, but his heart shaken. *Goodbye, Deirdre. Goodbye Patrick, Gracie, and Mom and Dad. I love you.* The two men forced him down a dark hall and through a door that led out into the night. The cold air smelled of winter: wood smoke, a crisp waft of frost. A clear, starry sky glinted through twisted tree branches. *Okay, God. Have mercy on me. Here I come.* He had just a little bit of life left …

*   *   *

Lewis's captors pushed him into the woods. After about fifty steps they stopped. Kole still gripped him. By moonlight, he saw him slowly raise his gun. Lewis closed his eyes, took a last breath, and waited for the bullet.

Pop! The tight hold on him abruptly let go, and Lewis stumbled. He heard another *bang!* and he opened his eyes wide.

Kole's body lay on the leaf-coated, woodsy ground, a dark lump. Mafioso was left. Faint starlight glinted on the gun he pointed at Lewis.

CHAPTER 34:
DEIRDRE'S PRAYER

It was about five o'clock in the morning in Newark, and Deirdre had not slept. Her heart had been so troubled with premonition that she could hardly breathe, much less slip into sleep.

She got up, moving carefully in the ark. Her efficiency apartment was tiny but since coming to Earth, she'd managed to acquire a full-sized bed, a chest of drawers, a white round kitchen table, and two wooden straight chairs. Also, on the kitchen table she'd laid a pot containing a forced scarlet amaryllis on the table, plus a cup holding a tiny pink-blooming cactus. Two dozen fresh cut yellow roses from Lewis filled a vase.

Light from the street illuminated the kitchen, and the room smelled sweet as

Deirdre sat, clasped her hands, and talked to God. Tears fell onto the tablecloth, and she spoke aloud.

"I know beyond a doubt that Lewis is in danger. The enemy wants him, his body and his soul. Please protect his life. I know that 'all things work together for good,' according to your promise. Please bring him home safely." Deirdre lowered her face onto her hands.

Although her mind and heart begged for Lewis's safety, she felt no answer. She knew that God was present with her, but he wasn't making promises such as, "Lewis is fine. He'll come home to you real soon."

Breakfast time came. Like a robot, Deirdre opened a pantry door and took out a packaged breakfast cookie. She put it on a plate. The cookie looked at her, and she looked at it. Slowly, her hand pushed the plate away. *Time to go to work.* She'd be hungry later. Maybe. Maybe not.

* * *

Elegant in a pale-yellow dress with a flowing skirt under a long heather gray coat, her golden hair twisted up into a bun, Deirdre locked her door and walked into the morning toward her bus stop to go to work. It was several long blocks away, but comfortable walking shoes supported her petite frame, and her steps were quick.

At the bus stop, she waited. Her backpack felt heavy with kids' homework and her own books. Deirdre adjusted the strap to make it more comfortable. She smiled as she imagined Alysha's expression when the girl saw her homework graded with an "A." Alysha read and wrote slowly, so Deirdre had told her that five to eight words in a sentence were fine, and she worked with her one-on-one to organize her thoughts into a paragraph of three sentences: The topic and purpose, the central idea, and the structure of the idea.

Shoving back her fears for Lewis, Deirdre tried to visualize her next lesson. First, she would give a brief introduction then have the students work singly on a small writing assignment. Next, they would divide into collaborative groups—

A strong odor interrupted Deirdre's thoughts, a perfume. It smelled flowery, sharp, heavy, disruptive, and almost overpowering. She suppressed a sneeze. Then her heart leaped with a jolt, and she looked up. The perfume came from … *Peggy!*

Wrapped in a hooded fawn-colored coat, Peggy's shoulder-length blond hair waved with a sunlit gloss. Deirdre admitted to herself that the woman's perfect skin and her large blue eyes were absolutely beautiful. *No wonder she charmed Lewis.* Peggy had a spell that even Deirdre could feel.

She stared at Deirdre with dagger eyes, leaning close toward her face. "You little sweetheart," she purred, "dear Deirdre, I know who you are. And I'm coming after you. I will ruin you, I will destroy you. Lewis belongs to me." Peggy tensed her hands into claws. With a twisted smirk, she cut the air in front of Deirdre's face.

Deirdre pinned the other woman with a steady, controlled gaze. "Lewis belongs to God, not to you, and not to me. And you belong to Him, too, if you would only trust that."

For a moment Peggy froze. Then she stepped back. "Your god is impotent," she hissed. "Saoma is god. Before we kill you, I will have you tortured. Then you will see just how 'powerful' your god is."

A strange pity filling her heart, Deirdre replied, "My God loves you. I pray that you come to believe that."

Peggy spat a thick wet wad of phlegm onto the sidewalk. Exuding hate like an evil fog, she spun around, and slid into her red Porsche. Screeching tires left black burn marks on the pavement as the woman sped away.

CHAPTER 35:
PATRICK FINDS HIS WEIGHT

Nark's knife descended slowly, slowly toward Patrick's hand that he held hard against the piano. Patrick closed his eyes, trembling, and waited to feel the cut. The edge of the knife reached his wrist. It pressed.

Then it lifted.

Patrick opened his eyes, expecting blood. He saw no blood and no cut. Nark lowered the big knife. The pirate king's expression was inscrutable, but his face regained its color. All of the Swethan magi in their maroon robes glared at Patrick, and Nark's council chamber susurrated with their whispering.

"Go ahead, Your Majesty Layhew," the one with the hooked nose urged. "Punish that insolent *bibat*." Murmuring of agreement rippled through the magi.

Nark's eyes dug into Patrick's, but the knife did not plunge into his hand. Instead, Nark released Patrick's wrist and noogied his head. "You *bibatoon,* get out of here. Go!"

Patrick slid off the piano bench and fled. But before he left the chamber, he glanced back. Nark's guards had seized Patrick's Blue guardian, and they were binding him. Instead of hurting Patrick, Nark would torture the Blue person.

*　*　*

Running into the alcove that he shared with the Blue guardian, Patrick flung himself onto his pallet. He pulled the rough blanket over his head. It took a while for him to control his trembling. Yes, he had deliberately provoked Nark because of the king's posturing in front of the nasty Swethan magi and his participation in the plans to conquer Bardia. But by pounding in a tantrum on the piano, Patrick had embarrassed Nark in front of the Swethan magi. Thus, he had caused the torture of someone innocent. Huge emotions crashed inside: Fear, guilt, self-hate.

Bibatoon. "Fat boy." Patrick could feel his protruding soft belly and see his plump hands. The greasy food, the many sweets, and inactivity were causing him to gain weight. Self-hate swelled in his soul like the calories had in his body. Under his breath, he cursed himself, using words he hardly ever used, sloppy, sick, obscene, ruinous words. He imagined dying. Dropping dead would be much better than this existence as Nark's slave.

When the paroxysms of self-hate finally tired, he moaned aloud, "I should be tortured; I deserve a painful death."

Like a flitting butterfly, an image slid into Patrick's mind: Jesus on the cross. He'd heard way back, before Lanthra, a presentation in church about the medical effects of the Roman torture called crucifixion, which nailed a person to a wooden structure to struggle on and on until the effort to pull oneself up on nailed hands and feet to breathe failed in fatal exhaustion. The excruciating torture could last for days. When the doctor recounted the gruesome details, one girl in his group had even fainted and had to leave the room. "I deserve *that!*" Patrick told God.

Yes, you do, and so do many others, the thought came to him.

Patrick's soul squeezed in agony. He closed his eyes. Now he thought that he could hear the Blue person screaming as Nark's torturers twisted his body. "Yes, I deserve to be crucified!" he exclaimed.

Suddenly a new thought smacked him. He whispered, "*Jesus* was crucified! And why? So *I* would escape punishment!" Patrick's mind still pictured Jesus suffering on the cross. But for the first time, that awful image held, not fear and outrage, but hope. Yes, *hope.*

Astounded at the new perspective, he thought, *All this time, I thought Jesus wanted me to be good. Live the 'What Would Jesus Do?' mantra. But Jesus isn't about being good. He came to save bad people—like me.*

Patrick's brain felt like it had tilted 90 degrees. He sat up, eyes seeing twinkling light in his alcove. For the first time he noticed that the lamp on Nark's table sparkled. Small rainbows formed on the walls around the cut and beveled clear glass lamp. Not only that, but the inlaid abalone shell tracery on a little box glowed. It was the first time he'd noticed it. The bit of kitsch intrigued Patrick. *Nark likes pretty things. What's in there?* Rainbows of hope, perhaps.

A chain of creative thought flashed in Patrick's mind so quickly that he could hardly breathe. He might be a slave, but he could build himself up better. He might not lose weight, but he could get stronger. He couldn't rescue the tortured Blue person, but he could be respectful of the other Blues. And … he would find out where Nark caged Prince Christopher. There had to be a way to rescue him and save Bardia. "Well," Patrick decided, "I can't miraculously teleport to Bardia and warn them about the invasion; I can't snap my fingers and make the prince free again. But … I'll check out that box!"

CHAPTER 36:
THE WARRIOR GIRL

The ship *Westwind* rocked softly on the small waves of the Bay of Thesare as it floated on the ocean called *Tessappa*. It was tied up to one of the Port of Kyrie's jetties, with its gangplank in place. In the late afternoon light, ship after ship anchored at those long cement bars that lined the bay's coast like the tines of a giant comb. The sailors from *Westwind* walked in chatting groups toward the city for their leave.

But before Mim could set foot on Eleaemanan soil, she endured a lecture—a stern set of instructions—from Captain Lu. His cabin was hot and humid in the tropical afternoon despite the open ports, and her sweat dripped into her eyes as she stood at attention. On *Westwind,* Mim was not the princess; she was crew and under orders.

The captain paid exacting detail to who had the authority in her next actions. "When we return to Bardia," Captain Lu began, "you are my superior. But on this ship— and during our stay in port—you are under my supervision."

The cabin door was open, and while the captain talked to Mim, the first mate, Wei Chou, waited just outside the door but within earshot for propriety's sake, *No one can accuse Captain Lu of inappropriate sexual conduct,* Mim thought. *He's not at all like that miserable Lord B.S. and his lecherous looks.* But, as she listened to Captain Lu, except for the occasional "Aye, aye, captain," Mim realized that she was going to be practically a prisoner at the port of Kyrie.

After that, Mim could not concentrate. Grief and anger welled up as she pictured her father before all the trouble started. King Norhe was tall, broad, and had a balding head. He could be gruff, but not with her. He like to say that she was his "sunshine," and he included her in his schooling of her two brothers. He often told them: "One of you will rule after me; all of you will know how." Mim pictured him with Mom, beautiful dark-haired Queen Katharine, kissing her when he didn't think the kids were looking. Her older brother Chris was of medium height, trim, dark like Mom. He kept busy, but sometimes he shared adventures with her, like the time they went high-diving together off a rock quarry ledge, and like the excursion down the Bardian coast on his sailboat.

But the good memories didn't linger when Captain Lu emphasized the dangers "out there" in this foreign port so close to Nark's island. In a flash, she saw her father's dead body crushing the flowers in the courtyard. She saw her mother's sick, thin face and felt her bony white hands with the loose rings later clutching hers in that awful carriage ride to the cemetery. And she imagined her brother Chris as a captive on that looming Isle of Mercy. Mim thought, *I can't bring Dad back from the dead; I can't heal my Mom! What can I do? How can we rescue Chris?*

"You must not leave the hotel." Captain Lu wrapped up his talk, and Mim's mind snapped back to attention. "Do *not* wander outside. There is too much at stake for Bardia to have another of its royalty captured or killed!"

"But," Mim blurted, "How can we rescue my brother?"

Captain Lu answered, "I have many contacts in this area of Eleaemana. Let me work through my channels. *You* are to take care of yourself and obey orders." He addressed the first mate, "Wei Chou, come in."

The first mate stepped inside Lu's cabin. As usual, Wei Chou was quiet and his expression unreadable. Mim knew that the captain trusted this man, and she had sensed a wholesome strength in him. Captain Lu instructed his first mate: "Wait until late, past the twelfth hour when the dock is deserted, to escort Mim off the ship. I will already have gone to the hotel. Take her to the room I've reserved on the third floor of the Harbor Hotel."

His gaze boring into Mim's, he went on, "You'll find your room attractive with all amenities. But, while you stay at the hotel, you must stay in your room except for meals. Keep the door locked. If someone besides Wei Chou or myself comes to your door, do not open it. There is a peephole. When it is time for a meal, Wei Chou will bring you to a special dining room. Do you understand?"

Mim fought the urge to stamp her foot. *Somehow, I must see Fean Bogoswega.* Forcing a neutral expression, she nodded. "Aye, aye, sir." She quickly added, "And what may I do, while I am, er, sequestered? You said that it's going to be several days before we return to Bardia."

Captain leaned back and raised his thick black brows. "You may do anything you like—in the confines of your room. Use your imagination! If you ask for anything— books, journals, pens and paper, snacks, it shall be given to you."

Mim shuddered at the idea of spending the next several days as a recluse, no matter how valuable Captain Lu felt she was. She held back any retort, but she couldn't restrain a big sigh. "Captain, while I'm keeping safe, I'd like to have illustrated books about Eleaemanan botany—and journals and pens."

"Botany?" For the first time ever, Captain Lu looked puzzled. "What—?"

Mim began, her passion for the kingdom of plants rising and making her eloquent, "Eleaemana has some of the most beautiful and useful plants on Lanthra in its fields and tropical forests. The best medicines in Lanthra are made from its exotic plant species. Maybe I will learn something of their healing properties. I want to be a healer. If God is willing and we live, I want to go to the university in Kingsport and study medicine!"

*   *   *

Dusk gathered early in Eleaemana. The latitude here was only a few dozen *linath* above the Lanthran equator, which made for short evenings. While Mim waited for the twelfth hour before she could get off *Westwind,* she stood at her favorite spot in the bow by the rail. On the starboard side she could see the forest peak of the Isle of Mercy—where Chris might be a prisoner. A ray of light from the brief sunset shone on the hillside, making it look lush and green.

The sun set below the black, barren volcanic Heights of Merimnas. But over the heights' jagged edges, a long optic pink cloud lingered. Was it a sign of hope? No. Mim narrowed her eyes and frowned as she watched the cloud grow larger and grayer. Sunlight quickly faded. The cloud hid the stars and the moons. Soon the ship's lanterns made small pools of illumination scattered in darkness. And she was still stuck on the ship.

Just as she began to turn from the rail to wait below and hopefully get a snack from the galley, Mim felt a cold touch on the back of her neck. "What—?"

Before she could spin around or jump away, a man's hand covered her mouth. "Don't scream!" his voice breathed into her ear. His arms held her tightly. She smelled the biting odor of a man's cheap perfume and recognized Alli, the arrogant, narcissistic sailor she'd avoided as much as possible despite his advances.

Mim couldn't make a sound. But Chris had taught her some fighting tricks. She flung her head back to knock his face and jabbed her elbow into Alli's side. He emitted a satisfying grunt of pain and stepped back. "Alli! Get away from me!" she hissed. She spun around to face him. Her voice rose as she exclaimed, "What are you doing on the ship? You're supposed to be on leave in the port!"

The young sailor's hand grabbed her right wrist and squeezed it so hard that she cried out. "It's just me teasing you a little. I don't mean any harm." In the lantern light, Mim saw his eyes and white teeth. He reminded her of a wily, hungry hyena—and she was the meat. *Where is Wei Chou?*

"Let me go!" Mim ordered loudly, struggling.

Alli twisted her wrist and pulled her close to him. Mim could feel the rough texture of a rope. He planned to tie her up!

In an instant, Mim realized that Alli meant more than rape—he intended to force her to shore and sell her to the Horned Edge, who would be delighted to own another heir to the Bardian throne. A bolt of fear threatened to weaken her, to make her struggle futilely.

Mim resisted the fear. Before Alli could bind her, she stomped her booted foot hard on his toes. Then she kicked him right above the knee, and he tottered.

But Alli quickly righted himself, and he still grasped her wrist. "We're just having a little disagreement, my dear *princess.* Come with me. I'll take you to shore to meet my friends! We'll have a party!" His grasp tightened so hard she was afraid he'd break bones, and again she felt the rope on her skin.

No one was coming to help. The watchmen seemed to have vanished; Wei Chou was apparently waiting below deck for a deeper dark to take her to the hotel. Mim shouted, "Help!" No one came. Alli began to drag her across the gangplank.

Then her free hand felt the handle of a big knife at Alli's belt. She knew that, if she kept a clear head, she could pull it free. "If you don't let go of me, Alli, I will kill you." Mim spoke with certainty.

"Oh really?" Now the rope was looped around her left wrist.

But Mim swept her right hand down and whisked the man's knife from its scabbard. The night was so dark she could not see the blade gleam, but she felt it firm in her grasp. "Alli," she promised, "I will kill you."

"You really mean it, don't you?" he responded, with some surprise. "Too bad. I've got you now!"

Alli reached to grab her free wrist and tugged her toward him. Instantly, she stabbed him in the kidney with his knife, thrusting it deep into his waist. Alli jumped back, tripped, and collapsed onto the deck.

What a mess! Alli lay on the deck, bleeding, still holding the rope that he'd used to bind her. Mim shook the rope off her hand. She dropped his knife, and finally, Wei Chou and the watchmen came running.

"Where were you all?" Mim demanded, her heart racing. But a tsunami of shock hit her, and she shook. Wei Chou hugged her to his chest, and she sobbed, "He was going to sell me to the enemy. He almost succeeded!"

"I'm so sorry," Wei Chou kept saying. "I'm so sorry! I went to gather some books for you before the shops closed. I had no idea—"

"Somehow Alli knew that I am a …" Mim gulped, and bit back the word, *princess.* She let out one more big sob, which embarrassed her. But Wei Chou's arms were warm and safe.

Wei Chou ordered the watchmen, "Call the dock security. Have them take away the body, and also see that they clear anyone lingering around waterfront walkway. Call the captain. He needs to know about this. Also, assign guards to accompany us to shore."

Finally, the situation was clear and guards were present. Wei Chou patted Mim's back and let her go. "Let us go to the hotel now." He sounded so kind. "Your room is ready. And so are your books and journals."

"Thank you," Mim said. Now she felt numb. Wei Chou took her arm, and they with several armed sailors proceeded down the gangplank.

CHAPTER 37:
DER BUND

In the wintry woods behind Lord Charon's estate, Lewis heard night sounds, tiny rustles of beech leaves, a soft sighing of wind. The starlight behind the bare tree branches glinted on Mafioso's gun. Two bodies lay motionless on the frozen ground. Lewis waited to be killed, and time stretched like a Mobius strip, on and on and on.

But the gun waved to one side. "There are others about," Mafioso whispered. "Keep quiet and follow me."

Shocked into cold-decision mode, Lewis understood what happened. He was not dead. His brains were not scattered over the forest mold. He was being rescued. Without a question, he turned and let Mafioso lead him to … wherever.

*   *   *

Mafioso dropped Lewis off at the Teterboro airport with a one-way, economy ticket to the Dallas/Ft. Worth and the instructions: "When you arrive in Dallas, wait at the baggage claim."

"I don't have any luggage."

Mafioso drove off without answering. Lewis wondered who and what he would encounter at the baggage claim in Texas.

He found his departure gate and boarded the plane. Tight accommodations in economy seating cramped his long legs. Acute hunger pinched his stomach, and despite the courtesy coffee, Lewis felt thirsty. When the steward came up the aisle again, he asked for water and the man brought him some. While Lewis sipped the ice water, a thought warmed his soul: *Thank God I'm alive!*

Orange sunlight began to peep upward from the deep blue eastern sky as Lewis's plane landed at the Dallas/Ft. Worth airport. Despite the spacious airport interior full of shiny glass and the large Crystal Mountain sculpture, Lewis felt rumpled, unshowered, cramped, and bone weary.

But now that he could move around, it felt good to walk. As soon as Lewis arrived at baggage claim—with no baggage at all—he saw someone holding a large sign: "Lewis Brahmindura."

Gravitating toward the sign, Lewis tensed with apprehension. The man holding the sign was a stranger, Hispanic, medium height, grave. But next to the man stood none other than Lewis's former mentor and friend, Dr. Abel Zhartha.

Dr. Zhartha threw out his arms. Lewis leaned into a firm, warm, and enthusiastic hug from the elderly scientist. The man's wrinkled face beamed. "I was so afraid for you. *Der Bund* told me you were in danger. I told them to bring you here."

Confused, Lewis asked, "You mean the liberal Swiss newspaper?"

"No, Lewis, I do not mean the newspaper. I mean my network of friends who consider themselves neither liberal nor conservative, but, ah …" Dr. Zhartha paused to choose his word, "faithful."

"I'm utterly grateful to your Der Bund, then. The Horned Edge nearly executed me last night."

Dr. Zhartha examined Lewis closely. "No blood. No bruises. That's good. But your skin is grayish and you look ready to fall over."

"I feel ready to fall over," Lewis said. His voice sounded hollow in his ears.

Restraining his usually peppy walking pace, Dr. Zhartha began a slow andante gait, walking side-by-side with Lewis out of the sliding door. They approached a waiting black Cadillac limousine outside the baggage claim area. As they reached the limo, Lewis felt dizzy. He grabbed the door latch. *Please, please, do not let me have a seizure now.* Alarming darkness and pressure filled his head.

"Close your eyes. Breathe deeply," Dr. Zhartha ordered.

Lewis stood, his mentor holding him up while he followed instructions. His head cleared. "I can get in now."

Dr. Zhartha opened the rear passenger door like a valet, and Lewis slipped inside. The Hispanic limo driver glanced back but said nothing. Dr. Zhartha slid in beside Lewis. As the limo pulled away from the curb, the famous scientist soothed in his deep voice, "You might as well get some sleep. Later you can have a meal. We have plenty to do after that, but you need to recover."

Lewis sighed and felt his tensions ease in the limo's comfortable road rumble. He put a handy pillow behind his neck, closed his eyes, and began to tell himself, one body part at a time beginning with his toes, to relax. *Wiggle, toes on right foot. Wiggle, toes on left foot. Stop. Relax, feet. Relax ankles. Relax knees and thighs. Relax* ... and his mind drifted into the cozy dark place called sleep.

Lewis awoke when he felt the limo slow and turn and then stop. He sat upright, yawned, stretched. "I feel so much better!"

Dr. Zhartha smiled at him. "Welcome to my GPC!"

Lewis's "wherever" destination turned out to be the Graviton-Phonon Collider that had been completed under Waxahachie, Texas. Lewis surveyed the GPC scenery as he and the older scientist exited the limo, which drove off. He saw a grassy plain under partly cloudy sky with a horizon of modern, tastefully landscaped buildings. The air felt brisk, yet much warmer than the New Jersey winter; Lewis enjoyed being able to walk outside without his coat.

Dr. Zhartha escorted Lewis through a sliding glass front entrance into a large lobby with lots of brass and glass. Lewis saw an attended formal reception desk, a chair and sofa arrangement, and white ceramic planters filled with palms, fig trees, bromeliads, orchids, pathos, and many blooming tropical plants. One black glass wall flowed with water that fell into a pebbled trough.

"This is the 'human area' of the GPC," said Dr. Zhartha. "Although the government shut down the old Super Collider in 1993, we began construction again. In under ten years, thanks to our huge grant, we completed this beautiful, fully functional accelerator of gravity particles." The scientist huffed into his bushy white moustache. "What is new about the GPC is that it uses sound—yes, *music,* if you will—as a gravity particle stimulant."

Lewis nodded.

Dr. Zhartha went on, "Using a gravitational resonance idea I heard from *you,* no less, we investigate string and brane theories and much, much more. The addition of phonons—"

Lewis stumbled, and Dr. Zhartha caught his arm. "I'm sorry. I'm very hungry," Lewis confessed. "I haven't eaten since … well, since before your lecture at Harvard."

Dr. Zhartha nodded. "I'll take you to our cafeteria."

While devouring a large chicken-salad croissant, a blueberry yogurt, a packet of veggies with hummus dip, and two packages of Twinkies downed with a cola, Lewis learned a great deal. He soaked up Dr. Zhartha's discussion like a hungry sponge.

Dr. Zhartha told him about their latest research findings. They had identified so far six branes—layers of the universe—and they were sure there were more. Scientists conjectured ten or eleven strings in the fabric of space-time. Dr. Zhartha believed there were ten, and that the eleventh was yet another, separate unique dimension of the universe.

The discussion stirred Lewis. His heart beat fast, and he listened closely. *My job in biophysics sidetracked me, despite its noble purpose,* he thought. *This area of physics is where my heart is. Enabling time travel—by adding Lanthran technology to this Earth system—is what my heart dragon has been telling me to do.*

Dr. Zhartha kept talking. Lewis's mind fixed on every concept, integrating what he heard with Lanthran sonic computers and locating technology. However, he nearly flew out of his seat when Dr. Zhartha told him that the GPC could teleport physical objects. *So close, I am so close to realizing my dream!*

Dr. Zhartha noticed his excitement. "So far, we have transferred objects the size and weight of refrigerators across a distance of a thousand kilometers." The scientist grimaced. "Once in a while a teleported object disappears across a brane, never to be seen again. That's a problem you can help us solve. We cannot have that happen if we want to teleport humans!"

Lewis's moment had come. Deep inside, his soul dragon pressed so hard that he felt ready to burst. He sensed that somewhere in the universe, angels were holding their bright breath, waiting for him to act. Seraphim stilled their great wings. Cherubim stopped wheeling and gazed at him with their many eyes.

Lewis's mentor spoke again, jogging Lewis back to the ordinary world. "Remember the piece of plastic you slipped to me after my lecture?" Dr. Zhartha asked. "I have it." He reached into his suit coat pocket and pulled out the plastic curl of data. He placed it on their table and smoothed the crinkly surface. "What's this? A candy wrapper?"

"If we develop this," Lewis stated, "we shall be able to transfer people and objects accurately across galaxies—without spaceships. And we can connect them safely in a near instant of time."

Dr. Zhartha stared at Lewis. "Where did the technology you say is embedded in this 'candy wrapper' come from? The Chinese? The—"

"From another world. Lanthra. That's where I went when, uh, terrorists kidnapped me several years ago."

Lewis could see that Dr. Zhartha believed him. The cafeteria noise of rattles and conversations faded. Quiet descended over them like a discreet cone of silence.

"I have a million questions," Dr. Zhartha finally said.

"Me, too," Lewis confessed. "The technology embedded in this piece of plastic creates an entire generating, computing, locating, and connecting system. Imagine! With it humans could colonize our moon, Mars, and onward through the vast reaches of the universe."

Dr. Zhartha smiled, his face radiant. "We could meet intelligent life, even other species of humans!"

Lewis leaned forward, excited. "There *are* other species of humans! There are blue hair covered people on Lanthra, imported centuries ago to be slaves. They have long red tongues, and apparently no vocal cords, because they always use sign language to communicate." Lewis described in detail the slender, graceful peaceful Blue People of the species he called *homo azure*. "I've looked their world through the *Thoyo-on,* er, the Lanthran locating system. The Blues' planet has lots of wetlands, some mountain ranges; one large ocean. The people live in grass and clay huts for the most part. And the sky … From the surface, the sky has a pink hue."

A catch came to his throat, and Lewis could not speak for a while. Eventually, he forced out the words that pressed in his heart night and day, "Help me develop this technology as fast as possible and add it to the GPC. I must connect to Lanthra and rescue my brother Patrick. I have a strong feeling that there isn't much time before something terrible happens to him." The urgency that rose in him drove him to stand up. "When can we start? *How* can we start?"

"Yes, you need our help, and we need yours." Dr. Zhartha added, "but first I must ask my question. *How* do we translate that little plastic thing into an entire working system?"

Lewis nearly bellowed, "It's read with *sound!* Just like you use in the GPC."

People in the cafeteria stared at him, so he sat down and lowered his voice. "This 'candy wrapper' is read like MRI technology that reads the body with magnetic resonance! Only, reading this information is teased out by sound particles… phonons. It's all here…" He tapped the curl of plastic. "All the instructions!"

Then Lewis sat down, but waved his arms to indicate the entire GPC construction over Waxahachie. "By coincidence—or not, what you have here is *exactly* what we need to develop the system for instant space travel."

Dr. Zhartha smiled, a big happy grin that spread out his moustache. His eyes shone with joy. "I don't believe in coincidences."

"Using sound to interpret the structures," Lewis added, "we tease out the schema. It's like the diamond needle that causes the grooves of an old record on a turntable to actualize a symphony." He could hardly sit still. "You already have the technology to do that. A week of steady effort perhaps, and we could finish actualizing the data on this plastic 'candy wrapper' and use it to open a portal …"

Lewis stopped talking and closed his eyes.

Dr. Zhartha asked, "What is it?"

"I have to get back to New Jersey and bring Deirdre here! If the Horned Edge have hurt her …" Lewis's heart pounded and his voice rose. "I have to bring her here with me! I have to protect Mom and Dad and Gracie! And I have to rescue Patrick! Oh, my God, I have so many things to do and think, so many places to go—I don't know where to start!" The high anxiety made him want to beat his head against the wall.

Dr. Zhartha put his hand on Lewis's arm. "Calm down, son. Calm down. One thing at a time. You have friends. We can see that your family and Deirdre will be all right."

Suddenly Lewis remembered Dr. Zhartha's short description of his "faithful" friends. "Dr. Zhartha," he began, "you started to tell me about a network you're associated with called Der Bund. I know that means 'The Brotherhood.'" He paused, leaned forward, a little afraid of his thoughts. "It can also mean 'a conspiracy.' What *is* this Der Bund?"

The old scientist's brown eyes twinkled. "Der Bund is a loose collection of people throughout the world. It's like the Horned Edge in that we work in our vocations of education, science, politics, sales, cleaning services, retail, computers, day care, nursing, farming—in every kind of endeavor. It's *not* like the Horned Edge because we don't seek to control the world. We encourage people to control themselves. Der Bund strives for one thing: *excellence* in all that our hearts, minds, hands can accomplish. Yes, that includes spiritual excellence, love that translates into actions."

The scientist continued, "We are definitely *not* a conspiracy. Our values clash with the Horned Edge's. Oh, many people in the Horned Edge are just ordinary people who want to reestablish what they think of as 'a nation under God.' The leaders seduce the ignorant with lies about establishing a utopia. But their ravening desire is for control. The Horned Edge strategy is to divide people with all-or-nothing thinking, to weaken trust and community life—until they have the opportunity to strike. Then they will begin a major war of world conquest."

"So, Der Bund is a sort of anti-Horned Edge movement?" Lewis interrupted. He wasn't sure whether he could trust this new entity. "Trying to take over and make over the world?"

Dr. Zhartha's face clouded. His eyebrows drew together, then the scientist relaxed. "No. The forces that rebel with unethical force against a dominance are in hegemony; they become part of the oppressive system. We don't fight that way. We stand on codified principles—the Torah, if you like—and exercise our power through doing our jobs and doing them very, very well …

for God."

"Lewis," Dr. Zhartha went on, "Der Bund is not equivalent to a group like some Christian Nationalism. People from all walks of life and affiliations take part in Der Bund—all who advocate love like Jesus commanded." The scientist smiled and quoted, "Love one another."

"So, you are a Christian?"

Dr. Zhartha paused, tilted his head as if listening. "I don't know. However, I know this: The organization of space-time is so beautiful and symmetrical that I must believe in God." The man's deep brown eyes glimmered with his thoughts. "I am not ready to become a rabbi, but I will satisfy my soul. I have signed up for some theological courses and I shall see where that leads. To Christianity, perhaps." He fell silent.

"May I tell you about my own experience?" Lewis asked.

The scientist nodded.

Lewis described his epiphany during the Christmas Eve church service, when powerful words were spoken over the baby Jesus. "God of God, Light of Light, Very God of very God ..."

When Lewis finished, he and Dr. Zhartha sat back, each immersed in his own thoughts. Dr. Zhartha did not comment; he appeared to be processing. Lewis thought, *I'm a Christian now, but perhaps I could take a private class where I can ask all my many questions* ... The face of the pastor in that Newark church appeared in his mind: A man in his sixties, African-American, with the tense alertness of a highly educated person and the relaxed peace of a satisfied soul.

*　*　*

Dr. Zhartha excused himself for a moment. While he waited, Lewis scrolled his phone's contact list. "Let's see ...," he murmured to himself, "I can't remember the name of the pastor, but I'm sure that I have the phone number of that church."

He found the number. It was about mid-morning, New Jersey time, and he was pretty sure he could reach the church office.

"Redeemer Church," came the voice of the church secretary.

"May I speak to Pastor ... um...?"

"Pastor Cooper is his name. I'll transfer your call."

In a few seconds, a rich bass voice resonated over Lewis's phone. "Pastor Cooper here. How may I help you?"

Lewis came to the point quickly. "I attended Redeemer Church for a Christmas Eve service. It spoke to me, a former atheist, and I'd like to know if I may meet with you sometime soon."

"Thank you for telling me about yourself. I'm here at my office weekdays, Monday through Friday, and by special appointment as needed. What time works for you, Mr. …?"

"Just call me Lewis," Lewis replied. He did not want the pastor to recall that strange person named "Lewis Brahmindura" whose mysterious public disappearance in Newark had been caught on a video that went viral.

After a short conversation, Lewis disconnected the call. He had an appointment for Wednesday morning with Pastor Cooper. *Der Bund … Excellence … Resisting evil by simply standing in the Good.*

*   *   *

When Dr. Zhartha returned to their table, Lewis's mind felt clear. "I need to go back to New Jersey right away for Deirdre," he said. He pushed the curl of data toward Dr. Zhartha. "Keep this and develop it …" his voice caught, "in case I don't get back."

"Go well, then, Lewis." He accepted the plastic curl and returned it to his pocket. "Then come back. Bring your love, Deirdre." Dr. Zhartha grinned. "Yes, we know about her. The Horned Edge are not the only ones keeping track of you."

CHAPTER 38:
LEWIS MEETS WITH A PASTOR

On Wednesday, a cold, clear January day, Lewis arrived in Newark. He ached to see Deirdre, but first … an urgent task compelled him. Something inside insisted that he visit that church where he'd attended the Christmas Eve service. *I must talk to the pastor; I've got to resolve some questions I have about God.*

His Lyft first stopped at the drugstore to pick up his seizure medication. Quickly he downed the round white pill with a bottle of spring water and ate a large Snickers bar. *Thank God, I've had few side effects from this med. And no seizures since …*

As Lewis entered his second taxi to Redeemer Church, his breath came out in a white cloud, and he pulled his coat tighter around him. For a moment he imagined himself having a seizure during his interview with the pastor. Lewis knew that, if he did, the world would go black, and he would not exist until he woke up with a terrible headache. The pastor would be horrified to watch him kick and convulse and scream on the floor. Lewis shuddered. *I could skip this self-assigned torture.*

But his gut demanded that he try. Squaring back his shoulders, Lewis resolved, *I'll ask those questions that keep bugging me!*

Perhaps he could start with a question like, "How long did it take to make the universe? Was it just six days—really? How can any intelligent people actually believe that?" The pastor would roll his eyes, then glare at him with the pinched mouth and scornful dark eyes of far-right, judgmental religiosity.

Immediately, Lewis's stomach felt unsettled. Fortunately, he'd kept the paper bag that had contained his pill bottle.

Clutching his abdomen, Lewis surged into mental darkness. Up surged, not vomit, but an evil memory—the memory of himself standing, shivering just night before last, in the cold woods behind Charon's huge mansion, guns pointing at him while he waited to be executed. That picture made his breath come quick and his heart pound. *This is no good. I'm starting to have a panic attack.*

With little mental shake, Lewis called out in his heart, *Deirdre ... Soon I'll see you, my love.* To his great relief, the nausea subsided. He remembered Dr. Greer's advice: *Take out your wracked brain and put it on a shelf. Look at your thought as if it were an object and evaluate it.*

He clasped his hands in concentration, then pantomimed himself taking out his brain. His brain sat on the shelf, resembling a withered poisoned green apple. Breathing deeply, Lewis studied the miasma of shame and fear that swamped him. But fear, judgment, and ridicule didn't have to be the only possible realities. He needed to select a different thought for that brain.

Searching for something positive, he concentrated on the passing view from the taxi's window. Even through smeary salt spray, the morning sky rose a sweet, clear blue dome, with cheerful sunlight yellowing the world from the east. Bare tree branches made intricate patterns on the sky. Lewis calmed.

The taxi dropped him off at the church entrance. Lewis made his way through the red front door into the large reception room. There, he stopped. Larger than his entire apartment, the area glowed with warm sunlight from floor-to-ceiling windows. On the right side, a sign read "Sanctuary," and on the opposite wall, "Offices and Classrooms." Beside that, Lewis read, "Restrooms." *Good!*

Before finding the pastor, Lewis visited the private Family Restroom. He leaned his head against the wall and closed his eyes to think. *No, don't think,* a soft voice whispered. It sounded like Deirdre, and he smiled. *Feel.*

Leaning and relaxing, Lewis took in a deep breath and let it out slowly. He closed his eyes.

His imagination took him to a view of the Alabama hills near home. A real memory took over: He'd been hiking. Above, clear blue sky peeked above the silver tree branches. In particular, he noticed a young beech tree. The silver bark and clinging golden leaves reminded him of exquisite jewelry. Behind the beech soared a huge oak, great twisty brown branches fanning the sky. Then, looking down at the path, Lewis noticed a wet patch of oak leaves in a bowl of rock. The leaves in the middle swirled. Curious, brushing the leaves aside, he saw that clear water filled the depression. A tiny whirlpool bubbled up from a hole in the bottom of the stone bowl. Lewis got down on his knees, cupped his hands, and drank. And drank again. And again. A verse from a poem came to mind as he got up, wiping his mouth.

Deep Spring, will you, eternal living drink, refresh the dead?

The Bard of Bardia had sung that song, far away on Lanthra at the Red Oak Tavern. Lewis's heart swelled. He stood up straight. Courage flowed into him, and he squared his shoulders. "Time to see the pastor," he told himself.

* * *

Once he found the church office, Lewis saw a generously-built black woman with braided hair and a red dress suit operating the copier. Her desk's name plaque read: Keisha Bennett.

"Hello?" he called.

She hit the pause button on the copier and stared at him. "How may I help you?" Her voice sounded efficient but warm.

Lewis tensed. "Hi, Ms. Bennett. I'm here for an appointment with Pastor Cooper."

"He's on a call right now," she told him. "Wait a few minutes, and then I'll tell him you're here. What is your name?"

"Lewis Brahmindura."

Ms. Bennett repeated his name, but mispronounced it. "Lewis Bramdoora. I'll let you know when the pastor's ready, love."

"Brah-min-du-ra," Lewis enunciated. "It means 'justice of God' in Hindi. But I'm American."

Ms. Bennett directed him to the big reception room, saying, "I'll call you, Mr. Bramidoora."

For long minutes, Lewis stewed, torn between his pressing questions and the desire to walk out in anger. He waited and waited. He drank some cold water from the cooler. He played with his phone. Delay, delay, delay …

Just as he stood up to leave, Ms. Bennett entered. "Pastor

Cooper is ready to see you now." The lady smiled and exuded such kindness that Lewis forgave the long delay. He put away his phone, and she escorted Lewis to the pastor's office. The pastor sat behind a desk, but when Lewis entered, he stood, moved forward, and offered his hand. "I'm Pastor Cooper. And you must be Lewis Bramdoora?"

Taking in the room before he spoke, Lewis saw tomes packed together on built-in walnut bookshelves and a new MacBook Pro laptop on the desk next to photos of cherubic grandchildren. Framed certificates and diplomas on the walls showed that Pastor Cooper was titled a "Reverend Doctor" with a Ph.D. in psychology. The titles intimidated Lewis.

"Ah, … my last name is pronounced Brah-min-du-ra," Lewis said. "But, please, call me 'Lewis.'"

"Have a seat, Lewis!" Pastor Cooper gestured to a chair. He himself rounded the desk and sat across from Lewis on a similar chair. His brown face was deeply creased with age lines, crowned with short curly white hair, yet because of the way he sat up straight and alert, he radiated power.

Pastor Cooper's intense gaze bored into Lewis. He suddenly exclaimed, "Oh! You are *that* Lewis, the physicist who disappeared two years ago along with his brother and sister and a friend!"

Lewis, taken aback, nodded.

"And around this Thanksgiving, you disappeared and reappeared in front of dozens of people on the highway. Well, well, well."

Lewis steeled himself, as an avalanche of memories hit him. He couldn't express his emotions in a few words, so he concentrated on his purpose for coming here. "Pastor Cooper, I had called myself an atheist, but during and because of my traumatic experiences, I began to believe in God. I think I'm a Christian. But I have a lot of questions."

Pastor Cooper replied, "Tell me more."

Lewis blinked. *Will he judge me? Does he expect me to be hostile because I have doubts about God? What if he's the hostile one?*

His mind flashed back to Lord Charon's cave chamber on Lanthra—the beautiful amethyst crystals, the tall obsidian monitor a portal to the worlds. Then, the glory of the stars shone on that monitor. He'd felt that another Person perceived the diadem of glory that was the universe and rejoiced over it. Once again, the "Lord of the Dance" song rang out:

> *I danced in the morning*
> *When the world was begun,*
> *And I danced in the moon*
> *And the stars and the sun,*
> *And I came down from heaven*
> *And I danced on the earth,*
> *At Bethlehem*
> *I had my birth.*

Resolute to have at it with his questions, Lewis dove in. "At your Christmas Eve service, I heard the baby Jesus called 'God of God, Light of Light, and very God of very God.'" He took a deep breath. "Was Jesus really God?"

"Yes, he *is* really God. True God, and true man."

"How do you know?" Lewis countered.

The pastor's wrinkles deepened in a smile. "To quote an old song, '... *for the Bible tells me so.*'"

"But how can you believe the Bible? How can you separate fact from fiction?"

Pastor Cooper explained, "The 'historical grammatical method' of interpretation that most evangelical Christians use assumes that the ordinary Bible reader can discern the authors' intended meanings and styles. In some cases, the authors wrote history or factual discussion; in other cases they used symbolic or poetic styles."

Lewis's doubts surged, and he pressed, "But how can you tell if it's *true?* I mean, what about the stories of Noah's ark, Jonah and the whale—

The pastor interrupted with a smile, "It was a big fish, not a whale."

Lewis chose to pass on that one. "What about the resurrection of the crucified Jesus?" He paused, flooded with memory of the night his once-spurned Bible had called to him. "What about that account in Ezekiel about seeing beings like winged wheels full of eyes, and a 'son of man' on a throne? That stuff sounds just plain weird! How can any intelligent person possibly believe all that?" He heard his voice getting loud, so he stopped, waiting for a sharp retort.

Instead of judging, Pastor Cooper empathized. "So many questions! You're really struggling about trusting Jesus. A lot of people say that you just have to 'take it on faith,' that you just have to 'trust and obey.' Yet you need answers. The Bible says, "'Argue with me,' says the Lord, 'and see if you can be proved right.' That's from Isaiah 43:26, one of my favorite verses."

The pastor went on, and his voice sounded soft, "You don't know if you can trust the Bible. However, the Old and New Testament are scientifically plausible."

Lewis sat back in the chair. The office got quiet. "How so?"

"For instance, the ancient prophecies came true, over and over. For instance, the prophet Isaiah named the Persian King Cyrus hundreds of years before the man's existence. Likewise, Isaiah informed the Jewish King Ahaz that there'd be a virgin birth. The prophet Hosea wrote of the resurrection, saying, '*After two days, he will revive us; in the third day he will raise us up, and we shall live in his sight.*'"

Lewis listened as Pastor Cooper went on, "From a probability point of view, the words of the Bible are accurate. They were very, very carefully copied from the originals. If an Old Testament scribe made a mistake, he or she started from the beginning. Plus, most of the manuscripts say the same things. For instance, there are about ten thousand ancient manuscripts that now constitute the New Testament. These copies agree textually with the astounding correspondence of at least 85 percent. Yes, there are variations, even important and conflicting ones, but the probability of such an agreement, both textual and thematic, among so many copies over so many years is absolutely phenomenal!"

Lewis chewed on the information. As a scientist, he understood the importance of probability in affirming the likelihood of a hypothesis. He understood reliability and validity in research. *Is the Bible more trustworthy than Plato's writings or Shakespeare's plays?* Pastor Cooper's words sank deep inside, and he could not deny that the pastor comprehended the science behind having faith in the Bible's divine authorship.

For another hour, Lewis peppered the pastor with question

after question. To his growing amazement, time after time, the pastor answered. Instead of losing his temper, the man got more patient. *Christians aren't as stupid as I thought,* Lewis decided. *I could respect this guy.*

His questions weren't organized, but he fired away.

"Do miracles still happen?"

"What about all the people who never heard of Jesus?"

"Why do Christians revere the cross—an instrument of torture?"

"Surely Christians believe in evolution!"

Time after time, the pastor answered in a clear, reasonable tone. The light from the office window had swung into shadow when Pastor Cooper sighed, leaned back, and stretched. "Lewis, you've worn me out."

Lewis nodded. "I've worn myself out, too, Pastor Cooper." He stood up. "Thank you for this conversation."

Cooper stood, too, asking. "When can we schedule another visit?"

Lewis shook his head. "I'm going out of town, and I don't know if I can get back to see you—ever." He pulled on his coat, then met the pastor's dark eyes. "But we can see each other virtually and talk, if you're willing. I have another question, a big one."

Pastor Cooper's face creased with a big smile. "Go for it. If I can answer, I will. But it's up to you in the end to trust what the Bible tells you." He gave Lewis his card.

* * *

Lewis hurried to yet another ride. He had one more destination in this city before he could take Deidre with him to safety. And what he planned to do next was not safe.

CHAPTER 39:
A CEO WITH A GUN

"Mr. Gnudst can see you in just a few minutes, Lewis. He's on a call right now."

Lewis said, "Thank you, Chas," to the friendly male receptionist at Gnudst & Cranz Pharmaceuticals and surveyed the large company's lobby. It reminded him of a five-star hotel: a high ceiling, a waterfall wall, large healthy potted tropical plants. Everything was clear glass and white walls, airy and transparent, filled with light. He'd come through it every day, five and sometimes six days a week. Usually, he'd hurried to the lower level of cubicles where the techies worked. But today he was going to the higher level of plush offices where management worked. Gnudst & Cranz did not emphasize a classless culture. Lewis knew he was low on the ladder.

The air inside the lobby felt cool and smelled clean, just like his lab. While he waited, Lewis tightened his dark gray suit jacket and adjusted his blue tie. No longer would he wear his dust-blue tech coat—he'd come to formally resign. Not only that, but he wanted to present his idea to CEO Roger Gnudst and apologize for the bitter end of the relationship with his daughter Peggy.

The receptionist wore one wireless ear bud and typed into a computer at his desk: the latest Apple model. He smiled but otherwise ignored Lewis, who decided to relax his jitters by concentrating on the soft rush of the waterfall. Finally, "He's ready for you, Lewis," Chaz said.

Lewis took a deep breath, lingered just an instant longer by the waterfall, then tapped his badge at the security panel and walked through the waist-high turnstile. There was an elevator, but he didn't like enclosed spaces, so he trotted up the curved staircase.

Soon he stood at the CEO's office. The heavy teak door was open. Lewis glanced at the pewter plaque that read, "Roger Gnudst, Ph.D." Roger, too had an ear bud. He was talking to someone on the phone, so Lewis knocked softly.

Roger threw him a sharp nod, raised one finger, and continued his conversation. By the strained look on his face, he was either getting chewed out by his board president or he was dreading his talk with Lewis. Or both.

Lewis waited, concentrating on his breathing, trying to quiet his thoughts so he could speak naturally. He felt off balance because Peggy's father radiated energy that filled the office—negative energy. *Is he furious with me for breaking Peggy's arm?* Roger's bulky navy suit and large shoulder pads generally made him look bigger than he was, but now that barrel chest looked deflated. His expression darkened as he listened to the caller. "All right, all right, I'll do it," he snapped, and the call ended.

Roger waved for Lewis to come in. The CEO's expression immediately altered to a cheerful glowing smile. "I'm glad to see you!" Roger said, extending his hand, and gave Lewis a firm handshake. Lewis resisted the temptation to excuse himself and flee.

"One of my brightest people. Tell me, Lewis, what's on your mind?" Roger waved for Lewis to sit in the padded blue IKEA chair by his desk and angled himself into an open posture.

Lewis sat, astonished at Roger's quick transformation from … what? fear? horror? … to welcoming.

"Mr. Gnudst—"

"Call me Roger."

"Very well, Roger," Lewis began, deciding to be blunt, "I came to offer my resignation." Roger started to speak, but Lewis quickly added, "But, please listen to me first."

Roger leaned forward. At first Lewis thought he would tell him off, but instead the man nodded and clasped his hands together in an attentive pose. "Go ahead. Tell me what you have on your mind."

"Since I've worked for you, I've had an idea that may help you come up with a new treatment for Alzheimer's. Not only might the treatment slow the disease down, but it might even bring it into remission."

Roger listened attentively, his face impassive but not discouraging as Lewis painted a proposal to develop an AI animation program to investigate the Alzheimer's ß-protein deformation process at the atomic level. At the end of the short presentation, Roger said, "That sounds like an excellent idea! Write up your proposal, Lewis, and send it to Mr. Cranz." But his voice sounded rather off, forced.

"I will!" Then Lewis hesitated. "Why Cranz? Why not you?"

Instead of answering, Roger unclasped his hands. One broad hand with stubby fingers lay spread on the table. Lewis noticed that it trembled, and he wondered if Mr. Gnudst was getting Parkinson's. Very gradually, Roger's other hand reached into a desk drawer and drew out a gun.

Lewis's jaw dropped and he scooted back in his chair. "Mr. Gnudst, what are you doing!"

Roger wore a weird grin, more like a twisted grimace as he said, "I had big plans for you, Lewis. I'd intended to groom you to rise in this company, even take my place someday with my daughter Peggy at your side. At that Christmas Eve party, I'd thought you and Peggy would announce a wedding date, but instead ..." Roger choked, coughed, began again. "You broke my daughter's arm!" Roger's face distorted. "And now I have orders ..." His intense blue eyes narrowed, and he gripped the gun and pointed it toward Lewis. He raised the gun, began to pull the trigger …

"No!" Peggy screamed from the doorway.

The gun fired. Lewis leaped away, got tangled in his chair, and fell over. Lying on the floor, he felt a searing pain in his right upper arm. Although Roger was only a few feet from Lewis; he must have jerked or wobbled at Peggy's cry, because he had missed the target.

Peggy ran to Lewis. He heard the skirt of her smart red dress suit rip when she knelt down to check if he was unharmed. "No, no, daddy, no!" she cried. "Don't kill him!" She started sobbing.

Shaking, Lewis stood up, Peggy clinging hard onto his side, tears pouring down her cheeks. Blood dripped onto the plush white carpet—his blood. Lewis's arm felt stiff, but when he bent it everything worked, and he realized that the bullet had barely grazed the flesh.

To his horror, Roger pointed the gun at the two of them. Peggy had her arms around Lewis, and she stood between him and her father. "Don't shoot your own daughter!" Lewis shouted.

Roger's face looked swollen and gray. The blue eyes were bloodshot, but they drilled into Lewis. "You've ruined everything!" he snarled. "You've wasted your whole life— and mine!"

Lewis whispered to Peggy, "Step away from me. I don't you to get hurt." The young woman moved several feet away to Lewis's left, toward the office door.

Roger steadied his hands, aiming again at Lewis's heart.

"Call security," Lewis called to Peggy. "Now!"

She ran out of the office and clicked surprisingly fast down the hall in her spiked heels.

Facing Roger, Lewis expected to be dead very shortly, not just wounded. Mentally, he waved a goodbye kiss to

Deirdre, to his family. The sunlight beamed through the window, and he wondered what death would feel like, what type of afterlife awaited him. *I believe in the resurrection of the body ...*

Then to Lewis's surprise and horror, Roger's grip on the gun changed. Slowly, the CEO moved his hands until he had pressed the nuzzle to his own ear. Roger closed his eyes tightly, wrinkled his brow, pressed his lips together ...

"Stop! Roger, don't do it!" Lewis tensed to go for the gun.

Peggy's father opened his eyes. His features relaxed, and color returned to his face. That barrel chest heaved once, then deflated. The hand with the gun wavered, lowered, and Roger dropped the gun onto the desk with a loud clatter.

Roger sighed and spoke. "Go away, Lewis. My commander told me to kill you because you no longer cooperate with us, but I didn't want to because you are a decent man. I don't know how they will handle my failure, but right now I don't care crap! So—go! Now!"

Lewis considered for an instant. *Run away?* But he jerked his chin in a tight nod and exited the office. He dreaded to hear another gunshot, in case Roger changed his mind, but none came. Deciding that the best strategy to get out was to act cool, to look as calm as possible, he used the elevator down to the lobby. Chas was at his desk, talking on his phone, sporting the ever-present earbud.

"Hi, Lewis," he called, pausing his call. "How'd it go?"

"Just fine," Lewis sighed. "Just fine." He took one last look at the beautiful waterfall, flipped the glossy big leaf of a peace lily and exited the Gnudst & Cranz building forever, he hoped.

CHAPTER 40:
FINDING THE PRINCE

Patrick had been a slave for forty-five Lanthran days. On Earth, that amounted to over three months. He knew because he had scored daily marks under his pallet in the alcove off Nark's bedroom and guessed at the time difference between Lanthra and Earth. The Blue Person no longer kept watch over him. Patrick knew he'd been tortured and probably killed, … and it was his fault. His heart ached and he cried—but stifled the sounds—night after night, especially since his "angry piano tantrum."

Today, as the Lanthran sun rose in optic purple-to-pink-to-gold, Patrick strolled—rather, limped—on the beach of the Isle of Mercy. King Nark let him exercise now. There were plenty of guards around the causeway to make sure that he couldn't walk away, and the rest of the coast was too far for his swimming skills, not to mention the rip tide. The dark sand felt soft under his bare feet, but less traction—even when he kept to the surf line—made for tougher going. That pesky ankle bothered him more and more, and it had reddened and swelled. But he kept going anyway, walking as fast as he could even though he had to nearly drag that one foot.

Just call me fat boy, Patrick slammed himself, squeezing the soft bulge around his belly. King Nark clothed him in tight Eleaemanan cotton pants and a loose sleeveless shirt. A kerchief caught the hot sweat dripping from his head; his shirt had big wet stains down the chest and under the armpits.

So intense in his thoughts that he could hardly see straight, Patrick didn't savor the tropical beach environment. His eyes brushed across the black sand, black rock outcroppings, the sun glittering on the water, shore birds skittering around him, and multitudes of little coquina clams that burrowed in the beach as the waves withdrew. Usually, the susurration of the surf could comfort his anxiety. Not today.

Patrick had only two more days until the invasion fleet sailed—two more days to find and rescue the hidden captive prince of Bardia. Need rose up from his stomach like heartburn as he stared at a flock of white gulls. He prayed hard to the warrior Angel of the Lord against the impending invasion of Bardia. *God, send the Archangel Michael to defeat the powers of darkness, all the bezubs, and King Nark, and the Horned Edge magi.*

From Nark's bragging, Patrick knew that he had chained Prince Christopher in a cave somewhere under the island, and he'd heard that cave's entrance was near the shore. *Help me, Lord, to find Prince Christopher and set him free to warn his people.* Patrick felt deep in his spirit that the young man would be a good ruler—but only if he were free, not a hostage puppet.

As he walked, Patrick listened for changes in the noise of the ocean; he peered at the rock outcroppings for telltale cracks and crevices. Somewhere on this island, Chris was being held in a chamber that flooded at high tide. He imaged the prince in a dark hole while water filled up the cave until he had to breathe out of a tube—or drown. Patrick was sure that Chris had wanted to drown many times. But twice a day, the young man had chosen to live until this very day … he hoped.

"If I find him, how will I free him?" Patrick muttered to himself. "Nark said that he's chained. And how will I get him off the island?"

When the time comes, he heard deep in his heart, *trust me.*

Speaking of time … his was up. Patrick had less than a half hour before he must play the piano for the pirate king. Time to turn back. He hurried as best he could to his chamber to take a super-quick shower and change into his one courtly robe. *Maybe, just maybe,* he thought, *what I hear today will give me a clue.*

* * *

Patrick's strong fingers tinkered on the white grand piano the rest of the morning while Nark held audiences with various dignitaries—especially those wrangling Swethan magi. He figured that the nasty Horned Edge guys would nag Nark until he agreed to help them share control of the Isle of Mercy's *thoyo-on*. And then, not only would an invasion fleet hit Kingsport in a few days, but ground armies and heaps of weapons could follow almost instantly.

Oh yes, the Swethans craved Nark's technology. Last year, there had been a rare earthquake and the Swethan technology on the southern continent had cracked so that it no longer functioned. That's why their Horned Edge wanted so desperately to control Nark's functioning system.

Patrick shook his head in frustration while he listened. Nark played hard-to-get. Hooked-Nose flattered Nark incessantly, tickling his ego at every turn. Patrick could sense the pirate king's iron control over his island's sovereignty weakening. The suspense made him grind his teeth.

Somehow the Swethan magus had gotten Nark to brag about his valuable Bardian captive. Patrick didn't dare to stop playing, but he listened with all his attention. "T'was the neatest trick I've ever done," Nark bragged. "I threw the crew overboard to walk home—if they could, *haha!* But the prince is mine, and my spies say that the Bardians think he's dead. The boy'll be a valuable bargaining piece when I produce him. I can picture the gaping mouths and white courtly faces! He'll be a hostage, my puppet."

A quick glance toward Nark's throne showed Patrick that Hooked Nose frowned at the image of Nark having the ultimate power over Bardia. "Do you really have this prince, or is he indeed dead?" Hooked Nose challenged.

"A few days ago, the *bibat* threatened to kill himself," Nark told them, with a spew of sadistic glee. "He said that he would let himself drown when the tide comes in. But when I went down to check on him yesterday, he still lived, the coward."

Patrick tried to keep playing. He held his breath while Nark's gravelly voice continued. "Yesterday the prince told me, holding the tube, his face barely above water, 'I shall be free by tomorrow—*Radyah* sent one of the *foroyah* to tell me that I shall certainly leave this place safely.' I had the laugh of my life. My belly shook until it hurt. I told the little royal rat … I told him, 'You have faith in that invisible nonentity, that flatulence of poor men's dreams? Their go-to opiate?'"

Patrick dared to glance up from the keyboard. Hooked nose

was grinning. Nark's blasphemy apparently made him happy.

"You should have seen his white face fall," Nark bragged. "I broke him. I knew that he wanted to die, to end his misery. But he did not have the courage. When the tide came in, he thrust the tube into his mouth as fast as if …." Nark added something in Lanthran that Patrick didn't understand, except that it sounded obscene.

Patrick caught a wicked gleam in Hooked Nose's eyes. The Swethan magus had an idea to regain control. Waiting for the ploy, Patrick let a minor progression ripple through his fingers. The Swethan magi gathered around Nark like ants around a cookie.

"I don't believe that you have Prince Christopher Reynolds," Hooked Nose accused. "You play up your importance by sheer fiction."

Nark's dark bearded face flushed red, and he swelled with a flare of rage.

But Hooked Nose leered at him. "Ha! I am right. You have nothing."

Nark radiated a supernova of anger. He pursed his lips as if to spit on Hooked Nose. But his anger hardened into control. "You will see. I will take you to him."

He gestured at Patrick to make him stop his music. Patrick stopped. "You! *Nobo* boy! You come, too. See what will happen to you if you defy me." The pirate king sneered. "And after that, I may show you the Blue *cilanthoon* who received what you deserve. He's not blue anymore!"

With a shudder and an awful ache in his heart, Patrick slid off the piano bench. He hurried as best he could, limping. But, although his chest heaved with the effort to trot behind Nark's train, mentally he talked to that "invisible flatulence of poor men's dreams"—the only power he had left to lean on. *Lord Jesus, I hope that what Prince Christopher heard from your angel comes true!*

*   *   *

Via a low tunnel, Patrick followed Nark's entourage of three Swethan Horned Edge magi and six weaponed guards through the Isle of Mercy's interior honeycomb of fluted lava caves. Patrick lagged because his ankle hurt, and one of the guards punched him.

They filed out of a Blue-guarded metal door to the outside world and faced the ocean. At high noon and low tide, blazing sunlight sparkled off the waves. Patrick squinted as his eyes adjusted. They all paraded across the sand into a tangled cluster of giant black boulders. Where the path twisted, he saw a crevice in one of the rocks, just large enough for huge Nark to scrape through sideways. The others and Patrick squeezed through after the pirate king.

At first all was dark. Nark clapped his hands, and Patrick blinked. The cave lit up as bright as the most fantastic holiday light display. But its decor was the dramatic opposite of a merry Christmas. In the scary red actinic light, Patrick saw a fluted lava cave riddled with little dark holes and clusters of very sharp and ugly spikes. He shuddered. *Those spikes could rake skin like Wolverine's claws.*

About fifty feet away, Patrick saw a young man bound with chains, sitting, covering his eyes against the bright red light. Patrick saw that he could walk about a few steps, but the chains were bolted fast to the basalt wall. Near the prince's hand lay a flexible breathing tube.

The prince did not speak when they approached, but he stood up. In the awful red light, despite matted dark brown hair and torn clothes, Prince Christopher Reynolds, heir to the kingdom of Bardia, projected majesty. Yet, at that moment Patrick knew to the bottom of his heart that the prince would either die that day or be free.

CHAPTER 41:
SNEAKING IN THE DARK

Patrick felt that it was always night in the lava chambers under the Isle of Mercy, even though Nark's electric lamps were always lit along its many corridors. But people still had circadian rhythm; they—including Nark—had to sleep after the sun outside set on the Lanthran horizon.

That night Patrick did not sleep because he was sneaking. He crept around in Nark's bedroom in the dark, feeling this and that, searching for the keys to Chris's chains. *I'm sure he keeps them here somewhere!* His heart pounded while the pirate king snored. Although he could imagine the beating—or worse—that he might endure if he were caught, he scouted about, touching everything he could reach until … until that box on Nark's bedside table called him.

It was eerie: The box was kept in plain sight, kind of pretty, with its inlaid abalone tracery. He'd seen day after day and discounted it as a keepsake or kitsch, or even a container for false teeth. Patrick knew too well from Nark's breath odor that the brute had terrible teeth. But he also knew that the man didn't wear dentures. Now, in the hour when Prince Christopher must be rescued or die, that small box shone in Patrick's mind so vividly that he knew, he knew …

…That's where the keys are!
Nark's ugly greasy head rested on a pillow only a foot from the box. Patrick crawled inch by inch toward that spot. If he made a noise, if he thumped or bumped or made the box lid creak when he opened it, Nark would see Patrick's bugging eyes staring at his

face. He'd explode! Patrick's remaining life would be nasty, poor, brutal, and full of pain.

Taking a deep breath, Patrick lifted his hands to the box. Yes, a burst of foul air hit him from Nark's snore. But he steadied himself. Right hand grasp, left hand grasp … lift the box millimeter by millimeter—and the box was his.

The box lid shifted with a tiny *rasp.* Patrick froze, heart thumping. Nark snorted, blinked, and rolled over.

I've got to hurry! He had maybe an hour, maybe two, to free the prince before Nark's usual wakeup time. *Yes, I might get caught,* Patrick admitted, repressing a sudden urge to pee. *But I've gotta do this.*

With the keys in his pocket, he limped out of the bedroom, into the hall, and to the corridor that led to the outside of the island. His progress seemed so terribly slow!

The do-or-die action pumped Patrick's heart harder than it had ever worked, even when he'd jogged back home. *With Nark's space-connecting technology, the Lanthran Horned Edge can spread armies and weapons anywhere. Nobody could stop them from taking the whole of Bardia. And if they take Bardia … there goes the rest of Lanthra!*

Patrick reached the corridor that would take him outside to the beach. Breathing so fast that he began to hyperventilate, his hand clutching the keys so they wouldn't clink, Patrick padded barefoot, silent as a stalking cat. Dim recessed lights showed him the path, the power generated by the sonic computer system that resonated with Lanthra's gravity. *I will run into guards. I might get caught and skinned alive like the Blue Person.* When black spots swarmed in front of his eyes, Patrick paused. *I might just faint before I get anywhere. I'm so scared!*

Remembering a first-aid blurb he'd read at school back on Earth, he cupped his hands and breathed into them, slowly, deeply. His brain cleared. Patrick kept going.

Sure enough, two large Blue guards stood at the door. They had been bred to be enormous, about eight feet tall with ropy muscles under their blue-haired skin. One Blue guard bared his sharp needle teeth and stuck out a long red tongue. He twisted it, warning in sign language.

"Ola, taboon aya," Patrick greeted them in both words and in signs. He deliberately used *"aya,"* the word that the Horned Edge only used for sentient life—that they religiously omitted when referring to the Blue People. Patrick wanted to show that he regarded them as intelligent, wise, and fully human.

The guards waved their tongues again. Patrick held his breath and waited. The guards might arrest him, beat him, and drag him to Nark, who might … Patrick slowly exhaled as the taut moment stretched on. Would Nark flay his feet perhaps? Or his hands? Or some other parts? He knew Nark wanted to keep him alive to torment Lewis, but the beastly man might not keep him whole.

The Blue guards pointed Earth guns at him—disgusting revolvers with attachments that would let them fire a machine-gun volley of bullets. Already the Horned Edge demon-worshipping magi had traded some weapons with Earth.

In Blue sign language, their tongues demanded to know, *"What are you doing?"*

Patrick whispered, *"Maradorya Baradyah aya."* Biggest Blue ordered him to go back to Nark. Patrick repeated, "I will save the Bardian human." Again, he emphasized the word, *"aya,"* to plainly insinuate that the Blue People were completely human, just like Prince Christopher and himself.

The two Blue guards, not just blue-haired mute aliens but intelligent humans, *homo azure,* lowered their weapons. They slowly turned their backs on him and stared at the tunnel walls as if he were invisible.

Rushing forward, Patrick thrust open the metal door. Immediately, humid, thick, salty ocean air swathed his skin, and he passed through to the beach outside.

* * *

After navigating the rock cluster, Patrick slipped into the lava tube. Slimy seaweed brushed his sides. The rank, salt odor of the tube under the island made him hold his nose for a while, but he dared not to slow down. He knew that either he would succeed in freeing Prince Christopher *tonight* or the young man would drown himself at the next high tide.

The hideous red light glowed when he clapped his hands.

Patrick knew that Nark could have set up the "on-switch" for only his own DNA, but Nark had cruelly made the light operable by anyone—except for the prince. Patrick's insides squinched as he thought of Chris chained in the dark for weeks, even months, enduring the inexorable rising of the tide and deciding twice a day not to let himself die.

Suppose Nark chained *him* in that lava tube? *I'd drown myself at the first high tide,* Patrick thought, shivering.

Shaking off fear and funk, Patrick picked his way toward the prince. Christopher saw him coming and jumped to his feet. Sweat soaked the young man's face and his chest; he—even in his chains—had been working out to be ready for the hope of escape.

"I've got the keys," Patrick whispered.

"Excellent," the prince breathed. He spoke in fair English.

Patrick said, "But I don't know how to get you away from the island. They say that the current is too dangerous to swim, and I know that the causeway and the docks are full of Nark's guards."

"We *can* swim," Chris replied. "We *can* reach the Bardian Embassy near the Ploiyon Jetties."

Patrick did not comment. Moment by moment ticked by. He imagined footsteps and enraged cries coming to get him, but he couldn't give up.

After Patrick unlocked the fetters, Chris rubbed his hands and feet, then surprised Patrick by wrapping him in a tight hug. "*Radyah ye hegetlua!*" he shouted so loudly that the rocks rang.Patrick cringed. "What are you doing?" His whisper hissed with panic.

"Blessing you," Chris replied.

Suddenly, Patrick wanted to weep. *The prince looks so happy!* He ordered, his voice breaking, "C … come out with me. We'll figure out what to do."

Chris nodded. Patrick and he proceeded through the lava cave into the night. Patrick clapped; the awful red light went out. To his surprise, he and Chris could see each other in the bright starlight. Chris's white teeth shone in a delighted smile. "Thank you."

Patrick breathed fresh ocean air. He listened to the small waves lapping on the shore and surveyed the dark line of *lanthra,* the horizon for which the planet was named. "It's low tide."

Further out, though, he heard the *boom!* of larger waves. When he imagined the long swim away from the island, with currents, sharks, riptides, maybe an undertow. Patrick began to tremble.

Chris stated, "I'm a very strong swimmer. You, my friend, only need to relax. You and I will make it to the Bardian embassy—and I'm certain that Eleaemana, which has not officially joined the Horned Edge, will honor our protection." He started for the ocean.

Patrick couldn't move. His knees weakened at the looming possibility of drowning in the sea. He imagined paddling and thrashing wildly like a hysterical animal, waves smashing his mouth and nose, breathing in salt water, and finally, while his lungs screamed for impossible air, dying in inexorable pain. *Will I go to heaven?* He hoped so, but … because of him stealing that hot marble, all that trouble in Lanthra had started. Because of him throwing a piano tantrum, a Blue Person had died horribly.

Chris came back. He grasped Patrick's shoulder with a gentle hand. "What is your name, *bibat*?"

"P … Patrick."

"Do not fear, *luean* Patrick." The prince's Lanthran pronunciation sounded like *Patris*. "I will help you. Let us walk out into the water together." A note of humor graced Chris's low voice as he added, "I'm an exceptional lifeguard—I watched the training videos from Earth when I studied at the College of the Magi."

Patrick limped with Chris into the surf. He muttered, "I hope you had some real practice as well as watching videos." The prince laughed.

*   *   *

Patrick felt the bottom drop abruptly after a few yards. Soon he and Chris would be in deep, deep water. He tried to stand, to keep his balance. At first, small waves lapped at his chest because there was little wind tonight. More confident, he dared to swim forward off the shelf. He made it about fifty yards. But at the coral reef that surrounded Nark's island, the waves got rough. Patrick began to flail. A cold wave slammed against his face. Close to blind, unreasonable panic, Patrick thrashed. Another wave splatted over his head, and he began to gulp salt water.

Chris's confident voice reached him, "We've got this,

Patrick. You and I have got this. Relax. You must relax! I can tow you. Here … catch!"

With a huge effort, Patrick forced himself to listen. He quit struggling and screaming. Chris tossed him a cloth—his shirt. Patrick's hand caught it. Chris said, "That's good, just hold on." Patrick felt himself moving behind Chris's tow, and the waves no longer smacked into his face. He calmed, tried to act like a floating raft.

"I'm going to hold you," Chris told him after they passed the reef. "Relax!"

"Okay."

A firm life-preserver of a hand wrapped around Patrick's armpit from behind. "We can do this!" Chris kept saying. "I'm strong, and you are brave."

The prince coached him on how to breathe while being towed. He learned to manage some face-slapping waves while Chris pulled him onward. Continuously, after each several breaths, Chris said, "We've got this. I'm strong, and you're brave!"

Eventually the steady breakers rolled them toward the Eleaemanan shore. Chris let go of Patrick. "Ride the waves, pretend that you are a surfboard." He put his arms in the diving position, lay flat, and the big foamy surf thrust him toward the beach.

Patrick imitated him. Wave after wave glided him closer to the shoreline despite his awkward swimming. Finally, Patrick slogged out of the shallows onto the beach.

Chris was already there. He grasped Patrick's hand. "Come with me as fast as you can. Nark will pursue us."

CHAPTER 42:
THE EMBASSY

Dawn brightened with Lanthran purple and crimson glory and sparkled on the Thesare Bay. "The Bardian embassy is nearby," Chris said as they walked along the beach toward the city. "Only about a mile."

Patrick stifled a big groan. His ankle smarted, but he pressed his lips together and kept up the pace. As they advanced, he scrutinized the people around them. His chest and stomach tightened when he imagined a horde of Horned Edge guards chasing them. "You said that Nark will come after us?"

"I'm sure he will." Patrick glanced at the prince, but Chris did not show any fear.

A few fishermen with buckets and poles and bamboo lawn chairs graced the shore. Patrick noted a family playing on the beach, with several little naked children. Some women walked along the beach in colorful saris. They reminded him of Sadie Gregory, whose family had adopted him and Gracie when they first arrived on Lanthra. *That* was an anxious time, too.

Because Chris was light-skinned and he was dark, Patrick feared that they would stand out like salt next to pepper. Yet the two walkers got few glances and no glares of suspicion.

The Bardian embassy was *not* close. Chris and Patrick walked and walked down the beach, not talking. The morning sunlight beat down and glittered blindingly on the bay. Just as Patrick thought he must flop in a heap onto the sand, a lovely strong breeze cooled his face and chest. He thought, *That's a God-Thing, like Eric from church talks about. Otherwise, I'd collapse.* He quickened his pace.

"Here." Chris pointed toward the dunes. "We'll go up those dock stairs, cross the highway, go down one street, and we'll be there. Pray that Nark has not put guards around the embassy—yet!"

Huffing up the steep steps, Patrick followed the prince to the dock. From there he made his way through a path through the sea oat-covered dunes to the broad main road that paralleled the bay. When his bare feet stepped onto the hot brick road, he yelped. "Ow, ow, ow!" He could smell the heat as he ran to the sandy berm on the land side. Traffic crowded the road, but it was Lanthran foot traffic—not Earth's cars or trucks or other motorized vehicles—and they could weave their way through. Chris and he dodged a donkey weighed down with cargo, three horse-drawn carts, a small herd of long-horned cattle driven by a team of cowboys, and colorful men and women balancing baskets on their heads. Someone with boiled eggs called out to them, even tried to block their way, but they slipped past. At another time, Patrick would have loved the tropical experience, but now his heart pounded, and he gasped for breath.

"There!" Chris pointed. "The Bardian embassy!"

Chris and he approached the large white building. Patrick saw five large armed men standing beside great brass-bound doors under a shady gold-and-green striped awning. None of them were Blue hulks. *Thank God!*

"We're Bardians!" the prince cried. "Let us in!"

The embassy guards turned and stared at them. Just as one started to speak, a few *wisto* away, screaming Swethan magi and formidable Blue soldiers swarmed forward. Patrick and Chris raced at top speed toward the embassy doors.

The guards pulled open the doors, and Chris grabbed Patrick and rushed through. The guards rushed inside, too, and slammed and locked the doors. Patrick heard pounding outside. He recognized Nark's deep, angry roar, "Hand over the traitors!" and his heart pounded so hard he thought he might faint.

The doors held fast. More Bardian guards hurried into the lobby, filling the room with defenders should the mob break inside. By a mahogany counter, a middle-aged female in a red sari gestured for them to follow her. Her eyebrows rose as they passed into the depths of the embassy, and Patrick felt conscious that they were dressed in wet rags and smelled like brine.

Chris talked to her as they hurried through a corridor, "We're Bardians, seeking asylum! I am Prince Christopher Reynolds. This boy is my friend, Patrick. We beg you, take us in. And arrange transport to Bardia as soon as possible—even today! There is an invasion fleet about to sail to seize Kingsport!"

* * *

Chris and he passed deeper into the embassy, and Patrick could no longer hear Nark's screaming. "I'm Genni," the woman told them, locking the doors after they passed through and leading them into yet a deeper sanctuary. "*Eaye gan Falu,*" but people call me Genni when they speak English."

"Thank you, *Falu* Genni," the prince said, and bowed.

She spoke in such a low voice that Patrick could hardly hear her. "Stay in here. Be quiet. Ambassador Dalath will take care of you, Your Royal Highness, and you, Patrick. Keep quiet. My staff and I will handle King Nargoleh Layhew's people."

* * *

After Chris reported to the ambassador, Patrick and he were escorted to a small room. The two Bardian guards who crowded in the room with them bore sonic guns—new Lanthran-made weapons—and were prepared for lethal force.

"Hurry up and wait," the prince joked, and Patrick managed a laugh. His extreme tension relaxed a bit. And they did wait, for hours.

The small, bamboo-paneled hiding place smelled stuffy. It contained no windows, no artwork, and only a smokeless but dim lantern on a shelf on the wall gave them light. Patrick's head whirled with adrenaline and his wet, salty clothes made him itch. But noticing that Patrick stood with pain, a staff Blue person, a willowy female with a pale dandelion puff of hair, brought in chairs. She gave them cold coconut water and sugary fried plantains, and then left.

Finally, Ambassador Dalath came into their room. "Nark and his mob have retreated," he reported. "But we dare not take you outside until dark."

Patrick and Chris waited for several more hours. Patrick's stomach rumbled with returning hunger. He jumped up with gratitude when Genni entered, bringing a light supper wrapped in banana leaves. She smiled and curtseyed as she served them their "plates."

More time passed—*boring!* Finally, Ambassador Dalath returned. With him came a tall Bardian ship's captain in full dress uniform. Patrick noticed that he had a sword at his side, and a holstered sonic gun in his belt. The captain's face shone with recognition when he saw Prince Christopher. "My lord and king! By *Radyah,* we thought you were dead!" He fell to his knees before the seated prince.

Chris touched his shoulder. "Captain Lu, father of my friend Darwin, please stand. I'm not the king yet. And I am so sorry if I am in any way responsible for the loss of your son. I … I cannot undo what happened. Captain Lu, I need your help; I need it now! The Horned Edge magi and Nark plan to invade Bardia and seize Kingsport!"

"My son Darwin lives," the tall man told Chris as he straightened. "But we thought you had drowned." The captain's brilliant dark eyes examined Patrick curiously, but he addressed the prince. "My ship *Westwind* came to trade here. We are fully loaded and were ready to sail today, but … his chiseled lips smiled slightly, "we were delayed. Thank *Radyah* for the Blue Person who dared to come and warn me! There is a secret, safe way to my ship. I will take you to Bardia."

"Is the Blue Person safe?" Christopher asked quickly. "Nark is very cruel to those who frustrate his plans."

Captain Lu nodded. "She is on my ship, and my crew are well armed. My lord, we will sail today! The *Westwind* is designed after Earth's clippers; 'tis the fastest ship in my company. Not only that," a small smile crossed his Asian features, "I've signaled the other Bardian ships that are in this harbor. Your Royal Highness, a small fleet will sail with us to Kingsport. We may arrive to warn the city a day before the coming invasion."

"May it be," Chris answered. "Thank you!"

CHAPTER 43:
GRACIE AND MOM

School was over for the day, and Gracie was home in her bedroom, holding a book. Afternoon February sunlight streamed through her southwest-facing window, perfect for reading. For once, her soul rose with happiness, even gaiety. She'd checked out a Christian sci-fi book from the library, *Firebird* by Kathy Tyers, and she knew she'd really enjoy the adventure. The book could have been fine chocolate, and the experience of reading it would be absolutely delicious. As she settled on the yellow quilt that cozied her bed, she slowly opened the novel.

Just at that second, Gracie heard Mom's voice calling from downstairs, "Gracie, can we talk?"

"Mom," Gracie whined, "I'm just starting a good book!"

But Mom called again, "Gracie, please." Mom didn't sound forcing, coercing, demanding. She probably just honestly wanted to talk.

Yet, since Mom had started treatments for aggressive breast cancer, Gracie had been avoiding her. In fact, a terrible pressure built up in her chest whenever she saw Mom or heard her voice. That pressure began right now and, clutching the book to her chest, Gracie thought, *oh no. Mom must have some horrid news. The chemo isn't working. There's no hope. She's going to die!*

Mom called again. Groaning and grumbling under her breath, Gracie tossed the book onto her bed and headed downstairs. Eighteen stomping steps later, downstairs and standing by the grandfather clock in the hallway, she glared at Mom's feet. *What's Mom doing in running shoes? She had been wearing her fuzzy slippers every day. What's she thinking? Mom's absolutely in no shape to run with me.* "What do you want to talk about?" Gracie growled.

As usual this awful winter, Gracie didn't want to even look at Mom. She didn't want to see the drawn face, the dark circles under her eyes, the bald head.

"Come into the living room with me," Mom invited.

Gracie complied, dragging herself into the family area with its sofas, armchairs, and television. She reluctantly noticed that Mom had turned on the bronze table lamp. It glowed on the wood-paneled walls, which made an intimate ambience.

Mom gestured toward Gracie's favorite chair, the wooden rocker. "Sit down, my love."

Gracie couldn't resist whenever her mom called her, "My love." Rebellion eased a little, and she sat down. Rocking in her antique oak rocker with the plush gold pillow soothed Gracie's spirits even more than Mom's invitation. It had been a good while since she'd sat there to watch television or read or just hang out with the family. Without Lewis and Patrick at home, she felt a yawning abyss in her heart every time she entered the living room. Plus, to avoid encountering Mom she'd been hiding out in her bedroom except for meals.

Mom sat in her own favorite chair, the blue lounger, but she didn't put her feet up. Instead, she leaned forward. "Gracie, I love you; I want you to be in my life."

Gracie couldn't reply. The lump in her throat felt like she'd swallowed an apple whole. *Your short life,* she thought. So far, she had managed not to look up at Mom's face. Gracie rocked a little too hard. The rocker bumped against the wall, and Gracie scooted it forward again. "This chair always bangs the wall" she grumbled.

Mom declared with an emphasis that surprised Gracie, "I am *not* going to die. At least not before my time, the good Lord willing."

Suddenly Gracie stopped rocking. She leaned forward and stared at her toes. "You mean you are *not* going to die? How do you know?"

"The last scans could not find any cancer. My blood work was completely negative for markers. And I feel different; I feel better. Something good is happening. I'm recovering."

For the first time today, Gracie dared to glance at Mom's face, whose expression radiated serenity. Gazing fully at her mom, Gracie wondered what was going on. The living curtains were open, and sunlight highlighted Mom's face like a pink jade cameo. Suddenly, Gracie noticed the bright golden curly short hair that covered Mom's head! "Mom! Your hair is growing back!"

"Yes, it is. And I'm much stronger. While you were at school, I've been exercising. I feel I could go for a run with you!"

Suddenly big tears welled up in Gracie's eyes. "Mom! That's wonderful!"

Mom came forward and caught Gracie's tears in a small cut-glass bottle. Mom quoted, "God keeps all our tears in his bottle." She added as more tears streamed out of Gracie's eyes, each treasured by the bottle in Mom's hand, "Gracie, I know you've been avoiding me because you felt such agony since I told you that I was sick. Cancer is not pretty. Chemo's effects aren't pretty. I've been a mess this whole winter! But, Gracie, even if my body weren't turning around and healing, I'd want to see you and talk with you! Please, stay with me—with your eyes and in your heart!"

Gracie sniffed, and Mom handed her a tissue. "Mom," Gracie cried, I'm sorry, I'm so sorry. I hate myself for the lying and the sneaking, and … for getting drunk! I don't understand why … I mean, I'm only ten years old! What's wrong with me?"

Mom reached over, put her hand on Gracie's, and Gracie covered it with hers. Mom said, "You have experienced more pain in your young life than many people do in a lifetime! So far you have told me and Dad that when you and your brothers were on Lanthra, you were a prisoner, even a hostage in daily personal danger. You could have been raped. You could have been killed. You lost your brothers and were afraid they were dead. Oh—" Mom's voice broke off, then returned stronger, "When you all returned home from, ah, your adventures, life appeared to settle down. But, Gracie, all that fear and hurt lay inside of you. Then, at Thanksgiving time, you lost your brother Patrick—again! Your brother Lewis moved away with his new job … You and he were so close that I'm sure you felt abandoned. Trouble piled up on trouble. Because I got sick—with aggressive cancer no less—your system had more than it could handle."

Gracie cried out, "I should have been able to handle all that! After all, I believe in God. He stayed with me in Lanthra; and he got me back home. Why should I have become an ..." her voice fell at the gravity of the words, "... a stupid alcoholic!"

Mom hugged her. "Gracie, you did have God with you through everything. But some things are too big to stay 'between just you and God.' You needed to talk; you needed people you trust to help you manage your grief. I wish that as soon as I got sick Dad and I had started going to counseling with you. We could have *all* gone for help."

Gracie wept again, tears streaming down her cheeks, nose running, eyes puffing. Kneeling before her rocker, Mom held Gracie and stroked her hair. "Gracie, I ask you not to do one thing: I ask you not to *should* on yourself. Nobody needs that."

Despite herself, Gracie laughed. Comparing "should" to, *ahem,* "poop" completely described the feeling she had when she used that word on herself. But her laughter choked into a new thought. "But, Mom, how can I quit *shoulding* on myself? I've been a ... a big liar. And, if I love God, I'm supposed to try to be good?"

Mom answered, "Gracie, you've brought up a complicated question. The *rules* say we *should* be good in all our ways. But the world isn't the same as it was when God created it. It's messed up because of what English-speaking people call 'sin.' That's an ancient reference to archery ..."

"Huh? I don't get that. Sin is related to archery?"

Mom nodded. "Our life—our bow—is defective. Bent. Crooked. And we keep missing the target. Some of our arrows are even dangerous to others."

At Gracie's blank look, Mom sighed. "I could go into deep detail. But right now, the doctrine about 'sin' is too much to take in. Just remember that people are not and cannot be perfect without God's help. Jesus came and died on the cross to 'save us from our sin.' He is our help."

Mom took a deep breath, and Gracie knew that she wanted to try to explain the whole God-package. The part about the defective bow didn't sink into Gracie's mind very well, but she knew about Jesus. He was a good man and also a good God. *All right,* Gracie thought, *I believe in Jesus. But I don't know what he can do to help us.*

Mom went on, "Remember that Jesus didn't stay dead. He is resurrected from the dead. He's alive, Gracie! And his Easter new life has already started inside of us."

"Okay," Gracie mumbled. The intense God-stuff was about to overwhelm the rest of her ragged emotions. "But I still do bad things."

Mom kept talking. "Rules can't help you. The ruined bow is just that bad—you have to become a brand-new instrument. But God's loving Spirit can build us from the inside out. Gracie, you have the Holy Spirit. Trust him. And …" Mom emphasized every next word, "*Don't* forget to *talk* about what's going on inside to trustworthy others!"

By then Gracie could take in no more God-talk. She knew that Mom must have sensed it, because with a final hug, Mom got up and headed for the kitchen to fix supper.

While drawers opened and pots clattered in the kitchen, Gracie still rocked gently in her rocking chair. Her body felt exhausted, like she'd been on a long run. She didn't understand all the thoughts and ideas that had piled into her mind while Mom talked to her. But, at the same time, like Gracie had finished a good run her body glowed inside.

Gracie waited a while in the living room and listened to Mom's cooking noises. It would be dark outside by the time Mom and Dad, and she finished supper, but now a shaft of light poured in through the big window and made a glowing pattern on the wall. The pattern was shaped like a golden cross. With a big sigh and a deep cleansing breath, Gracie rose and went to help Mom in the kitchen.

CHAPTER 44:
FLIGHT

Deirdre got off the bus at the stop and walked briskly toward her apartment, her open coat swinging with her steady stride despite the winter cold. Today had been a triumph. The Lanthran strategy of guiding her students to learn each at each individual's level in the class showed success; it kept all the students too busy to misbehave. The least adept student, a big boy who had been ferociously truculent at first, had even begun to smile and hum as he wrote his little action-figure illustrated essays. *He might yet grow up to be the next Stephen Spielberg,* she thought.

A dark gray Volvo drove up and parked as she approached her front door. At the top of the steps, about to tap in the door code, Deirdre tensed and turned to see who had arrived. *Peggy? The Horned Edge?*

The Volvo's back door opened. A tall, dark, and handsome figure unfolded his long legs from the back seat and got out of the car.

Deirdre's heart glowed with pure joy. "Lewis!" she shouted.

Lewis ran toward her and wrapped his arms around her.

"I'm so glad, I'm *so* glad that you are back!"

His lips met hers in a tender kiss. "Deirdre," he said softly, "We have to go. Today! We have to go today! The Horned Edge will hurt you to get to me."

A lead weight sank in Deirdre's chest. "But my students ..." She thought of their progress, their smiles. Who would take her place? Would they be able to follow her lesson plans? Would they treat those rowdy kids with kindness?

"I know," Lewis told her, touching her cheek. She felt a

teardrop roll down her skin, and he brushed it away. "You love your students. But you will not be able to help anyone if the Horned Edge kidnap or kill you."

"But—

"Please, Deirdre, make the arrangements today! Tell the school you have a family emergency—because we do have an emergency! You pack. I'll call a taxi and we'll get to the airport."

Deirdre nodded. Holding hands, they climbed the steps to her building. She tapped the keyless entry and the door lock whirred as it opened. Once they entered, she turned and kissed him again, her entire body surging with warmth.

* * *

They hurried up three flights of stairs. Deirdre's apartment door also had a keyless entry, and very quickly they filed inside. Sunlight beamed through the big south window facing the street. Deirdre glanced at her plants, already planning her ... flight, their fleeing escape! The yellow roses from Lewis had begun to droop. Those she could let go of in the trash. But the little cactus and the gorgeous red amaryllis would have to be given away. She had a neighbor who would take care of them. Now ... *Stick to your main priority—make the call.*

Letting Lewis take over the kitchen for his phoned arrangements, Deirdre made for her bedroom. Sitting on her yellow quilt, she called her school. "I can't come in tomorrow," she told the secretary. "But let me speak to the principal."

Fortunately, the principal could come to the call. Deirdre told her succinctly what she had to do. "A serious family emergency has come up, and I will have to leave my job right away."

Dodging the woman's questions, Deirdre went on, not letting her urgent desperation seep into her voice. "You have my lesson plan for the rest of the school term. You have been very supportive of my innovations. I'm so sorry that I cannot finish with my students. Please be sure to tell them that I love them." Trying to keep from trembling—and having her voice tremble, she let the principal talk for a second. Then she interrupted, "Now I must go. Thank you for all you do!"

By the time Deirdre broke off the call, Lewis had called for a taxi to arrive in thirty minutes. Plus, he emailed her the details of their flight to Texas. Their escape plan was set.

Deirdre and Lewis held hands longingly. Her body yearned for him, for his caresses. "Not yet," she sighed and looked away.

"Deirdre," Lewis broke in, "I have a question for you."

"Okay." Her breath caught when she noticed that eyes sparkled—with tears!

Lewis lowered himself to one knee. "Will you marry me?" From his jacket pocket he drew out a small box. "I know that you and I are in a hurry, but—when we get to our destination, I know a church …"

Deirdre's hands flew to her mouth as her heart leaped. "Oh, my love, yes! Yes, I will marry you!"

Lewis opened the box and took out a simple ring with a flashing diamond in a yellow gold setting. The ring pleased her at first sight. Lewis put it on her left ring finger. It was a perfect fit. Leaning into Lewis's arms, Deirdre kissed him on the mouth. "I have always loved you, yet my love grows with each day! *Ra pasa, plit, poth, boonua-oya!*"

Lewis smiled. "*Lu Noreth e Lanthra, boonua-oya!*" His baritone resonated in her small apartment like a smooth cello.

Finally, he let go of her. "Grab some clothes. Our taxi will take us directly to the airport." His voice became urgent. "Do you have all the information, including the address of where we're going? And Dr. Zhartha's phone number?"

Deirdre checked. She did.

Going around her apartment and gathering this and that, she called to Lewis, "Please put the plants in front of room 307!"

She saw Lewis's smile flash again. "You do love your plants," he teased.

*   *   *

Lewis carried Deirdre's blue suitcase as he and she trotted down the stairs of the three floors to the front entrance. He spotted their taxi waiting at the curb, and it was the vehicle he had ordered. Its license plate matched the texted number. *Good,* he thought. *We're ahead of the enemy.*

He and Deirdre hurried out of the apartment building toward the car. Even in his hurry, Lewis checked the license plate again while the driver opened the tailgate and helped with the suitcase. Lewis made sure that Deirdre got in first, and then he sped around to the other passenger side door.

Just as he reached for the handle, something grabbed him. Something strong; something inexorable, a giant set of invisible pliers. Shocked, Lewis cried out, *"No!"* But a heavy curtain brushed against his skin, a blinding light flashed, and he fell.

CHAPTER 45:
NARK TRACKS LEWIS

Lewis found himself sprawled face down on a cold floor, a tiled mosaic floor, with an obscene image leering at him. The cold penetrated his clothes, his skin, his deep muscles, his face and hands. He shook with it. Above him, a deep, rough voice growled, "I hate you, Lewis. You murdered my brother Barth and drove me from my home. Now 'tis your turn to suffer."

Lewis heard the familiar accent and knew: *Oh great. I'm on Lanthra again! With Nargoleh Layhew!* He summoned courage and, before turning to look up at Nark's ugly face, retorted, "I did *not* murder your brother! And, not I, but the people you oppressed drove you from your home."

Nark's booted foot nudged him in the side. "Get up, *Fean.*"

Exhaling, Lewis pushed himself to his hands and knees, then managed to stand up. Before facing Nark, he recognized the place: It was the same hideous locating chamber where he'd been kidnapped with Patrick by Blue thugs that November day. Ancient frescoes ornamented the walls and ceiling. Their brilliant colors showed contorted, horrid faces of various demonic deities like Mayan gods.

Looking away from the frightening frescoes, Lewis glared at the same two muscular Blue thugs who had kidnapped him and Patrick before. The Blues stuck out their long, long red tongues and mocked him in sign language. Coming forward, invading his body space, they bound his hands behind his back.

Not far away gathered a murder of cordovan-robed magi. Lewis saw that their sleeves dangled and flashed indigo linings. *Swethans!* Their hands displayed gold rings with black diamonds—*Horned Edge magi*. One of them, a short man with a flat, squashed nose, stood at the control console, smirking. *The new location expert?*

To his left, Lewis saw a white grand piano. *Patrick has been here.* His heart lifted. *Maybe I can find and rescue him!*

However, to his right, Lewis saw what he did not want to see: *Nargoleh Layhew.* Even though Lewis stood tall, Nark towered over him. The man wore a crown, a massive gold and purple velvet puff with a large gold star at the top. The star had five needle-sharp points. *King Nark,* Lewis groaned to himself. *A Horned Edge ruler and a worshipper of Saoma.*

The man's greasy, wiry black hair cascaded down his back and a great beard surged out of his face. Nark's full lips looked too, too red, as if he wore lipstick. And in a trick of the light, Nark's deep-set dark eyes glowed red with demonic brilliance.

Lewis's stomach cowered, but he straightened in the grip of the Blue thugs, took a deep breath and whispered, "God, help me!"

He expected immediate calm strength; instead, he stood wrapped in fear. A shot of despair drilled into Lewis's mind. *Will he torture you? Will he humiliate you and finally kill you?*

Yes, Nark might torture and kill me, Lewis realized. *In fact, he probably will—he's so vindictive!* Lewis could see spittle drooling down the man's dirty black beard—Nark literally salivated with the anticipation of inflicting a painful revenge. Lewis knew that Nark's favorite torture was to skin his victims from the waist down and let them die slowly. If Nark flayed him, Lewis knew that he would certainly scream and plead for mercy, that he'd feel all of the pain.

Protect yourself! You are too important to lose! stressed an inner voice.

A way out of his situation sped through Lewis's mind. The first time he had ever encountered Nark, the man was the Baron of Torgard. Lewis had felt as small as a hobbit before a big orc then, but he'd acted cold and brave. To protect his brother Patrick and sister Gracie, he had joined the enemy. *Don't let him torture you! Choose that strategy again!*

More impressions filled him all in an instant. Lewis felt a presence like Lord Charon, a loving admiring mentor. Lord Charon loved him. If he joined the Horned Edge again, Lewis would be okay. Charon's presence suggested, *That squashed-nose magus at the controls doesn't know half of what you know about the Lanthran system, dear Fean. Think of what you could do with it if you volunteered for Nark. You could defeat him from within! You could be a major force for good!*

Lewis considered the option: *Join the enemy. Pretend to work for them, but actually you'll be one of the good guys.*

Again, Lord Charon spoke to him from within. *Why let that filthy Goliath torture you? No. Come with me.*

But a different thought slipped into his heart: *Don't repeat a bad decision. You do not have to join anyone to save yourself and your family. Never again live in fear. I am with you.*

Lewis shook his head to clear out all the voices. He had to choose. And he had to choose a Right Thing now! *I can't live in fear anymore, either fear for myself or, worse, fear for my family. Whatever happens, I will just be myself, on the God-side of the Abyss.*

Lewis calmed. His knees which had been melting strengthened. The small voice again edged through his consciousness, *I have a purpose for you. You will know it when the time comes.*

Will I die? Will I be tortured?

He knew of no promise that he wouldn't suffer. But he did have the promise that he'd be loved and helped through anything—through *anything!*

Time moved again. Nark ordered with a blast of sour breath, "Take him to the *abagib*." As the Blue People dragged him out of the locating chamber and the Horned Edge magi snickered, Lewis resigned himself to a violent, painful death. He thought about his loved ones: *On Earth, Deirdre is safe with Dr. Zhartha. Gracie is safe, too, with Dad and Mom. But what about Patrick? Is he here?*

Lewis knew he couldn't help his family. He couldn't control what might happen to them. He couldn't even control what would happen to himself. Control was not an option.

*   *   *

The Blue People locked Lewis in the *abagib*. It had been a new Lanthran word, and he had thought it meant a torture chamber or a cell. But now he knew exactly what it meant: a closet. Not just any closet, but a bedroom closet. And not just any bedroom,

239

but Nark's own personal quarters. *What in the world does Nark intend to do to me?* Terrible possibilities made him squirm inside the stifling space that was filled with Nark's rancid-smelling clothes. Plus, there was an even fouler odor, as if other people had been locked in this ... *abagib!* Claustrophobia had only slightly bothered him in elevators and small spaces, but now he was sealed in a stinking upright coffin.

Will I have a seizure in here? No, I'm not that lucky. Lewis kicked the door over and over. The door didn't budge. The cords on his hands behind his back tightened so much that his hands were numb.

Leaning against the closet wall, Lewis began to weep. He made no noise, but huge tears rolled down his cheeks. His greatest fear had come upon him. *Is this an oubliette where I will rot away, deliberately forgotten? Where are you, God?*

Lewis again considered joining Nark. *If I cater to Nark, I could find Patrick! I could get my brother out of this awful place—even if it kills me!* Lewis felt certain that he could bargain with Nark, probably work his way into a position of power so that he wouldn't be flayed. But something in Lewis's deep self knew that, if he used Nark to save himself, trouble much bigger than he now faced would burst upon the universe. Patrick might be saved. Lewis's own life might be spared, but ... all of Lanthra would fall. And Earth would not escape the trouble. It, too, would become subject to the cruel, *Saoma*-worshipping Horned Edge. Plus, he knew that other worlds would fall, innocent worlds that had never yet suffered the devil's power. Making himself relax as much as possible, Lewis quit struggling. An empty mind felt much, much better than one trying to figure everything out.

*   *   *

The closet door flew open. Nark's huge, dark form filled Lewis eyes. Startled, he cried out. Rough hands jerked him into Nark's bedroom.

Nark slapped him. "Steady up."

And Lewis steadied. *I'm out of the closet, the claustrophobic closet.*

"Come with me." Nark pulled him by the arm out of the bedroom and through the corridor. The motion of walking in the open space penetrated his thick cloud of fear so that Lewis breathed deeply and regularly.

He and Nark stopped in the locating chamber. They were alone. But the technician or someone had already made a connection between far coordinates in space: The monitor glowed with innumerable galaxies. The dazzles of stars pierced Lewis's fear. *Stars ... infinitely scattered through the universe, and intelligently designed by ...*

An old song welled up from deep inside from music he'd heard at his parents' church. Words with the old Shaker tune came:

> *I danced in the morning*
> *When the world was begun,*
> *And I danced in the moon*
> *And the stars and the sun, ...*

Could he identify that song? *Yes, "The Lord of the Dance."* Who danced in the song? *Jesus.*

The words warmed Lewis's heart as Nark took him toward the cabinet by the control panel and pulled out a marble. "Here is the *noretha* you must use. *Pigolanor.* You will connect to Earth. Then you will do what I tell you."

"You will have to untie me," Lewis said. To himself he breathed the comforting words that he'd heard during that bright moment on Christmas Eve, "Jesus. God of God, Light of Light, Very God of Very God."

But Nark heard his murmur. "Yeh-suss," he echoed. Like a typical Lanthran, he could not pronounce a "j," and like the unique Nargoleh Layhew, his final "s" was sibilant. Nark cocked his head as if he'd heard a familiar word. Then he shouted, "*Radyah!*"

Memories flooded back to Lewis from his first encounter with Nark in the baron's fortress, Torgard. He had been exhausted and terrified, but he had also been defiant and proud. He'd even bragged about his scientific skills, saying: "I can design weapons of war that you've never heard of! Just imagine a nuclear bomb detonating in the bowels of your fortress, the rock vaporizing, this mountain melting for miles into the bedrock, and your atoms scattering into the thick, poisonous mushroom cloud!"

At the time, he'd sounded brilliant, capable, ruthless. Now

his old pride made Lewis sick to his stomach.

A worse memory came up like bad gas. When Nark asked about *bizeor,* demons, Lewis had replied, his voice snarky, "Perhaps there are spiritual beings, but science cannot find evidence of those." When Nark had questioned him repeatedly about God, Lewis had considered himself such a very smart atheist who so scorned an impotent supernatural force labelled as "god" that he had refused to tell him anything.

Lewis's pride caved in. He despised his old arrogance. *I've been such an intellectual snob! How much suffering could have been prevented if I had just told this man about Christianity, if I had just been willing to satisfy his secret burning desire?*

Nark freed Lewis's hands. Obeying his captor, Lewis took *Pigolanor,* the little piggy, the marble that had the spatial coordinates to Earth, and inserted it into the control panel. He adjusted the controls so that Earth's beautiful blue horizon grew close, but he didn't connect fully because the coordinates were set out in space where there was no air. "What do you want to see?" he asked Nark.

The huge pirate king insisted, "Go close. Go to a ... a *radath.*"

Lewis mentally translated, *A radath is a body of Christians.* Alarm bells rang in his head, and he blurted, "What do you want to do to them?"

Nark only thundered, "Now!"

His hand shaking, Lewis reset the control to the locating system so that it still connected to Earth, but only by a quantum brane dimension; nothing could pass through. The monitor went dark.

Nark gasped, "Nooo!" His arm raised to strike Lewis.

"Wait!" Lewis commanded, and to his surprise, Nark's fist relaxed. The glaring eyes narrowed, and Nark stood before him, listening.

"Earth is the Planet of the Curse," Lewis stated, "the headquarters of the demons who serve *Saoma.* I could find a Christian gathering for you, even pick up a broadcast worship service for you to watch. But that might not help you. Christians aren't perfect—they may even offend you. Plus, the bezubs would certainly interfere. Instead, let me *tell* you about Jesus, *Radyah,*

Earth's Treasure!"

"Tell me," Nark panted, drooling into his beard, "or I will strip your skin now."

Lewis didn't doubt it. Nark was unstable, close to insane. "First of all, God the Father, *Ba-on*, exists, and he loves all the things he made. That includes you! Nargoleh, you and I are both twisted people, full of pride and murder. People hate us, and we hate them. Yet God sent *Radhegoyah*, his son, to Earth to rescue us from *Saoma*—and from our own malice."

Nargoleh stood before him, long arms dangling, his breath sour and heavy. But he listened.

Lewis could feel his heart strengthen as he went on, "Evil people killed Jesus on Earth. But, because he is God, he made that death a sacrifice for sin. *You* understand sacrifice. You sacrifice Blue People to please demons so that they won't hurt you and so that you might have good luck. But God doesn't need sacrifices of animals or Blue People or any kind of people to help us; he sacrificed *himself!*"

Nark growled, "Then *Radyah* is dead. There is no hope." His face darkened. He seemed to swell, and the glowering deep red demonic light returned to his eyes.

Lewis shouted, "He is *not* dead! Jesus is God! He didn't stay dead; he came back to life on the third day. He is *labath,* alive! Oh, please trust me; I don't have time to tell the whole story from the nativity to Pentecost. Just believe me: *Radyah* is Jesus, and he is alive, never to die again. He loves you. He rescued you from your own death, promising a resurrection of your body. Trust these words!"

The locating chamber rang with Lewis's urgent voice. However, the vibration ceased. The air became heavy and stale, and Nark's rank odor grew even more powerful. *He doesn't believe me.* The grotesque chamber filled with the presence of bezubs, mocking, threatening.

Nargoleh retrieved the cord. He reached for Lewis, and Lewis cringed. He knew that the ruler might bind him again and order his torture and death. "Whether by your hand or not, you murdered my brother," Nark stated, and Lewis's stomach sank. But, as he backed away from the pirate king, the small voice that had often guided him said, *Even if he kills you, trust me, Lewis.*

Nark grabbed Lewis's arm. But instead of tying Lewis, the man wrapped the cord around both of their wrists to loosely bind them together. His deep-set eyes glinted into Lewis's and his red, full lips smiled. "We belong to *Radyah* now. You and I are brothers."

Shocked, Lewis saw a radiance glow on Nargoleh's face. The pirate king's voice boomed, those beady eyes shining, "I will call off the invasion. I will help Bardia, and I will—"

A flash of silver crossed the chamber, and Nargoleh screamed. He stumbled forward onto his knees, pulling Lewis down, too.

Lewis saw a long shaft of a spear in the man's broad back. "No!" he shouted.

CHAPTER 46:
SAILING TO BARDIA

The evening after their floating haven *Westwind* sailed, Patrick and Christopher Reynolds ventured from their cabin and climbed topside. As soon as the bosun saw the prince, he told him, "Come up on the quarterdeck. Captain Lu asks to talk with you." The prince left with the bosun; Patrick stepped to the port rail and watched the gorgeous Lanthran sunset. Small, rosy-fingered clouds floated low on the horizon. Gradually the light morphed from bright pink to optic pink with glowing streaks of orange. After everything that had happened since last night, Chris's rescue, their terrifying swim across the Thesare Bay, and holing up in the Bardian embassy while Nark's people swarmed to recapture them, Patrick felt physically battered, and worse, worn out and mentally bruised.

Another person stood at the rail and admired the sunset. The boy had short, thick auburn hair. He appeared to be about fifteen, short and slender.

Patrick and the other exchanged a glance; the boy came over to talk with him, graceful as a dancer. "Hi, I'm Miriam," he said— no, *she* said.

Immediately, Patrick felt his whole body flush. *Wow! She is so beautiful!* He stuttered, "G … glad to meet you, M … Miriam." The stuttering made him choke, so that he had a coughing fit.

She waited for him to control his cough, and then asked, "Are you all right?"

"Well, I just got … I just thought … er, I'm okay." He couldn't tell her how amazing she was. "I'm kind of all right. I've had a rough time lately, but I'm so glad …"

"I've had a long story, too." Her hand touched his arm.

Patrick felt himself quiver; he felt physically excited. *Oh wow. This is love at first sight! But she's older ... but maybe she could like me.*

Miriam smiled. "Just call me Mim. What is your name?" She had the relaxed grace of a girl who was comfortable with herself, and Patrick admired her all the more.

"Uh," he said, "I'm Patrick."

Her eyes widened. "That's not a Lanthran name! *Pa-triss,* you are from Earth!"

A quick thought assailed Patrick. *Yes, I'm from the world of the Curse.* Taking a deep breath, he admitted, "Yes, I'm from Earth. But that's a long story."

"You're from the world of the Treasure!" Mim exclaimed, and her eyes shone with admiration.

To call attention away from himself, Patrick gestured toward the quarterdeck. "I'm with Prince Christopher Reynolds. He and I escaped from King Nark. We made it to the Bardian embassy, and Captain Lu hid us on this ship. He'll take the prince back to Bardia to be king."

To his surprise, Mim's eyes went wide, her mouth fell open, and she leaped up straight. "My brother Chris! He's alive!"

Patrick swiveled until he could see Chris and the captain deep in conversation. "He's your *brother?*" How did *you* happen to be here?"

Miriam poised like she wanted to dart up to the quarterdeck, but just then her brother and Captain Lu disappeared from view. Tapping her foot, she told Patrick, "All right. My name is Miriam of the Reynolds family. I am the daughter of King Norhe. And, after his murder, I ran away from home."

"Wow." Patrick knew he was smitten. The way she carried herself, the way she talked with her lilting Lanthran accent ...

The sunset faded quickly. On the ocean's surface still glimmered shades of pink, then those turned dark. Overhead, along with a few bright stars, Patrick could see two moons, one a coppery disc, another shining white like a large star. He and Mim stood face-to-face in the gathering dark. Afraid to admit his strong, mixed-up emotions, he poked at hers. "Tell me how you got here."

He could no longer see her expression as she told him, "Everything began when my brother went on a voyage to Eleaemana and his ship disappeared." Patrick watched her petite outline on the forecastle lamp. She had a nice figure. Mim's voice sounded flat in the humid darkness. "Everyone—except me— thought Chris had drowned after his ship was seized by pirates."

"I'm sorry to hear that." Patrick thought of his own brother, Lewis. An ache hollowed his chest, and he swallowed back a lump in his throat. "But why did—?"

"I run away? There's more to the story." Mim paused. "Right after Chris was lost, my father King Norhe died suddenly. They said it was a heart attack." She swallowed, as if choking down her grief. "During his funeral, I walked behind the casket with my mother, with all the mourners of the kingdom staring, and my heart was eaten up with rage … because I knew Dad had been murdered!" Mim paused.

Patrick had no answer. He could imagine what it would feel like if he lost his dad, and his heart went out to Mim. In the lantern light and in the brightening moonlight, he could see her profile. A tear glistened on her cheek.

Mim continued, "Besides all that, my mother got sick. Her hair became rough and her skin grayed. She could not keep down her food. Fearing death, she appointed a regent until I could come of age. The regent, Lord Sipes, made a lot of changes in a great hurry." Patrick picked up on the sharp edge to Mim's voice.

"What kind of changes?"

"For instance, he arranged to marry me. I'm only fifteen; I do not want to marry anybody yet, and I especially do not want to marry *him!*"

"So you ran away. Wow. But …" Patrick began to worry. "Won't he pursue you? I mean, if Lord Sipes is as you say and knows you ran away, won't he seize you when we get to Kingsport?"

Mim shivered. "That could happen. I dread to think of it."

Patrick wanted to hug her, comfort her. But he held back as she went on. Her voice grew stronger, "My brother is alive! We're going back to Bardia, and Chris will be king. The people love him. Brute Broton Sipes's mischief will *stop!*"

Meanwhile, light dazzled over the ocean from a rising third

moon. Patrick appreciated its great, pale opalescent orb. He saw Mim turn her face up toward its light, and there were no tears on it this time.

"*Noreth*," Mim said. "An omen of good to come. She is beautiful, and rarely seen."

Patrick thought, *Like you. You are beautiful ... and I hope I get to see you a lot!*

For a while their conversation stilled, and Patrick leaned on the rail beside the girl, staring at her rather than the moonlight that rippled on the water. For now, just for now, he captured the moment.

The moment ended when the bell chimed for the next watch. Patrick and Mim reluctantly drew back from the rail. "Time for us to get some sleep, Patrick," Mim said. "Day after tomorrow, we should arrive in Kingsport. And behind us is an invasion fleet. We will have to fight them."

"Yes." Patrick did not feel sleepy. He felt like his universe had shifted sideways. *I'm in love!*

Mim slipped away. But ... she hugged him first. His heart vibrating, Patrick descended the ladder to his hammock in the crew's quarters.

*   *   *

The next morning, sunlight sparkled on the ocean when Patrick again made his way to his spot by the ship's port rail. Mim had already come. "I'm so glad to see you!" he exclaimed.

"And I'm glad to see you," she answered. They chatted a while, making light small-talk, taking in the morning freshness. Then Mim dug into deeper conversation. "It's time for you to tell me your own story. What happened to bring you from Earth?"

Patrick stalled. "I'd rather hear about you." He waited, hoping that she would talk, and he could avoid reliving a lot of anguish. But Mim persisted, "Tell me your story, please." She stared at his tattoo, and he cringed.

I don't want to, Patrick balked, but a small urging countered his reluctance.

Do it. Tell her. Begin at the beginning, the nudge came.

"Okay. But I've gotta start at when the hot marble entered my life. I was a little kid, ten years old—Earth years. I'm thirteen now. Anyway, I saw a flash in the sky down the street, and my sister Gracie and I walked down and found a hot marble in the grass." He paused, memory washing over him. "It felt creepy in that field! I guess the marble had a bad spirit around it."

He glanced over at Mim. Sunlight glowed on her short red hair and showed some freckles on her cheeks. "Do you believe in evil spirits?"

"Yes. The *bizeor*."

Patrick shivered. "And all the trouble after that was my fault—I stole the marble before my brother could ..." *I let the bezubs tempt me,* he thought.

Mim waited for him to continue, so he swallowed his big wad of guilt and said, "It took me from Earth to your world. It took my brother Lewis, my little sister Gracie, and my brother's friend, Fred. And when I landed on Lanthra, something gave me a push and I fell. That's when I first injured my bum ankle. First I probably just sprained it, but later, after I was kidnapped and tried to run away, I fractured the same ankle."

"You were kidnapped? How horrible!"

Patrick turned toward Mim and saw that her eyes were wide. He was probably bug-eyed, too. Retelling his story felt like summarizing a horror movie. The events filed from one to the next in his mind, and fear and tension grew with each.

"They—the bad guys from the Horned Edge—were after my brother Lewis, but I was with him, so I got taken, too. And Lewis set it up so I could escape, but I botched it. I caught my ankle in a root and fell, and it broke. The skin was broken. I got an infection."

"Is that why you're limping now?"

"Yep." Patrick waved away the ankle business and quickly added, "I got treated by some doctors in Moorway. They helped me get rescued. But I was stupid." He gulped down a toad of self-loathing. "I went out on my own, got captured all over again, and ended up in Lord Charon's dungeon. Lewis was with me."

Mim exclaimed, "How can you tell that so calmly?"

Patrick shrugged. He didn't feel calm. Nope, he felt like a pot of water boiling under a tight lid.

"How did you escape?"

"The Bardians invaded Lord Charon's castle and rescued us in the nick of time."

"Thank *Radyah!*"

"Amen!" Patrick went on, desperate to wrap up the story and quit remembering what a turd he'd been, "We got back home to Earth, and life began to get normal—for a while."

"What happened after that?"

Although Patrick could still see the morning sun glittering on the ocean, clouds surged toward them from the west. A rising wind kicked up rowdy waves that hit the ship with big slaps. Patrick choked out: "Nark sent Blue thugs to kidnap my brother and me. My brother got away, but I didn't."

Suddenly Patrick's hand swept up to cover the ugly tattoo on his neck. "All right," he said, skipping the nasty part of his story, "I did get away, because I'm here now on this ship. And your brother Chris is safe."

"I'm glad you are here with me." Mim saw the tattoo—how could she not?—but she smiled and reached out for his hand.

Patrick wanted to touch her, to take her hand. But he just couldn't handle all the feelings hurtling inside right now. He turned away. "I'm going down to my quarters. See you later." He hurried below.

*   *   *

The whole rest of the day Patrick spent in misery. He tried not to cry because he thought the crew would laugh at him. But he snuffled and rocked back and forth, and sometimes he moaned. The big slave tattoo on his neck—he was stuck with that for the rest of his life! And he missed his family back on Earth. *Earth— the planet of the Curse. I'm cursed, too.*

Evening came. He wanted very much to see Mim before … before they had to fight Nark and the Swethan fleet. Shoving away his funk, Patrick got up. He made his way to *Westwind*'s bow rail.

Mim was already there. The lamp light showed her vixen face and glinted off her red hair. Just the sight of this girl made Patrick's heart beat faster.

"The moons glow orange tonight," she said. Patrick heard a catch in her voice and wondered why. She added, "Wega, is always orange, but Noreth and even bright Aine are on fire."

Patrick stared up into the night sky. He saw three orange moons and fish scale-like clouds coming up from the west. "Altocumulus clouds. Plus, the air is full of a lot of particles. That

250

filters the light and makes the moons' intense colors."

"I don't like it. This weather reminds me too much of war."

A gust of wind beat against Patrick's back as he turned toward her. It fluffed his thick dark hair and brought tears to his eyes. Despite the wind, however, the air felt hot.

"Move away!" shouted a sailor. He motioned for Patrick and Mim get out of the way so they could work. As the crew swarmed into the rigging to lower sails, one of the sailors called, "*Fomath-oon!*" His finger and his bushy beard pointed to the west. Patrick saw a long line of deep purple clouds, its edges glimmering as it began to cover Aine. The gusty wind powered up. Its shoves made the waves punch the ship hard. Patrick held on tightly to the rail.

"Terrible storm coming," Mim translated in English. She seemed so taut and frightened that Patrick's heart beat hard, and he put his arm around her.

"Let's go below," Patrick urged in English. She didn't resist.

The old-timer threw him a dirty look, then turned away with a hiss. "*Pigolanor.* The *bibat* speaks a tongue of the Planet of the Curse." He spat. Then he joined the crewmen, who hauled on ropes and managed the winches, their muscles rippling and straining.

Mim wasn't moving. Patrick repeated, "Let's go below."

But Mim seemed frozen.

Patrick wanted to yell at her and force her to find shelter, but he took a deep breath and said softly, "Dear princess, please come down with me."

Mim answered so low that he could hardly hear her over the wailing wind. "I'm afraid of drowning down there in the dark ..."

The crew finished taking down the stay sails. They began to heave out a big fabric parachute from the bow.

"Get off the deck!" a sailor yelled.

Big drops of rain splatted on Patrick's head. Suddenly, rain came down hard, pounding against him and Mim. A wave smacked the ship, forcing them to slide into the scuppers. Strong, gnarly hands gripped Patrick and pulled him upright. "Get thee below!" the bearded guy screamed.

Patrick grabbed Mim and fled through the hatch. A great

splash of sea water ran with them down the steps. They grabbed the handrail against the ship's rocking, then tottered through a wood-paneled passageway. Even there, water oozed under their feet.

She led him to her cabin; they rushed into the cramped little room.

"Stay with me," Mim pleaded, trembling. "I'm so scared."

Patrick slammed shut her cabin door, trying to balance against the ship's movements. They sat on her bunk. Just then, the little lamp went out. Dark enveloped them.

She whispered, "The storm reminds me too much of what's happened back home. I'm so scared that we'll die before we can set things right. And I'm afraid of what will happen if we fail. That Broton Sipes … What a slimeball!"

Mim shivered in her soaked clothes, but to Patrick she smelled like clean soap and a warm croissant.

I'm hugging a girl and loving it. Despite the noisy creaking, groaning, and heaving of the ship, although the air in the enclosed space made him sweaty, hot, and stifled, Patrick thrilled with pleasure.

The ship tossed and shuddered. Feelings of romance vanished. As time crept by, the ship's crashing and smashing became so violent that Patrick was afraid it might break up. He held Mim close in the dark, seeing only flashes of his circulation behind his eyes.

Boom! Thunder vibrated through *Westwind*'s thick timbers. Mim let out a piercing squeak and gripped him like an octopus. Suddenly, a great force rammed their floating haven, and *Westwind* rolled sideways. Further and further the ship tilted, until Patrick and Mim were smashed against the bulkhead.

Mim screamed, *"Radyah! Maradoyra!"*

Jammed into her, Patrick waited for The End: *Westwind* keeling over, sinking. He'd seen the old movie *Titanic.* He could imagine ice cold ocean water creeping under the door, filling up the cabin until …

The ship seemed to hover on its side. He and Mim screamed.

Then, with a great *groooan!* the ship righted. *Westwind* quieted and eased its rocking.

CHAPTER 47:
KINGSPORT

Westwind entered the mouth of the Winerush River in the next afternoon at the nineth hour. Making his way to the starboard bow of the weather deck to face the northern bank, Patrick joined Mim and Chris. Even now, although the storm had passed, the wind blew fresh and hard from the west so that they battled for every *wisto* as the ship tacked to make headway up the wide river.

The royal siblings and Patrick didn't talk much as they watched the occasional villages and wetlands recede. Gold and green marsh reeds covered the water at the banks, and flocks of white egrets stood in the water. Many of the birds flapped their wings and flew in great clouds. Gulls circled overhead, hoping for some trash. A long line of brown pelicans floated past, heading seaward. *Westwind* sailed under a high and blue sky studded with scattered puffs of clouds like cotton balls.

"It's so pretty now," Mim commented, breaking the silence. "But I'm still scared. We might fail, be captured, and …"

Patrick remembered vividly her fear of last night. Feeling tender toward Mim, he rested his hand on her shoulder. She snuggled into his arm.

"We have a respite before the battle, thank *Radyah!*" added Chris, turning toward them. "And we are not alone." He gestured, and they saw a dozen ships following them, their sails bright and full, their Bardian flags stiff in the driving wind. "More than that, we have the power of the *foroya*—God's angels—with us." His face alight with joy, Chris gazed into the distance as if he could actually see a host of angels following them.

Patrick examined the prince closely. His cheek bones stuck

out of a thin face, still very pale. There were dark circles under his eyes. His straight black hair had grown over his ears. But compared to how he had been while a captive in the lava cave—like a pallid ghoul … he looked powerful! Chris had great posture, and the way he lifted his chin—*We can do this!*—made Patrick's own stomach calm and his body straighten.

Captain Lu had provided them all with clothes worthy of the Bardian royal court. Instead of rags, Chris wore a fine white cotton shirt with a black leather vest, close-fitting dark gray trousers, and high, slim boots. The young man carried both a long, narrow sword and a stern knife in his belt.

Like her brother, Mim readied to challenge the usurping regent. Her red-haired, brown-eyed beauty was enhanced by a light pink, long shirt embroidered with small gold rosebuds over ivory pants. A feminine ivory pashmina wrapped her neck and shoulders. Mim, too, wore a short sword with a cloisonne pommel. Patrick thought with a rush of warm admiration, *All she needs is her tiara!* And she watched, not her brother, not the scurrying sailors on the *Westwind,* not the gathering Bardian fleet in the distance, but *him!*

Captain Lu and Chris had decided to present him as a young noble, the prince's personal attendant. They'd found a gray outfit with a white vest that set off his dark skin and hair. Patrick fingered the gold necklace that Captain Lu had given him—real, heavy gold. The captain had found a sword for him, too. He took the sword out of its sheath to examine it and imagined himself fending off parries, thrusting it past an opponent's defenses. The weapon was long and light, of bright steel. Patrick ran his finger along the sharp edge and saw a thin line of blood. Quickly, he sheathed the weapon and wiped the finger …

On his rather tight gray pants. A wave of self-hate rocked his mind, and he pulled at his belt. *I've gained so much weight since Nark caught me! Just call me Dough-Boy. I'm going to be useless. I don't deserve to be Chris's attendant. Mim will never love me. I'm short, I'm fat, all I know how to do is play the piano.* His hand—his plump hand—swept up to cover the black tattoo on his neck.

Chris caught his attention with a sharp gesture as if he knew exactly what Patrick was thinking. "You look noble—you *are* noble. Now … we need to go over our plans. *Westwind* will reach Kingsport in about an hour."

Patrick took a deep breath, and the miasma of self-doubt dissipated. "What do you want me to do?"

"Soon I will lay out our strategy for our whole effort to all our company—but, first, I want to encourage you. Patrick, you have been very brave. Do not worry about being a warrior! We will defend ourselves if we must, but I prefer that we depend on our guards to surround and support us: you, Mim, and me."

"But what if—"

"Patrick, your role is to be my companion. You have good eyes and ears. You have a bold heart. You are loyal. You just stay with me and go where I go. After all, you rescued me. I am forever your friend." His eyes sparkling, Chris grasped Patrick's hand and squeezed it.

Next Chris stopped a sailor and asked him to tell Captain Lu that he wanted to address all of *Westwind*'s crew, and even the Bardian fleet. The sailor hurried off, and Chris plus Mim and Patrick climbed up to the forecastle.

Captain Lu summoned the crew. He signaled the fleet. The Bardian ships neared, and each sent representatives to hear the prince. The crew assembled in ordered ranks; boats rowed or sailed toward the *Westwind,* which had been transformed into a flagship of the fleet. Soon, a large company crowded *Westwind's* deck.

Standing high on the quarterdeck with Chris, Mim, and Patrick, Captain Lu announced, "We have brought Prince Christopher Reynolds back to Bardia from captivity in the Laestes Isles."

The assembly cheered. Captain Lu continued, "One of our own lords betrayed him: Broton Sipes. We had thought the heir to be dead, and when the king died, we allowed Lord Broton Sipes to be designated as regent. But now the prince is safe with us, and we know that Lord Sipes is a traitor. In a few minutes we shall arrive at Kingsport. Let our prince tell us what we shall do."

A hush came over the ranks. Chris began in his carrying voice, "This ship, *Westwind,* will dock at the Royal dock. However, the rest of our ships will land at the main port docks. Immediately, you must contact the Criers Guild to do two things:

The Criers will proclaim our arrival to the whole city, and they will warn the Kingsport garrison of a large, imminent Horned Edge sea invasion."

A murmur rolled from the gathering. Captain Lu called their attention on the young prince, who continued, "*Westwind* will anchor at the royal dock. I and my company will go into the palace. I'll remove Lord Broton Sipes from the regency in front of many witnesses. The other ships will head to the port, and you will be armed and ready to fight. However, … only if necessary will we harm our own people!"

The crowd cheered again. When they quieted, the prince went on:

"By the time the Horned Edge fleet arrives—which I expect will be late this afternoon, the city will be ready to meet them. Be aware: The Horned Edge may have advanced weapons."

A great hush fell on the assembly. Patrick could almost hear them breathing, feel their sinking hearts, and see their fevered imaginations of the fighting: swords and knives and bows against guns.

Chris lifted his chin. "But we'll have the advanced technology, too! High Magus Daniel contacted me. He tells me that he has already sent a sizeable force with new Lanthran weapons. They'll arm you when we land. It may be that the Horned Edge will surrender without a fight when they see that we are ready for them. But maybe not. We will fight if we must." Chris paused. Patrick held his breath. Then Chris shouted, "But we shall win!"

Loud shouting and applauding filled the air, and some of the crew threw their caps. Patrick could sense their support of Chris, heir to the throne. After the hubbub calmed, Chris, Mim, and Patrick quickly descended to the main deck while Captain Lu distributed orders and the fleet leaders returned to their ships.

Patrick's imagination began to run wild. *Invasion. Battle. People are going to get hurt.* Before he dragged himself back into fear and doubt, Chris suddenly hugged him. The young man's strong arms circled Patrick's shoulders and squeezed. "Dear friend and rescuer, don't forget that we have our own edge on the Horned Edge!" Chris lowered his voice to private mode. "The High Magus Daniel spoke to me via—what would you call it?—

via the Lanthran portal before the storm."

The prince turned to Mim. "Remember your letter to Daniel?"

Mim's eyes widened. "Yes! Right about the time of Dad's funeral! I was desperate!"

"Yes," Chris said quietly. "We both were. Anyway, Daniel responded to your letter with action. As Captain Lu said, he'll meet the invasion with a large company of Bardian soldiers that have advanced Lanthran weapons as well as our own …" he smiled and touched his sword, "more primitive weapons."

Patrick blurted out, "How could Daniel talk to you across an ocean? This world has no satellites, no cables under the ocean, no wi-fi, no phones …"

Chris grinned. "Don't forget the *thoyo-on* at the College of the Magi. The Bardian magi can connect space and travel instantly better than the Horned Edge can. We'll have communication, weapons, and reinforcements."

Patrick remembered the Lanthran *thoyo-on,* the teleportation system from his previous journey to Lanthran. His heart surged with hope. *This might turn all right after all!*

*   *   *

When *Westwind* approached the Royal Dock, Patrick saw several dozen uniformed and heavily armed soldiers waiting for them. His mouth ran dry with adrenaline rising. *Will we have to start fighting right away just to get off the ship?*

"Will those soldiers try to arrest us?" Patrick asked Chris, who had a short moment alone with him and Mim while the crew prepared to anchor and tie up to the bollard.

"No," Chris answered. "Look, Patrick!" He pointed to the soldiers' uniforms. "Sipe's palace colors are gold and white. But these are brown. Can you see their oak-leaf and acorn insignia? They are Bardian special forces from the Nutman garrison of the Rockeerie Province." His face broke out into a smile. "See their salute!"

All of the soldiers raised their right hands. Their voices rang out, "Hail to Christopher Reynolds, prince of Bardia!"

Patrick followed the prince and Mim as they stepped down

the gangplank. Captain Lu and a phalanx of well-armed men flanked them before and behind. They strode down the long waterfront walk, through the rose garden, and past the gazebo. The roses were in full spring bloom, plump and gorgeous. Willows had been planted around the gazebo; the crabapple trees that lined the walk were bursting with pink blooms that waved in a light breeze. It was high noon, and the spring sunshine warmed Patrick from above.

Patrick tried to walk with proud composure, but he couldn't avoid limping. His ankle had begun to ache when he stood on the ship's deck; now it stabbed with pain. To keep from lagging behind, he gritted his teeth and walked faster.

Chris noticed. He slowed; the entire contingent of the armed forces matched the prince's stride, and that act of kindness made Patrick want to weep.

At first, there was no fighting. Some of the palace staff in their white and gold followed them along the walk to the palace entrance. So did beautifully dressed nobility. Many of the nobility projected hostility with crossed arms and sullen faces. One of them shouted an ugly curse: "Go back to the pirates, you little dictator!"

But then a group of women, possibly palace employees, waved scarves and cheered and sang, "Hail, Prince Christopher! Hail Princess Miriam! Welcome home!"

Chris saluted the crowd as he walked. Miriam waved. Patrick smiled and limped. As they neared the palace, the throng grew, both the sullen and the joyful.

The river walk ended in a stacked stone wall that fronted the palace. At the river-facing iron gate, the prince stopped. He called, "I am Prince Christopher, home to claim my kingdom."

White-and-gold uniformed guards amassed before and behind the barred gate, bearing swords and spears. Everyone stopped. Patrick held his breath.

Then Patrick heard Chris tell his guards quietly, "Lord Sipes has chosen to waste time until the invasion fleet can arrive. He plans that I will be caught between the invaders and himself. The Horned Edge wanted to set me up as a puppet to rule Bardia through me. But Sipes wants me killed so that he can stand as regent or even receive the crown from the Swethan Horned Edge."

His expression grew drawn and stern. "I'd begun to hope that we would not have to fight; that Lord Sipes would mutter to himself, back down, resign, and return to his southern province."

Chris turned to address the Regency-supporting palace guards. They stood as still as rocks, faces uncertain but weapons drawn.

"Lord Sipes is obsessed with the ruling position," Chris said in a very loud voice so that his guards, the Bardian company, the palace guards, and all the crowd could hear. "His ego will not let him be anything less than absolute ruler of Bardia, and Sipes is certain that the invasion will cement his power. He plans that the Horned Edge invaders will seize our capital, then our province, then our entire country."

The prince's supporters shouted. Those who supported Sipes snarled.

Suddenly Chris stepped in front of everyone to address the palace guards. "I do not want to fight you. Let the Horned Edge plan slaughter, not we Bardians who worship Radyah."

Most of the guards in front of the gate lowered their weapons. The guards behind the gate did not. Hot sun shone on them all; the Winerush River sparkled in the strong light, so that Patrick narrowed his eyes. Everyone stood frozen, and no one spoke for a long while. Chris needed support before he could breach the gate.

The prince stepped forward toward the gate. "Let us in," he ordered. "You know that I am the rightful king of Bardia." He held open hands toward the guards. Silence again thickened the air.

Suddenly Chris's retinue and all the people surrounded the prince. Patrick tensed and put his hand on his sword. But Chris waited, and suddenly they shouted, "Crown the son and heir of King Norhe! Crown the king of Bardia!"

Somebody in the crowd shouted, "Hang Broton Sipes!" Others took up the chant. The palace guards opened the gate, and people began to surge forward like a mob. Swords clashed; people cried out in fear and pain.

But Chris yelled, "Stop!"

To Patrick's amazement, the throng grew quiet. Chris ordered, "We will *not* hang Lord Sipes, or anyone else! Disarm anyone who opposes you, fight if you must, but let us proceed with order, not chaos. Our goal is peace, not slaughter!"

Loud cheering came from the crowd. In an ordered manner, Chris, Mim, Patrick, Captain Lu, and their company surged through the gate. Guards in the gold-and-white uniforms fell back. Some of Sipes's people threw down their swords and fled. Others began to fight. But Chris's supporters pressed forward. Patrick estimated that two-hundred or more people accompanied them as he limped, and the prince strode—still kindly keeping pace with him—from the gate into the gracious wide foyer that led to the main chambers.

The prince's crowd reached the ballroom's great double doors. This was the main event room of the Kingsport palace; here—when it was time—the coronation would take place. Chris and his large following entered. What a noise! People began shouting and screaming. Patrick wanted to cover his ears. He held his sword ready, but as yet the fighting had not yet reached him.

Captain Lu quietly advised the prince and Mim and Patrick, "Stand by the great fireplace and let your soldiers do the fighting." Then he left to help lead those loyal to the prince.

From his spot at the fireplace, Patrick saw that the grand ballroom was bright inside despite the milling people, with floor-to-ceiling windows overlooking the Winerush River. Gold and silver tapestries hung on the white stone walls. Arches on three sides opened into hallways that led into the other rooms and chambers of the palace. But Patrick's ears told him that violence was fierce in those hallways, with Lord Sipes's people pouring in, and the invading fleet would arrive soon. He fought down panic. *What good can I do here? And what will happen to me if we lose?* If the fighting reached their protected huddle and he and the others were captured ... or killed ... Patrick swallowed hard.

CHAPTER 48:
THE BATTLE FOR BARDIA

Mim, princess of Bardia, stood next to Patrick in the back of the big, bright palace ballroom with her sword drawn. She could see little of the action past the large Bardians who guarded them. Taking Patrick's warm hand, she forced a smile, although her body was as tense as a bowstring. She examined his grave round face with those magnificent brown eyes and loved him. "We're going to be all right; we'll win!" She didn't sound convincing, even to herself.

A deep pang of anxiety made Mim's hand tighten on the pommel until her knuckles turned white. If Lord Broton Sipes were to kill Chris, the heir to the Bardian throne, then their country was sunk; the Horned Edge would gain a strategic foothold on the world, and she ... Would she survive? Would she even want to survive? Or would creepy B.S. carry his loathsome plan of forcing her, all of fifteen years old, to marry him? The thought made her want to retch.

And what would the Horned Edge do to Patrick, who had just escaped them? Give him back to Nark?

Suddenly, Mim saw bright flashes, heard some sizzles and pops of weapons. Two of the guards who surrounded the royals collapsed. At her left, Chris exclaimed, "Lord Sipes has breached the royal supporters and he's close ..."

The clamor in the ballroom grew even louder. One of their guards thrust guns at Mim and Chris, saying, "The High

Magus has brought these new weapons. Use them!" The guard handed one to Patrick. Although at first Mim saw that Patrick tried to push the offered gun away, she was relieved when he accepted it.

Chris practiced firing into the fireplace behind them. At each well-aimed flash, a bit of rock evaporated. Then he told Mim and Patrick how to handle their guns. "Just point and press the trigger."

Mim got the method right away. But Patrick couldn't find the trigger. The Lanthran gun fit in the hand like a sword hilt with no sword. It was made of some type of ugly purplish gray plastic. "Chris," he said, "I'm afraid I'm going to shoot somebody!"

Chris said, "I'm afraid that's the goal. There, Patrick. That bump on the side is the trigger. Touch it when you aim—be careful!"

Patrick had pointed the little hole end of the gun at him.

Mim practiced three shots into the fireplace. The invisible rays punched holes in the walls and the fresh logs stacked on the hearth began to smoke. Flames shot up from the logs. Patrick shot once. A gaping hole appeared on the hearth. Mim heard Patrick mutter, "I can imagine what these guns would do to people!"

But Mim could, too. Their guns' blasts would sever arms, punch chests, obliterate heads. She gulped.

The action drew much closer, for the royal guards tightened their ranks around them. The invasion forces had joined Sipes's people, and their two-hundred odd supporters—who included civilians—were grossly outnumbered. Mim laid her sword down on the hearth and kept the gun. Fencing skills she'd learned growing up with Chris and Dad; the gun felt unfamiliar, and unpleasant, but it was definitely the more potent weapon. *Point and shoot. No skill needed to kill.*

The hostiles pressed deeper toward their position in the ballroom. Mim screamed when two of their guards fell, then three more. Only three more guards protected them. Then they, too, collapsed. The floor was covered with blood and body parts and the ballroom stank of death.

To Mim's utter disgust, flanked and fronted by his own gold-and-white uniformed guards, Lord Broton Sipes appeared. He wore scarlet clothes and fawn-colored tall boots to battle—ever the dandy—and he held a gun. The regent stared into her eyes. She saw the man's long, full lips curve up, his tongue touch his lips in a message of lust especially for her, and Mim shivered.

At Sipes's command, all of Sipe's guards turned their weapons toward Chris. Chris pointed his gun at Lord Sipes. So did Mim. Patrick stepped forward to join them.

The regent's party and Mim's trio aimed at each other, but no one fired … yet. Mim knew that to fire at Sipes would mean Chris's instant death. Patrick would die, too, and she herself might… A thrill of fear surged through her. She might survive.

"Surrender, or we kill the prince," Broton Sipes drawled. His stare roved over Mim again, then he waved his gun at Patrick and demanded, "Who is this boy?" His long teeth and red gums showed in a sneer. "Another heir? A forgotten brother?"

Holding her gun, Mim looked toward Patrick and caught his eye, hoping that he might receive her love and be comforted before the end. Lord Sipes noticed.

"Why, dear princess Miriam, I see he's your fat little boyfriend!"

Mim growled, "Yes!"

But to Mim's surprise, Patrick's expression was hard and cold. In a flat tone, he stated, "Lord Sipes, be gone, or I will kill you now."

Shielded behind one of his henchmen, Sipes laughed until tears ran down his cheeks. His guards, steadfastly aiming at Chris, laughed as well. Mim saw a wicked gleam in B.S.'s eyes. He stepped to one side and his gun whipped toward Patrick.

Without another word, Patrick tapped the trigger.

Sipe's head exploded. Mim and Chris shouted. The regent's guards remained; Mim was sure the traitors would kill them all.

But they didn't. Mim saw all of the battling soldiers turn toward one of the hallways, their faces white. Blue warriors sat down, unwilling to fight any more. Shouting as loud as a filled stadium, and a chant filled the hall: "The High Magus Daniel declares Christopher Reynolds to be king of Bardia!"

Guns and swords through the mob clattered to the ballroom's marble floor. The enemies surrendered immediately or they ran, trying to retreat to their ships. In only a few minutes, the ballroom was clear of the Horned Edge invaders. Mim breathed rapidly, as if she had sprinted fifty meters, but she recognized Captain Lu and Daniel the High Magus of Lanthra approaching and knew that the war was over.

"The good guys won," Patrick said. Now he smiled, and Mim embraced him. They stood together, her head nestled on his shoulder, his arms wrapped around her while Chris greeted his supporters.

CHAPTER 49:
THE CORONATION

A week later, the palace was clean again—or, in Patrick's mind, clear of blood and gore and basically put back together. But the palace was not clear of ghosts. Too many people on both sides had died. He could sense them, even picture their anguished spirits groaning invisibly in the walls. And ... he'd killed a man. Patrick felt as haunted as the palace, even as the victorious coronation of Prince Christopher Reynolds began.

Patrick stood with the Chris and Mim in the great palace courtyard, which was filled to overflowing with Bardian townspeople, robed magi, plus high-status visitors from Polunking and Smythe and even Eleaemana. He again was being treated like a member of the royal family, including the Queen Mother, Katharine. Mim had told Patrick about her mother's illness. He thought that the Queen Mother looked beautiful but thin, but according to Mim, "Mom is a million times better! Her face has color, her hair has luster, and she is active again!"

The crowd's murmuring filled the outdoor courtyard, and a gentle breeze from the Winerush River cooled Patrick's neck, The sun shone on luxuriously blooming flowers and green-leafed trees, glorious as the Garden of Eden. But Patrick saw the world through eyes full of darkness. Even the brilliant afternoon looked wavery or dim, as if there were a full solar eclipse.

While Patrick waited and shifted his weight away from his aching foot, staff with slow steps approached, bearing the royal crown on a velvet pillow. He saw that it was made of gold inlaid with many jewels. It looked heavy, but he figured Chris would look magnificent in it. Chris had treated him like a close friend and companion, so Patrick stood up straight with dignity despite the cloud in his brain.

The ceremony went on and on. Patrick listened to speeches and blessings and a very long prayer from a fervent young bishop. Finally, Chris knelt. Lanthra's High Magus Daniel, wearing a shimmering gold robe, lifted the crown from a small pillar next to the prince.

Now the high magus raised the crown high to show it to all the people. A solemn hush stilled the ballroom, and Daniel lowered the crown … into Patrick's hands.

Patrick nearly fainted with surprise. He took a slow, deep breath to master himself while his swirling head cleared. *Don't you dare drop the crown!* With reasonable precision, Patrick placed the crown onto Chris's head.

Chris stood. He lifted his arms in triumph. All the people shouted, "God bless the King!"

Mim hugged Patrick, eyes sparkling. Daniel smiled at him, even while he spoke a blessing over Chris. Patrick asked the high magus, "Why … why did you choose me to crown the king?"

Daniel replied, "Christopher specifically asked me to let you have that honor. Without you, none of this could have happened."

Mim leaned forward to kiss him, but suddenly Patrick felt funny, as if his brain were sliding down a greased slope. Mim's eyes widened; she began to say something and grasp him harder, but the world darkened, and Patrick could see nothing.

Suddenly a great light exploded around him. A thick velvet curtain brushed against his skin, and he slammed against a hard surface.

CHAPTER 50:
PATRICK FOUND

Patrick lay still for a long moment, breathing hard, still seeing the red and orange spots against his closed eyes. When he opened them, he saw darkness, but he felt as if he were in a large, open place. The air smelled damp. *Where am I?* Curling up like a threatened caterpillar, he began to panic. *Oh no! I'm back at that awful Isle of Mercy. What will Nark do to me? Cut off my hands, like he threatened to do?*

But no massive, clawed hand gripped his wrist. No evil voice mocked him. His ankle throbbed and swelled, but otherwise he seemed all right—just alone somewhere at night. Somewhere outside, high above the ground; someplace familiar.

Slowly, he straightened and pushed himself upright. His sight had adjusted so that he saw that he had landed on … Earth. He was safe on the walking and hiking path called the Skybridge—close to his home in Huntsville, Alabama!

"It sure wasn't Nark's system that brought me here," Patrick muttered to himself. "Then who brought me back to Earth?" He turned and searched the horizon to oriented himself. *Home is that way, toward the city lights. Oh, groan. Two mile's walk!* His ankle throbbed wickedly as he pressed onward. "Just eat this elephant one bite at a time."

When Patrick got to the place where Skybridge sailed over the busy Memorial Highway, he stopped to rest. Below him, despite the night hour, cars and trucks zoomed and roared up and down the highway's many lanes. "Not too far to go now," he sighed. "I've got this. Go, Patrick, go!" The vista lightened as the clouds overhead broke up; he saw Venus sparkling near the horizon. "I'll get home; I'll see Mom and Dad and Gracie." He imagined the surprise, the delighted hugs!

Then his stomach clenched and growled with hunger, and his imagination turned to food.

The food at Nark's table had been terrible: bland and greasy. The worst school cafeteria offered better food groups. Maybe, at home after all the greetings and before he fell into his comfy bed, he could eat a big peanut-butter-and-jelly sandwich, oozing with grape jam. And drink a big, sweaty glass of sweet tea. *No ... not sweet tea; it will keep me awake. Chocolate milk! Yum!*

The cloudy sky lightened even more, and the twinkling city lights dimmed. A wee-hour jogger and a pony-tailed lady walking three big dogs passed him. At last, Patrick came to the stairs that lead down from Skybridge to his neighborhood. He descended the steps, came to the street. Birds cheeped and twittered; a black cat sped across his path. "Home, just five more blocks!"

But he felt so very tired. "Four more blocks." The street seemed endless. He wanted to stop and sit on the sidewalk. *Well, go ahead and rest for a bit,* a little voice said in his head. Patrick shook his head. "No, no, no. I'm going home!"

Around the corner, and his street stretched down a curving slope. "It's my street! I'm getting there!"

Sunlight peeked down with long, slanty rays on green suburban lawns, and the trees were blowsy with fresh new leaves. A new spring had arrived in Huntsville on Earth just as Patrick had left a later spring in Kingsport on Lanthra.

One house across the street from where Patrick walked had a flower bed full of red and purple tulips. The driveways on his block sported lots of parked cars; a few on the road passed, probably going to work, as Patrick limped down the sidewalk along the asphalt street.

At last! He saw the two-story red brick and white siding suburban house where his family lived. Patrick limped up his driveway, onto the walk that led to his front door, up the step, between the holly sentinels, to the welcome mat before the front door. The sun had barely risen, but somebody should be up. Patrick pushed the button for the doorbell.

*   *   *

Gracie in her pink pajamas opened the door. Patrick saw her

face get so pale he thought she might faint. Suddenly, she hollered, "Mom, Dad, come here! It's Patrick!"

For that blessed moment, they were all home together. The hugs happened. So did the juicy peanut-butter sandwich and the chocolate milk, plus five chocolate chip cookies. Patrick's family gathered all around him in the living room, asking many, many questions. But Patrick almost nodded off in the middle of answering, "I landed back on Lanthra, and … well, this guy named Nark made me his slave. That's where I got the stupid tattoo …"

Patrick heard blood rushing in his ears. The lights dimmed. Between one breath and another, he felt himself falling over sideways on the sofa, and then it got very dark in his head. He knew he had fainted, but he wasn't quite unconscious.

"Call Dr. Miles and see if he'll meet us in the ER *asap!*" Patrick heard Dad say. The blood flowing in his brain seemed so very heavy.

Dad carried him out from the living room to the Tesla SUV. Patrick felt cool leather on his skin as he lay across the back seat. All jumped in the car. With slamming doors and a whirring motor, the Tesla bounded forward. It felt funny to listen to his ears ring and feel the slight bumping against his face as his family raced him to the hospital.

Patrick slept or blacked out during the ride, but awareness returned when Dad transferred him from the car to a wheelchair. That pesky ankle flamed, even though he wasn't walking on it. And he felt cold.

"He's shivering," Mom's voice said.

"I'll get the blanket," Gracie volunteered.

"We're here at the hospital," Dad told Patrick. "Dr. Miles is here."

The blanket's made him relax. Patrick let his head droop. "I'm so tired," he mumbled.

"We'll get through this! You're going to be okay."

A blood pressure cuff pumped around his arm. A thermometer brushed his forehead. He felt better, but he felt so heavy that he could hardly move; his eyes could see but couldn't focus worth a hoot.

"What's his blood pressure?" he heard Mom ask the nurse.

"It's 80/50," the reply came. "Pulse is 145."

Dr. Miles sat his long, slender frame in front of Patrick and used the stethoscope on his chest and back. He lightly examined Patrick's neck, "A tattoo! This kid is too young to have one—unless …"

Dad replied, "He told us that he was trafficked." Patrick was grateful that Dad didn't mention *Lanthra.*

More questions followed. Then he heard Dad say, "You can see how swollen his ankle is."

"Yes, the whole leg is swollen and red. There's a hard knot of pus over the malleolus." Patrick heard Dr. Miles sigh. "We need to get some x-rays of that ankle. And we'll have to inform the police, too."

Inwardly, Patrick groaned at all the fuss. Why couldn't he just stay at home? And the nosy police weren't going to be happy if he told them the literal truth: He'd been kidnapped, forced across the universe to another world, and enslaved by a nasty pirate king who had a grudge against his brother.

Plus, there was something even worse. While Patrick had played background music for Nark, he learned a lot too much about the Horned Edge's plans for Earth. His family was deep in a pile of trouble if word got out that he knew …

CHAPTER 51:
AN ANNOUNCEMENT

On Lanthra, Lewis's cry echoed through the Isle of Mercy's locating chamber. The obscene carvings of Saoma's evil gods leered down at him as the big body of Nark Layhew lay still. Lewis threw a profane gesture toward the carvings and knelt by the body, his wrist still secured to Nark's dead hand. "What have you done!" Lewis shouted. Fear evaporated and his heart burned with rage. "Whoever killed this man—your king!—show yourself!"

From a dark crevice in the locating chamber, a muscular Blue Person stepped forward. With his long scarlet tongue, he signed, *Wicked master is dead. You go home now.* The hairy *homo azure* unwrapped the cord that tied Lewis's wrist to Nargoleh's and threw it against the lurid wall.

Then Nargoleh shuddered on the chamber floor, and a thick trickle of blood sprang from the wound. A low growl of pain rumbled from deep in his throat.

Lewis wanted to help Nargoleh, to save his life. But before he could touch the speared man, the Blue Person yanked Lewis up to his feet and signed, *Go!*

Lewis resisted, pulling against the Blue's iron grip. "No! I've got to help Nargoleh. The man might die; but he might live!"

The Blue signed with his tongue, *You cannot help him. Go! The boy you seek is no longer here. He escaped!*

Stunned, Lewis froze. His heart beating wildly, Lewis let the Blue guard push him to the control console. He sighed. It horrified him to see Nark writhing where he lay, the spear's shaft sticking out of his side. But he willed himself to go. Lewis's finger brushed the console's surface, and the connection to Earth was completed. There was no time or way to search for a familiar place

...

Lewis walked to the obsidian monitor. He passed through the nexus, feeling the brush of the curtain of the brane. A great light flashed. His body felt a huge jerk, and Lewis found himself kneeling on Redeemer Church's red-carpeted altar area.

*   *   *

From the church in Newark, New Jersey, Lewis walked slowly on a sidewalk along the highway, reviewing his options. *How can I get home?* Nark had taken his phone, ID, even his handkerchief. Lewis searched his pockets. In his pants pocket he had a thin wad of cash. *After all, Nark couldn't spend U.S. dollars on Lanthra,* Lewis thought with a brief flash of humor. "What next?" he muttered. Because he'd been stuck in that awful *abagib,* he stank. "Okay, I'll buy new clothes. And, so, ... on to a Dollar Store."

A mile or more down the road, Lewis found a Family Dollar. After paying cash for a cheap long-sleeved t-shirt and a pair of sweatpants, he left the store and made his way to a Raceway gas station. He stripped in the bathroom, washed himself with soap and paper towels, and dressed in the new casuals. Gladly, he hurled his rancid *abagib* clothes in the trash.

Lewis had also bought a burner phone at the dollar store. His own iPhone was lost somewhere in Lanthra. *Probably a Swethan magus will try to reverse-engineer it,* he thought, at first with humor, but then he paused, troubled. *Once again, Earth technology can contaminate Lanthra. What if the Horned Edge got phones and the loyal Lanthrans didn't.* He took a deep breath and prayed, "God, I can't help Lanthra. I can't help Earth. What can I do?"

The answer came, *Trust me. I will use you.*

Pausing in the hospitality area of the Raceway station, Lewis tried to keep calm. He considered his next step. He wanted to see his family in Alabama, and he wanted to be with his fiancée Deirdre. Either option meant he would have to find a flight. *But how can I get home!* He had nearly exhausted his cash. He had no ID. He couldn't fly anywhere. It wasn't safe to thumb a ride.

"I've got one good option," Lewis said to himself. "Call Dad."

Standing to one side under the Raceway's eaves on a gum-spotted cement sidewalk while people headed in and out, Lewis phoned his father with the new burner phone. To his great relief, Dad picked up. He blurted, "Hi, it's me, Lewis!"

Dad's bass voice boomed out, "Lewis!" The noise of Gracie's background cheering burst through, and Lewis nearly yanked the phone from his ear.

Dad exclaimed, "Lewis! Lewis! Where are you? Wait—first, get this: Your brother Patrick is home. He's safe!"

If Lewis had dentures, they would have fallen out. "Dad … How? When?"

"He came to the front door this morning like the prodigal son in the story." Lewis heard bright joy in Dad's voice. "Oh, Lewis, he was so—!" Dad's voice broke off, and Mom got on the line.

She sounded strong, warm, not sick at all. "Lewis, not only are we all at home—but you have a guest here named Deirdre. She rang our doorbell and introduced herself just a few minutes ago! Oh, where are you, Lewis? Can you get home?"

"I need help. Right now I'm in Newark, about a thousand miles away. Is there any way that you could—"

"Yes!"

The spring sun warmed Lewis's face … and his soul. Suddenly, not only did he see gum stuck on the sidewalk and oil stains and cars trying to park, but he could see trees and bushes planted along the perimeter of the property and flocks of little birds pecking on the pavement. While Dad talked, Lewis grabbed the pen in his new nerd pack. Scribbling fast, he noted how to handle the cumbersome TSA process he would have to go through to fly home without his ID.

Dad added, "I'll send you money. Are you near a station that can send it?"

Looking at the front of the Raceway, Lewis saw the small sign. The store had—thanks be to God!—a Western Union station inside. "Dad, thank you so much!"

*   *   *

In less than an hour, Lewis got money through the Western Union services. Next, he took a cab to the library and checked his email on their computer. "Ah, wonderful!" Dad had emailed copies of his birth certificate plus several photographs of business envelopes addressed to him. Now he could face the inevitable questioning by TSA officials.

By early afternoon, apprehensive, trying to quiet his churning mind, Lewis made it to the airport. He consulted politely and at length with TSA people at multiple points along the airport algorithm. Finally … *finally!* … resting in a chair at his gate with a latte and a huge chocolate muffin, Lewis called home again. He heard his voice as raspy, but he *was* husky and raspy and tired. He told Dad, "The plane is delayed two hours because of weather between here and home—maybe more. I've got a boarding pass and I'm okay!"

But the flight was cancelled. So was the next one. "Hurry up and wait," Lewis muttered to himself. He changed gates several times, eventually found a spot on the carpet near the boarding area and slept.

*   *   *

It was mid-morning the next day when Lewis got out of the Lyft, strode up the front walk to his parents' brick two-story house, and stood between the red-berried holly bushes at their front door. With a quiet murmur of joy, he fingered the lush yellow begonia that Mom had bought to celebrate spring. Savoring every second, he raised his hand to ring the doorbell, leaned on the door—and toppled inside when Gracie yanked the door open.

"Lewis!" Gracie hugged him so hard that he gasped. "We're so glad to see you!"

"I'm glad to see *you!*" Lewis wrapped his long arms around his sister. Her auburn curls smelled sweet. He drew back a little to look into her hazel eyes. "Oh my God," he exclaimed, "I am *so* glad to be home!"

Mom hurried to the front hallway to join in the hugging. "Come on in," Mom said. She had gotten thin, and her curly sun-colored hair was a small corona on her head, but she looked healthier than he'd seen her since … since last year! "Sit down. And I'll bring you a drink."

"Wait—!" he began, but Mom bustled off to the kitchen.

Lewis plopped on the living room sofa. Gracie sat on the green, plush carpet at his feet, chattering. Mom brought him ice water. As he sipped, he enjoyed the morning light that streamed into the room and glowed on the Chinese-bone-white walls.

Light footsteps sounded down the stairs. "Lewis! I'm here—Deirdre!"

Lewis jumped up, sloshing ice water onto his lap. He could feel his smile about to crack his face in two when Deirdre's hugs and eager kisses engulfed him. Then she took his arm and led him back to the sofa. Her golden hair glowed as she sat next to him, her gray eyes sparkled, and her hands on his arm felt deliciously soft and warm.

Another set of steps clumped into the living room. "Patrick!" Lewis spilled the rest of his ice water and ran to his brother. Patrick was taller, more rounded than ever, and his skin had an unhealthy grayish hue under the brown. Although the boy smiled, Lewis saw an ugly black tattoo on his neck: An "N" wrapped with a nasty snake. By the squinch on Patrick's face, Lewis could see his brother's suffering; it wrenched his own gut. "Bro', I'm so sorry, so very sorry that happened to you."

"That's 'N' for Nark." Patrick stated, and the light left his face. "He made me his piano-boy." He lowered himself onto an armchair, swept his unkempt dark brown hair from his eyes. "It's a long story ..." Patrick's voice fell off. "But I don't feel like telling it right now. Here's The End: I got yanked back to Earth.

"But how?" Lewis exclaimed. "Who brought you home?"

Beside him Deirdre shifted and smiled. "Dr. Zhartha and I did. He built the system from your instructions. We had your DNA from the FBI database, and with that we were able to find Patrick on Lanthra."

"Yes," Patrick added. "But—"

"But we weren't accurate enough with location yet to focus him to this house," Deirdre broke in, a bit rueful. "He landed—"

"On the Skyline," Patrick finished.

Everyone started talking at once, then Lewis noticed who was *not* there."

"Where is Dad? Is he at work?"

"He was here at home working in the study," Mom said. She looked worried. "I wonder ..."

Just then Dad entered the living room, holding up his phone. His face was dark with anger. Lewis exclaimed, "What's going on?"

But Dad shot him a warning glance. Motioning them to keep quiet, he put the phone on speaker.

"Frank Brahmindura, I'd like to speak to Lewis," said a silky voice. "I know he is with you."

Lewis recognized that voice. He leaped up and grabbed Dad's phone. "Tahei Charon!" he shouted. "What in the world do you want from me?"

"I want *you,*" Charon told him. "I understand that you are with your family now."

Lewis wanted to throw the phone at the wall, to step on it and smash it—as if he were smashing Charon's face. *Will the Horned Edge ever leave me alone?* He took a deep, deep breath to control himself before he spoke to Charon again. "You gave orders for my execution! Did you change your mind?"

"I did *not* give orders for your death. We talked, and I had my people escort you out to go your own way."

"That's not how it appeared to me," Lewis seethed.

"Oh, I know about der Bund," Charon continued. "I've heard that they've recruited you. And I'm glad that they did—I appreciate their efforts for good, and I look forward to working with them. Their—and your—talents will enhance all our endeavors to help this sick world."

Lewis opened his mouth to protest, but Charon continued, "Dear *Fean* Lewis, you belong with us. You've heard of the Deep State? It exists, and it's worldwide. We are their opponent. No, there is no silly Illuminati. Yes, there are evil forces working in and under this world; we oppose the people who want to remake society in their amorphous image. The Horned Edge is the real power in this world, as it is on Lanthra, and we shall eventually have them under control. Imagine: The lands healed, violence subdued, countries at peace, God honored and worshipped. That's what we stand for. Don't fight us. Come to me. I can have someone pick you and Deirdre up from your family's house there in Huntsville."

For a moment Lewis could not speak. He listened to Charon's voice continuing through the phone. It was hypnotic, persuasive. An odd thought took over Lewis's mind. *If you embed yourself in the Horned Edge, if you join Charon to control the world's violence, you will save many, many lives. You may even be able to convert Charon himself!*

Now *that* was tempting. Lewis could picture his former mentor dedicated to God, all because of his influence.

Charon talked in that hypnotic smooth tone, "Der Bund resembles a creative but weak startup, too small to be effective. Overcoming war and violence needs a bigger venue, and the Horned Edge has the resources."

Lewis thought, *Maybe I could work for Charon after all. He wouldn't hurt my family, and I could sway him to do good.*

Suddenly, he realized that he, Lewis Brahmindura was just not that powerful. He was one guy, not God, and he could not control the Horned Edge. *What should I do? The Horned Edge seems to be everywhere! God, help me! I know who the real power behind the Horned Edge is: It's Saoma, Satan and his demons. I cannot fight them myself; no one can.*

He felt rather than heard the answer, *Charon, like his demonic lord, is a liar. Get on with your life as you planned. Leave Lord Charon and the Horned Edge to* Me*! I am quite able to manage the universe ... all of them.*

Lewis heard Charon pause. Then: "Lewis? Lewis? Are you there?"

Lewis shook himself to clear his head. He was no longer Charon's understudy, his laboratory leader, his pliant expert, and it was not up to him to save the world—make that the worlds, either. *That* job was already done. He told Charon, with a tinge of compassion, "Goodbye." *Click.* Lewis ended the call.

He surveyed his family. Everyone sat still, shocked. "Dad," Lewis said, "Please pray for us, right now. Charon—the guy that called—wants me to work for the Horned Edge, and I won't do it. But he may come after me again ... and he might threaten to hurt all of you."

Dad stood. "I know. I'm proud of you for your decision. But what can we do?"

Lewis emphasized, "We have to get out of here as soon as we can. I know some people who can help us. Then I ..." He reached out for Deirdre's soft, firm hand gripped it in his. "I want to make wedding arrangements."

CHAPTER 52:
WORKING TOGETHER FOR GOOD

That night, Patrick couldn't get comfortable even though he was safe at home and in his own comfy bed. His ankle throbbed and Dr. Miles had scheduled him to see an orthopedist in two days, but meanwhile he was loaded up with antibiotics. Dr. Miles had mentioned "osteomyelitis," and Patrick knew what that was: A bone infection. His private, frantic internet search mentioned extreme treatment: antibiotics, maybe surgery … *maybe even amputation.*

His head whirled a bit, and his skin burned with heat. *Why am I so hot? I had a shower. No more body stink. And the air con works fine.* Patrick rolled onto his side. He curled up, straightened out, thrust his legs over the side of the bed, moved them back to center. His brain craved sleep, but he couldn't. When he closed his eyes he imagined exploding airplanes. Plus … he was scared.

Lewis's clash with Lord Charon had stirred him up. *When will Charon try to force Lewis to work for him? And what will that man do to me and my family?* Patrick remembered being a prisoner with Lewis in Lord Charon's cave chamber. He recalled Charon's flat dark eyes like two bottomless pits … *Yech! Get a new thought.* But a worse thought popped up: *Suppose Nark makes another connection to Earth and captures me again? Would he skin me alive?*

Patrick squirmed on his bed, but the ugly thoughts wouldn't stop.

What would he do when he had to go back to school? He remembered the bully in his class, calling him the "N"-word and threatening to beat him up. School would eventually engulf him, with all the agony and constant humiliation from that big kid. *I hate me!* Perhaps he could just die first from the bone infection. Oblivion would be sweet because he was so disgusting, so worthless, so vile, so … fat.

As he lay in bed, Patrick's hand pushed aside his sweaty thick hair to touch the tattoo on his neck. It was a jet-black "N" to remind him permanently of being Nark's slave, with a nasty, coiling snake. *I'm only thirteen—and I have the ugliest tattoo in the world, right where everybody can see it. That bully in my class is going to point it out to everybody. Then after school he will beat me like a flabby football.*

Like lightning, a yearning for death shocked his brain. Obeying the compulsion, Patrick got up and stood at the window. There was a dead fly on the windowsill. He flicked the fly away, raised the window, removed the screen, and leaned out. The driveway surface lay two floors below. It would be a quick fall and a good, final smash at the end.

Pulling up a chair, Patrick began to ease himself through the window.

*   *   *

In her room, Gracie blinked awake. *What was that noise? Some kind 'a scrape. Not my room; the sound's from Patrick's room. Why'd he start pushing things around his room in the middle of the night? That pesky Patrick!*

Irritated, she listened, but the noise didn't repeat itself. Gracie nestled into her covers. Just as sleep blissfully cloaked her mind, *another* scrape woke her up. Instantly, she tensed. The strong thought came: *Patrick's doing something dangerous!*

Leaping out of bed, Gracie ran down the hall. *Thank God, he didn't lock his door!* She yanked it open and screamed. Patrick was halfway out the window!

"No! Don't!" Gracie yelled.

Patrick growled, "Get out of here, Gracie!" His arm and one leg were already outside.

Gracie ran and grabbed his leg, bawling, "Dad! Mom!" But Patrick kicked her away.

Dad came first. He flipped the light, ran forward, and wrapped his long arms around his son's torso. Patrick fought, kicking and hollering. He punched Dad's face!

Gracie imagined hideous bezubs howling and pushing her brother forward. "Patrick!" she cried again. His head and the other arm now hung out of the window.

Next, Mom, Deirdre, and Lewis stormed in and joined the tug of war. Finally, grappling and pulling, the family got Patrick back into his bedroom.

Dad and Lewis held him down until he quit struggling, then Gracie and Mom and Deirdre joined them. They breathed hard as if they had sprinted a mile.

Gracie glanced at each of her family. Lewis and Deirdre hung onto Patrick. Lewis was saying, "We've got this, Patrick. You're going to be okay." Mom's tears ran down her cheeks. But Dad … Dad's face was swollen and red. There was a bruise by his eye.

"Why are you so angry?" The words broke out of her anguished soul. She couldn't bear it if Dad tore into Patrick at this awful moment.

But he didn't. One of his big hands wiped his face; tears welled up in his eyes. "Yes, Gracie, I'm angry," he told her. "But not at Patrick—at myself. I didn't see this coming; I knew he'd suffered, but I didn't pick up on his pain." With a deep, deep sigh he added, "Family, we need to talk. Come downstairs to the living room." He put his arm around Mom's waist, hugged her, and they left.

Patrick could hardly walk. His entire body sagged as if he had no bones. Lewis helped him down the stairs, and Gracie followed, biting her lip to hold back sobs. Her heart still pounded.

Soon the family gathered in the living room in their pajamas, scared and disheveled. Dad's dark wavy hair haloed his head in sweaty short curls. Mom's face was white beneath her new-grown crown of golden hair. Patrick—well, Gracie thought her brother looked like a bulging sack of gray potatoes.

Gracie sank onto a big floor pillow, and Deirdre and Lewis bookended Patrick on the sofa. Mom and Dad sat in their armchairs—but no one leaned back to relax. The room smelled funny, like … not quite like fear, but like a mix of fear and sorrow. Heavy. Gray-blue. No one spoke. The silence vibrated in Gracie's ears. She caught herself holding her breath.

"Patrick," Dad began at last, his voice edgy as if what he

said hurt him very much. "We have to take you to the hospital."

Gracie tensed. "Why? He's not hurt!"

Dad looked only at Patrick. "You might have died from a fall out of the second-story window. Or you might be crippled for the rest of your life. The point is, you were trying to kill yourself, and that's very, very serious. It's a symptom of deep psychological pain, a bigger pain even than the one you have in your ankle. We'll have to check you in."

Patrick closed his eyes and his head drooped. He didn't cry out or argue. Gracie saw that he was exhausted. His skin looked dull. Then Patrick whispered, "Dad, I … I … couldn't stop … It's all my fault! Everything went wrong from Day One when I found that stinking hot marble."

"Listen!" Deirdre broke in. "It's not your fault, none of it! Evil started it—and Goodness ended it and brought you back home." She put her arm around Patrick in a hug. He didn't resist.

Lewis and Dad started to speak at the same time, but Dad waved to Lewis. "Go ahead, son. You first."

"Okay." He turned to Patrick. "I love you. I want you to be alive and with me. I don't just love you, I *enjoy* you. I want you around for a long, long time."

Then Lewis looked to Dad, who nodded and began, "Patrick, here's what to expect: We'll take you to the hospital and have you admitted."

Patrick's eyes got wide. "Will they cut my foot off?"

"I very much doubt it," Dad said. "The medical people may give you a sedative—you were pretty wild up in your bedroom, which might have partly been the fever—and they'll also probably start you on some strong intravenous antibiotics for that ankle."

Mom added, "In a lot of movies, people go through extreme dangers and come out smiling in a happy ending, ready for the next episode. But you've got to understand this, Patrick: It doesn't work that way. I know that everything, even the dark things, can work out for good, but recovery from something as traumatic as you've gone through isn't instant. Healing takes *time!*"

Gracie saw from her perch on the pillow that Patrick's eyes glistened. He was crying.

"The internet says that a bone infection is really serious!" Patrick exclaimed. "And … and if the doctors can't get it under control, they might have to …"

Mom shook her head. "The medical people will do everything possible to heal your ankle without the extreme case of amputation." She rose. "I'll get dressed. Then Dad and I will take you to the hospital."

"Can we all go together?" Gracie asked.

Mom's eyes sparkled like Patrick's, and Gracie's stomach contracted. "Don't cry, Mom!"

Gently, Mom said, "Gracie, sometimes it's fine to cry, and tonight we definitely have a crying occasion. Yes. You can go with us to the hospital. Once Patrick is checked in, though, Dad will take you home. I'll stay with Patrick."

Gracie pounded upstairs, nearly tripping on the steps. In her bedroom, she threw on jeans and a shirt. These "normal" activities seemed bizarre. Like a hologram that wouldn't go away, she kept picturing Patrick bunched into his window, aiming to go *splat* on the driveway below.

At last Gracie was ready to go. Except … just to find something, *anything* to ease her jangled thoughts, she flipped open her Bible to a random place. The book turned to Romans 8:28. She read it carefully, and summarized softly, "God makes everything work together for good. Everything!"

Gracie closed the Bible. "The perfect verse," she whispered, putting the book down. "Everything's gonna' be all right." She sighed and ran back downstairs.

AUTHOR'S NOTE

The Horned Edge refers to a fictitious evil society infiltrating groups, organizations, and churches throughout the world. Combating this evil "movement" with fiction felt appropriate after the attack on the Capitol building on January 6, 2021, a bad year of world-wide rancor, economic stress, and the Covid-19 pandemic.

This story is written to encourage you that you can overcome trauma. Your journey will be hard work. Cleaning out the deep wound may feel awful. But, as Lewis, Patrick, Gracie, and I have learned, God, not the Horned Edge, is in control.

ACKNOWLEDGEMENTS

Thank you, dear folks, for your constant support and encouragement to write and finish *The Horned Edge*. My publisher, Cynthia Hickey of Winged Publications, a best-selling author of such books as the Misty Hollow series, has cheered me these last two years. My grown kids, Peter, Amy, and Mary, have hung in there with me through the four-plus decades since we started together! Family members who have loved me throughout include Cathy Elliott, Patty Johnson, and Jane Bergman, plus Eileen, Zach, and Leslie Althoff, and Heather and Jackson Wood. Friends, you have supported me in word and deed. Some of you include fellow writers like Linda Porcello, Dianne Miley, Claudine Bailey, Jennifer Cotney, Raymond Russell, Paul Watson, Teena Myers, Ingrid Green, Pauline Wells, and co-author with me of a new book-to-come (*The Judge's Dilemma*), Xavier DeSoto. Others who've offered me the great gift of confidence are Nancy Gill, Dan & Mashell Brown, Kathy Bragg, John Lewis, and Daisy Orth. Special thanks go to my beta readers, Cathy Elliott, Xavier DeSoto, Tony DeSoto, and Claudine Bailey.

Last, I want to thank my dear husband Skip, who long ago, when I was being negative about myself, said one of the lines that made me fall in love with him: "Don't ever put my girlfriend down!"

WHAT'S NEXT …

Book 4: *Silence into Singing:* Lewis Brahmindura has been successful in his instant space-travel research and happy in his new marriage to Deirdre and the birth of a child. Now he works with the wholesome Der Bund (the brotherhood) for a better world, combating the Horned Edge's plots. But, after a serious auto accident and deliberate malpractice brain surgery engineered by the Horned Edge, Lewis can no longer speak or write coherently. He cannot work. He cannot communicate his amazing ideas for time travel. And the enemy is not finished with Lewis. They will recruit him to conquer the universe—or destroy him.

* * *

For news and updates about my writing, look for my website at *https://rosemaryalthoff.com*. You can sign up for my monthly newsletter there. Also, to find out more about me, search for Rosemary Althoff on Amazon, Goodreads, BookBub, Facebook, Instagram, or Twitter.

Book 1 (*The Hot Marble*) and Book 2 (*The Cave Chamber*) of the Soul's Warfare series are available at Amazon.com. My books may also be ordered at Barnes & Noble, from Walmart, or wherever books are sold. Please rate and review my books after you have read them.

A Soul's Warf
THE
HOT MAR
Rosemary B. A

THE
CAVE CHAN
A Soul's Warf
Rosemary B. A